The Many Lives & Loves of Hazel Lavery

A Novel

by

LOIS CAHALL

This is a work of fiction. All characters, locations and events in the narrative - other than those based on actual historical people - are products of the author's imagination and are used fictitiously. Where real historical figures, locations and events appear, these have been depicted in a fictional context or based on actual recorded historical resource material.

First Edition published by Historium Press

Images by Shutterstock, Imagine, Promeai, & Public Domain
Cover designed by White Rabbit Arts at The Historical Fiction Company

Visit Lois Cahall's website at
www.loiscahall.com

Library of Congress Cataloging-in-Publication Data on file

Hardcover ISBN: 978-1-962465-62-5
Paperback ISBN: 978-1-962465-63-2
E-Book ISBN: 978-1-962465-61-8

Historium Press, a subsidiary of
The Historical Fiction Company
New York, NY / Macon, GA
2024

ADVANCED PRAISE

"*The Many Lives & Loves of Hazel Lavery* sweeps the reader along in a riveting tale of thwarted desires, crushing duty, and inescapable destiny. Lois Cahall captures beautifully the echoes of past conflicts resonating anew."

– Amanda Foreman, author the prize-winning bestsellers, *Georgiana, Duchess of Devonshire* and *A World on Fire: An Epic History of Two Nations Divided*

"Lois Cahall is a storyteller of verve and vibrant enthusiasm, and that is precisely who is needed to tell the tale of a woman who lived so many lives on a worldwide stage. Hazel Lavery is a larger-than-life heroine who is not content to remain within the confining roles of debutante and society hostess, instead following her heart—even when it leads her into scandal and politics, and yes, even a rebellion. Cahall tells the story with evident love and admiration for her intrepid subject, and Hazel Lavery is a name that we should all know."

– Allison Pataki, New York Times

bestselling author of *Finding Margaret Fuller*

"I love reading historical fiction about people who actually lived. This is one such book, and what a life! Spanning the Victorian era through the roaring twenties, Lady Hazel Lavery defied convention at a time when society judged more harshly than today. However, that did not slow her down. Thank you, Lois Cahall, for bringing this amazing story to light."

– **Kathleen Grissom, *NYT best-selling author,* *The Kitchen House & Glory Over Everything***

"The novel begins by tracing Hazel's early life, but it really takes off when her world collides with that of Collins; she played a role in the peace process, she grew very close with him, and she was overwhelmed by grief when he was assassinated at the age of 31 in 1922. Author Lois Cahall says in her author's note that she felt a deep kinship with Lavery, and that warmth and attachment shines through on every page."

– Kristin Harmel, *NYT best-selling author*

"Like one of John Lavery's portraits, Lois Cahall's *Hazel Lavery* oozes love and passion, intrigue and imagination. To that canvas add chiaroscuro—loyalty and infidelity, diplomacy and assassination—and you have a novel almost Shakespearean."

– Larry Loftis, *New York Times* bestselling author of *The Princess Spy*

"*The Many Lives & Loves of Hazel Lavery* by Lois Cahall is a powerful and at all times eminently readable book, a fine work which will undoubtedly win the praise and plaudits it so richly deserves."

– Julian de la Motte, author of *Senlac* and HFC Reviewer

For Rebecca Dunn
(My beautiful, brilliant friend)

&

For Michael "M Lem" Kennedy
(Now with God, he skis only in powder)

The Many Lives & Loves of
HAZEL LAVERY

The Irish Times

FUNDRAISING AUCTION TO HIGHLIGHT THE PROPERTY OF HAZEL LAVERY

By James McEleney — August 14, 1950

A photograph of Hazel taken in c.1916

Portrait entitled Woman in the Golden Turban

Hazel depicted on a hammock in a later portrait entitled The Red Fan

The daughter and only child of Lady Hazel Lavery - Alice Livingston Trudeau, of Kilkenny - is preparing to auction never-before observed paintings, jewelry, and Irish-themed valuables of her late, beloved Mother. Until recently these most anticipated treasures were carefully stored and memorialized in Ms. Alice Trudeau's home in Kilkenny, Ireland.

It is estimated that Hazel Lavery posed for four-hundred-plus paintings for her husband, Sir John Lavery, which have found their permanent residence in museums worldwide including the National Portrait Gallery, London; and locally in Rothe House Museum, Kilkenny. The September auction will feature the highly sought-after-never-before-revealed properties of Hazel Lavery, expected to fetch high-thousand-pound figures.

"There was a warmth, a radiance, about my mother, Hazel, from her birthplace of Chicago to London to Dublin," says Ms.

Trudeau. “She was a wife, Mother, Stepmother, friend, fixer, lover and so much more.”

All proceeds will be donated to charities near and dear to Ms. Trudeau’s late mother’s heart including those for education, hunger, and peace missions. “One cause is in memory of the Great Famine,” says Ms. Trudeau, “and financing the Irish Sisters of Charity hospital in Cork.”

When Hazel and John Lavery visited Ireland, the couple became enthralled with the drama surrounding the ‘Easter 1916 uprising.’ It was there that rumors circulated that Hazel stole the heart of freedom-fighter, Michael Collins.

Love letters from Collins to Lavery will be available for auction and are set to start the bidding at 1,000 pounds each. “it’s always been believed that I destroyed Michael Collins and my mother’s love letters, but I’ve kept them carefully preserved until now.”

Says auctioneer, Matthew Mongovern, “We’re very excited at the undiscovered treasure trove. Hazel Lavery’s life, which spanned the Victorian Era through the roaring 20s, has the makings of a legend, except all of it is true!”

The auction will commence at 11 a.m., on Saturday September the 9th, 1950, James Adams & Sons Ltd., St. Stephen’s Green, Dublin.

Chapter One
Hazel

I've been told I was problematic from my first breath, torturing my mother with two days of strenuous labor like a giant crocus pushing its tiny, purple head, through the soil.

"Push, Mrs. Martyn, pushhhh!" begged the midwife to my mother who writhed in pain and dripped with perspiration amid blood-soaked towels. Finally, she let out a shrill... an agonizing groan... encapsulating the past forty-eight hours.

Mustering one more thrust. Then. Right then, I ripped through my mother's torso.

I was born younger than early spring, March 1880... and just like my birth month, I came in like a lion and out like a lamb.

My father, Edward Martyn, waited outside the door until the nurses finished bathing me. As the nurse cradled me into my father's arms he declared, "Ah, she's a vibrant but serious spirit. Like a shot of Irish whisky." He moved to kiss my mother's forehead, still drenched with cold beads of perspiration. "Bless you, Mother," he said, "We must decide upon a name."

But they couldn't. She couldn't. Mother was exhausted, dehydrated, and fell back on the pillow, caring less about my welcome into the world.

Finally, and only to satisfy that year's census on my otherwise nameless birth certificate, they called me 'Elsa' which meant 'pledged to God.' But Elsa didn't serve me well. With my big, seductive eyes, fervent with a 'hazy' gaze and muted as an Irish winter's landscape, my appearance forced them to rename me... Hazel. Hazel Martyn.

We moved from Boston to Chicago, the land of opportunity. It was there along Lake Michigan where we settled; where the trade routes bustled alive with horses and open carriages for the poor, and horses and buggies for the rich. We fell someplace in between. And it was in Chicago that I blossomed into a future beyond the pages of Huckleberry Finn, Father's favorite, which he read to me by candlelight before tucking me in for slumber.

"Can we visit Missouri? Where Huck lives?" I asked.

"No, no, my child, it's very far from Chicago. But someday soon we'll visit a much grander and farther place...Ireland...the great land of your ancestors." I curled my shoulders up to my ears, drawing the duvet to my neck in satisfaction. "Sweet dreams, my sweet Hazel…"

I was Daddy's girl as far back as I can remember, always leaping into his arms and stroking his goatee, at times his beard, often his muttonchops, or whatever facial hairs were stylish that particular year. But Father left our home promptly by 7 a.m. on weekday mornings, as I squatted to spy him through the staircase spindles. As he ran his arms through the sleeves in his overcoat, he'd glance up at me on the landing to declare, "Do not try to make it a good day, Hazel; make it a splendid day!"

"Where are you going, Father?" I asked, my chin trembling.

"To work."

"To work where?"

"Armour & Co.!" he exclaimed proudly. Then putting a finger into the air, "The finest pig meat-packing firm in all America!"

I didn't like the sounds of it...packing pigs...until he'd bring home treats of ham and cured bacon which were salty and scrumptious. And according to Mother, naughty foods.

As the shores of Lake Michigan exploded with opportunity Father eventually became Philip Armour's Vice President which translated to travel abroad, leaving me to my reading. Solo.

Granted, the position allowed my father to be thought of as

prestigious, prominent, and society's absolute finest. Or, in other words… we were suddenly rich.

Our next home had groundskeepers for the lawn and gardeners for the roses and topiaries. There was a tree surgeon on retainer and a man to tend to the outdoor tennis court and croquet station. There was a handyman to oversee the wading pool and fountain where a large exotic goldfish named "Meg March" resided. The fish was named for the heroine in Alcott's book, Little Women… the story of a young woman coming of age...

"I forbid you to read it!" exclaimed Mother.

"But..."

"But nothing. It's too risqué!"

I pouted and stormed to my room. All the more reason I snuck the volume. And named the fish.

Feisty, formidable, and stubborn Irish blood coursed through my veins due to my father's desire to instill a love of Ireland into every tale he told me.

As the family's pride and joy, I was the spoiled only child until one day Mother uttered the most dreadful of words, "Meet your little sister, Dorothy Hope."

"Hope? What a peculiar name," I declared, staring into the bassinet. "Hope for what?"

"Eternal happiness," beamed Mother. She was a far prettier baby, demanding my parents' attention, though nothing swayed me from being the family's dominant child.

"Goodbye, don't cry," said Father, as he snapped his top hat from the coat rack. I just hated when he left… me… calling after him at the door, "It would be better if goodbyes could be killed, Father. I'd have murdered this one." Father would chuckle at my boldness, but his departure always broke my heart like a stab wound.

By my teenage years, I possessed a good deal of misplaced flippancy, uncertain where I might funnel it, though while attending the Chicago's World Columbian Exposition I believed I'd found the answer.

"Stay by my side," insisted Mother, as I moved through the displays and crowds, eager to move onto the next. My fingers flitted across the silken strings of the French tapestries. "And don't touch anything!"

"Look, Mother," I declared, as I witnessed exhibits from Columbus's contract. "It's to do with Ferdinand and his clever wife, Queen Isabella!"

"She was notorious," snapped Mother. "Not to be a role model."

"Why not?" I asked, as Mother pulled my hand from the tapestry.

"Isabelle's life was more inclined to justice than to mercy and far more rigorous than forgiving," explained Mother.

"Then I adore her," I declared, inspired by her world, and longing to be royalty, too.

I didn't know much of the world, since Mother home schooled me, except for my dance studies at 'Bourniques' where a courtly, nimble man named Colonel Bournique taught ballroom decorum to society's children. He led us at an awkwardly long arms-length – step one two three, two-two three, three-two three – before pulling me into his chest, his halitosis breath fumigating my neck and hairline. Nevertheless, Mother's tutoring eventually led me further afield to Kenosha, Wisconsin, to a proper boarding school situated on a Great Lake. There I learned to really care about what mother called "those common people" sprinkled amid us well-to-do, and it was there I learned – no, I preferred - the common people. And apparently it was there at Kemper Hall where I learned poise, to stand shoulders back and heart forward with a bold eagerness to conquer the world.

After I earned the title "The Most Beautiful Girl in the Midwest" and surprisingly named the foremost authority on 'form' in all of Chicago, my beauty shone brightest in a good heart. And, I was determined to always have a good heart.

At Christmas, I took the train back home where Father, the brightest heart of all, returned from business. Since a celebration always abounded whenever Father was around, I posed as a mini grownup with intentional pedigree. I got to eat dinner late, hold fake cocktails adorned with toothpicks of orange and cherries in the drawing room, and retire to bed past ten. Adults listened to me, and when the adults spoke, they treated me like one.

Mother's friends circled around me in admiration and curiosity. One named Mrs. Crewe smiled and nodded, her eyes traveling in earnest over my turquoise, squared-neckline evening gown. "Your gown is lovely, my dear," she said. "How are you getting along with your lessons?"

"Quite well," I said, tipping my mocktail at Mrs. Crewe's Tiffany goblet. "I've found myself quite fond of the poor girls' humble beginnings set against our rich prejudices and..."

Mother glared at me, cutting me off mid-sentence. "Hazel will be traveling to Manhattan soon," she declared, waving her opera-length-gloved-arm between us.

"Oh..." said Mrs. Crewe, "Do tell..."

"Well, I'll..." I started to say, but Mother interrupted me mid-sentence. Again.

"Hazel will be..." said Mother, next interrupted by Father.

"My Hazel," said Father, placing his arm proudly around my shoulders, "Why my Hazel will be attending Miss Masters, a finishing school in Dobbs Ferry-on-Hudson."

The oohs and aahs of approval ensued.

"It's just outside of New York," Mother added, her voice dripping with arrogance.

"Splendid," said Mrs. Crewe, toasting Mother's goblet. "Finer education is everything, my dear." Everyone tipped their crystal glasses towards me, and I obliged, knowing full well I would be utterly bored. And knowing full well it was the age of innocence in Victorian society come to an end. Perhaps that was a good thing...

Father leaned in, impeccably dressed as ever in navy waistcoat and polished shoes, and kissed my forehead as he whispered, "I love you."

How I adored him. "I love you, too, Father."

But I didn't love fine education which was utterly exhausting! Between my French and Latin language lessons, and my personal parlor dramatics, I performed and starred in school recitals for the Players Club. I loved acting. I loved the attention. I loved the way the stage light cast a Geisha-like powdered dusting across my fragile features, my ruby red lips punctuating the spotlight glare as I spoke, the click-clacking sound of my heels across the stage, the crisp feel of the script in my fingers. How I loved the power of words, but it was in the silence of art where I found my forte.

Drawing was my hidden talent. Whipping up charcoal sketches of the girls in the dorm, I made the plump girls skinny, the skinny girls bosom-y, and the homely girls beautiful. The power of interpretation from pen to parchment was all at once captivating as it was exhilarating.

On weekends I escaped Dobbs Ferry to attend Manhattan lectures and opera with my roommate, Madeline. "Look, Maddie!" I exclaimed as we traversed Central Park. "A circulation plan! For horseback riding!"

"Do you?" she asked, "Ride a horse?"

"No. I'd rather drive a pleasure vehicle."

"Have you driven a car?"

"No, we have a driver," I said, disappointed in my answer to Madeline, who was admiring the cherry trees, and the ice cream vendors that appeared with other carts of lilacs and blue bells. We dodged the streets sans traffic lights and few traffic rules, block after block. Horse carriages zig zagged in all directions as we stopped at an intersection trying to determine which way to cross.

"My feet hurt. Where are you taking me?" asked Madeline.

"To Broadway," I said, folding her arm underneath mine. "It's a surprise."

"What's Broadway?" she asked.

"A street. Used to be in Madison Square but they've gone and moved it," I said, craning my neck to assure the direction. We rounded a dusty corner where train lines spewed coal dust. Suddenly, there it was in all its splendor. "Look!" I declared, "Times Square! Ta-da!"

"Such a silly name," said Madeline.

Her disparaging comment widened my eyes, but so did the pulsating lights that beamed from the marquees. "They're electric lights!" I shouted out, spinning like an aristocrat in a garden from the pages of *Pride and Prejudice.*

"And we're meeting movie stars?" says Madeline, her tone suggesting she didn't believe me, while she struggled to keep up with my stride.

"No," I snapped. "Broadway stars. Theatre stars. Father has arranged for us to meet them," I said, pointing to the dazzling blue and yellow marquee with the names Edwin Booth and Lilian Russell.

As we slid to our center first row seats – excuse me, thank you, beg your pardon - I gazed up to the stage to witness Lillian gallivanting for the audience as she strutted across the wooden stage, her lace corsets and ballet flats pointed playfully from beneath her purple chiffon gown. She had the 'it' factor. A brass walking stick supported her flamboyant personality and physical antics as she tossed her head back with laughter, as if to brush off everything. Yes, she certainly had my attention, especially when she winked and blew a kiss to the elderly gentleman seated to my left, who nodded with a grin.

"She must be flirting," I whispered to Madeline. "I've witnessed Father do that with other women." There, perfectly positioned, I studied Lillian's facial expressions...her sly mouth, demure batting eyes, tip of the head, raise of the brow - expressions I would learn to practice in the mirror back at the dormitory.

But while I appreciated the best actors in all of America, I was most fascinated by the prostitutes scattered along the avenues who served a wide variety of clientele from playboys to sailors on leave. New York was at the height of its dirtiest and most rotten in all of history.

"You young ladies shouldn't be out here alone," said the Officer from The Broadway Squad, helping us cross the intersection after the show.

"We're fine, Officer, I can assure you, we are," I said, unsure of anything but willing to venture on. Soon I caught voyeuristic glimpses of prostitutes as I traversed the city from Washington Square to the 'Tenderloin' below 42nd where a high tolerance for unlicensed liquor and illegal card gambling ensued. "Father told me that upscale horseracing tracks were allowed, here, too," I said, wondering how he knew all that but I assumed it was from his business trips.

"Oh, my!" Madeline exclaimed, as she gushed at the pornography postcards spinning on a rack.

"They're outrageous," I said, snapping one from the stand and dropping some loose change in the peddler's hand. "And they're so alive!" As I studied the photograph, the toothless vendor pointed his finger to another one.

"See that one there," he grinned.

"Which one where?" I asked, pulling my purse strings closer to me.

"She's Irish," he said.

"And?" I asked, a note of sarcasm.

"A ballet dancer," he sputtered. "First she dances on one leg, then on the other; between the two she makes a living." He raised his brows to suggest sex.

"Despicable!" said Madeline.

"She earns wages because she has talent," I said, correcting him, as Madeline dragged me by my arm with all the force that she could muster.

"C'mon, Hazel! We've got to get back to the study hall."

But I didn't want to go back. Certainly, Manhattan had more education to offer. I was most drawn to the rebellious and the change-makers determined to leave their mark on our world...

Yet, all the privileged lifestyle in the world didn't prepare me for the worst...

When Father contracted pneumonia, I was summoned from school by my nanny, taking the long and frightening train journey alone from Manhattan to Chicago, with only a coachman there to greet me at the station. From the buggy, the horse hooves pounded cobblestone for what seemed an eternity as the whistle of the driver's whip hastened the horses along.

Finally, we were at our front door. There the driver groped in the darkness of the carriage for the little bell in his pocket signaling orders to the house staff to come out and gather me.

The looks on their dismal faces said it all. Whisking by them, I darted through the long halls calling out in desperation, "Father! Father!"

No answer. Dead silence.

The housekeeper in her grim baritone voice, delivered the news... "Miss Martyn, Mister Martyn is gone."

"Gone where?" I questioned, and she lifted her eyes to the heavens. "But I didn't get to say goodbye..." I said, trembling, the tears flowing heavy before turning to gulps. Mother was nowhere in the vicinity to hold me. The housekeeper moved in – there, there, child - but I pushed her away, dashing instead to the stairs, and pounding breathlessly up each step with such purpose to the children's wing of the mansion. Returning with a pile of my bedtime books, I plunged them one by one into the fire. Without Father there to ever read to me again, it felt as if my childhood had now gone up in dramatic flames, too.

As I watched my books ignite, I sobbed and threw myself on the velvet loveseat. I could hear the adults outside the glass door. "He worked himself to death," said Mother nonchalantly.

When she saw me through the glass, she came to my side, pulled me in for a hug, and declared, "Now, now, you can cry when the dog dies. But not Daddy. You must be strong."

Staring up at her with disdain, I was horrified by her stoic manner. I scowled back, "But he was my father?"

As soon as the formalities of Father's burial were completed – the white roses tossed on his casket, cranked, and lowered deep into the dirt of the earth – my mother promptly sent me back to Dobbs Ferry. At that moment, left to tend to my grief alone, I hated my mother for separating me from my home and from my sister, Dorothy… and for making Father's death lighter than a dog's.

Father's passing pushed me further into fantasy, though

eventually it was understood that royalty couldn't be obtained that easily – well, short of marrying a Prince or at the very least a Duke – so I chiseled the idea of a place where women ruled. Because of the memories of my father, I knew the importance of businessmen. He taught me the necessity of earning respect and creating power, but for him, travel was everything.

So, I would travel. And what better place to absorb all that is culture and couture than to visit Paris during the height of the Belle Epoque. And to escape Mother.

"Mother please let me go...it's all I want!!"

"One semester. Just one," she agreed, the tip of her finger in my face. "No quarrels about this. Though you have the travel bug of your father, rest in peace."

I clapped with delight, deciding that I almost liked her for letting me go...

It was there in the Salons of Paris that I attended the shows of the Impressionists – Manet and Monet - their style 'en plein air' fascinating me; their technique of shadow and light and bright playful colors exhilarating my very soul. The French were marvelous at experimenting, something I didn't experience in the confines of Chicago.

While I felt Paris expanded my senses, when I returned home that winter, Mother insisted on my debut into society.

"We'll have a debutante ball... for Chicago's finest," she said. "It's what your father would have wanted."

"I doubt it," I said, knowing Father would never have pushed me onto other men.

"Oh Edward, Edward," she sighed with exasperation. "Why must you live on in this child of ours?"

"Fine, I'll do it, but only if it pleases you, Mother," I said, unable to accept the idea of fine suitors lined up for consumption. Sons of prominent lawyers, athletes, and heirs. Boring.

When the day arrived, the ball met my negative expectations.

While circulating through the room, I noticed Ned Trudeau, a medical student who stood at the corner of the mantle admiring me, his smile expressing his desire to worship all five-foot two inches of me. I may have been petite, but I had the presence required to own a room. With my flaming red hair, hazel almond eyes and the tiniest of waistlines, I flirted and curtsied with ease... the way Lillian Russell had done it. This of course was not the expected etiquette. Ladylike girls were supposed to wait along the walls while potential suitors circled them. Ladylike girls were expected to stand in the wings next to their father...except, my father was no longer there.

Society women somehow managed to fill their days with nonsense routines that left little room for mistakes, let alone for spontaneity or expression. There were dress fittings. Boring. Cotillion balls. Boring. Theatre tickets and operas galore. Yawn, yawn...

How I longed for gay Paree as my permanent residence. How I hungered for its naughty Bohemian studios and cafes. Now on an accelerated trend of my own doing and as my name began to grace the pages of society columns, I returned to Paris for one more semester, where the study of etchings was undergoing a sudden Renaissance.

Evenings, I sipped Lillet Blanc, an aperitif from Bordeaux, with fruit liqueurs and flavored with quinine, while watching cabaret acts, a new dominant form of entertainment offered in the Folies Bergere. Admiring the outspoken women dressed in red, revealing, and opulent clothing who sang and danced, I loved the spirit inside them, though I never let on to my mother. Instead, I wrote that I was busy organizing French fetes to raise money for hospitals and charitable organizations. But I took to my studies with a fever, immersing myself in paper and charcoal, I studied the dry-point style of printmaking technique.

It required a hard-pointed needle of sharp metal for engraving, like using a pencil. Once I conquered it as my medium, I was able to build a clever portfolio.

By the time I returned on the long journey back home to America, the Chicago Daily News declared, "Men who know pictures are enthused over her work."

With great aspirations, I intended to be taken quite seriously.

As an artist, I would earn a proper place in history. Or so I thought.

Mother agreed, despite little understanding of why a woman might want to be self-sufficient and achieve success by her own right. No, Mother pacified me for now, until a proper husband – one who secured the finest tables with the Maitre-d at the finest restaurants – came along...

Chapter Two
John

John Lavery's birth certificate had discrepancies. In the register at St. Patrick's Church in Belfast, his birth was listed as 1856; yet years later, in the official list of Members of the Royal Academy, it's recorded as 1857.

"Either way, you're an old man. A quarter century my senior," I once teased John to which he retorted, "And either way I chose St Patrick's Day for my birthday as being, for an Irishman, easy to remember." Then swigging his whiskey, he swallowed, chuckled, and added, "No doubt my first years do count... but I cannot account for them." He told me his fondest and saddest childhood memories long before he became the Knighted portrait artist...

John's father, from what little he remembers of the trestles and barrels in the wine-and-spirit shop, was a wine merchant, where he learned the adage that one can never get enough of a fine burgundy. And his father loved to drink! But he abandoned John and his siblings early on, leaving his mother to care for a four-year-old brother and John, only three, with his sister Jane, age two. Relatives and friends divided up the children...John was raised by an uncle, Edward Lavery and his wife, Rose.

"The poor wee orphan's a bit of a sad sack," said Rose, looking him up and down. "Come on then. In the tub ye go." It was from the tub where John heard his aunt talking to his uncle. "Smells like a sopping wet bag of barley," she said. "Shall we tell 'em?"

"That he smells like barley or that his mother died of grief?" asked the uncle.

Apparently, John's father, Henry Lavery, drowned on a ship to America. He'd been sailing on the Pomona, described as a splendid clipper ship of fifteen hundred tons. Thirty-seven deck hands and three-hundred and seventy-two passengers were onboard. Henry Lavery was one of them. But only twenty passengers were saved from the waves when the ship sank. Henry Lavery was not one of them.

John's Uncle Edward was a farmer with a kindly face, a simple life, and a prized pitchfork. On occasion John was beaten… sometimes out of outrage, sometimes over the economy. The Laverys hadn't much money though life was hopeful when the railways began to appear in Ireland. Aunt Rose was fascinated with the trains.

"Let's rename the farm 'Train View Moira,'" she said, toasting a glass of fermented peach juice through the windowpane at the distant railway workers. "Adds a bit of class to our life to have a train, don't it? Yeah?"

John's uncle and aunt had two other children whom they dressed with scrupulous care though John frequently went barefoot, agonizing over the thorns, thistle and flint coming to live in the bottom of his sole. John never remembered much of those days except that the year he turned ten, Aunt Rose sat him down.

"Young man," she said, "I'm sending ye off to England for an education, yeah?"

"England? Education?" asked John, perking up.

"You've a very rich cousin, who has a big house with solid golden balls hanging from the front door."

"Like a palace?"

Arriving at his destination via the cabin of a Belfast-Ardrossan passenger and cattle steamer, John imagined what the palace might look like as the realistic smell of cow dung penetrated his nostrils.

But the palace turned out to be just a simple brick house. He gazed up at the portal, with indeed, the golden balls albeit not perverted at all, but made of cast-iron and painted gold leaf. Above were these words: 'Union Loan Office. A pawnshop.'

John's uncle had a remarkable clientele of miners, negroes, and sailors, who came to pawn banjos, picks, shovels, guitars, knives, and pistols. But John especially loved the traveling theaters that descended upon his town. For just three-pence to a shilling he'd relish in the artistry of their plays...the noise, the music, the comedy of it all with a touch of naughty nature.

In his late teens, John decided that he'd had enough of his common life and robbed the till to hightail it off to Scotland. A week after arrival and with no idea the cost of living, he found himself hungry and broke, without board or lodging, sleeping in Glasgow Green on the benches.

Wandering yard to yard he rummaged through the bins, found food scraps, washing them in the fountain when daylight came, and washing himself in the evenings when the town squares went dark.

As a smallpox outbreak surfaced, John contracted the disease. Immediately a policeman took him, with fever and fatigue, to the attic of a "Sairey Gamp" whose treatment was kind but rigid. Tying his hands behind his back so he wouldn't scratch madly at his sores, she bathed him in whiskey. Having been blind for a week, John found he could see again and as the fever broke, he escaped without a scratch or pockmark.

Sadly, he was shipped back to his uncle and aunt at Train View Moira, where once again he tended to the cows and livestock. Yet a longing burned inside. Every genuine artist creates the circumstances necessary for fulfillment. And, so, John was determined to run away. Again.

But to flee is a simple adventure. The difficulty is to get something to do after the running has come to a halt.

"There's opportunity for ye, lad," said his uncle. "Glasgow Mineral Department, yeah?'

"Please, let me go, Uncle, let me go..."

"Let 'em go," said his aunt to John's Uncle. "We can't feed another mouth, so off you go then." With that she moved to the cupboard and handed John five pounds. "For a gloomy day, Johnnie. Make good of it. But with a real job. Paintin' is a past-time..."

"No, it's an earning, I promise," said John, looking down at the money in his hand. "Thank you, Auntie, thank you Uncle." And with that he was off.

Of course, John was overflowing with elation, and couldn't resist celebrating a bit, so he took the money – more than he should have – and entertained his Belfast cousins with theatre and meals. "Chablis and oysters all around!" declared John.

"Johnnie, ye rich!" said a cousin, toasting him as the fine wine poured and trays of delectable dishes arrived. Hours later the bill arrived, too.

"Six Quid!" said John, flabbergasted. "Quick boys, we'll make a run for it." And run they did...out the back door through the kitchen.

As they safely rounded the corner and down the alley, John leaned breathlessly onto a brick wall. A sly grin crossed his face. He'd had a taste of the wealthy life in a Galway oyster bar and knew he'd somehow follow that path...

John ended up in a low quarter of the town on the Road to the Gallows, the area lined with dilapidated mansions which once housed Aristocracy now sheltering the poor. John meandered through the streets via the streetlight gas lamps, passing through the half-open door of one of the houses. As he stepped up the rickety, mildewy, garbage-strewn staircase, he passed a drunken man and the lodging housekeeper. As luck would have it, the housekeeper tossed the soused man out into the cold, thus making space available for John.

As he observed his fellow roommates - Navy chaps from ages sixteen to sixty - he sat round the fire to keep warm until the housekeeper kicked at him. "Weel, me lad, where's yer money?"

John dug into his pocket, producing barely enough to buy a bowl of porridge.

"Could I have the share of a bed?" asked John.

"C'mon then." And with that, the man led John down a long hallway to a room that was even filthier than the main quarters. The candle in the man's hand exposed a makeshift mattress on the floorboards. "There ye are, ma wee man," said the housekeeper. "Ye'll be as snug as a bug in a rug."

The squalor was sickening. John glanced at the sardine bodies packed next to each other, the smell of vomit and sweat occupying every orifice of space. But John was grateful, washing himself at the 'jaw box' – a sink at the window with barely a basin in which to wash though not a bar of soap. He did the best to freshen up with his waistcoat before undressing to sleep in his shared bed.

With his trousers under his head, not for substitution of a pillow but to prevent the snoring man next to him from stealing them, John determined to be more than a jack-of-all-trades. He would find his craft. He would be rich.

He would one day sleep in the grandest of rooms with a feather bed, with fine linen sheets and even a quilt with intricately woven embroidery like the ones he'd seen in store fronts when the owners shooed him away.

But for now, John Lavery just had to pray to high heaven until morning and leave behind the lowest of the low. As John turned onto his side, a lone streetlamp outside the window cast the shadow of his profile onto the wall. His finger touched the cracking stucco where he traced his image. Deep inside he had always admired anyone who could draw. And deep inside, he knew he possessed that skill, if only he had the financial means to attend art school.

The very next morning, when scrounging through rubbish barrels for food, John came upon a crinkled ad in the Glasgow Herald: "Situations Vacant." His dirty finger with dirtier fingernail moved down the advertisement to read: "A smart lad with knowledge of drawing wanted. Apply with specimens of works to J. B. MacNair, Artist and Photographer, 11 West Hill Street."

John dashed for the first train to Glasgow. All aboard! Fate was calling... fate and a three-year contract that paid up to twenty pounds per annum.

"Uncle?" He rang from the tele. "I've a job. A real job! As an apprentice."

A pause and then John added, "I'm practicing blob work." He laughed. "With a brush and modeling with some putty!" On the other end of the line his uncle offered to pay the rent. "You will?... I'll take good care of the flat… I promise... Thank you, Uncle. Yes, love you!"

As he learned to illustrate – drawing leaves, flowers, and plants – the practice taught him to draw intelligently and respectfully. He phoned home regularly though his aunt and uncle had little clue what he was referring to when he said, "Auntie! Art is not a dead thing, but a thing alive, with a babyhood, a childhood, and a manhood..."

They were happy that he was happy. Simple as that.

Completely sketched heads came next, and then hands and feet, drawn in outline. In all the lessons, John found his forte. Oil painting. And enough income for the purchase of colors. Inside the art store he asked the clerk for "a tube of yellow ochre, crimson lake, Prussian blue," John cocked his head sideways, ..."and a cobalt blue, er, the ultramarine, and what else?"

"Raw sienna or burnt sienna with lampblack seems to be a favorite," said the clerk.

"Right, then. Raw sienna and Lampblack it tis."

And with that, John began painting people.

Portraits.

He was on fire with passion.

At times of course, like any artist, John's spirit groaned, the heart failed, the mind went numb, but the hand, well, the hand went on inspired and automatically.

Chapter Three
Hazel

I was twenty-three before Mother started taking my sketches seriously. On the verge of being published, I begged her to let me spend the summer in an artists' colony in Brittany. Mother agreed but only if she and my sister, Dorothy, accompanied me to the coastal villages between Concarneau and Pont-Aven, a place where the highly sought after artist Gaugin painted his hillsides.

Oh France! Je suis a Paris! Je t'aime la France! I spun around the cottage foyer before forcing open the window shutters, their glass panes sooty and in need of a good seasonal scrubbing. Alas, here I was, my dream coming true, as I continued my exploration of Impressionists who once vacationed right here in Brittany, with its majestic rocky coast and dune covered beaches. Breathing in the sea salt air... This was heaven! I was in heaven!

"Dorothy," I said, turning to my sister. "I hope you love France as much as I do."

"Do you suppose I will?" asked Dorothy, always in amazement of me.

"Well, the last time I visited France, I spent a banker's holiday in Barbizon. Mother doesn't know I ventured there, but it's such a charming bucolic village just south of Paris. You know, it's just a stone's throw to this massive Chateau in Fontainebleau. Someday I'll take you. Wild boars dart through the forests..."

"Wild boars? That's preposterous!"

"Oh, no they do exist," I said. "I swear they do! Almost died at the tusk of one chasing me through the courtyard."

"You speak silliness."

"Fine, it didn't quite chase me, but Barbizon, well, you'd adore it. A sanctuary for us leisure class types. But oh, Dorothy, it's a true magnet for the painters – Cuvelier, Millet, and Father Corot. They created an entire art movement towards Realism!"

"You speak gibberish, Hazel. I have no interest in artists."

"But, don't you see, Dorothy," I said, moving toward the window and smiling out at all the world had to offer. "It was in Barbizon that painting was achieved in the open air of the warm-weathered countryside, amid the Irises, the wisteria. It was where artists could feel nature rather than copy it. Pure heaven!"

"Don't let Mother hear you. You sound crazy, my beloved sister. We're in Brittany now."

"Yes, I've longed to try the seaport lobster and my first bite of Moules Frites."

"Mules, who?"

"It's French. For boiled muscles and potato fries."

We giggled and then there was Mother, who always had a plan...

"I've a tradeoff," said Mother, quite curt.

"Oh?"

Mother cleared her throat. "In return of my gift of allowing you to study at the colony I've commissioned an artist, John Miler-Kite, to paint a portrait of you and Dorothy."

"Never heard of him, Mother."

"An Anglo-French artist. Quite promising."

"Must we?" I begged.

"Yes, you must."

"But..." I whined.

"Have I made my position clear?" Mother stood firm.

"Yes, there'll be no quarreling," I whispered, turning to leave the room while under my breath I murmured, "You're an obstacle to my happiness."

"What was that?" she asked.

"Nothing, Mother."

The very next day, Dorothy and I sat for hours, facing each other like twin flame-soulmates, perspiring in Mr. Kite's one-window studio, our hands clasped in our lap, our eyes fluttering heavily from our state of boredom.

"Still, ladies, not a breath," said Mr. Kite, who, ironically, had little problem capturing Dorothy's delightful image but had much trouble capturing mine. "Hazel," he said, "your eyes flicker color-change like a sea of light and storm."

And so, Mr. Kite called upon John Lavery, a highly regarded and established colleague who'd been painting for years. When John entered the room, he looked at me as if he were not seeing Dorothy and me at all but instead envisioning the finished painting already in his head.

I'd first set eyes upon Mr. Lavery from our hotel's veranda, watching him struggle past with a six-foot canvas strapped to his shoulders and a gentle smile attached to his face. He wasn't particularly tall, as a matter of fact, he wasn't tall at all. But he had a thick stock with thick limbs, and far from handsome but somehow artsy, or call it, Bohemian handsome, if that makes any sense.

Mr. Lavery took a lot of time mixing colors with his palette knife.

"Does it always take so long?" I asked, squirming.

"Truly," said Dorothy, "Hazel and I are exhausted. Isn't there a compromise?"

Mr. Lavery chuckled before replying. "The word 'compromise' is not acceptable in that of the artist and his subject, as the artist sees and does what he must."

Dorothy rolled her eyes toward me, but I liked the way Mr. Lavery worded his thoughts... driven by something far deeper, something only a fellow artist could comprehend.

Mr. Lavery attempted to capture the most delicate traits of our young, perfect womanhood. "One mood is all that a portrait needs," said Mr. Lavery, "but I don't feel I've found it."

"Good, then I must use the lavatory," said Dorothy, breaking our pose, and hastening to the next room.

In the end, and after my new-found addiction to the smell of linseed oil, our Dorothy and Hazel portrait was three-quarters Milner-Kite and one-quarter John Lavery, who was displeased with his portioned result.

As we prepared to go about our holiday, it also displeased Mother to find Mr. Lavery and me in a heated conversation about art and life in Paris. In truth, I found him to be a brilliant man, even though twenty-four years my senior. I adored his intelligence as I had always adored cerebral, big brainy men like Father, and now, as luck would have it, like me, John was an artist. As old as my father.

"Tell me about your version of Paris," I delved, hovering at the sink as he cleaned his brushes.

"I have a fairly intimate life but on rare occasions I socialize at Café Guerbois, in Montmartre."

"On the hill?" I asked, my voice rising in excitement.

"Yes," he smiled. "It's where a new group we call 'The Impressionists' gather. For quite a while. Long before your time."

"Tell me more," I begged, as he moved to pack up the paintboxes.

"I began frequenting in the 1890s."

"Your style is different than theirs, no?" I asked, "I can imagine the perpetual clash of artsy opinions."

He paused from speaking, instead impressed by my sentiment, my understanding of artist to artist even if he was decades ahead of me. His raised eyebrow told me that he saw me as more than the young woman he was hired to paint. He told me how he moved into his artist life having met a friend in Paris, John Singer Sargent, through James Abbott McNeill Whistler or "Whistler" as John called him... yet I could never understand why John called him simply "Whistler" but on the other hand, referred to Sargent as "John Singer Sargent" in full name.

"You can just refer to him as Sargent, otherwise it's a mouthful," I suggested.

He smiled down at me as he continued, "A couple years prior I'd contacted Sargent with an invitation to become an Honorary Member of the Royal Academy, but Sargent got all huffy about it, his ego bigger than his palette, having been only invited because another lesser-known artist had resigned."

"Ego for certain," I declared.

"Yes," said John, "Apparently, there were egos galore in those Impressionists-in-the-making and certainly in the case of the Edwardian-eras' American expatriate..."

"...the premiere portrait painter, John Singer Sargent... er, Sargent."

"Indeed!" he said.

Listening to John was artistry to my ears. "Tell me more!" I begged, but he insisted his day's work was done.

At the same time, Dorothy, having sat patiently listening on, begged me to go for a stroll but I shooed her off. My heart pitter-pattered and my mind was lost at the telling of his artist's gossip, not so far-fetched from the Queen-Bees who made newspaper gossip famous in the society pages of the Chicago Tribune. No, this was real and raw. Not a fur and pearls event but a thinking event with depth and soul...and canvas.

A few days later, Mr. Lavery, now referred to as "John" and when we were in private, escorted me to Pont-Aven, a lovely nearby village where Paul Gaugin depicted the seaport town in a painting called "Watermill in Pont-Aven." The Aven river sliced through the village like a source of inspiration...a huge powerful flow of genius with all that energy force coming up from the earth. John's greatness made me feel like I lived in society's smallness. I longed to go big.

I didn't know it just yet, as I'd played emotional games with boys of the past, but this… well, this must be love.

Chapter Four
Hazel & John

The day of that stroll there was so much to learn about this fascinating man whose genius hid beneath his surface. Just brushing up beside him I could feel his brilliance.

As we turned the corner of a cobblestoned street, past the oyster farm at the fish port, I reached out for John's hand, and he took mine, letting down his guard.

According to John, he painted his very first picture around 1876, just shy of the four years before I was born.

"If you must know...I painted Death of Charlton for Thomas Chatterton. I first spied it in a magazine," John explained, speaking like an emotional tour guide while squeezing my hand into his. "He was an unsuccessful poet whose suicide became a sort of symbol for blighted artistic genius. Chatterton was in purple silk knickers, strewn on a divan, his right arm swung to the floor as though he were dead, having drunk poison."

"That's what inspired you?" I asked, slightly mortified. "How bizarre and brilliant all at once!!"

"Agreed. It spoke to my soul!" John folded my arm under his and tucked it close to his chest. I could tell by his exhales he knew I was a challenge. Yet, John carried on speaking comfortably in my presence. "By that point in my history I had come a long way from the squalor at the boarding house at Road to the Gallows. I had many employers. Some kind, some not so kind, but it was art school that propelled me to fine-tune my craft. Yet it didn't come easy, Hazel. Nothing does. It took arduous work, substantial amounts of discipline, and sometimes physical starvation to eventually find the delayed gratification of success. As a proper artist."

"Or a starving artist!" I chuckled.

"That and a studio fire, put another fire, well, under my arse..."

And he told me the story…

It was with a stroke-of-luck that once, while renting a studio in Glasgow, a burly Highland policeman entered the dining room where John was having a sumptuous supper with a friend. The officer looked hard at John, "Are you Lavery?"

"Why?" asked John, "Do I owe you money?"

"No," said the policeman. "But you're gutted."

It was the Officer's tender way of breaking the news that John's studio had burnt to the ground along with what may have been his first masterpieces.

John was oddly elated at the news since the studio had been insured for three-hundred pounds… more money than he ever had in his life. With it, he could pay his rent, long overdue, along with his present sitter, a city merchant who'd grown tired of sitting for practice portraits.

John carried on in life, fluctuating between on-the-spot sketches and studio clientele with enough income to afford a small flat in a tenement house in the west end of Glasgow. Above the door knocker, a brass plaque read: "John Lavery, Artist."

As our walk slowed to a leisurely stroll in Pont-Aven, which translated to the American words 'River Bridge', and as we crossed over one, a boat carrying fish and bricks floated by underneath. "Bonjour! Comment ca va?" I called out, asking how they were, and waving with such delight at the thought of being uncaged from Mother.

"Bonjour! Tres bien, et vu?" the fisherman called out waving, as they lowered their nets.

It was so glorious to be away from the familiar, to be around so many public people – townsfolks, fishermen, shopkeepers and of course, John. All my life, except for boarding school, friends and family surrounded and forced me to behave in a certain way. John was Bohemian in life to my Bohemian soul. This friendship was destined to be divine.

I turned back to John as we moved into the market square full of shopkeepers selling their wares. "Your stories are from some alternative universe, one I so long to be a part of..."

"Let me see... it was the winter of 1880 –"

"The year I was born!" I teased.

"Yes, that too, my child," he said, pausing as though considering the fact of our age difference. "Wisdom is the only benefit of growing older, my dear." He moved his fingers to my side for an inappropriate tickle and our teasing tapped into the obvious vein of possibilities.

"You were saying..." I said, deliberately moving my hip out to move away from his fingers.

"Yes," he said, gathering his composure. "I made my debut as an exhibitor at the Glasgow Institute of Fine Art. I remember well this particular painting of the back view of a girl – quite like you – but kneeling on a high-backed Jacobean chair gazing at an oval portrait of the Madonna and Child."

I smiled at his comparison. Reminiscent of my father during our bedtime stories.

Except John was larger than life. And anything else would be an oversimplification of all that was John Lavery...

"Hazel?" he queried, "Where did you go?"

"No place," I said, snapping back from my memories and

thinking on my next line of questioning in order that I might sound intelligent. "What painting made the grandest difference in your life?"

"It was called *The Tennis Party*, and it depicted women of the bourgeois swinging racquets on the green, spectators watching on. There was nothing particularly inspiring about it, Hazel," said John, "though the social significance of the sport can't be underestimated."

"You're suggesting tennis is an opportunity for younger women – like myself," I pouted, "to be forced to fit into a mold of polite conversation with potential and eligible partners." I rolled my eyes. Utterly boring.

But John stayed serious. "The composition was relaxed and realistic – nothing labored – instead confident, alert, and alive. Or at least that's what patrons told me." His tone suddenly turned snobbish in nature.

"Oh," I said, my voice falling off, disappointed. Why didn't he take to my flirting as bait like with the Chicago boys? Including that Ned Trudeau boy.

"It's a funny thing," said John. "I was the only artist completely unaffected by the Impressionists. Manet perhaps, for his thoroughbred grace, but quite honestly, I have horse allergies, and had little desire to do studies outdoors. I'm an indoor type of man." John chuckled. A silence that fell between us as I processed his words...words unlike any I'd ever heard before. Certainly, more meaningful than the chatter of the boys back home that I knew who talked sports, boats, and investments.

Two gulls sidestepped toward us on a distant seawall. I paused, attempting to slow down John's walking pace to mine, taking in the cawing of the gulls dropping seashells to the rocks; nose diving to devour the clams in one swift gulp.

"I don't mean to sound star-struck, but can you tell me about Whistler?" I asked, imagining his social circles far more exciting than mine.

"Ahhh... my Whistler," said John. "What a character with his thick mob of black ringlets and one white curl in the center. You'd have liked him, Hazel. He always held a monocle up to one eye to correct his vision. With his volatile personality you never knew what you'd get." I chuckled but John's words softened. "Though he adored me and taught me to make beauty out of the everyday. He'd have painted the air if it were possible."

"Oh, how divine! What beautiful words to capture him," I said, getting as daydreamy as he was about Whistler.

"He would have liked you just fine, Hazel. Nevertheless, the two of us worked together with little friction. It was in London, by chance, in Piccadilly Circus, that I bumped into Whistler for the first time."

"One doesn't just bump into Whistler..."

"Oh, but we did. We artists… well, we all knew of each other," said John, reminiscing. "And we shared a brotherhood of 'Art for Art's sake' so when Whistler asked me to come have a cocktail, how could I decline? That cocktail turned into dinner and more cocktails at my hotel until 4 a.m."

"I can imagine the conversation," I giggled. "One of women and spirits, not as in ghosts but as in liquor!"

"The conversation was more along the lines of politics, horses, and art," said John with a stern tone. "Mainly the newly formed politics at the society of which Whistler resided over."

"Oh, I see," I said, disappointed by his sternness. "And the Queen...?" I asked with anticipation, changing the subject. "Mother read that you've met her."

"Yes, painted Queen Victoria. For six hundred pounds."

"Six hundred pounds doesn't seem like much money," I said.

"Six hundred pounds was a financial lifetime," said John. "There I was, painting her, high on a platform, with a peep hole in a curtain as the elderly monarch, wearing a widow's bonnet and looking rather severe, was wheeled into the exhibition in a royal chair. Her face was concealed from my view," explained John. "I was so fearful I was to be in the same room as Her Majesty, in her very presence! Me! John Lavery."

“You, the orphan farmer child,” I teased.

“Precisely,” he continued. “The by-standers bowed as the Queen was announced. Silence. No sooner I began to paint, and my hand started to shake; a movement of the curtain caused Her Majesty to glance over at the drapery, giving me just a brief glimpse of her facial features front on.”

“How did the painting turn out?” I asked, as we crossed back over the bridge heading toward home.

“Fortunately, I was able to deliver *The State Visit of Queen Victoria* painting to the International Exhibition, Glasgow, as a recorded work of history. Of course, when the painting was completed, 10 feet by 8 feet, and shown to the Queen at Windsor, she claimed that I had made the head too big for the body, and that there was too much red carpet in the foreground, otherwise, and after a deep annoying exhale of sufficiency, she anointed my work a success.” John bowed. “And there you have it. That’s how I became a famous portrait artist, though I do highly detest that word.”

“Artist?”

“Famous.”

“Famous?” I questioned. “But everyone wants to be famous...”

“Let’s just assume that painting launched my official career as a society painter and anything else was clear sailing,” said John. “That was until after many requests that there must be an official portrait of Her Majesty that would satisfy the people, at long last she succumbed for one brief session, at two o’clock one unexpected afternoon.”

“The Queen came to you?” I asked with skepticism.

“Yes,” said John with certainty. “She arrived at the tick of the door opening to my studio and wearing the bonnet she’d worn at Glasgow which would allow me the same position of the ‘State Visit’ sketch. Her eyes traveled up and down, judging me. ‘What view?’ asked the Queen, in as few words as possible. ‘May I escort you to a chair?’ I asked. She raised a hand ‘no’ to stop me. Again, she repeated, ‘What view?’ She remained standing. ‘Profile,’ I replied, 'If it pleases, Your Majesty.'"

"Did she speak?" I asked.

"The only conversation was with her two ladies-in-waiting – something about flannel undergarments – until she finally said 'Enough,' and stormed from the room, after only twenty minutes, whispering annoyance under her breath that she had a country to tend to. When she departed, the Ladies-in-waiting curtseyed and batted their eyes.

"And the portrait?" I asked.

"I was pleased with the portrait because her profile was like that of Caesar. On the Roman coin."

I giggled and turned into John just then, inhaling his scent of Bergamot and lemon oil. Masculine with an underlying gentleness.

My eyes met John's and he leaned in to kiss me, ever so gently at a garden gate... our day trip to Pont-Aven came to an end, and I was fully versed in all things John Lavery. Well, except for the one thing I most wanted to know as I pulled back from the kiss. Smacking my lips, my gaze lowered to the cobblestone. Then looking up, I got the nerve to ask a question as we moved on to a row of turreted buildings, one housing a creperie.

"Is there a Mrs. Lavery?" I asked, attempting to sound innocent though calculating in my inquiry.

"There is, well, there was," said John, glancing back at the waterwheel of a mill in the distance. His eyes misted. "Best to keep those stories in our hearts." Then he changed the subject. "Have you experienced a crepe?" I shook my head. "Ah, well then, let me be your first," he said, another play on words. "Galettes and crepes are to Brittany what pizza is to Naples. This shop prepares the most-savory crepes with buckwheat flour. Shall we?"

Share a crepe we did. One with runny egg and salty ham and then another with lemon and honey for dessert. But my mind wandered back to the mystery of Mrs. Lavery.

Later John would tell me that he had been exiting an artist's color shop early one morning on Regent Street, London, when he saw a young girl with a bright red shawl over her head like that of a gypsy woman. She carried a basket of flowers which she was selling undoubtedly for survival. Her angelic face caught his attention.

The next day she turned up at the studio, stunning John with her exquisite beauty. She explained she'd escaped a convent and that her name was Kathleen MacDermott. Her appearance and accent suggested she was an Irish lass, and John asked her if she'd consider leaving London and coming to Scotland to be an artist's model. She jumped at the idea, and a few days later, off they went by train to Glasgow. Eventually, despite being at times a desperate nuisance flitting in and out of his life, and with a hacking cough from the Glasgow dampness, John took pity upon the girl. And, well, next thing he knew it was -- "I John Lavery, take you, Kathleen MacDermott as my wedded wife..."

A daughter, Eileen was born shortly after and just behind that, when Kathleen was all but nineteen, she died of acute Phthisis.

John's friend, Patrick Whyte, a witty, albeit honorable military male who John always called "the finest man I have known" played nursemaid to Kathleen through her illness, from one health resort to another, eventually becoming the nursery governor to little Eileen. Whyte took a house in the country and lived with Eileen and her nurse through her baby years while John, with his head in a paintbox, resided in London.

"Well, here we are," said John, one block from my family summer cottage. "And here I've been going on and on about myself and know very little about you."

"In due time," I said, realizing my wealthy miniscule existence in Chicago all paled in comparison to John's massive artist life.

"Good night, sweet Hazel," and he kissed the back of my hand. "Thank you for the loveliest of days I will most certainly and always cherish."

I would cherish it, too. Having been netted like a fish by the fisherman, I'd been taken away from the 'school' that was Mother, if only for a day. How I longed to divulge that longing but instead I simply said, "Thank you and good night, Mr. John Lavery." I was back to the formalities of Mother.

Chapter Five
Hazel

Mother spat under her breath. She forbade me to indulge in the "quarter-century-older John Lavery," and "a widower, no less." But I ignored her. Afterall, I was twenty-three years of age, thus able to come to my own mature decisions, thank you very much.

And by day four of his acquaintance, I was certain this was love, or whatever love was supposed to be.

John's friend Milner-Kite – the artist who'd been painting the portrait of my sister, Dorothy, and me - referred to Mother as "The old Chicago Dame" which applied more to Mother's attitude since her forty-six-year age was a year younger than John Lavery. Perhaps Mother had eyes for John Lavery herself. Perhaps Mother was just jealous.

Before my family's journey back to Paris, I wrote John a letter, handing it off from my bosom to Milner-Kite for safe delivery. My calligraphy penmanship deliberately included some suggestive words which somehow just spilled out onto the parchment page:

"...And you are not to mention the ever-embarrassing fact that it was I who was the first to discover that you wanted me to come into your garden..."

The "garden" would soon become the romantic code word in our love letters.

As the train rattled from Brittany to Paris, slowing up from station to station, something told me that beyond instinct, beyond logic, there was a constant nagging like the chugging of the train, a void at the core of me. Whisking through sea to countryside to city opened some chasm of longing to my childhood. From Jane Austen and her nonsense flirtations to the Bronte sisters and their real literature, and then of course, Shakespeare… could it get any more poetic?

I'd been reading the book John gifted me for the train ride – *The Count of Monte Cristo* – by someone named Alexander Dumas. I could certainly see why John was attracted to the book given his own rise to fortune –from that of a peasant orphan - though honestly, I could also see that like human nature, art is improved by strife and danger, and it must shift to better itself.

The truth was I had trouble focusing on the book, wondering all the while why I was so attracted to John, a disheveled, albeit successful and brilliantly minded painter. Was it my longing for the attention of my dead Father? Probably. Perhaps. Likely. Yes!

Either way, John felt it too, and as a result, followed Mother, my sister and me to Paris, inviting us to lunch at his hotel. But the lavish meal of chicken, duck, and root vegetables with various sauces, pastries and jellies, was a disaster. Mother made it clear with the clank of the fifteen pieces of silver cutlery between us, that she did not approve of John for me.

The next day John decided to depart hastily for London. I couldn't let him go, so I told Mother a fib, that I was feeling ill from shellfish poisoning. Leaving her to have tea in the dining room, I made my way from my hotel, Le Meurice on Rue de Rivoli, down Rue Saint-Honore and crossing the Pont Neuf. His Hotel, Residence Henri IV, was located on the left bank.

Arriving covered in perspiration and desperation, having dashed on foot, with much difficulty, I was thankful my structured day dress gathered at the hem so I could sprint! Twirling my pink parasol, I explained to the concierge in a flurry of urgent broken French that I made my way through Saint Germain des Pres and the Latin quarters, arriving the 3.6 km breathless journey into the lobby to see John Lavery. There you have it. My chest heaved as I caught my breath. Then announcing loudly, my voice echoing in the foyer, “I must see John Lavery. Tout suite!!!”

The desk clerk studied me as the desperate American girl. “Ah, *Mais bien sur.* (But of course). Allow me to see if Mr. Lavery is available, *Mademoiselle*.” His tone was one of appeasement. Clearly the doorman suspected I was some deranged fan, so rather than stir a foyer fuss, and upon John’s arrival downstairs, it was suggested that John take me by the arm to the outdoor curb. He stood near me, beating his walking stick nervously against his boot-top, all the while pondering my adoration and my promise to write.

We were cordial. “The weather is lovely,” he said.

We were kind. “You are the most delightful person I’ve ever met,” I said.

We agreed to correspond. “Yes, at the very least, we’ll write,” said John.

Staring up at his facial expression, studying him for memory, his grey eyes were like the winter’s sea flickering a candle. His ski slope nose pointed down. His skin shaved clean from the barber, no sign of a beard or moustache, and his dark hair was neatly tucked back behind the ears, just receding at the temples like my father’s hairline. This was the face of a man I would care to remember. Forever.

I watched his horse-drawn carriage move further away from me, carrying John to the port and ferry. The sight of him disappearing from my view shredded my heart to tiny bits, as it did when I lost my father.

Reversing back to the hotel, I strolled this time like a ‘*Flaneur*’ - the French word for wanderer. I was lost in my little girl fantasies.

Back at the hotel, only Mother recognized the widening of my already almond eyes and suspected something. “Just where here have you been?” she asked, hands fisted at her hips.

“Nowhere in particular,” I said, and slammed the door to my bedchamber where I sat at the writing secretary, immediately postmarking a letter to the concierge for John Lavery.

> Dear, dearer, dearest and all sorts of other love names, John,
>
> I am still in your garden, still incorrigibly and unwarrantedly and unconcernedly sitting in the middle of your best flower bed, just as though I had been properly invited. I have one eye on the gate of your garden, John. You were foolish to leave it unlocked but perhaps you did that purposely…

John was all the wiser and cautious of my invitation, having married, stupidly, the once young Kathleen who turned out to not be nineteen but only seventeen – she lied; and turned out to be Welsh, not Irish - she lied again; thus, making his portrait of her entitled *The Irish Girl* a lie, too. Her real name was Annie Evans, but it would be another decade before I would find compassion for a woman like Kathleen who would go to such desperate measures to fib for survival. When Kathleen died, she left John with the responsibility of an infant girl. Sadly, the last bit was true. John thought he was walking into a similar trap with a young anxious girl, although unlike his first wife, I came from solid Chicago stock with a respectable history.

Nevertheless, he was self-deprecating albeit direct in his response:

> Well dear, I am busily engaged in looking for the key and wondering how you would feel to be locked up in such an old garden with all the flowers to tend to and the funny old paths to keep straight, and if you wouldn't, after a time, get tired and want to climb the wall, getting out one fine morning and leaving it to ruin?

Chapter Six

Hazel & John

Mother often said that "love was foolish. That the heart is just a muscle..." And I believed that the heart is an organ of heat. The heart wants what the heart wants, and I wanted John as he seemingly wanted me.

Deeply pained and vulnerable, John not only lost a wife, but his dear friend, Whistler passed away that very year we met. I saw John's vulnerability as an 'in' for me to win him over, even if it meant listening to more of his gushing admiration of Whistler. John did, after all, deliver Whistler's eulogy:

When my daughter, Eileen, was merely seven and returning from boarding school at Sacred Heart Convent, Whistler would call out to her, "Hello Little Lady of the Holy Heart!" And then proceed to lower to the floor to play dolls with Eileen, teaching her amusing rhymes about a tooter who tooted the flute.

Come to think of it, it was Whistler who saved a portrait of my daughter Eileen from destruction. Once in my studio, Whistler noticed a painting in a dark corner and exclaimed, "John, what's this?" I sheepishly wheeled it out into the light - a painting called *Pere et Fille* (father and daughter), the smell of linseed oil still present. Whistler clapped his hands, "Bravo!" and upon closer observation of the 7' x 4' canvas of the man sitting behind a small child as if pondering life, declared, "At last my dear Lavery, you have done it! Keep it as is. It is beautiful! It is complete!" It had pained John to be pallbearer at Whistler's funeral, but it also made him proud. And so, I utilized the weakness John felt for his dead friend as a source to gain his trust. In my next correspondence I wrote:

> Each star follows its own God. Whistler was yours.
>
> You are mine.

It was time he knew that I took him and his emotions very seriously. Besides, I didn't want complacency, I wanted urgency. Certainly, John would adore me with romantic urgency when the time was right. How spectacular it might be to be adored! Society didn't have room for anything other than practicality, but John wasn't practical at all.

There was one final memory (letter) of his mentor, and then John asked me to not ask him about Whistler anymore. It was time to put Whistler and his memories to rest. But this was by far the finest story of all... because years from now my grandchildren would see Whistler's work in the Musee d'Orsay:

Whistler's mother had posed for the No. 2 painting while living in Chelsea, London. Apparently, Mother Whistler had been a replacement model for a woman who hadn't kept her sitting appointment. Little did she know the French would love the portrait entitled "Whistler's Mother" and she'd someday be considered the "Victorian Mona Lisa" all from that sideways profile sitting on a chair with two Pekingese lapdogs.

Dorothy lay next to me under the duvet, as I read through John's letters. Her hand came down hard on the paper, crinkling the sheet. Her face beamed over the page at me.

"Mother is furious about Mr. Lavery," she exclaimed, with that insinuating look of sibling agitation on her face. But I fell back on the goose down pillows, letting the letters cascade to the floor in surrender. Gazing at the ceiling now, I said nothing. "Hazel?" Dorothy quipped, "Say something!"

"You know I don't want to love him," I said, "But I have to."

Silence.

Then Dorothy began to cry, "Why must you love him? You can't love him! You'll leave me all alone! With Mother."

"You won't be alone. You'll always have me," I said, more an appeasement than a fact.

"How? Chicago is a lifetime from England or France."

She was right. But I said nothing, instead pulled the gold chord of the lamplight. The room went black. "Hush, Dorothy," I whispered. "Time for sleep, my dear one."

Dorothy clung to my backside like a wounded animal, snuggling in for protection.

Our suggestive love letters moved back and forth from London to Paris, Paris to London. I was most anxious to visit John in England, in what John called "the usually most delightful month of October," when rain was at a standstill, and crisp blue skies prevailed.

John wanted to assist in helping me achieve additional lessons in dry-point etching, as well. Together, we'd be two artists, lost in love, and lost in each other, though John, being more practical, insisted we'd also try a second round of a portrait sitting in South Kensington rather than Paris. He was most comfortable surrounded by his own brushes, his own easel, and the familiar lighting of his studio, unlike some makeshift place like that in Brittany. He wanted nothing more than to capture me on canvas as he now felt for me in life... straight from the heart.

But was I just a 'muse' to John? Quite the contrary, John was more the realist and I, the usual dreamer, the romantic, and the most melodramatic of creatures, with opinions and snobbery, thus offering little stability in a painter's craft.

As luck would have it, Dorothy was shipped off to boarding school while Mother – tired from late summer's heat – refused to accompany me to London. All the better if I could travel solo. I adored the circle of friends John ran with – John Singer Sargent, yes, but now the sculptor, Rodin, as well. I adored the fame he acquired, a fame making its way to our American newspapers. I adored the clientele of royalty and the top echelon of society who trusted him with their portraits. And I adored the anticipation of being John's lover, my first official lover, but I was nervous at losing my virginity, and told him so in that next correspondence...

It has caught me now, John Lavery, the storm, and the panic.

All my fine recklessness and gay courage is gone. I am even no longer incorrigible! It is my turn to beg, 'Wait, wait, I must have time.' I am only a girl who is afraid to become a woman. And I am alone. I belong to nothing or no-one in the world – I could not bear to belong – and yet the very thought of giving myself is terrible and sweet. If I dared.

But Mother was her usual furious self, accosting the postman and snatching our correspondence.

"I forbid you to carry on with him!" demanded Mother, pacing around me where I rested on the divan, dreaming of John, and now forced to stand at attention.

"But he humanizes me from your fake society."

"I beg your pardon?" questioned Mother.

"Heavens to Betsy. Talking to you is as cumbersome as a tiny ant hauling a twig."

"Hazel Martyn!"

"I beg of you Mother, don't you see? I want to make something of my life. Be a painter, live abroad, be someone important in this world..."

"You can find something worthy to do in Chicago," she snapped.

"Like what?" I asked, "Gardening?"

"No, nothing quite so desperate."

"You're impossible," I pouted.

"Not at all. I'm attempting to stop our friends from gaining a whiff of scandal. He's a desperate old man..."

"He's a famous artist! How little you understand," I said, my arms falling limp and my voice trailing off in disappointment.

"No darling child, how little you understand," said Mother, pointing at the cushion for me to sit. I obeyed. She stood above me shadowing over my sunshine. "All this newfound gaiety over love is no basis for a romance. You must be sensible over emotion. Being sensible will afford you a life of culture, couture, a proper home, a staff, and a wardrobe suitable for your fundraisers and galas."

"But John is sensible, Mother. And he can afford culture. He is culture. Just not the type you strive for. He's an artist. I don't care about a wardrobe or a proper home. I'd live in a shack naked if I must. For love."

"Oh, good God, you've lost your mind, Hazel Martyn! There will be no more of Mr. Lavery and that's the last we'll hear of it!" With that she placed her mauve gloves on, one finger at a time, then struggled at the wrist to secure the velvet buttons. She sighed, "To think I trusted him to paint your portrait... not to steal my daughter."

From that moment on, tensions grew in our Paris hotel. I hated every fiber of this wicked widowed woman, explaining to John, it was doubtful London would be a reality.

John telegrammed: No, Hazel! Stop. Just the other way around, it would be madness and lunacy not to come. Stop. Do please trust yourself...

John waited for a reply.

None came.

And then a brief telegram arrived to him by courier from, of all people… my mother. "Very sorry, Mister Lavery, but impossible to go to London. Stop."

Chapter Seven

Hazel & John (& Ned)

Ned Trudeau showed up overnight in Paris, having received a note cabled from my mother: "Come immediately, stop. Or you'll lose Hazel for good. Stop."

Ned packed his bags in such haste that he sailed from America without even an overcoat. He'd been pursuing me since the last society event in Chicago. As for John Lavery...Mother followed her short, rude, and abrupt telegram with a proper letter:

> Dearest Mr. Lavery -
>
> It was no idle decision that I sent by telegram this morning. Hazel is truly a wreck, and I am unnerved over the worry and anxiety this question has caused us – I alone am to blame for her not going up to London, and though the inducements in every way serious and otherwise are great, I simply cannot allow to let her go now – the situation is sudden and tremendous. I do not want to trust the added glamour of the atmosphere there if she were to see you in your home.
>
> That Hazel cares a great deal for you there is no doubt, but it is the question of a lifetime. I hope you will believe that I am doing what I feel will be best for the happiness of you both.
>
> With kindest regards,
> Mrs. Martyn

John crumpled up the parchment letter as if the gesture might end the news it contained.

He collapsed into the chair at the fireplace, staring at the rise of the flames to the page. Then he stood. And paced. And paced - back and forth in front of a portrait he'd been tampering with of a lady in a green coat. He wanted to slash the emerald composition, to destroy it and all his creations.

He moved to a beaten cherry wood table full of telegrams. Picking one up to examine it, he was surprised to find that he had little interest when Rodin – asked to be President of the International Society, since Whistler was now gone – wrote a cordial and jolly note to John accepting the position:

> Mr. Vice President,
>
> I am very grateful for the honor you have paid me in offering me the International Society of Sculptors, Painters, and Gravers of London, and I beg you to receive my acceptance.
>
> In expressing to you the interest with which I will follow the movement of the Society, I beg you, Mr. Vice President, to receive the assurance of my feelings of highest consideration.
>
> Auguste Rodin

"Bollocks!" mumbled John, crinkling that note and tossing it into the fire, too.

Then he unstopped a metal flask and pressed it to his lips, sipping the warm whisky.

John Lavery couldn't pick up a paint brush for days. His fingers only able to run through the brush's bristle… thinking, pondering. Hazel, Hazel, Hazel...

One week later a letter arrived from me to John. Up until now I was completely unaware of Ned's arrival to us in Paris… until that very day.

> Oh, my dear John,
>
> To complicate matters, there arrives in Paris from America the one man in the world my dear Mother would not think me more than mildly insane to marry.

Unable to write much more, I took to a darkened room, sobbing and distressed, reminiscent of all my English heroines in all those Jane Austen novels.

Mother and Ned beat at the door. Even Dorothy tried to persuade me, but I went forty- eight hours without food or water. Only when they coaxed me out with Lobster Thermidor carefully packaged up from Chez Marie's, did I finally emerge, ravished and wilted.

But there was no stopping Mother or Ned. They were determined to make me Mrs. Trudeau...

A lavish dinner followed to fix any further starvation and celebrate our family's reunion with Ned. We strolled along Rue de Beaujolais and dined at Grand Vefour, Mother's favorite. The restaurant was the jewel of Paris in the Palais Royal, full of charm but dignity, too, in all its glory, gardens and arches.

Ned sat to her left, me to her right, with Dorothy still at boarding school. Leaning into Mother I whispered, "How many of these dreadful dinners do I have to attend?"

"As many as it takes until we find you a proper husband," she whispered back.

"We?" I asked, with sarcasm.

To annoy me even more, Mother kept raising her Bordeaux goblet in a toast of cheer. In duty I raised mine, to keep up appearances, glancing from Mother to Ned with a pasted smile.

Upon studying Mother's face, I realized that no amount of rouge, pancake powder or lipstick could mask her determination. Surely Father had left enough money not to marry me off to the first 'John' who came along. I suppressed a giggle by biting onto my fork tine. I did indeed want the first 'John' who came along. John Lavery.

As multiple courses arrived on silver trays – caviar, Jerusalem artichokes, duck – Ned's kind eyes rested on me like that of a butterfly to a flower.

Smiling demurely, my face softened from the strain that I was not giving him what he wanted. It's not that Ned would make a bad husband. Quite the contrary, of all my Chicago suitors, he had been a delightful medical student with a pedigreed resume. Educated at St Paul's school, then at Yale, and finally at Columbia University in New York, Ned was the son of the famous Dr. Trudeau who once treated Robert Louis Stevenson when he had his breakdown.

Yes, Ned was one to admire – tall and handsome with a long, droopy, masculine face like that of a Bassett hound. He had dark hair and beautiful blue eyes, always dressed appropriately in a full woolen suit, white crisp shirt, a tie, and his father's pocket watch close by in his vest pocket. By society standards he was a gorgeous catch. And I suspected I'd have to go along with the plan for now.

The next day it was decided we were returning home to Chicago, so I posted one final brief and melodramatic note to John before we set sail:

> My dearest John, my love,
>
> *Malheureusement* (French for 'unfortunately')
>
> "I am helpless more so than you know... I cannot breathe when I think of crossing that dreary sad gray ocean."
>
> Au revoir.

And so, the Martyn women, including Dorothy, set sail with Ned Trudeau for New York. Every inch of the journey took me further and further away from John.

Shortly after arrival across the pond, Ned, a house surgeon at New York Presbyterian Hospital, whisked me to meet his parents at their hunting lodge in Saranac Lake, just north of Troy. I'd never witnessed so many pine trees and mountains. It was so unlike Chicago. It was a glorious sanctuary on the lake, and it made me long for a simpler mountain life, and the imagery of what it might be like baking pies and tending to a house for a husband without the accompanying staff.

Despite their odd love of sailing, swimming, and hunting, the Trudeaus were lovely people with all the proper etiquette. Their home décor was the most modern of Victorian furniture characterized by ornate and intricate carvings. The fabrics were luxurious, and as I sat in the morning room on the green damask, Mrs. Trudeau made us tea. I watched Ned and his father talk chummy in the distance of the drawing room, their hands clasped behind their backs just above their coat tails in similar father and son fashion. John had even begun to grow mutton chops to mimic his father's matching facial hairs.

Oval gold-framed portraits of Trudeaus lined the hallways in the distance. I'd be next. A predictable life. Eventually on a wall. Was that such a terrible thing?

As Mrs. Trudeau called the housekeeper for a tray of biscuits, my hand reached out to some decorative pieces on a side table. A silver cache with a reptile that resembled a snake-charmer's snake. It was hideous, but to its left was a delicate silver mirror. Picking it up and examining its backside I appreciated the feather pattern in enamel with sapphire trim catching the rainbow light from the windows. Flipping it over, I didn't appreciate what I viewed in the glass ... a sad woman reflected like a haunted ghost from a Dickens novel, longing for the life I would never have in London, seeing my future but knowing it would be officially over before it began.

Clearly Mother had won...

"You'll come to Newport this summer, yes?" asked Mrs. Trudeau trying to break the awkward silence.

Placing my China cup down, I replied, "Perhaps. Though I was hoping to attempt some charity work in Manhattan."

"Don't be foolish. You'll miss the women's sailing league. And the dinners with the most elite of families from the Carolinas. The Vanderbilts throw the most glorious of all soirees."

"Yes, true. But I thought Newport was designed for women

who otherwise had no power in politics or business... to be presented and hopefully snatched up for a favorable marriage. I'm not that. I have Ned now."

The tone in the room changed. To what I wasn't certain. "More tea, dear?" asked Mrs. Trudeau.

Obediently I nodded, the liquid pouring into my cup. Our eyes stayed glued on each other as she sized me and my truth, up and down.

Traveling home to Chicago I wrote to John Lavery, the final note, though I had trouble moving the pen across the page, pausing, correcting, and crossing out the words until I brought it down to the right amount of brevity.

> Goodbye John Lavery –
>
> As I came into your life suddenly and without warning, I leave and there is silence once more. For I must go, and you must not cry out or lift your hand to bring me back – it is not to be – let us forget.
>
> Before you read this I shall belong to Edward Trudeau, utterly irrevocably. I may not tell you my reason and you shall not ask; this is at once a command and an entreaty.
>
> John Lavery, believe in the truth of my every thought and word and deed toward you. There was no stain of falseness in there.
>
> Once you said it took a long time to become young, but one can grow old in a single hour. I am old and very tired. Please keep my letters. They are the real, real, Hazel. You can remember her without bitterness – I have gone and again you are alone."

John wrote a desperate telegram which arrived on December 1st. "Any Hope?" but I ignored him. I had to.

He followed up with a cable to my mother, "Please delay

proceedings. Stop. Her future happiness possesses undoubted proof. Stop. Delay can injure nobody. May prevent grave mistakes. Do consider. Sailing shortly. Stop."

Mother ignored him, too.

John always believed that if he had six months left to live, he'd paint faster. His art being everything. Yet, it was at that very moment, John Lavery realized that painting pictures was nothing.

It was love that was everything...

Chapter Eight
Hazel

One might imagine my wedding to be a massive over-the-top society event, but my heart wasn't aligned with the nuptials. Nevertheless, Mother saw to it that despite only a mere intimate gathering that we remained the most fashionable event of the holiday season.

The Chicago Tribune wasted no time alerting all the news in their next social column:

It was not unlike the bride, who is noted not only for beauty and popularity but also for her artistic taste in all things, to select such time-honored songs as *Annie Laurie*, *How Can I Leave Thee*, and *Drink to Me Only with Thine Eyes*. Instead of a modern love song as a setting for the holy words of matrimony, a simple old German melody softly played overtaken by the stirring wedding march from *Lohengrin* as the bride appeared down the aisle.

Refusing to allow Mother to compensate for Father's absence, I walked down the aisle of St. Chrysostom's alone, wearing a delicate gown with garlands of orange blossoms around the bodice. A rosebud clasp ensemble secured a flowing tulle veil to the top of my head. Dorothy said I looked ethereal under the pale winter sunlight which struggled through the stained-glass windowpanes.

Father Snively, my family's Preacher, who gave me the sacrament of confirmation years before, greeted me with a smile and a nod from the altar.

Handsome and perfectly appropriate, tuxedoed up in black and white, Ned waited for me, nodding a sign to Mother that they had won.

But in my death-sentence-of-a-walk to the altar, all I could reflect upon was the letter I'd posted to John back in England, that morning...

> And this is my wedding day. I suffer.
>
> There is no such thing as joy or goodness or justice in this world and it is not true that hearts break, they merely grow more, keep with pain, and ache through one's whole life.
>
> It is not true that duty should be a primary consideration.
>
> I am yours, the soul and the breath and brain and bleeding heart of me are yours – and my life will be lived for you whether you will or not – and you shall think and long despair with me – always – always – always.
>
> No law can hold my soul. No human creature can touch me.
>
> I am yours. Your letter came this morning. God is indeed cruel to me. And I have nothing but bitterness in my heart.
>
> My love, my best beloved, do you suffer with me? Or are you in your wisdom and greatness pitying me for my mad grief and unreasoning anguish?
>
> I am not a child. I am a woman and I have suffered as much as you have in your whole life – I know.
>
> Dearest, I wish my heart had stopped beating forever that night at Pont Aven. I remember how I trembled all the night through and prayed to God to let me be happy and have my heart's desire. I knew then that I was to suffer... I never dreamed too much. I love you supremely. I am not an ordinary woman and I do not love in ordinary ways. - As ever, Hazel

The Preacher cleared his throat. "Repeat after me... I, Hazel Martyn, take you, Edward Livingston Trudeau Jr., for my lawfully wedded husband, to have and to hold from this day forward, for better for worse, for richer for poorer, in sickness and in health, until death do us part."

I repeated the words verbatim. My "I do" was followed by an inward gasp, as if I were holding my breath under water. As if I was drowning.

"I now pronounce you man and wife" was clarified. Ned raised my veil as his newly appointed wife and kissed my lips. On December 28th, 1903, I became Mrs. Hazel Trudeau in St Chrysostom's church... until death, really until death – which I hoped would happen soon – we would part.

Alas... be careful what you wish for...

As newlyweds in wedded bliss, we moved to a furnished Park Avenue apartment, a wedding gift from Ned's parents. From the window I could see Grand Central Station where just the year before, two locomotives collided because the smoke coming from the steam trains obscured the signal. Somehow it felt apropos of my life.

Nevertheless, my new home was welcoming, with a black and white checkerboard ceramic floor upon entry and lovely floral arrangements tucked in every portal down the hall. Emerald green toile wallpaper made it cheery, and the bedroom had a four-poster bed so tall it required a step stool to climb up.

The apartment was equipped with a small studio with sufficient light for my painting, though my painting skills felt a million miles away, someplace with John, someplace in Europe. Ned's parents doted on us, and thought we were the most handsome couple in all of America.

Ned was a renowned surgeon at Bellevue Hospital, working brutally long hours. As a result, I spent brutally long hours missing my Chicago life, my English life, and my Parisian life, too. But how could I complain since Ned had given up his life to serve others who were mentally challenged, poor and homeless at Bellevue's public hospital space?

An epidemic of disease and pneumonia was gaining strength in Manhattan, and I worried about Ned's health. He worked near his dying patients.

Only a few months after the wedding, maybe because I had prayed that I would die, or that he would die, or we both would die, it was Ned who contracted pneumonia and did.

Die.

It was a brain embolism compounded by the fluid in his lungs. We'd been sitting in the parlor, sharing an evening sherry, when without warning and in a very dramatic way, Ned collapsed to the floor.

I screamed. And screamed and screamed. More for my wicked thoughts than the fact that he'd collapsed. As the medical workers attempted to save him, I was certain that all my wishing for death was transparent. God would never forgive me. God would someday punish me.

But by the next day, I knew I couldn't think of that guilt. As a girl raised with solid values and discipline, I knew that I must follow protocol, follow ritual, and behave like a lady, so I contained my underlying happiness and with grave concern, wired a cable back home to Chicago. And one to Troy, New York.

The next day Ned's parents arrived. Within days Mother arrived with my sister, Dorothy.

Ned's parents tended to the arrangements, devastated beyond repair.

Dorothy and I dressed for the wake, where she cornered me in my bedroom, between the dressing table and the washstand, practically hissing: "This is what you wanted, isn't it?"

"How could you say such a thing?" I questioned, taken aback by her bold accusation. "Shame on you, Dorothy. Ned was my husband."

"On legal paper, perhaps," snapped Dorothy, "but your heart is elsewhere. Dorothy cast her eyes down to my waistline, watching as I rubbed circles around my belly, now rounded with pregnancy. She softened. "I'm sorry," said Dorothy. "I shouldn't have."

"It's quite alright," I said, tears welling up. "Emotions run high at funerals as they do at weddings." We stared at each other like the twin flame soulmate sisters we once had been. My bottom lip quivered for the next outburst of sobbing. Suddenly I felt forlorn for a husband who would never know his unborn child and a child who would never know its father. "Dorothy? Where do you suppose he is?"

"In his casket," she said, affirmatively.

"No, no, no," I said, "I have to believe there's a heaven and Father is there to greet him..."

"That would be ever so nice," said Dorothy, arms outstretched and then pulling me in with her own sobs. She held me and we stood swaying for a long bit – two sisters - tears streaming down each other's shoulders.

I pulled back first, "I've an announcement to make." I wiped my eyes and corrected my posture. "I think it's time for me to come home."

"To me?" asked Dorothy, excited.

"Yes," I said, certain I was no longer welcome to stay on in New York amid the remaining Trudeaus. "I'm coming home to Chicago."

Ned's funeral took place on a sunny spring day at a church in the village of Paul Smiths, only a short distance from the Trudeaus' Saranac home. It was a beautiful hamlet in Franklin County, New York, just on the gentle Lake of the Adirondacks, a place Ned so loved.

During the service, Mrs. Trudeau caught my glance, knowing all too well I was not in mourning but in silent celebration. It was understood and unspoken, but I knew what it would mean for me and that of my unborn baby. Mrs. Trudeau did not know of my pregnancy, nor did I intend to tell her. Years later I'd understand the selfishness of keeping a child from its grieving grandparents, but until then, I had a lot to learn about empathy and compassion.

After the ceremony I moved home to our Martyn family's new and smaller home at 566 Division Street East in Chicago. I felt a sudden gratitude I'd never known as I lit the evening lamps in the parlor. Seating myself on a pale gold and brocade wing chair I methodically counted the cabbage-rose garlands on the wallpaper, realizing we'd had similar paper in our past home but that I never cared to really take notice. Now the roses signaled belonging, safety, family.

It was a relief to be surrounded by childhood furnishings of rosewood consoles. The mahogany bookshelves reminded me of the years us Martyn's read books alone or to each other. And I paid special care to Father's Irish history books, now properly dusted and placed on a shelf of their own. He used to tell me, "You can always tell someone by their collection of books or the lack thereof."

From the edge of my porcelain teacup, I watched with delight as the parlor maid freshened the fire with more coals, poking vigorously to stimulate the flames, as the flames within my heart knew I must wait just an appropriate amount of time longer. The recommended length of time mourning a husband was up to two years. By contrast, men had it much easier. Widowers mourned for up to six months, sometimes less. And they were encouraged to remarry more than widows.

I would mourn, yes, but decided I would mourn more like a man.

Chapter Nine

Hazel & Alice

My mood never improved with the baby I carried, despite its active kicking and knocking about, alerting me to its existence. I tried not to moan too loud, as Mother taught me that we "never complain and never explain." But I felt I was bearing some massive punishment... as if the baby was really Ned kicking at me in truth and in spirit.

As I grew larger, walking in heeled shoes was impossible. Social events were intolerable. Life was unbearable. I took many hours to bed until finally, one October day, as the leaves turned gold and orange at their peak, labor came, hard and fast.

Birth was a living hell. How did women before me experience this and still survive? No wonder my own mother emotionally tortured me so...

Truly delirious, writhing in pain, the only thing to save me was the large oak tree outside the window, so magnificent in its autumn color... my focus on its falling leaves. The nurses administered twilight drugs, which saved me, but later I learned that I had almost died as my pelvis was too tiny to pass the baby's eight-pound weight. They had to use forceps to practically rip her from me. Worst of all, I'd longed for a son and ended up with the pink, sticky, blob of a daughter... Alice Livingston Trudeau. Born October 10, 1904.

But as I held Alice in my arms, all pain, suffering and longing for a baby boy was forgotten. She was mine. Beautiful little Alice, her mouth struggling for air and sucking on her delicate pink fists. As was natural, she squirmed and rooted towards my breast. I felt such a mix of emotions. And exhaustion. On the one hand, I felt melancholy, wishing her father had lived to see her born, to be a father, but on the other, I longed for John Lavery to be that father figure.

In the days that followed, something wasn't quite right. I needed many herbs and medicines from the apothecary, including an elixir with dried elder flowers, to assist my lack of energy. But, to no avail, I developed nephritis, a post-natal condition with severe side effects like face and ankle swelling, migraines, and blurry vision, diminishing me to near blindness.

As Chicago's chill whipped its winds and winter dragged on, so did my illness. An unexpected darkness gnawed at my sanity. For no apparent reason I'd find myself sitting in a corner, staring at nothing, days away from being catatonic. An overall sadness took me to some unexplained dark side. My obstetrician informed me of postpartum depression, common in women following childbirth.

Napping helped restore my energy; Alice slept often at my side.

Finally, around late February I began to resurface as Hazel, only a different Hazel, a maternal Hazel, one foremost protective of my infant girl, and the world that surrounded her.

Even Mother was kinder to me, or perhaps it was me who appreciated Mother. Able to finally rise from bed, I joined her for breakfast in the solarium. Spooning marmalade onto my toast, the sound of my knife against the bread was the only sound occupying the room. I looked into Mother's eyes. My expression? Sad, distant, and very changed from the social animal I used to be.

"What seems to be the matter?" she asked.

"Please, Mother," I begged. "Please write to John and let him know I'm a mother now. And a widow."

Placing the spoon down next to the soft-boiled egg on her place setting, mother pondered the idea as though I was certain she would say 'no.' Instead she surprised me, and with a delicate smile said, "I shall."

"Oh, thank you, Mother," I said, the first bit of enthusiasm I'd mustered in months.

Except that I didn't know Mother's correspondence would be so brief...

> Dear Mr. Lavery, Hazel barely lived – improving – daughter born. Stop.

As I swaddled with my newborn daughter, I thought about what John would feel hearing from Mother. I wondered repeatedly what type of wonderful father he might be to Alice and to me. And I wondered what he was up to in his European life. Was he alone in his studio or had he taken a lover, or worse, a wife? Barely able to contain much more curiosity, I sat at the desk and wrote while little Alice slept in her cradle:

> My Dearest John,
>
> How good you are, John Lavery, and how beautiful your garden is...

My wrist stopped moving. My fingers wrapped around the fountain pen, debating whether to start with that opening sentence or not. By comparison to all that I'd been through, the sentence seemed trite. I wanted honesty, sadness, and truth, not persistence. And so, I began again...

> My Dearest John,
>
> I have been so very far away, and my suffering and my need have been great. I am groping my way slowly back to the world and to life although it may be weeks and months before I am strong again.
>
> Alice is a darling. She is very wee and ugly and queer, but her ears and hands are beautiful, and her mouth and chin like that of a 'V'."

It was unusual for my behavior... carrying on and on in the letter about little Alice... able to mix a woman's needs with that of a mother... something I never realized is the true essence of what makes a woman finally become a woman: Motherhood.

A new appreciation of my own mother continued to grow in those months following Alice's birth, as I found myself fascinated with how she raised us after Father died. She was alone. And undoubtedly frightened. No wonder she wanted the best for me with a man like Ned who could provide security.

This time, when I sealed the envelope and handed it to Mother, I just knew in my heart of hearts she would be sure to send it through the post on my behalf.

And she did.

As spring sprung in 1905, my health had improved immensely. Alice was strong and eating healthily, crawling around between the chair legs and the dining table, gurgling, and cooing to all our delight.

We were busy packing for spring and summer holiday, so I wrote only a brief note to John asking him to reunite with us. We were traveling to England, to the Malvern Wells, a health spa in Worcestershire near Stratford-upon-Avon...

The motor car carried us through the civil parish and town of Worcestershire, England, down the foot of Malvern Hill, an area of outstanding rugged mountainous beauty, when we came upon a small town. We stopped outside of a pub with a thatch roof, the signs out front beckoned for us to come in – 'two-for-one pint on Tuesdays.'

What was a pint? We had no intention of drinking, but Mother and I entered so she might use the ladies' relief area. As the patrons stopped to stare at us, dressed in our daytime finest, Mother refused to meet their eyes. She moved straight ahead staring her way to the woman's powder room, if one could call it that… more a rusty basin area. Before moving through the door, she reprimanded back, “Do not touch a thing. It’s filthy. Arms at your side.”

Alice was in the motor car with the driver.

I awkwardly stood in the center of the plank floors of the pub, smiling and meeting the eyes of the patrons, knowing they’d overheard her. I smiled again, wondering who all these people were. What did they do in this life? Did they work? Or did they take European holidays like our Martyn family? They stared back, some nodding, some whispering about me, but all of them dressed in working clothes with dirt on their trousers and sweat on their backs. I suspected they were ‘wage earners.’

The women were in a separate room, in the back, sharing drinks, since their presence was a potential threat to male camaraderie. Even upon entering the pub, I noted there was a separate entrance that read “Ladies Entrance” though Mother and I didn’t use it.

“Hello, Lass,” said one, approaching with apparently, a pint.

“Hello,” I said, “Lovely to meet you.”

His eyes lit up with hope. I smiled graciously.

“What’s in a pint?” I asked, smiling.

And then Mother was there, swinging my arm in the other direction, escorting me out the door, her gaze held firmly on the exit.

“Do not speak to those people...” she said.

“But they’re...”

“Commoners are what they are,” Mother said, practically pushing me out of the door frame. “They’re outside our social class.”

“But they’re just being friendly,” I said, waving back to the gentleman mouthing the words, ‘I’m sorry.’

“Friendly, sure! They could only dream of having a wife like you.”

“But they’re people. Just like us!”

"Enough," said Mother, "now get into the motor car."

"I'd prefer not to breathe," I whispered, lifting my dress to step into the backseat.

"Excuse me?" she asked.

"You're incorrigible," I said.

"I take that as a compliment," she said, and then I watched as my mother lifted her dress hem to reenter our isolated existence of wealth, upper class, and snobbery. Ironically, footmen had become a thing of the past, now considered extravagant, which was of course, Mother. And motor cars had changed everything since a carriage horse was limited to the fixed radius of the distance it could handle to go and come back. But motor cars were extremely expensive. Moments later, with a putter and a rev of the engine, we were on our way. But I couldn't help but turn around and watch the thatched-roof tavern grow farther from view, until it was out of sight.

"Turn around," said Mother, bouncing Alice on her lap.

I did as I was told, slamming my back into the seat, and smiling at little Alice, observing me. I wasn't sure that this was what I wanted for my daughter. Why was it I was allowed the luxury of riches while the folks in that tavern worked hard, undoubtedly saving and budgeting their earnings to share a 'pint' at the bar, or fish and chips. Would Alice never know the other world?

Glancing at Mother there was something more... I couldn't put a finger on it, but it seemed it might be that the pub women had little interest in each other's clothing whereas women always dressed for women in Chicago circles. But not here. No, those women were about each other. Not the jewels, the finest Milner's, or the bonnets - the ones that bordered on ridiculous like a meringue on top of the head from a pastry shop. At the heart of me, I'd be fine in a frock. I'd always been an artist, happiest in love, happiest to be with John, in the seaside shanty of my dreams, if we must...

"Ahhhh, yes, we've arrived," signed Mother, taking in the spa which was a lovely and wonderful respite of stillness despite

England being a dinner-giving-society. At Malvern she would be more relaxed. Thank goodness.

The days folded into one another...

I spent long mornings reading in my sleigh bed as Alice napped at my side after a game of "peekaboo, Mommy sees you!"

Mother and I dined with Alice, quietly, often in our room or on the private balcony, overlooking the hills and the serenity of the countryside, a cool breeze always moving in on cue. There is a time of day from afternoon to dusk when for just a few minutes everything is bathed in a vivid blue with a purple hue. "Magic light" is what I called it. Magic light fascinates; never disappoints...and as an artist it stirred something inside of me.

One morning, out of the corner of my eye, and as I spooned oats and apple sauce into Alice's precious little mouth, I noticed Mother admiring me. As a woman. Woman to woman. And at that, I turned and smiled, and she returned the gesture to both of us, holding the gaze for quite a while. Our eyes shifted to Alice in adoration.

Maybe Alice would be the one little person to finally bond us in all this society boredom.

Mother cared for Alice most daytimes which allowed me the luxury of finally picking up a paintbrush. It had been so long. My first subject was none other than my daughter, Alice. The painting titled *The Brown Baby* for the enormous topiary sitting next to Alice's pram which sheltered her from the light. The reason I called her 'the brown baby' was because her bonnet was white and her skin darker in tone, like that of her father Ned's. Oh Ned, poor Ned. To die so young and never know his little girl. Such a sin...perhaps we would have been happy...

But John was beginning to step up, sending the baby a parasol to protect her from "Father Sol" and a portfolio to carry my canvases. Mother delivered them from the hotel concierge with an added bounce in her step, as though she approved of the showering of gifts.

The unspoken was now obvious...

Dearest John,

Today has been such a wonderful day for I painted all morning and walked in the hills all afternoon. If you could have been near me, I should have asked nothing more of the very Bon Dieu. But I am so wildly excited about painting! It surely is a fairyland, and the brushes are fairy wands that have the power to make everything change and become beautiful.

Thank you for your thoughtful and generous gifts... do say that you'll visit soon...

Chapter Ten

Hazel & John

During my convalescence John visited Malvern Spa. He dropped his bags on the rail station's platform at the sight of me approaching in the distance. I longed to fall into his arms and share a long overdue and most passionate kiss, but John was reserved, cautious, with a stiff upper lip. I did, however, emit a soft gasp at our proper embrace.

"There, there," he said, finally softening and lifting his right hand to my temple to tuck a wisp of hair behind my ear under my velvet black hat. "Still as beautiful as ever, Hazel..."

"I've missed you so much... more than you know, John Lavery," I replied, my voice dripping with desperation and sadness for having grown up.

As we strolled to the carriage and followed the footman, I moved silently, John gazing over at me to make certain I was alright. He could see that I'd aged much since the last time that he and I were physically together. The death of Ned, the birth of Alice, and fighting my ongoing illness does that to a woman weathering many storms.

When our eyes dared to catch one another all I could do was smile, looking up at him, from where I rested my head on his shoulder; breaking the moment with a giggling sigh of relief. Thank God he was here!

We spent the mornings playing croquet while Alice crawled around the green. Mother spent her afternoons practicing archery or playing bridge with Dorothy, while Alice napped.

As for me, and to make John's visit official business, he decided to capture my mood in a painting now known as *Dame en Noir* or *Woman in Black*. Sitting posed and somber, my eyes as hazel and wide as ever, albeit hooded from lack of sleep, my nose dipped slightly, pointing straight-on. As a widow I wore all black, as was to be expected, but my lips were ruby red and moist, longing for passion. It was a tremendous juxtaposition between duty and defiance... between the losing and the living. John loved how I stared at him, and when he smiled, his face was like that of an open window allowing the sun to stream in.

The day when we were to begin the portrait, he didn't.

Instead, he folded his hands in his lap and simply sat, studying me intently. Consuming his subject. He saw things nobody else could see...a light on my face...suggesting a hopeful future for a widow, torn between the dependable old and the unknown and unreliable new.

Finally, after much deliberation he began, telling me to look straight on. I did.

But I was looking beyond him at a table in the corner where one lone candle burned to the base. He reprimanded, "Don't look at whatever is drawing your attention. I can see it in your eyes."

Immediately I changed my gaze to a new direction, straight into an intended void, except my mind was ticking thoughts of him... of what our life might be, of what my father might have thought of John. Would he have approved?

"Hazel, you're doing it again," said John. "Don't think, because it alters your expression."

"I don't know what I'm to do," I whispered, more desperate than respectful. "I'm in love with you..."

John lowered his brush and sighed. "Yes, I'm in love with you too, my dearest, but I want you to close your eyes for a moment." Then sternly, as though my emotions were irrelevant, art being his first and most important love, he said, "I must capture your essence. I must capture your pain. Clear your thoughts. Breathe.

Think of nothing. Not even me."

Closing my eyes, I swallowed hard against the knot in my throat and did as I was told.

A long moment's pause.

"Now open," he said.

I did. My mind, a clean slate.

With a deep exhale he began. Brush to canvas.

First, he applied an *Ivory Black* oil color, one that would provide a sad and forlorn widow's backdrop to surround my alabaster skin. It was the only solo hue in the portrait peering out from the misery of darkness. A *Lead White* pigment for my cheekbones gave the appearance that I was very much alone, almost ghostly, and my daunting hazel eyes revealed that I very much wanted love.

"You said you loved me," I whispered when I knew we were done for the day. "So casually you said you loved me."

"And love you I do, Hazel, with every fiber of my heart, my soul and loin."

A couple of days later, Mother circled the painting, finger to her chin, examining and studying the finished product. Her head moved up and down, left to right. Finally, she announced, "It's void of emotion."

"What I was hoping for," said John. "To capture Hazel in mourning."

He was correct. What I saw in seeing my portrait was an empty woman, lonely, isolated, like a doorstop for living.

They say that black on black is the hardest painting to recreate, and yet John Lavery had accomplished it effortlessly.

"Well then," said Mother, leaving it at that.

Later that day, alone, we shared tea and scones. As I passed the cucumber sandwiches, I asked my beloved, "What might it be like to be common? To have a simple life?" But the question widened his eyes, and he sat back away from me.

"Why does this question arise?"

"I can't be certain. But I was so fascinated by the pub where we stopped on route here. The people were so happy. Even amid nothingness they were relaxed. Joyous."

"They don't know what they don't have," said John.

"I was envious," I admitted. "What they have seems to be all they want."

"For me, as an artist, I believe it's not having things. It's having stories to tell, not possessions to show." John leaned forward to refresh my tea's hot water. "Come to think of it, Hazel, the older I get, the more I realize that it's quite all right to live a life that others don't understand."

"I'm learning that in loss and in living, it's best to expect nothing and appreciate everything." With that, I reached my hand across to John's. He gently squeezed my fingers in his. "The best things in life aren't things, Fath..." I almost said 'father' – almost called him 'father.'

"Hazel, I..."

But the moment was abruptly broken as Mother stormed the room. "Darling girl, it's time to dress for dinner," she said. "Roasted quail is tonight's main dish."

"Yes," I said, leaving John's fingers to linger. "The scent of fennel is everywhere." And then turning back to John, "Will you join us?" I asked.

John shook his head, "No, no, my dear. As they say, I am as full as the Butcher's dog."

Mother moved again to the finished portrait of me. "Mr. Lavery..." she said, pondering a moment.

"Yes, Mrs. Martyn..."

"Shall you call it *The Widow*?" Mother's tone suggesting caution and reminder of my status.

"*The Dame en Noir*," he snapped, not moving from his chair, but fixating his eyes on mine.

"The woman at night..." I smiled. "I love it!" "Lovely," said Mother, with just a hint of sarcasm and a lot of concern in her tone, as if she held the monopoly on honor.

Later as I changed into dinner attire, the first formal dinner since our arrival, Mother approached me at my vanity where I sat clasping my pearls. From the mirror I could see her reflection behind me. "Just say it, Mother. Say what's on your mind."

"You look lovely, dear. Wonderful to see you back to your most authentic self."

"That's not what you're thinking..."

"Fine," she huffed. "This salacious behavior... this, this cavorting with Mr. Lavery is not good for your reputation..." She left the sentence to hang.

"Cavorting? Oh, Mother, please," I said, handing her the string of pearls over my shoulder as I struggled with the clasp. "You have such rigid morals! Honestly, we've had a delightful time, you, and me. I've been a dutiful daughter and I finally felt as though we were of the same mind. I very much want your full support of our friendship."

Clasping the necklace around my neck Mother wiped at my shoulder blades to straighten my dress sleeves before lowering her face to mine. Glancing up we were cheek to cheek in the mirror. "Darling daughter," she exclaimed, "He was fine at a distance but seeing him in person is deplorable. It's not been a respectable amount of time since Ned's passing."

I stood up from the ottoman, turning to face my mother, then took her hands in mine. Studying the front and back, the fine blue veins of her hands; the similarities of our features.

"Might you imagine duty and happiness together?" I asked.

Mother looked confused.

"Duty in memory of Ned, and happiness in the hopes of a future." But Mother said nothing. "I promise you," I said, my tone mild with adoration, "no, I can assure you that for the moment, John and I are only interested in each other for our shared artistic endeavors... our pursuit of color on canvas and all its miracles." I bent over to gather my summer stole and evening clutch from the chair. "Romance is not considered an option just now, and quite frankly I'm surprised you'd even suggest it." Mother rolled her eyes, knowing full well I was lying, knowing full well I was writing to John Lavery again… and again and again.

"Come now, Mother, we'll be late for appetizers, and you so love prawns."

"They're serving Welsh Rarebit," snapped Mother.

"All the better," I said, dismissing her fears, and fetching her jeweled clutch purse which she took from me with resignation.

Chapter Eleven

Hazel & John (& Mother)

My father once told me that everything should be understood by means of self-examination... but my 'self' had grown tired and discouraged. While I felt close to John, I still felt so far. And I wondered if I had played into the tug-of-wars that brought us together as well as kept us apart.

The very next morning, before the crack of my soft-boiled egg, Mother abruptly announced that we'd be departing for France.

"France?" I asked, twisting my face in an expression of confusion.

"Yes," she said, "To Etretat. If we have time, we'll stop in Paris."

"Paris?"

"Yes, why do you keep repeating me?" she asked, aggravated. "Coco Chanel's making headway with her new hat collection. Apparently, her 'chapeaus' are surprisingly understated. It's all anyone's speaking of..."

"Good, we could use some simplicity," I murmured.

"I beg your pardon," said Mother.

"Oh please, I love you... but there's more to life than Parisian hats," I said, stabbing my silver fork into a bowl of berries.

Mother snapped at the housekeeper and nanny, demanding they alert the staff to a list of about twenty intentions and instructions for our departure. I could not help but catch the maid and the butler sharing a look, one that said they were utterly exhausted in catering to our every need and our short-term whims, complaints and demands. Utterly ridiculous.

As Mother requested the immediate removal of the breakfast tray– yes, Ma'am, right away, Ma'am – the young waiter attempted to lift the silver tray overflowing with dishes, cups, and glasses in need of washing, but Mother's commands made him nervous.

"Hurry along," said Mother, "we'll need to dress!"

"Yes, Ma'am," said the young waiter, the tray jiggling until a spoon fell to the parquet floor. Upon trying to balance the dishes and gather the spoon, the entire tray crashed, too. Dropping to his knees to gather up the mess, Mother sighed. Instinctively I stood from my chair and dropped to my knees to help him.

" *Malheureusement, Mademoiselle*," he said, glancing up at me – French for unfortunately – and avoiding a stare, tears forming in the corners of his eyes, his hands moving swiftly to the glass. "Will I be fired?" he whispered in his best broken English to which I shook my head no.

"Careful you'll cut yourself," I warned, trying to pick up the shards of glass.

"*Oui, Mademoiselle*," he whispered.

"Is this your only job?" I whispered back. He nodded.

Mother chimed in, "It's the worst way to make a living. To work."

I shot her a look that said she was being heartless, but she stood up and clapped her hands, ordering everyone not to make a spectacle of the spectacle. Time to pack.

It was then I formed a love/hate for my mother. On one hand I appreciated all that she had given me in this life, but on the other, it was clear that anger and loneliness ruled her.

Proud people bear sad sorrows for themselves... I'd read that once.

As I helped the nursemaid pack up Alice's wardrobe and toys, I wondered exactly how much time and care went into running a resort like this? A hard-working-class who serviced our rigid itineraries of socializing nonsense. Let's see... There was the bellhop, the footman, the receptionist, the chefs, the waterboys, the waiters, the maids, the concierge, the gardeners, the laundry workers, the women who ironed our sheets, and our dresses. Finally, there was the nurse for Alice. And if one went riding? Well, the mud-splattered clothes had to be scrubbed for hours on end.

"Stop your dilly-dallying, Hazel," said Mother. "Get to packing our wardrobe and the nurse can organize little Alice."

I had become accustomed to quietly tipping the staff – a pound here and a pound there –but always behind Mother's back. Jane was the maid, Saoirse the housekeeper, Colin the bellhop, Thomas the concierge, Matthew the gardener, and so on. I snuck each of them loose change the past week and ever since that pub experience. No wonder I'd witnessed the maid slip a banana or croissant from our unwanted breakfast trays. Poor dears. They could barely make ends meet.

Mother kept a close reign on me, keeping me in the boudoir but I struck up a conversation with Charles who was about to carry our variety of suitcases and attaches. The many changes of clothes required much heavy luggage. Proper dress was a preoccupation of the rich, while poor Charles, in one uniform, was from London and came from a family of six children. I tipped him, too.

As we departed for the train station, it was clear that Mother intended to waste little time in plucking me from John, and I intended to waste little time in dropping a note by the concierge, as we made our way out the door and into our carriage. I decided to go back to the romantic giddy way we once corresponded. It was due time:

> My Love,
>
> It is wonderful how much you have improved the garden, Johnnie! There are magic corners everywhere...
>
> And now on a whim of Mother's we are off to Etretat, France, where I'm sure gardens abound...

John wasted no time in responding either and wrote right to the point. "We will elope if we must!" refusing to lose me twice in one lifetime.

That message was already waiting when we arrived at Le Hotel des Roches Blanches in Cassis.

But Etretat, oh Etretat! A place known for its chalk cliffs, including its three natural arches and a pointed formation called L'Aiguille on the Needle. When the tide is low it rises some seventy meters above sea level and seemed to mimic John's sudden stirring for me.

Strolling the grounds, I had to admit, the resort was magnificent. The hotel took its name from the limestone rocks that lined the coast from Cassis to Marseille and had the most breathtaking view of the majestic cliff of Cap Canaille. Staring out at it all, I just knew there was a higher life, a much bigger purpose for me than the perspective of life seen through Mother's eyes. "Truly it's every artist's inspiration just sitting there waiting to be painted," I said, but Mother shrugged, uninterested. Art and vision weren't her strong points.

Once settled at Le Hotel des Roches Blanches, and after hanging my day dresses in the wardrobe, I sat to write to John. Mother and Dorothy went to tea, and my little Alice was napping. Dipping my fountain pen into the ink jar, so anxious to write, even the scratch of my writing instrument racing across the paper was moving faster than I could...

I wrote of E'trat, Gustave Courbet, and the Realism movement, and Alice, too.

This time John didn't respond. Days went by. Nothing.

"Mother!"

"Yes, Hazel..." she said with a crafty innocence to her tone as she sat brushing her hair one-hundred-and-one strokes. Not a lock out of place.

I stood behind her. "I've been conducting an illicit courtship with John Lavery." I paused for effect, before adding, "And I love him. I'm in love with him. We are in love with each other."

Mother paused, setting the silver-plated brush on the vanity. "Was the deception necessary?"

"You left me no choice," I persisted. "Had I married John years ago I wouldn't be a widow with a small child. Instead, the child would have been John's, and my husband would be very much alive to help raise her."

"One can't change or improve on destiny..." Mother said, her voice dripping with some sort of misguided wisdom.

All I could do was guffaw. "Your tone, the way that you speak... Can you not understand love?

"Yes," she said gently. "I understand love. I also understand practicality." And then she paused, inhaling and exhaling in such a way that I thought she might burst into tears. "I'll see what I might do."

The next day, Mother wrote to John:

> The revelations of yesterday were a terrible blow to me, but it is far better to be out and understood. We will be at home between three and four if you will come then. We will adjust matters – I certainly shall not stand in the way of Hazel's health and happiness.

Chapter Twelve

Hazel & John (and Dorothy)

What is the obligation vs the expectation in a relationship between mother and daughter? I wondered what Father might say to all this push and pull if he were alive to witness Mother's rules. Perhaps my mother didn't want to lose me to another continent?

These questions moved through my ever-concerned thoughts. Why would anyone want to control another person's happiness?

A week later, and so as not to make it too formal, John met us in a Brasserie for lunch; Mother and I sat on one banquette with John across from us in the other.

Mother's long-awaited support of our love had stipulations, and an agreement made that after a six-month separation period, if I still wanted John and he wanted me, she would not stop our marriage. In the meantime, Mother had more demands... we were not to correspond unless I became seriously ill or vice versa.

Of course, those were Mother's rules for Chicago, but knowing I was on the same continent as my love for the duration, I snuck one final note to him with our next address at Hotel Foyot in Paris, where we'd be staying for a couple of months longer.

Within days, John was in Paris, and on his way to Italy, longing to see me.

Finding any excuse to leave my sister busy sewing needlepoint in the room, I scurried down the spiral staircase, and spied him in the dining room in a corner banquette. I slid in breathless and smiled. We sat discreetly across from each other, in such a way that the mirror against the wall showed us who might be entering the restaurant. Or should Mother arrive, I would keep this strictly formal.

An odd tension arose, so I knew this meeting would be brief. John ordered for us a poached salmon in a lemon meringue, though I could barely eat nor really remember what else accompanied the fish on the plate. There wasn't much to be done except to honor Mother's wishes. Time was like a poetry theme, whether it's about the passing of time, the ravages of time, or the symbolism of a ticking clock. Our clock. Five months and thirty days until tick tock, we could be together.

For me it was a lifetime, but I had all the time in the world. I was young. For him, growing older before me, time was made more valuable if not shared with the one you love.

John took my hand in his and spoke first, "...time to make me grieve, let's part abide, and shakes this fragile frame at eve, with throbbings of noontide..." He let go of my fingers.

"Are you quoting someone?" I asked, confused.

"Thomas Hardy," said John, matter-of-factly.

"Whatever does it mean?"

"I suspect it means that Mr. Hardy writes about himself while looking in his mirror to see his wrinkled and aging skin, and..."

"Enough of that, Johnnie. I am in love with you. All of you. Old and wrinkled and wise."

"Like Mr. Hardy, the heart that beats in my aged head is that of a young man still capable of feeling love, and romantic longing..."

"Precisely," I said. "For now, I must go," I said, looking over my shoulder. "But know when we are next together... it will be forever."

Days later, a letter arrived from John from Italy where he was working on commission of a portrait of a Count and his wife. The letter was written in Italian, so I asked Dorothy, able to speak several languages including French, to translate. Plucking the letter from my hand Dorothy moved around me reading as only a younger sister might do to annoy.

Dorothy read that John spoke of the room he was renting... the furniture scanty while the walls were rich in tapestry. He found it remarkable what the ordinary Italian housepainter could do...to get a room done in plain color with a whitewashed ceiling was said to be more expensive than a sky with clouds and tapestry walls.

Dorothy dropped the letter to her knee. “This is dull. You call this love?”

“It’s brilliant,” I exclaimed. “Please carry on....”

Dorothy exhaled a long sigh, picked up the letter and continued, “He says, ‘I suspect that every Italian house painter is a scenic artist. The furniture was made as it is for the stage to be seen only from the front – all gold and glitter facing you – and the back not even planed or painted. It was a bit of a shock for me, coming from Scotland, where a piece of furniture can be seen with equal interest from all sides...’”

Then Dorothy paused. Her eyes still scanned the letter, eyebrows rising high.

“What? “I asked. “What does he say?”

My sister bit her top lip and continued. “Seems you have a rapturous admirer,” she said, her eyes quickly interpreting every word and then expressing them to me. “And he’s planning to visit you.”

“Visit?” I said, slightly panicked but at the same time elated. Dorothy could read the expression of happiness I tried to contain on my face.

“Mother will be livid,” she said.

“Mother will survive,” I replied.

“Mother will not survive,” said Mother, entering the room from eavesdropping. “I cannot let your future fall to shambles after the agreement we've made with Mr. Lavery."

"Agreement? It was your agreement, not mine," I snapped. "Have you any idea how following the guidelines of the one and only Mrs. Martyn has destroyed my life!"

"What type of a decent gentleman would do such a thing?" Mother paused to ponder her own answer. "To pursue you with such vigor after our pact."

"A man who loves, Mother. A man who loves!"

Dorothy's eyes moved back and forth between Mother and me. She enjoyed this.

"I'm not feeling well," Mother blurted, moving to the fainting couch at the window. "I'm feeling despair and fatigue." Dorothy quickly brought a silk fan to help cool Mother off. She sat for a long while fanning herself as we watched on dutifully before she finally stood up.

Alice woke up crying from her nap.

"Now then, ladies," said Mother, rearranging her dignity, "that will be enough upsetting Alice with talks of Mr. Lavery." She moved to her vanity to pin her hat into place. "You're to join me in half an hour in the dining room for high tea with our friends, the Smythe's. They've come all the way from Boston... and made the drive up the coast from Marseille."

"I thought they were summering in the Loire?" asked Dorothy.

"I'm not certain why it matters," said Mother, and with that she turned and departed, but not before handing the heavy gold door key to Dorothy who was left standing and staring at me.

"Well go on," I said, "Go join Mother and I'll be down after I freshen up." I put my hand out to gather the gold room key. She dropped it in my palm as I clutched my fingers around its weight.

Dorothy thought about it for a moment, then turned to leave, but not before turning back one more time. "You're going to write to him, aren't you?" she said, her voice with a tone of mischief.

"Perhaps," I chipped, containing a giggle. "Now go..." and I escorted her to the door. "Make conversation with the lovely

Smythe's of Chicago. They have a nice son for you, Dorothy. A banker, I think."

Immediately I dismissed my annoying sister and sat at the desk, dropped my head into my hands and sobbed. I longed to be with John but maybe it was not meant in this lifetime. Though how divine if little Alice might finally have a father. Then, with a deep inhale to start again, I dressed in such a hurry that I forgot my evening shawl but managed to stop at the front desk to instruct the staff to send a cable to John.

"Do nothing. Stop. She will never forgive you for writing an anonymous letter. In a disguised Italian hand. Stop."

This time John had had enough. He wrote directly to Mother:

> If you remember when I came to Paris to see you two years ago, I said nothing and because Hazel thought it hopeless at the time, that if she went home, she might manage our point better. You know the result...that she had made a terrible mistake, and now after two years of the most appalling anguish and the raising of a child single-handedly, she feels herself falling apart. For good. Both physically and emotionally speaking...

Mother returned his thoughts with a brief letter:

> Pardon my being frank, but I have been recently told things about you from Boston friends that makes it seem perfectly impossible that a sweet sensitive woman like Hazel would find lasting happiness with you...

John suspected what Mrs. Martyn was referring to though she refused to substantiate the rumors. John's mind whirled back to his youth; how he and his siblings were separated as orphans when he was a child. His brother did return from the Navy as a young adult, along with his sister Jane.

Jane had felt lonely when they reconnected years later, but he barely gave her a thought. When one day he found her weeping, she explained it was nothing, really, but John took notice that the happy bright and laughing girl had gone listless and hollow.

Jane had become pregnant by a pawnbroker's assistant and when she told him that she was pregnant with his child, the man tried to flee to America. But she found him, and he married her, returning to Glasgow to live.

On occasion John visited his sister and husband but he never approved of his brother-in-law. Granted Jane's husband talked advanced socialism, so he was educated, but there was something about him that didn't feel right to John.

Another baby came, and John decided he wasn't interested in being a part of their lives as Jane's husband was a hard and coarse man. When Jane asked her brother, John, to help her escape the marriage, John refused. "You made your bed. You can lie in it."

Within forty-eight hours her husband came to John to inform him that his sister, Jane, had drowned herself by jumping off Stockwell Bridge into the Clyde, and that John was wanted at the police station to identify the body.

Jane's death had always bothered him more than the passing of his young wife, Kathleen. He never forgot that haunting image of his sister, bloated from the water, but somehow still young and quite beautiful with her face showing a newfound sense of serenity. He paid for the burial and never spoke of it again. Except to me. But the word was out in the street that he'd abandoned her, and she committed suicide.

John tried to make excuses for his behavior. He even sought confession so that a priest might forgive him for his ambitions...for focusing on himself, a barely eighteen-year-old man, and a struggling starving artist going from boarding house to boarding house...

Yes, John was certain that was the story to which Mother was referring, and so he immediately wrote to her promptly, requesting the source in her letters, but she did not reply. John then wondered if it wasn't that story of his sister Jane at all. Perhaps it was of his young wife Kathleen, who also died under his care, leaving him with a daughter. Perhaps, John thought, Mother was trying to protect me from his misgivings.

In the garden, long ago John had quoted something first said by his friend, the Scottish novelist, Robert Louis Stevenson, that I would someday understand and use for my own misgivings. He said, "Art is so sacred that the love of it covers a multitude of sins, and so we excuse ourselves..."

Chapter Thirteen
Hazel

My mind was playing tricks on me. I'd been married to John Lavery so many times in recurring fantasies that it felt like I'd already been his wife. What did my future have in store? It was as if some great hands of fate – like those of John's friend, the sculpturer, Rodin – seemed to pull me from the cliff, mold me and then drop me to the mountain below, crushing my dreams. At the base of that emotional mountain, I became ill. Again. The nephritis returned in full force.

I was barely able to write to John, barely able to see the paper, let alone steady the pen; instead, I wrote to complain of neuralgic pain and blinding headaches. I had to endure bed rest and an all-milk diet which was a common cure since milk possessed a hydrating composition and was protein-rich with potassium and calcium that might help reduce the frequency of head pain.

It didn't seem to work.

John feared that while the doctors could diagnose the body, my mind headed for a nervous breakdown from my desire to fulfill a longing never satisfied...

A doctor from Rome came highly recommended and so, just like that, we temporarily moved to Italy. It was there that the trees seemed to wave at me, emitting vaporous, golden oxygen. I began to pray, succumbing to the inevitable, that maybe Mother was right, that this life was best lived without John Lavery.

Rome, like it's men, was a city that seduced me. It was like a near-death experience of the good kind, of the spiritual kind, with the Coliseum, the Pantheon, and Trevi Fountain all within reach, and there to coddle me. And yet, the Roman mythology which dated its founding to around 753 BC made me feel small in comparison... a modern-day woman from the city of Chicago established in a mere 1833.

Mother seemed happy here, calling Rome the *Capital of the World* or *Caput Mundi*. And for an artist like me, the Renaissance felt everywhere, except I was still ill. Watching the city from the inside of my bedroom window, one day I began to feel better and wanted to share my enthusiasm with John, who I was determined to keep as my friend, if nothing else. So, I wrote:

The sun, warm and yellow and comforting, is streaming into my room. The air is delicious, and I can smell Rome through the open window, a kind of exquisite compound perfume of pine and violets; full of so many memories and so many promises...

But eventually the winter's fog rolled in like a long, deep sigh. At times it felt more like London, or Chicago, with the winter an angry grey rain, or sleet, or both. As a result, I took a dramatic turn for the worst. With tonsilitis in December and with an unexpected draft from a church service, Mother feared pneumonia as Ned had before me.

By Christmas day I was able to sit up with the help of my nurse, and able to watch Alice open her presents with big red and gold satin ribbons. To make it feel festive, Mother bought a Christmas tree, and garland to strew along the balcony and staircase for hope of a healthy new year. Alice set up a tiny Nativity set sent by John. She arranged the Mary and Joseph statues, along with the three Wise Men around Jesus's manger where he lay in a bed of myrtle leaves, since straw was not available in Rome.

Amid the ribbons and wrappings, still hostage to my bed, I longed to again experience life as a young mother caring solely for my child… to study, to read, so I might again follow my dreams of world travel and attending art exhibits. After all, an artist needs freedom to capture, to explore, to feel industrious in the world, and not surrounded by herbal medicines.

Mother and Dorothy went to dinner often, leaving me to rest and coming home with tales of how Italians ate something called 'Macaroni' with their hands. And according to my sister, colanders drained long strands of what they call spaghetti which was a noodle slurped into your mouth. Alice adored the game of it, more than the eating of it.

But I had little appetite, instead picking up my sketch book as nourishment. Reading literature followed, too, since at this point, I felt that John Lavery was no more real to me than Whistler, or Jane Austen's Emma or even Napoleon, for that matter. I adored John more than the tangible people in my daily life, but I could no longer believe a personal relationship would develop into finality. It occurred to me that I had been brought up by a handsome man – my father – who was always the center of attention. Now I longed for the illusion of him in the forty-nine-year-old, John Lavery.

As my illness waned around February of 1906, and at twenty-six years old, while an old maid by normal standards, I was still attractive. That morning, I stood to dress myself by putting on morning clothes – a burgundy dress instead of my mourning black wardrobe. For the first time in months, I finally tossed my cotton nightgown to the bed. Mother had purchased the dress for me as inspiration to get up and live.

As I studied myself in the mirror, my petite frame, my complexion sallow from lack of air and sun, I wondered what an Italian woman of a village might wear. Subtle changes in silhouette began to occur in our womenswear with more tubular shapes which accentuated my tiny curves. The trend was an 'S' shape from the latest health corset. Lace was all the rage, and it framed my pale face with a soft glow. As I admired and feared myself, Dorothy looked on from the dressing room, until she caught my eye. "You've risen!" she declared.

"Like Christ," I teased.

"Shall we explore Rome together... two naughty sisters..." she asked, playfully, taking my hands and spinning me in circles but ever so gently so I wouldn't lose balance.

"Yes!" I said, "Right now this very second..."

The city bustled with energy. The San Remo bicycle race from Milan was in full swing along with automobile races that sped through the streets.

It was all a strange juxtaposition for a new country but a weak one. Aside from Rome, Italy was poor and there was little respect for the government. One couldn't imagine the Royal family being unsafe, but Mother told me their own King Hubert had been assassinated at the turn of 1900.

Ah, but Italy's ancient capital brimmed with history at every turn, and it extended especially to its socializing. People were warm, touchy, feely, and goodness knows they wanted me to eat. Besides, Dorothy convinced me that I must try my first macaroni. Or in other words, I'd eat, and she'd watch, since she dined most times the way a small sparrow might chew, pecking at tiny morsels and crumbs, pretending to eat at all, only maneuvering the food around on her plate.

One night we entered a new trattoria called *Rostorante Alfredo alla Scrofa* which had just debuted. The owner, Alfredo Di Lelio invented the classic pasta dish *fettuccine alfredo* as a reason to help his wife with a small appetite feel enticed.

He served the cheese-soaked noodles with his grilled sea bass so freshly caught that its gills practically breathed on the plate. Alfredo had me sample something called *gnocchi* and *prosciutto*, a dried and cured meat similar to the bacon Father used to bring us home from his curing company. Though I felt weak, my taste buds exploded with the culinary joys of flavor.

"This is divine," I said, sitting back like a stuffed pig. "But you've barely eaten."

Dorothy shrugged her shoulders. "I'm not very hungry," she

said. My eyes scanned her tiny, emaciated frame. She'd struggled with eating disorders for a couple of years but sitting upright with her, I could see how utterly transparent it was.

"Dearest, you must eat. You're looking too frail."

And with that she forced herself to sample the smallest portion of *gnocchi*, before spitting it discreetly into her napkin so that I wouldn't notice. I did.

For dessert I had my first *gelato*, an ice cream made with butterfat whole milk and sugar. Dorothy watched on, more apt to engage in spirits, as we shared a little too much *grappa*.

It was then that I saw him across the room, watching me...

Dorothy's eyes followed mine following his. "He's staring at you," said Dorothy, nudging me.

"Yes, he is," I said, discreetly glancing over. When he caught my eye, I fluttered my lashes and turned away demurely. The game of it all. Flirty banter with a man. Just like Lillian Russell taught me long ago from my seat at her Broadway show.

"Oh my," said Dorothy, grabbing at my wrist, "He's approaching just now!"

"*Ciao, bella*," he said, taking my hand, and then kissing the back of it.

His name was Leonard 'Len' Moorehead Thomas. Like me, he was American. Like me he was a tourist. Like my dead husband, Ned, Len was well educated at St Paul's and Yale, excelled in sports, but then one further... he'd even composed an opera.

"A Renaissance man" is what Mother called him when Dorothy and I returned home that evening, giggling and silly. Leonard was now employed as the second secretary in the U.S. Embassy. As a matter of fact, he was voted the 'Most versatile man in his class,' to my 'Most beautiful girl in the Midwest.' Yes, I was smitten, or just desperate to be held, to be kissed, to be out of the house, to be young and free again. And to finally know Mother's approval.

Night after night the red wine poured between Len and me. The comfort of macaroni was shared between fork bites, and the night strolls followed, where sunset brought an unexpected magic. The

Eternal city was so grand and monumental by day yet became Len's and my own intimate experience by night.

On one Roman night walk, we sat close to a bubbling fountain where the sound of crowds seemed to evaporate. It was there that he kissed me, first gently and then hungry with passion. His kisses, yet another flavor of Rome… were best enjoyed after dark.

This was *Amore*. Love.

A week later it was time to contact John.

Oh, if I could die before writing this to you...

My letter carried on that I was a coward and a fool but at least an honest one. My mind was full of Len. Perhaps it was the sudden escape of being bedridden. Perhaps it was the smell of the Italian nights, the freedom from Alice or all that simmering delicious foods. Perhaps it was the ambience or affection. But whatever it was, I was in love with Len. I couldn't lie to John. Not now. Not ever.

I ended my letter by saying, "I've wrecked everything, and my shame is so great I long to hear you tell me just what I am to my face. Lash me with your scorn John Lavery, and turn your heel and go... And then I signed off like a stranger, in full name – Hazel Martyn."

John, patient and wise, suspected that Mother was behind my decision which forced me to marry Len. John told me that he wanted me to let him into my confidence, asking me not to treat him as someone rejected or cast aside. He also said he wrote from Florence, having already arrived in Italy for a commission, and he'd be arriving in Rome soon.

I replied in a telegram: "Beg you – not to come or try to see me – await letter – H."

That very night, Mother, Alice, Dorothy, and I were celebrating a lavish meal at *Checcino* with Len to celebrate our unexpected engagement. Just yesterday he had proposed "impromptu" as he called it and I said, "yes" because I was romantic at heart and simply adored the institution of marriage despite my first husband, Ned. Rest in peace.

"This is the most brilliant news!" declared Mother, clicking glass after glass, and giving me a look that said I'd finally found the perfect man that would please her.

The restaurant patrons cheered and toasted – *Amore*! A few patrons came to kiss me on the cheek, so unusual given that Chicago people would never behave so openly. And the food kept on coming. Dishes on the house. *Checcino*, unusual in its fare like *con pajata*, a macaroni with tomato sauce and a delicacy of lamb intestines sprinkled with pecorino cheese, was a divine enticement. As a bottle of Barolo was passed around the table, and as we toasted, I thought about how selfish I'd been. When might I grow up and see true love for what it was? To understand how much pain I'd put John through? But more so... why?

I began to believe that if John Lavery represented my father, then I could never really allow him to be there for me since Father had abandoned me in death. Trusting John to love me until death-do-us-part was taking a risk I didn't think I was yet capable of taking.

But I also knew that John Lavery was the noblest of men.

As the heat of summer progressed so did the heat of love with Len. There is a sexually charged fever at its height; a constant all-or-nothing that accompanies sizzling summer love. Len was a whirlwind, knowing how to own me, and kiss me, which he did, in every place one would kiss a woman in Rome... the nape of the neck at the Piazza Garibaldi, inside the elbows at the Mouth of Truth, on the back of my shoulders at the Fountain of Four Rivers, on the tip of the nose at the Ponte Garibaldi, and passionately full on the mouth at the Termini Train Station, where we parted ways.

But the heat also encompassed our emotional intentions. Together, we'd build a culture in Chicago. Together we'd help the poor, the homeless. With Len by my side, I intended to step away from society events and focus instead on people-in-need. He didn't seem enthused at the time with my ideas, but over time I was certain I could convince him of what mattered.

By August's end my family joyously returned to Chicago to await Len's arrival.

It was wonderful to be back home on American soil, after coming out the other side of illness and finding love. This was love, yes? Not lust, right? Italian love with my American Prince?

Preparing for my wedding, this time we decided on a more formal affair. After various wedding gown fittings, I chose a modest dress with an S-shaped corset complete. Dorothy worried that the high-waisted empire lines might not suit my figure, but I made up for it with billowy sleeves to the elbow and an overall lace pattern. Everything was perfect, the way Mother wanted it, except on the evening of the ceremony. As the candles were lit, the guests seated in their pews, and the organ music a thunder, Len disappeared.

While my exterior displayed beautifully put together perfection, my insides felt clogged with slow spreading tar. I was pained. I was angry. I was just plain stupid.

Speculation grew amid Mother's and my society circles that he had been just a hot Italian lover. That I was a summer fling. That he was not an honorable man and that he had illegitimate children in every European port. Oh, dear!

But most of all, that I'd been stood up. At the altar...

In November, feeling foolish, alone, and frightened, I realized there was only one man aside from Father that ever genuinely loved me...

John Lavery.

The wise, kind, and patient, John Lavery. My tonic for hope.

But God knows he'd had enough of my antics. From Ned to Len, how many nuptials might I consider before I really and truly realized John was always my Mister Wonderful?

Chapter Fourteen
(A new) Hazel

While most society women might be embarrassed about protecting themselves from gossip, I honestly could have cared less. Instead, I took accountability for my wayward actions, writing to John that I was sorry and learning to pay for my mistakes. God had somehow worked His way to punish me for Ned's death by shaming me with Len. I also questioned if I even or ever understood what true love was.

At this point, I also suspected John had little use for me.

Much to my relief and delight, he responded in kind, though guarded in his romantic emotions:

Yes, Hazel dear, let's talk it over.

No, I don't see that anything is spoiled either finally or utterly, or that the situation is anymore changed than is customary with the hand of time...

During my correspondence with John, my maternal grandparents, the Taggats, fell ill. I could not, would not, sail to Europe. Even for John. Instead, I'd have to stay put in Chicago and learn to put my only selfish needs aside. I would care for Alice while assisting Mother with her elderly parents.

Up until now, life had been a constant and steady stream of suitors, boyfriends, fiancées, and a husband, albeit a dead one.

During those men and those years, I'd gone from girl, to woman, to wife, to mother, to widow...I was then jilted as a would-be bride because my emotional radar was damaged. So, I decided to focus on strengthening my inner core. To dig deep. To find my own identity without that of a man – or my mother - to identify with.

Even Dorothy suggested that every woman should be alone at least once in her lifetime. Certainly, she knew... poor, frail Dorothy, who'd become a skeleton of a girl with dark circles around her eyes. Anemia set in along with her food disorders. No man would even notice her.

As I cared for Dorothy, I did the best I could, regaining my place in Chicago society, by becoming a member of the Children in Need... those who were homeless. In spring of 1908, and since I was home playing nursemaid to all of them, I decided it was time to improve my education. Father once told me we should always be learning, so I enrolled in the Chicago Art Institute for lessons in drawing and painting. It seemed every art form had been explored but there was always something more to learn. My portfolio immediately received a few local awards, pleasing me to know I still had a knack for my God-given talent.

In the meantime, Dorothy had her 'coming out' debutante ball in fashionable Society, though it wasn't a ball at all. It was a small party which was what my sister wanted, since Dorothy was under the care of a physician. Around her full time now, I was getting a sense of how very much she really needed me; how she just wanted to be loved, to be heard, to be understood. Certainly, I could understand those needs.

At nights I'd rub her head until she fell asleep, her hair now brittle and lackluster. She had once been a lovely creature, full of hope and promise and exhibiting a great deal of talent as a writer.

Perhaps it was best to get my sister to write again? As I sketched, I gave Dorothy amusing scenarios to write about. Soon after, Dorothy began typing at the desk in the nearby study. I took joy at hearing her pounding away on her typewriter, the clitter clatter of keys. Finally, she delivered her first stage play. "Can I read it?" I inquired.

"No, it's a surprise," she said, smiling a sly grin.

Mother and I were so delighted to sit front and center on the first row at the theater for opening night only to find out that her play, Grove Eden, was based on her life with an overbearing society matron and a young heroine who cannot seem to choose between suitors. Me!

My Dorothy. Beautiful but broken, though highly intuitive. She too longed for the father she barely knew and had since been the shadow of my vine in life's events. But I justified my behavior of not providing 100% to Dorothy, because I had Alice and our own future to worry about.

Across the pond, John too, was busy tending to his only family, his daughter, Eileen. My letters inspired him to take a renewed interest in raising her and to someday see her off to university. Back in the late 1800s and early 1900s, John only saw Eileen as an object to paint – "the victim" as he called her – for many of his portraits. The problem with portrait sitting is that the subject often withholds conversation for the artist's sake, so Eileen was forced to be mute in his presence. Not good for a father and daughter relationship.

The most famous portrait was painted years ago for Eileen's First Holy Communion. She had posed tall and regal-like dressed in white with a delicate silk veil, to receive the host as the Lord, Jesus Christ. The portrait owed a debt to paintings like Velazquez and Courbet, in whom John found inspiration. Whistler had once admired the picture and suggested toning it down with a touch of charcoal.

But upon closer examination of the portrait, and no matter how brilliant the finished product, there was no disguising Eileen's face, long and lost. Her eyes cast down, practically bursting into tears, longing for the mother she never knew; longing for the father that was never present. John began to see a pattern in his paintings of

Eileen. It was time to see the young woman as his daughter. Not as art.

They traveled, father and daughter, to Morocco, to heal and discover the art of parenting together. John purchased a little property on the hill outside of Tangier, known to Moors as Dar-el-Midfah, because of a derelict cannon half buried in the front garden. He would make it his winter quarters for the next fifteen years... and eventually with me.

But it was now only June of 1909, and my life would change dramatically, delivering the darkest of times. Mother, myself, and my grandmother Taggart, now a widow, finally crossed the Atlantic to share a generational spring in Paris. Alice and Dorothy were with us as well, though my sister was fading to the backdrop. She'd become obsessed with fasting and despite my demands to make her eat, she remained stubborn to her cause. When she finally had enough strength to travel from Paris to London, off we went.

But no sooner had we arrived in London at the Coburg Hotel in Mayfair, Mother fell ill on our journey and collapsed to the marble floor of the lobby. Appendicitis.

Much of our time was spent by her hospital bedside. She had a post-surgical infection. Fear grew as the doctors failed to conquer her fever. I held her hand and talked to her, but to no regard, she faded into unconsciousness.

Before we could process what was happening, Mother died in England.

I never realized how attached and dependent on one another we were until her passing. I spent all my energy longing for a father who was never truly there. She was fifty-one years of age, having lived a lonely, long, but dutiful life raising us daughters.

Now the torch passed. To me...

Without my parents I was the new Matriarch. Without my parents I now understood what it was to want the best for my own daughter, and my wayward sister... to see them into a golden future, safe with a husband, much like Mother had always wanted for me.

As it was my duty to care for Dorothy and little Alice now, unconsciously I decided it would be best not to contact John. But it was Dorothy who one night persuaded me from our new hotel, on Cromwell Road at The Queen's Gate, to write. Our hotel was a little less posh, but very safe and secure for this time of emotional healing.

John had read about Mother's death in *The Times* and in a lower-middle-class paper called *The Daily Mail*.

> My Dearest John,
>
> Mother has passed away. It was all very sudden... I'm in much pain and the grief comes in acute and unexpected waves. Somedays my mind plays tricks with me... as if I'm seeing her enter a doorway only to find out it's a ghostly vision of my longing.
>
> We are staying at Queen's Gate. This hotel is so clean and comfy, and the food is so heavenly I could weep from sheer pleasure in the decency and daintiness of it all...
>
> I find myself not longing for riches. I don't long for society either. I just long for kindness, something often underestimated. And I long for family... you, John Lavery, have always felt like family...

And with that, John visited us. Our Hotel Van Dyke was close to his home...

Alice, Dorothy, John, and I spent most days together. At first arrangements needed to be made for Mother, and John assured us girls that we must not sulk. And so, at Alice's pulling at my hand, I agreed, and off we went. We picnicked in Piccadilly. We strolled through Green Park, took walks along the Thames, and shared ice cream in Shephard's Market, a place of ill repute after sunset, but which came to life with shops and butchers during the day.

One day John wrote me a brief note delivered by the Concierge as Alice and I were en route to the park to play:

> So sorry not to see you today, my lovely Hazel.
>
> From early morning till this moment, I have been in the hands of others and even now, I have had to explain that I have an important note to write, and I so wanted to write and tell you that I also grow in grace and realize more and more how wonderful my Dear One is. In haste but will see you soon. – JL

It was the last time John would write before becoming man and wife...

Chapter Fifteen
Hazel & John (and Dorothy, Alice, and Eileen)

I no longer belonged to my mother's world...
The calendar was marked - July 22nd - our wedding day. In attendance were the Priest, the children, and two artist friends of John's. There would be no beating-about-the-bush this time and especially after all these years. With my poor Mother out of the picture – God rest her soul – I could finally, finally, have my Johnnie...

...except there was Dorothy to contend with, almost a mini-Mother, though she wrote to John a very sweet letter filled with her bereaved emotions:

> Dear Brother,
>
> I am near tears tonight... because you are taking Hazel away... I am letting you take her without a word because I know that she will be happier with you, and that you will make her well, sooner than anyone else. You are the only man who could possibly make her happy. Mother knew this before she died. I know it tonight and have known it for an exceedingly long, long time... I send you lots and lots of love and I am wishing all the good wishes for you two tonight.
>
> Loving oh so lovingly, yours, and sister – Dorothy

No sooner she sealed the letter with the wax stamper, she telegrammed the Armours: "Hazel will be married tomorrow to John Lavery."

All of Chicago was abuzz. They had no idea of the longtime courtship we shared.

The ceremony took place at high noon at the Brompton Oratory, the second largest Catholic church in London – more a cathedral than a church, sitting magnificently just between Kensington and Chelsea. The four of us felt like miniscule church mice scurrying beneath the massive brick walls.

Dorothy and little Alice were our bridesmaids, dressed in delicate pink tulle summer fabric with tiny rosebud wreaths on their heads. John's daughter, Eileen, now age eighteen, didn't oppose our nuptials, but she didn't attend either. Instead, she was off to see friends at Sacred Heart Convent in Roehampton, a boarding school.

In her way of seeing things, it was not John Lavery who had been her father, but John's best friend, William Patrick Whyte, who had cared for her since infancy.

I understood the awkwardness of being her stepmother when Eileen had always fantasized about her biological parents being together. Now this marriage magnified the fact that her own deceased mother was never coming back. And besides, at eighteen years of age, tall, beautiful, and raven-haired like her feisty biological mother, I sent her off with a supportive note...

I love you my darling, and I always shall. I am going to be a happy girl... and you have helped to make me so... please do come and stay with us very soon. Warm regards, H

Walking down a noticeably short aisle to join John at the altar, I thought about how weddings somehow allow us to erase the past.

We spent a weekend honeymoon at Southend-on-the-Sea in Essex because I adored the seashore and it's where John and I first met. By the sea. It rained the entire honeymoon, and we battened down the hatches, but we didn't seem to mind. No matter what life had in store, at the end of today and the end of every day, I chose John, and he chose me... that's all that mattered.

I was, finally and officially, Mrs. John Lavery. And I had the marriage certificate to prove it, though I fibbed about my old age, declaring on the legal document that I was twenty-seven, rather than my true twenty-nine.

Just after the wedding, Dorothy, Alice, and I returned to Chicago to bury Mother's ashes and to settle the estate before winter came howling through. It was a long ship's journey. Our registered names on our tickets collectively created quite a brow-knitting curiosity to others – Lavery, for me, Trudeau for Alice, Martyn for Dorothy, and Taggart for Grandmother, who was growing weaker with each passing day and spent most of the journey resting in her state room.

One inquisitive Manhattan socialite thought she recognized me from my past marriage to Ned. She proceeded to follow us about until five-year-old Alice volunteered some information from her striped lounge chairs on the upper deck. "My Mother is the prettiest one and has been for a long time," said Alice, "but I have a dear new father just a week old!"

Trying not to chuckle at her faux pas, I held Mother's black urn close to my bosom. It was a ceramic with a Fleur-de-lis design, a symbol of French lilies my mother had always adored. It had been difficult to cremate Mother as she had always wanted a proper burial in her best dress and with viewing hours, but with the overseas death, we hadn't a choice. It was the only way to return her to America. And in returning her to America, I knew too, she would never see her beautiful granddaughter grow up to be a young woman.

God knows with each passing day Mother's death had certainly softened me. I was gentler and wiser. And while always confident, I was certainly at my most vulnerable.

John stayed behind in London, busying himself with painting and friends until one night he sat in his study and there was my portrait, *Dame en Noir* staring down at him, widowed and sad... the one he'd painted... the one Mother insisted be called *The Widow.* At that moment he felt ashamed that he let me take the journey alone to Chicago with Alice and Dorothy.

While the sail was clear skies and a calm sea except for a short bout of seasickness, Dorothy refused to eat. My only hope was that upon arriving home, she'd be in familiar territory with friends who might encourage her. But watching her holding onto the ship's banister for dear life, as a small steady wind practically took her overboard, was more than I could bear.

John felt that Dorothy was playing on my good nature, that she wanted me close by and would stop at nothing to not lose me. Thus, her dramatic antics. But I didn't see her odd behavior as such. I saw her drama as a call for help.

No sooner our ship sailed into the harbor of New York's port, friends were there to greet us... along with the Press. A little too pleased with myself, the reporters of *The Chicago Tribune* flipped the pages of their notebooks, scribbling as frantically as they could. Alice squinted from the bright camera bulbs. I leaned forward to speak as the reporter shoved a microphone under my nose, demanding, "Word has it you've abandoned Chicago..."

"My marriage to Mr. Lavery and the settlement of my mother's estate does not mean severing Chicago ties," I assured. "We couldn't have that, you know. "

"And Mr. Lavery," they inquired.

"Mr. Lavery couldn't come with us, but we plan to return for a lengthy visit next year. I must have him meet all my friends. Thank you so much." Placing my arm around Alice, I began to walk away, but they persisted so I turned back. "And now if you'll leave us, we must rest. It's been an extraordinary journey and we're so delighted to be home."

Ethel Hooper, a family friend, was there to greet us, having traveled hundreds of miles, along with The Hoopers, friends of Father's from Detroit. It was joyous to be hugged by loved ones who understood I'd spent the past year playing matriarch to my sickly family and shielding my sadness from Alice. It was joyous indeed, to just sink into their arms for long hugs, and the smell of familiarity... all those society parties and cotillion balls coming back with all those other annoyances I used to take for granted, that now, in hindsight, were the best times of my life. Turns out society would always remind me of Mother. And a world that was no longer.

In Ethel Hooper's arms I swayed and hugged, tears coming down full force. "There, there Hazel, I'm so sorry you've had to go this alone," said Ethel, patting the back of my head just underneath my bonnet, until finally, sniffling and pulling away first, I gained my composure.

Later in a hotel, with my feet up on the divan, and an arm across my forehead from a lingering headache, I explained the truth to Ethel, "It's been people, people, people, flowers, flowers, flowers, reporters, telephones, telegrams and under it all this sordid worry about money."

"I'd warned your mother many times, Hazel," said Ethel. "But she always lived in a big and lavish way, never counting dollars." Ethel sat in the easy chair near to me. "I hate to be the one to inform you, dear, but a couple of years before her death, she confided in me her growing concern about family finances."

Dorothy and I soon learned that our intended inheritance, the one from Father, had been spent on years of glamourous touring about, five-star hotels and five course meals. It was a lifestyle we simply could no longer afford. Or as the lawyer said over his spectacles across the desk from where Dorothy and I waited for the will to be read, "the word 'Budget' was not something in your mother's vocabulary."

To add to the stunning news, Mother had rewritten her Last Will & Testament when I was ill, and to prevent Ned's parents from attaching onto my future income. But what she lacked in realization was that she accidentally prevented her daughters from receiving 'the principle,' a reduced sum of $65,000, which, according to the lawyers, would be held in trust to begin after one year.

That wasn't going to do my sister and I much good. And it

didn't help with the mounting medical bills piling up through the gold-plated mail slot of Mother's foyer door.

The generous Armour family came to visit, offering to pay some of Mother's medical expenses now stamped 'past due,' and extending their hospitality in asking us to live with them, if necessary.

John suggested that I give Dorothy my share of my income until she was herself safely wed. But Dorothy continued with her fainting spells due to low blood sugar and lack of food. She fainted at the lawyers, she fainted at the cemetery when we buried Mother's ashes next to Fathers, she fainted at the bank tellers when we had to make our first withdrawal, and she fainted at the Doctor's when he examined her.

The attending Physician demanded I send her away immediately for at least a couple of months where she would be psychologically evaluated. I refused until he told me it was "that or death." Good Lord, when had Dorothy slipped into such a state?

At the same time, Grandmother Taggart was sent to a sanatorium for her increasing anddeadly tuberculosis. It would be where she'd spend her final days.

As for me, I felt helpless and alone, watching not only the last bit of family taken from me, but taken too, from Alice, the only family she'd ever known – the only moral support we had and had often taken for granted.

It pained me to sell the house, but it was listed almost immediately to pay for Dorothy's medical expenses. With the help of little Alice, finding humor in the crinkling of wrapping paper, we packed 'for sale' twenty-nine barrels of glass, floral bone china, as well as paintings, and crates of books, all our life's memories, now sealed off into a 20 by 24-foot storage facility for auction. Because taking everything was too expensive to ship, I would only take my father's favorite books about Ireland. In addition, the linens and silver would ship to England, having spent my life eating every meal from those utensils since the age of two… and planning to continue to do so at my new home with John.

There was a slapping realization that the entire reason Mother coerced me into marrying Ned was to keep our family on a hefty financial cushion. Dear Lord, why hadn't she told me?

The word 'sudden' was something I now understood whether it meant in this living life or in loss and death. But I had a husband waiting for me back in London, and for that I was hopeful and happy. When a reporter asked me what I thought of life with the esteemed painter, John Lavery, what advice I might offer young society women longing for a reputable husband, I replied in a way that would have honored my mother, "Women have the best out of life. A woman has only to know how to be helpless and some man will most certainly come along and look after her. She need not assume any responsibility; he will enjoy doing it. So, she has the advantage of being spoiled and of giving pleasure at the same time."

But those society words felt fake. I longed to be self-sufficient, to be financially stable, to be the powerful things women weren't allowed to be to make a mark on history, even though I loved John completely, not as my caretaker, but as an equal. There was a devotion to a man who let me see his art through his lens. A man who saw my life and pain and fears through my lens. But I still needed to be independent of mind… and of bank account.

No matter what I longed for I had people I was both responsible for and owed answers to. Life meant taking the risk to begin anew in a new country with my daughter and new husband. It meant turning my back, despite what I told the press about Chicago, as there was nothing left to be done. As for Dorothy, I was her only living blood family. I owed her the duty of care, and I would see to it that I did what was always in her best interest.

And Grandmother, well, I couldn't risk her death on the ship if we took her back with us. She was truly beyond repair, spent most of her time on oxygen and kept calling me 'Alice,' not for my daughter, but because it was Mother's name, too. She thought I was Mother and began yelling at me between coughing fits as to why I couldn't remember certain things from her Boston childhood.

And so, on September 1, 1909, with no other choice and

certainly no other money, I turned the key in the lock for the final time in Chicago.

Alice and I set sail home to England, where I would now be Mrs. John Lavery, assuming the duties as his wife.

Only God knew what life had in store.

As I stared out to the vast sea from the porthole of our stateroom, I saw America move farther and farther away.

On Alice's fingers we counted the days, "Just fifteen more sleeps and we'll be home to England. To Daddy."

Chapter Sixteen

Hazel & John

John had resided in what was now our home at Cromwell Place, South Kensington, since 1898 and it certainly felt as lonely as the bachelor he'd been. It was conveniently located across from the Victoria and Albert Museum and near to my favorite place, the Museum of Natural History.

When we arrived at our threshold, I took in the white block cement and cornice moldings on the exterior, the wrought iron fence at the entrance, and the arcade with columns in front of the slick black door with the bold brass knocker. The home had stunning long and lovely Venetian windows to filter light especially on the second floor, and a glass roof, to filter in more. Every painter's dream.

Back in the day it was John Singer Sargent who found the lease too pricey for his budget, but John, "In a fit of Irish recklessness" said "I'll take it" from the previous owner, Sir Coutts Lindsay, a fellow painter. And so, he'd lived there ever since.

Everything was as I imagined when Alice and I arrived. The interior was sparsely decorated though I'd promised John we'd change that. The Edwardian style era was ending. But for now, I knew Mother's linens and cutlery – a nostalgic nod to the past – would do just fine on the mahogany dining room table, though its style was in need of a revival. With autumn in full swing, the angle of the sun wasn't as broad, instead setting earlier with each passing evening and allowing John to finish his work by seventeen-hundred hours.

What interested me most was John's studio which possessed a table to the side, a stool on which to paint, a bookshelf covered in books, and a desk cluttered in papers. There were tins with brushes and a knife all arranged in an order next to the palette. One could imagine an artist's vigor if his subject was positioned and lit properly.

My new home had a number of paintings surrounding me from the moment that I entered the front hall. Back in Chicago, we had portraits galore, but spread out all over the house. Here they were collected in groups, lined up one vertically atop the other, leaning against the wall, or hanging, or sitting on various easels.

With a cup of tea in hand, I moved through his forty years of art which leaned, stood, and hung in various places, in which he knew where to locate each portrait...though ironically, he told me he had no idea who lived next door. Perhaps knowing neighbors might influence people and he preferred to keep people his 'subjects.'

It's clear his best works were that of painting women. Children's portraits came next, and finally those of men. His female portraits were arranged against the wall, single heads and half-length portraits, single figures indoors, single figures outdoors, and even one single figure of his daughter on horseback. There were portrait-groups outdoors and portrait-groups indoors.

Like strolling through a master class, I studied the paintings, each one. John's human figures stood or sat either lightly or heavily; the clothes that he painted brought to animation by hiding the limbs; his brushwork seldom got lost in the furs or feathers or accessories of which his subject was wearing. It was truly the human that rose to the top of each canvas. It was truly the human we fixated upon... the eyes, the nose, the expression, while all else in the painting faded away. Just then, John stepped into the room admiring me, admiring his work. Finally, he spoke, which alerted me to his presence, "Whistler once said that an artist begins a new career today and continues it tomorrow."

"That's lovely," I said, my voice going soft at the pain in his voice. "You miss him, don't you?" I said, turning to see his eyes.

"Every day," said John, holding my eyes for a beat. "He showed me how to limit the pigment on my palette, like he did with his mother's portrait in simple peaceful repose.

"An arrangement of just grey and black," I chimed in, and we shared a long happy smile.

John sighed, gazing up to the ceiling's crown molding as if it were heaven. "But old geniuses are like the sun with one power that kills and another power that ripens." Then he moved toward the window. "See there, Hazel?" John pointed to the sky. I joined him at the window, and he placed an arm around my waist, "The sun has template zones where we are helped by it as we work, as we create..."

"In my art classes," I said, "someone suggested 'to be modern in the fullest meaning of the term, a painter must blend as well as he can those very essential. I just can't remember what the essentials were..."

"Perhaps an unfeigned sympathy for popular life, for air and daylight color, and for freedom in the choice of management."

"Yes, I suspect that was it, though no one could express it like you, my Johnnie," I said, standing back to admire my handsome albeit older husband. It was like being in the library with Father all over again, when Father taught me about books.

And, it was clear John Lavery had studied, learned, tried, failed but accomplished the great traits he'd just listed.

John captured a wide range of women on canvas too, but as individuals. Each with a specific expression. And with pain. Not from being their parent's children but being their own self.

"To what extent is a human's character essential in a fine portrait?" I asked.

John kissed me tenderly upon my forehead. "It turns out the best portraits are a collaboration of two people... the painter and the sitter. And the moment and the mood must befit both. One mustn't be energized and one serene."

"Like our sittings?" I asked.

"Like our sittings," he confirmed. "The artist and the subject must meet their rhythm together, like two lovers, in a place that reaches the perfect height."

And sit for many portraits I did. Day after day after day. I loved his work almost as much as I loved him. In an odd way, his art became our love making.

John's friends filled our dining room and our life's circles. At the top of that list was the Prime Minister, H. H. Asquith, and his wife, Margot, whom I tolerated as she was snarky and often teased me, saying I didn't look twenty-nine but looked older than forty, which was like saying I was dead!

The fanciest of balls followed, with fancy-dress, but I'd found myself changed since the debutante society of Chicago. Unlike the others, hiring from the London fashion houses of Reville and Rossiter, dressmakers for Queen Mary, I came up with designs with the help of my maid, instead of hiring a tailor. My favorite pastime was sewing doll-clothes for Alice's 'Ms. Wimbles,' her doll with glass eyes that eerily followed us across the room.

The evening dress that was my favorite was the one that my mother had worn. The one she had left me that fit me the way it fit her. An evening dress that never goes out of style.

For one invitation to a formal affair, and to be bold, I risked dressing as 'Flora' to impersonate Botticelli's figure of spring, with organza fabric that flowed petal-like as I moved, with little silk flowers sewn in from head to toe. A photographer snapped my image, all white with cupid bow red lips. The press was impressed. Me, not so much. Instead, I worried about real life, not fashion, what causes I might immerse myself in, and most of all, worried about my Dorothy....

I had begged her to come live with us, but she chose instead to stay with Grandmother Taggart, who passed shortly after in November of that year from a massive heart attack. Now Dorothy floated to the homes of family friends, and at the age of twenty-one was already deemed an old maid.

There was some hope for her career in literature, and she worked for a bit for the novelist Kellogg Fairbank, but her illness caused a great deal of missing employment, until she eventually stayed home in bed. I tried to contact her daily, but communication was slow and far away.

Finally, one day I stormed into John's studio while he was in the middle of painting *The Lady in Black*, Mrs. Trevor. The two – painter and sitter – looked up stunned, and without apology I demanded that we sail to America tomorrow. I demanded that he understand Dorothy must come and reside with us. Immediately. I was sailing to America '*tout suite!*'

At practically the drop of his paintbrush, John joined me on this journey, and we sailed on the steamship arriving in only fifteen days. As the ocean liner reduced speed, and the port of New York came into view, I felt the pace of my heart steady. I was relieved. We had arrived. America was still my home.

Chicago was so hospitable to us. Portrait artists and landscape painters greeted us, but I had no idea the level of my husband's fame until I landed on American soil. They made such a fuss, especially when asked to guest speak at the Chicago Art Institute.

Back at our hotel that evening I ran my fingers through Dorothy's hair, giving her the head massages that she loved in childhood, reminding her of my love for her, and that she must move to England with me. She flatly refused, pulling my hand from the nape of her neck. It was as if she was punishing me for leaving her instead of recognizing the generosity that we could bestow upon her if only she'd join our London circles. Finally, after many attempts, I used guilt, convincing her we were all that we had – each other – which was true, and she must give it a go once. If she came and it didn't work out, I would agree to send her sailing back home.

Finally, she agreed by defeat more than by agreement.

Before we departed, and just to protect her financially in case she did return to America, I attempted to sell her unpublished manuscripts, carting pounds of paper around and up multiple staircases to Chicago's premiere publishing houses. When Dorothy found out, she shredded the remaining manuscripts and tossed them into the hotel room fire. It was as if I was watching her life go up in flames, all hope and love diminished to a smolder.

"Her spirit is broken beyond belief," I cried in John's arms.

"There, there, Hazel. It's mind over matter. Her mental depression is affecting her now emaciated body."

Taking her to London was useless. No sooner had we arrived, she cried and cried, demanding I send her back. There was no way to control her anymore short of putting her into an asylum, and I couldn't bring myself to do that. An asylum would be death for her though she was doing an excellent job of killing herself just a little more each day.

We delivered her back to the ship as promised.

There was a forlorn silence as I handed her a ticket, studying her in day clothes hanging loosely from her skeleton frame and wondering if this was how I must remember her when there was nothing left to remember. Pulling her in tightly, tears ran down the back of her shoulder as I pleaded once more, "Please don't leave me. I love you. Don't go..." But she said nothing, holding her body as dead weight, refusing to hug me back.

"It will all be fine, dear Sister," said John to Dorothy, handing her a roll of bills that would at least get her a first week's worth of groceries in addition to my inherited allowance I'd already relinquished to her.

"I promise to send you money every single week," I said, tears streaming down my cheeks, the salty taste but an ocean full of sadness.

John, Alice, and I waved at the ship. Alice looked up to see me still shaking uncontrollably. "It's okay, Mommy."

"I should have gone with her," I pouted, squeezing Alice's hand. I should have accompanied her back, but I was torn between my duties as wife and Mother to that of a sister who refused to abide by our wishes and just eat a meal. God helps those who help themselves and there was no helping Dorothy.

On October 9th I received a telegram that Dorothy was

admitted to St Luke's hospital.

Immediately I sprang into action, packing our family yet again, for another long sail to America. I couldn't bear the thought of losing her, too.

"I'm coming with you," said John. "I want to be there to care for our Alice while you tend to Dorothy."

"That's very generous my love, but we have the nurse and the maid."

"They're not a husband and a father."

I moved towards him and gave him a gentle kiss on the lips. "You're the most wonderful and patient husband, Johnnie."

"Thank you, Love, but the truth is I'm afraid if I let you go alone, you'll never return."

I chuckled. "I promise I will."

"We will all return. I'll get the Doctor to say she must have full time care. With us."

At that I stopped short. How wrong Mother had been to think this man, John Lavery, wasn't the perfect husband for me. How wrong she'd have been not to see he'd end up caring for our Dorothy, too.

But two days later, as we glided peacefully someplace over the Atlantic, there was a knock at our state room door. A deckhand sent a note from the captain delivering the news from The Inter-Ocean publication:

DOROTHY MARTYN: DEAD.

The cause of death was acute enteritis from all her years of self-enforced starvation. The worst of it was that the news later read, "Deserted by her sister, Hazel Martyn Lavery, Miss Dorothy Martyn passed away alone at St. Luke's Hospital."

To add fuel to the fire, the news that a prominent family member died in a public hospital flabbergasted our neighbors and socialites alike. The newspapers destroyed me, speculating I had abandoned her for love and money, speculating we had a wayward relationship and that I'd never been there for her, but the one speculation that wasn't speculation at all was that she died alone... with no hand to hold. And to me, that was the most painful.

What had Dorothy thought about me not being there as she lay dying?

It seems we measure ourselves through the eyes of the ones we love...

Our arrival was a dismal one and as Grace greeted us at the ship, porters followed with our luggage, and John moved me swiftly through the paparazzi. John arranged the funeral because I was numb and grieving, not for me, but for my sister, who had wasted a precious life, who had so much hope and so much talent.

Following a quiet ceremony, Dorothy was buried in the cemetery with Mother and Father. As they lowered the casket, I pulled Alice under my fur coat to shield her from the bite of the October chill. John and I shared a look, one that questioned, how did such a prominent family as ours, with so much to live for, end up broke, dead, and now, alone.

As we held our gaze, John held my hand as if to declare as loudly as possible albeit in total silence: "You'll never be alone, my love. You will always have me."

Chapter Seventeen

Hazel and John (and Alice)

Following my sister's death, I vowed never to return to the pain of Chicago, or to New York, or to America at all, for that matter. Though I would always continue to donate whatever my bank account might allow to the hungry and homeless of Chicago.

Back in England, I began to fall back in love again with what really mattered to me... John and Alice. But like a swarm of locusts devouring a crop, my previous life was wiped out, and I worried what Alice and I would do if anything happened to John. How could I survive yet another loss?

Immersing myself in all things John, I entertained my husband's friends and colleagues. It was said that together John and I created a culture of our own. John had a well-established clientele before our marriage, but he gained popularity after marrying me. Why, I don't know, as I never understood this, but perhaps because I pacified our guests' graceless faces with laughter.

John was often exhausted after a day with his sitters and had a challenging time making polite and political conversation over cocktails and dinners. By contrast, I loved talking, flirting, and telling stories of life back in America with my American accent, telling guests everything they wanted to hear about Chicago and New York. I understood why they needed that. The Brits were far more polite, less candid in their thoughts and in their judgment, which left me to put my thoughts and judgments in the open, like a true American.

Even the Prime Minister said to John, “Your wife is a delight. Any hostess who wants to have a successful dinner party need not worry about the champagne or the polished cutlery... just invite Hazel!” Yes, apparently, I was the “belle of the ball” though I was not interested… but I did my best to appease them all and to be useful to John’s potential clients.

But the world of England viewed John as boring despite being singly honored with a retrospective exhibition of fifty-three of his most important works at the Venice Biennale. They didn’t understand that an artist needs silence to go off and create. Not hoopla. If he’s ‘on,’ he’s giving off energy that would be best preserved for the canvas.

One Countess fanning herself, sipping a sherry in the corner, declared in a whisper, “despite everyone’s admiration of Hazel, she’d be all the more exciting if she hadn’t married the dull John Lavery.”

And then there was Alice... a spitball personality, reminding me of a cross between Mother and my younger self. On her first day of school, her playmates asked why her name was ‘Trudeau’ and her mother’s name was ‘Lavery.’ Embarrassed and struggling for an answer, she swallowed hard and explained, “Well, you see, my mother married a friend of mine and that’s how it came about.” Apparently, John had promised Alice that when she grew up, he’d marry her, and in the meantime, they’d be good friends. This was his way of not pushing paternal behavior on her. It worked quite smashingly.

John often painted Alice and me. Our favorite was the time we traveled for a week in Wendgern, a Swiss Alpine village in the Bernese Oberland region. Known for its timber and its chalets, not to mention its very Belle Epoque hotels, it was as close to a winter wonderland as Chicago had always been.

John was finishing up *Japanese Switzerland,* a stunning portrait of Alice and I holding hands in the snow. He placed the brush loaded with paint, dabbing dark shapes for figures – us – against the white snowy background. He stood back, admiring his work, taking delight in the visual drama.

And who wouldn't love the Alpine landscape? Except that Alice and I had to be extremely patient, despite the nipping air at our fingers and our toes inside our felt-lined snow boots. With a large sigh, Alice declared, "Isn't it a pity, Muffie, that we married an artist."

John, overhearing, burst into laughter, and it was contagious. I burst into laughter; the first time I'd really had a good laugh in many months. Yes, life was just glorious with the three of us, outside the society and politics of the world.

One day Alice wandered into John's studio where he was painting a portrait of Kenneth Clark, the then Director of the National Gallery.

"Hello," said Alice, pulling up a stool in which to climb upon and be eye level with Mr. Clark.

"Well, hello, young lady," said Mr. Clark, breaking his pose. "And who are you?"

"I'm Alice," she declared. "I'm Mr. Lavery's daughter, you see."

"How old are you?" asked Mr. Clark.

"I've just struck five."

He chuckled. "Did you 'ting' or did you cuckoo?"

"I cuckooed," said Alice, suddenly imitating a bird to Mr. Clark's delight.

"Hazel!" called John. "Hazel dear, can you come to gather little Alice."

Entering John's studio, I flung open the door minus my usual tiptoeing, and announced, "Darling," I said, "Take us to Tangier! You love it so. Let's go!!"

"But I thought you wanted to stay put," he responded, surprised, his brush held midair.

"I lied," I winked in Mr. Clark's direction. "The truth is I can't bear a long winter with talk of hemlines, the powdering of noses and political strategies."

"I'd love to see politicians powdering their noses," said John, chuckling at his own joke before asking, "And what do you think you'll learn in Morocco?"

Mr. Clark's head moved back and forth between us like a tennis ball.

"What will I learn?" I asked, repeating the question and taking Alice by the hand. "Well, come to think of it... I don't know. New food, culture? You tell me," I asked, putting it on him.

"You'll adore polo, but you might try pig sticking."

"Oh dear, what on earth..." I asked.

"It's the sport of hunting wild boar with a spear, typically from horseback."

"I'm squeamish at the thought..." I said, kissing John with a polite peck. "But I know our lives together have only begun!"

"What a lovely sentiment," said Mr. Clark, admiring John and I together.

"Tangier! Tangier!" clapped Alice with a rallying cry. "Papa is taking us to Tangier!"

"Brilliant!" said Mr. Clark. "And I can see you get your exuberant personality from your mother, little one."

Alice beamed, then kissed me smack on the lips. How I loved my little girl.

Victorian travel had always been about the politics of leaving home and escaping. It was a clear division of 'home' and 'away' and the difference between 'self' and 'discovery' or so I pondered that thought in a travel diary as our ship sailed closer to our new colonial encounter.

On the other hand, to run away is the simplest of adventures, the true trick is finding something to do after the running has slowed to a stillness...

One train to the port to Spain, and then a boat to Tangier – which sounds dreadfully long but in truth is only forty-eight kilometers, or thirty miles. That night, John's friends were thrilled to see him return though they asked if Eileen was joining us, so he explained she'd grown up and was away at boarding school.

Tangier-La-Blanca was our winter home and I instantly fell in love because we were far from the pain of illness and death. We shared wonderful meals of Couscous, Tagine, Zaalouk and so many flavorful foods with all types of travelers, early tradesmen, the first ambassadors, the painters, the novelists, and even the missionaries.

Alice, however, would have longed to dine with the corsairs. The Pirates!

Because John had previously taken his daughter, Eileen to Tangiers where they contributed greatly to the social life of the British settlement, it was there that they became close friends with Sir Reginald Lister, British envoy. Whenever John and Eileen were in town, Lister led a relaxed existence, riding horse back on the beach, and staging casual dinner parties for the British expatriates. Sir Reginald now welcomed Alice and me as family, too. My American stories amused him, and the way I captured John's heart as no other woman had before.

In Tangier, as the heat engulfed my body, America and Europe seemed very far off. A cloud of light grey dust emitted downward our existence, giving a dismal age to everything including the 'whites' worn by Arabs. Children's bright faces aged before our eyes as the white powder descended upon their brown mules and mangy dogs.

The hills above Tarifa on the Spanish coast made a stark, trenchant line across the cloudless sky beyond the Straits. Heaven must feel like this. Few tourists visited, and the dialect of Spanish mixed with Arabic surrounded us. Alice began to tune into their dialect.

John was often seated in the little winding path which led out to the Soco de Afuera surrounded by a crowd. Jews chatted, Moors stood and gazed, and Spanish boys flocked about while darting in and out of the crowds. Mules, laden with trusses of pressed straw, brushed by his easel. Now and then a camel sailed past, casual, and elegant, as John sat oblivious to it all, buried in his work. That was my Johnnie... like a King seated on his throne.

He sketched hard in Tangiers, and painted harder – street views, snake-charmers, the orange market, the Jewish quarters, a mosque in the moonlight. But his favorite by far had always been the painting of his daughter, Eileen, on horseback, which would later become *The Equestrienne* which later found a home at the Goupil Gallery.

Something happened in Tangiers. A spell was put on John, who painted many charming little portraits of native girls with colored draperies around their heads, and with a strange aloof wisdom in their eyes. It was people and humanity that inspired him the most and always would.

Like many artists before him, he felt a constant call to Africa or the East... And who wouldn't trade in the dismal winters of London for the warmth of Tanger-la-Blanca?

Eileen, that's who… surprising us one day that she was here to spend the winter. Alice ran with happiness to her stepsister's arms as Eileen swirled her around the terrace, knocking over several terra cotta planters of cacti.

We, meaning, us three girls, inspired John; and his resulting canvases gave little indication of haste.

He began formulating a painting idea that would be called *The Studio* of Alice, Eileen, our Moroccan maid, Aida, and me. He repositioned the idea several times before putting it aside, before moving to painting more leisurely and long in the warmth of the sun. Apparently, or so I later learned, the problem was me. He said I 'owned' the painting, commanding the viewer to draw their eye to me. And that's not what he wanted. He wanted the painting to be a balance of family. Instead, it was 'all about Hazel.' I wasn't certain what I could possibly do to alter that situation. And I was yet too naïve to fully understand the presence I had in his art, not just on canvas but in all of life.

Like a lioness with her cubs, my focus was on my daughter. And now, my stepdaughter. Alice, Eileen, and I strolled the gardens and studied and learned an entirely new geography full of deserts and mountains, and down to the creatures... the Fennec fox, the single-humped camel, the Dorcas gazelle, and the jerboa. Even the desert hedgehog, Alice's favorite. It was all quite different from a five-year-old learning about cats, cows, and chickens. This was an education beyond her wildest imagination, and she had quite an imagination. In an empty cigar box gifted from Sir Reginald, Alice housed a collection of dead insects and butterflies, having neglected to put holes in the sides for breathing.

One day riding 'Moses' her donkey, Alice was heard addressing him in Arabic with, "Go on, thou son of an adulteress," and similar epithets. In Arab.

It was our maid, Aida, who translated, and we later told John. It became a sort of house joke between us when someone needed to get something done. "Go on, thou son of an adulteress!" There was irony in that "adulteress comment," though I was yet to know it.

For now, life was everything grand beyond my wildest dreams. Was this really my life? I often asked that question, practically pinching myself to believe it, gazing out to the majestic mountains, tears in my eyes in all that I'd learned, all that I'd lost, all that I'd become and all that lie ahead of me...

Oh yes, life was perfectly grand. What more could I possibly ask for?

Chapter Eighteen
Michael

Long before Michael Collins was the *Most Wanted Man in all of England*, and the very founder of guerilla warfare, he was a mere boy, born in West Cork, Ireland, a place as traditional as it was beautiful, with colorful fishing villages dotting the hillsides. His family's farm, saturated in the rain-soaked landscape of dramatic greens, was nestled within the shelter of bays. Born in the traditional Gaelic season, October of 1890, Michael was ten years my junior and the baby in a family of his eight siblings. His old Uncle Paddy once declared, "Be careful of this child for he will be a great and mighty man when we are all forgotten." It's a shame his Uncle Paddy didn't live to see that truth come to fruition.

Michael's family had roots in both the bardic and warrior traditions of Ireland, where his jolly Irish family's heritage was a backdrop of famine and landlordism. The Collins clan was well-off by Irish standards, with a life of Catholic church on Sunday and farming their ninety acres of land all week long. Come Friday, Michael's father would place his hands on his hips, and exhale, "the land should always be owned by the people" which he instilled in his young son, Michael. "It's the way of the Irish. You got that, Mick?" Michael would nod his head though he was uncertain, because if the people didn't own the land, then who did? That thought stayed with him...

"Go bathe for suppa, Lad," his Uncle Paddy instructed, mushing a hand to Michael's head top. "And wash behind yer ears.

Can't have potatoes growin' back there, now, can we?"

While Michael never rough-and-tumbled or sang customary rebel songs in a pub, he was a steadfast, born leader from the get-go. When he and his cousins speared salmon, it was Michael who insisted on holding the pitchfork, charging the way. But he never learned to swim, typical of the Irish way of life since the ocean was seen as a place to create employment or to join the Navy, not to swim for leisure.

Michael grew up to be just under six feet tall; he loved football and hurling, and his nickname quickly became "The Big Fella." He excelled at the popular Cork sport of 'bowling' which wasn't with bowling alleys, but with an iron ball thrown down a country road. Jesus, Mary, and Joseph – he'd bless himself, hoping the ball would make a soft landing into a ditch.

Michael came from a world where nagging traditions were handed down from generation to generation. The school system of his youth longed to destroy the Gaelic language, training the children instead to become good British citizens with loyalty to the throne. But Michael knew early on that was not Ireland's destiny. Michael knew early on too, that Irish life fluctuated between happy and sad, famine and fed, hatred and love, and finally, reality and myth.

Michael was an avid reader like me, spending most of his after-school hours at the library. When he learned about the Irish Republican Brotherhood – the IRB – it swayed Michael to instill a spirit of what it meant to be born Irish. By age eleven he was already reading the writings of Arthur Griffith, the founder of Sinn Fein which stood for "We Ourselves" and the name of the Irish political party. Michael snuck the books late at night by candlelight, falling down a rabbit hole of information.

Like me, too, Michael lost his father, though he was only six, his father seventy-five, leaving him susceptible to the influence of outside men, including Uncle Paddy, to guide him into eventual rebellion against the throne.

Michael decided to take a shot at a bigger existence than one of life on the farm, so he prepared for the entrance examination for the British Postal service. He attended civil service classes in a nearby town called Clonakilty. For Michael, the Postal service was a way to see the world through other people's exchanges, and to find out what all the British fuss was about, too.

At barely sixteen, and with nothing but a weathered attaché case from the local priest and a worn duffle bag full of hand-me-down clothes, Michael raced down the pier to the lifting of the plank at the ferry.

"Ahoy!" called the captain, tugging at the whistle. "Ere she blows!"

Uncle Paddy waved from shore cupping his hands to his mouth and calling after his nephew, "May you have fair winds and following seas, me Lad!!" Michael put his finger to his ear to suggest he couldn't hear his uncle. Nevertheless, Uncle Paddy hollered out again. "Go on-éiri an bóthar leat," Gaelic for "May success be with you."

Michael saluted his uncle, watching him until the ship sailed farther away leaving Uncle Paddy and the Irish coast nothing but a dot on a distant map.

The ride was long, the sea choppy. When Michael wasn't hanging over the banister with queasiness, he admired the change of scenery, countryside to countryside, Irish green to English brown, until the city came into view as the ferry pulled into the harbor.

Excuse me, excuse me, pardon me, Mam. Michael made his way to the side of the railing and scanned the crowds. Finally, in the distance he spotted her. "Joanna!" he called, climbing onto the banister's second rung, and waving his arms overhead.

"Mick! Mick! Over 'ere!" called Joanna, "Welcome to England!!"

As soon as he gathered up his bags, he followed the crowds to where Joanna threw her arms around his neck. "Brother! How I've missed you," she said. Michael gathered her into his arms, spinning her around like they did on the family farm. "Oh feck. Put me down or I'll giggle to me grave, Mick!"

"*Ta go Brea,*" he said – 'fine' – placing her down on the cobblestone and gathering his bags. He walked alongside her, his free arm around her shoulders.

"I've secured you a job as a clerk in the Post office."

"Far from yer flat?" asked Michael.

"No, just in West Kensington. Close by to my place. Walking distance. Not that was ever a problem for you with those big feet of yers!"

"Big feet and bigger heart," he said, tickling her at the waist.

The year Michael took that job would have been the same year I went off to Italy exploring macaroni and men. And Len.

Ironically just a couple of years later and married to John, I would visit that very post office, just a few minutes from our home in Cromwell Place. There were two men working behind the counter, where I sidestepped to the glass-opening where a cheery, handsome young man greeted me.

"Top of the morning," said Michael with the world's most massive smile and flirty eyes.

"Good morning. I'd like to purchase fifty 'two pence' postage stamps," I said, unclipping my velvet change purse to pay him.

"Surely," said Michael, gathering several sheets of stamps with the face of King Edward VII stamped on their front side. His hand touched mine and my eyes lifted to his handsome face.

"Thank you..." I whispered.

He unleashed a grin. "Michael, Michael Collins of Cork, at your service."

"Thank you, Michael Collins of Cork. You're quite efficient."

"I try," he said, taking my coins. "I have other talents, ye know."

"Oh?"

"I type. I sew."

"Sew?" I asked curiously.

"My sister taught me because every man should know how to sew a button."

I sniffled, holding in a laugh. "You have a lovely day."

"Yer sure? There won't be anything else?" he coaxed.

"I'm sure," I said, as he handed me some change.

"Fine then, er, Miss?"

"It's Mrs. and it's Lavery," I nodded, holding the moment.

"Don't mean to be cheeky, Mrs. Lavery," he said.

I snorted to myself, moving away from the postal counter. As I stood off to the side at a table, licking the stamps for the dinner invitations, I watched Michael smiling, pushing his long fringe from his eyes, with that boyish grin, diligently assisting customers. He was possibly the most handsome young man I'd ever laid an eye on, with his square jaw, athletic build, dark brown hair, and a whirlwind of energy. The young women must go mad for him. Of course, he was all but a lad and I was ten years his senior, old enough to be his... well, his older sister...

But his real older sister, Joanna, took an interest in helping Michael complete his education and assisted in employment later. Michael was curious to learn his Mother Land's language of Gaelic, which was ironic that he had to move to London to learn the native tongue of his ancestors. It was said that the language represented the lower classes and poverty, but Michael wouldn't buy into that notion.

His other sister, Mary Collins, encouraged her brother's interest in the Nationalist struggle and guerilla warfare. Mary was attending school in Edinburgh and on holiday would tell him stories about how the gallant Boer farmers would end their days by taking part in an ambush and then return to milking the cows the next morning.

Like me, Michael lost his mother, too. In her case, to cancer, and in his case, he was just a teen. She suffered a long lingering illness and Michael always kept her funeral Mass card close to his heart. It read:

> Friend and stranger at her smiling board
> Found a welcome ever warmly stored;
> In her pulse the quickening rush
> Spoke the bosom's generous flush.
> An honest pleasure beamed in her eye:
> At her home 'twas ever so -
> Those who came were loath to go;
> Hers was Irish hospitality...

Michael once told me he was a lot like his mother, and he believed all his inherent goodness came from her. On her Mass card they had mistakenly written that she died at age 54, but Michael gently penciled in '52' next to it, though never crossed out the incorrect '54' so as not to ruin the card. But for a young man of only seventeen, that was quite a lot to lose. All he could do was carry on their legacy and their beliefs in the Irish way of life.

After his short-lived career as a postal clerk, his sister took him out shopping for a proper suit, tie, and shiny patent leather shoes, which he had trouble fitting his foot into since he'd grown up in hand-me-down boots. Nevertheless, when dressed and polished he looked like a true professional.

"Uncle Paddy? Uncle Paddy can yer hear me?" asked Michael, juggling the phone receiver to his ear, pressing at the hook switch of the landline. "I've a big job. A Stockbroker." (pause) "A big firm, Uncle. Work for the wealthy men, yeah? Making investments. (pause) Yes, I went to church on Sunday. Thank yer, Uncle. Thank you. (pause) I'll make you and the good Lord proud."

Michael also secured a position with his destiny, The IRB, a rising organization against British rule. In little time, he was promoted to treasurer.

He once wrote home to his uncle: "However happy I happen to be in a particular job, the thought is always with me that my future is otherwise that among the facts and figures of money. Yet I do not really dream of greater things... only the thought is always there."

Michael believed that character mattered most, and he believed in doing something bigger than just self-serving. Apparently, you can take the boy out of Cork, Ireland, but you can't take Cork, Ireland out of the boy...

Chapter Nineteen
Hazel

For the first few winters, Eileen joined her father and me in Tangier, but as any blossoming woman eager to explore the world, she also sought a life of her own. She'd often spend time with one of John's former sitting models in Casablanca, and it was through her that Eileen met a group of friends her age, including a young man, James Dickinson, who would ask John for his daughter's hand in marriage.

Alice, now age eight, was asked to be a bridesmaid and I was thrilled at the prospect of throwing a bridal shower for my stepdaughter. With the wedding ceremony, there were lists upon lists for the caterer, the florists, and a multitude of guests. We checked off everything right down to the flowers that would adorn the silk runner as she entered the parish. It was a bit overwhelming, and I wasn't certain if we should have the church bells ring when the carriage arrived or just after. Either way, I entered the drawing room gently separating the pages of the itinerary on the side table. John sat reading his newspaper in the stream of morning sunlight from the veranda.

"Johnnie, darling, we must spare no expense."

"She's really not that type of young lady," said John.

"But it's your daughter. It's Eileen!"

"She's informed me that she wants things simple. No horse, no carriage, no gown, just simple, simple, simple." I looked at John with dismay. John glanced over his newspaper, his spectacles sliding down his nose. "Hazel? I realize simple is not a word in your vocabulary."

"Well, if it's what she wants?" I said with disappointment, rearranging the pages and moving a couple of ideas off to the side. "We could forego the church, do the ceremony here? But that limits the guests," I said, answering my own question. "And what of the flowers then? Just some festoons of evergreen should suffice, for the veranda, I mean, if that's all she might want." My voice dipped to further disappointment. "But what of favors? For the guests?"

"Ask Eileen," said John, patting my hand. "I'm very touched you love my Eileen so..."

"You know Johnnie, I worry about her groom, James?"

"Why?" asked John, again glancing over his newspaper.

"He doesn't come from much solid breeding."

"He's not a horse, Hazel."

"And his education, a bit shady."

"As long as my daughter is happy. And she is."

My guest list included Sirs, Counts, Barristers, and a couple of Baronesses. The weather was ideal and after a small civil service in John's studio at Dar-el-Midfah, we had a lovely event at dusk, the pink sky playful until the moon and stars silenced it. James and Eileen made a dutiful couple, if I do say so myself, and I could tell by the look in his eyes that he loved her the way Ned once worshiped me.

But our happy occasion forecasted a dismal future. It would be our last event with our dear friend, Reginald Lister, having contracted malaria and who died shortly after. Suddenly the primitive charm of Tangier felt like the saddest place on earth, proof that death could follow me and Alice anywhere...Chicago, London, and even Tangier.

Returning home to London we asked our Moroccan maid Aida to join, which she did.

She was family to us and a constant in both Eileen and Alice's lives. Once home, John continued to work on what would be one of his largest portraits set in his lofty workroom. It was the same one of Alice, Eileen, Aida, and me. Even our family greyhound snoozed at my feet for the sitting... lucky the dog who could find a way to sleep during a boring sitting.

As John sketched and the painting formed, upon closer inspection, one could discern his reflection holding his palette and brush in the mirror, placed deliberately in the background of the scene. It had been a tedious sitting, John rearranging all of us several times to his satisfaction. First Eileen on the left, then later to the right, leaning on a table, in profile form yet hovering gently at Alice's side. She sat still with dangling feet as the bench seat was too high for her patent leather shoes. Then he added Aida, took her out, then added her again, this time with a basket of fruit in her arms.

I wore the same burgundy satin day clothes with strands upon strands of pearls, though my headpiece changed. A blue turban secured with a diamond brooch was the final choice. And in all the sittings, I was bored, completely bored out of my mind. Was this what life would be? Sitting for John Lavery? My spirit groaned, my heart sank, but his hand went on and on automatically, dot by dot, brush stroke by brush stroke until he was satisfied... After many alterations, he was… satisfied. Many considered the final composition a masterpiece, not only to John's longstanding love and relationship with Tangier, but because it contained prominent details to that of Velazquez's Las Meninas. And upon closer inspection, in all the renditions of the painting, though barely noticeable, there hung Idonia in Morocco above the mantel and a bust of Queen Mary, from the days of John's Queen Mary portrait in the background.

Number 5 Cromwell Place was home as home might ever be, and it was good to be back in London. John and I had created our own personal culture with friends, the theater, and the press. Our entertaining of friends sometimes seemed never ending.

The press felt I influenced my husband's creative output. When asked, I simply told them, "I have certainly posed a lot for him, and I suppose that saved him a considerable amount of trouble, but for inspiring him – well he was painting long before he married me, so I am not his muse. His travels are his muse. His works are a laid-out diary of his life from Ireland to Scotland to England to Tangier."

My life had been so consumed with my sibling, parents, lovers, and child, that lately I found I was happiest alone, finding my own self... pouring myself into our house, designing with a flair, a giant recapitulation of the styles of all countries in all proceeding periods. I plucked items to display from China to Spain, Boulle to Gothic, yet it was the bit of medievalism and Christianity that was considered the most fashionable... that and some intricate designed carvings from Tangier.

Finally, the house spoke to me, and Vogue saw it that way too, running a photographed piece called 'Notable Women at Home.' I sat posed on the silk arm of the divan in the drawing room. Tall palms staged around me.

In my interview I explained my design thoughts. "Spanish, Italian, and English influences are very apparent these days, which manifests little in the way of originality. But it's the moderne style attempting reluctantly to emerge for these forthcoming years."

"Will it still encompass Art Nouveau?" asked the journalist.

"Oh, very much so. For now," I said. "Modern remains experimental... a style of theorists. The new Deco is to be more a reaction... a successor of the Nouveau, but I'll always love the long organic lines of Nouveau."

"Seems you've maintained that in the back halls and the powder room," said the journalist. The cameras snapped and snapped as he nodded pleasingly at my comments.

But something for me was amiss. Like the modern style taking emotional elements from its past so did I find my life was just some ornamental vocabulary... some caricature form of past to the present. Something was wrong. I loved John, I adored little Alice, and I tolerated John's friends, but in slipping my shoes off at Number 5 Cromwell Place, while it was certainly home, a part of my soul was someplace out the door. But where?

"Mrs. Lavery?"

"Yes, I'm so sorry, you were saying..."

"May we see her Ladyship's sitting room?" asked the journalist.

"Yes, right this way," I said, breezing through the grand room and up the stairs. "To be honest," I joked, "I'm sure Mr. Lavery would prefer I spend more time alone here rather than the number of people I hold court for in our parlor. Namely the gentlemen callers."

The two shared a chuckle. Then the journalist asked, "Dare I ask, is it true that society women are highly competitive in the pursuit of husbands and lovers?"

"I haven't the slightest idea. I'm married." I thought before I continued to answer, and then coyly added, "Might we say that love affairs are acceptable, assuming they do not bring public scandal." The journalist scribbled my comments like mad in his notebook.

Chapter Twenty
Michael

It would have been just an ordinary Easter day with morning Mass, a lavish meal of ham, cabbage and corned-salted beef, except on this Easter Sunday in April of 1916, the Irish Volunteers and the Citizen Army marched to the General Post Office from Liberty Hall.

James Connolly, P.H. Pearce and Joseph Plunkett, along with Michael Collins, in his polished captain's uniform, led the group. Michael looked like a soldier - tall, handsome, good posture and an attitude of assurance that none of the others seemed to possess.

The General Post office (GPO) was now the headquarters for the army of the Irish Republic. They possessed handcrafted shotguns, and revolvers along with some obsolete German rifles. The army had planned to set up sieges in various areas south of Dublin including Counties Wexford, Cork, and Galway, but sadly as Michael said to one of his comrades, "Tell God you have a plan and..."

British troops moved into Dublin to crush the Rising, with the center of the city unexpectedly and completely encircled. By that night, the streets were burning. Havoc and death ensued. As one building was being evacuated, Michael made a short escape through the smoke and gunfire out a side door onto Moore Street, while many of his mates who weren't so lucky, were shot dead or being brought out on stretchers. The stench of blood was everywhere, with town civilians dressed in Easter Sunday best, moaning, and wallowing in pain. Unbeknownst to Michael just yet, one of them was his best friend of his boyhood days, Sean Hurley.

The entire atrocity was a pivotal turning point for Michael Collins.

The next day and to prevent further bloodshed, and with Michael leading the way, the insurgents surrendered using a white flag made of rags, marching down Moore Street, where one by one, each Irish soldier laid down his arms to the British Army. Michael took note of the number of men in his army, whispering to one of his comrades, "The more they shoot, the more people they bring to our side."

Huddled together, they were arrested and taken to Richmond Barracks by the Metropolitan Police of Dublin, who were brought in to identify the leaders of the Rising. Some of the leaders were executed but were canonized by the Irish as martyrs for the cause.

Michael was among two hundred other men taken to a cattle-boat at the North Wall and deported to an internment camp in Wales, called Frongoch.

While the English thought they were doing the right thing, lassoing these Irish followers of Sinn Fein – the "We Ourselves" movement – it became an excellent breeding ground for Irish camaraderie. Michael joked that the arrest had led to all of them being in "Frongoch University." Many of the prisoners were skilled or well-educated men so Michael took it upon himself to learn French, Spanish, and his most beloved Gaelic, the language that would make Ireland not only free, but speaking their God-given language as well.

But the conditions of the prison were dismal, dirty, and the food inedible. As a result, and after much complaining from the inmates, Michael was one of the four to speak to the home office about the conditions.

While not a Senior Officer yet, Michael was granted permission to formulate an army, picking and choosing who might be right for various positions. While at it, he took advantage of the guards, soldiers, and wardens in Wales, getting to know them, and figuring out how they might fit into his bigger plan.

"Have ye seen the destruction the bastards left behind," said a forlorn fellow prisoner.

"Yes, I surely have," said Michael, who stood up on a stool rising above the other prisoners, "Don't worry you, old cod," pointing to the man, "we'll rebuild the whole city in ten years if necessary!" There was a sense of camaraderie as everyone broke into much-needed back-patting cheers.

"But they're the world's power, ye know?" said another prisoner. "The Brits power stretches over two-thirds of yer globe."

"It surely does," declared Michael. "And their most troubling colony has always been the one closest to them... Ireland." More cheers came up from the prison floor.

By the late fall, the British Government believed that continuing to house these Irish derelicts wasn't worth their reputation, wasn't worth what the rest of the world, and especially what America, might think of them. And besides, World War had started, and the English had a more important agenda. So, they set the Irish prisoners free, but not before demanding in a lineup that they give their names and addresses. The prisoners cast their eyes down, not sure what to do, glancing over to Michael Collins for directions. "I speak for all of us," he said. "You'll get no names or information from any of us, so you can let us rot in this hell hole or you can set us free."

That week of amnesty was Christmas, so the men were released back to their families. Michael arrived home to his siblings on Christmas morning, his nose swelling with the inhale of country soil, his heart swelling with Irish pride, and his stomach soon full of the roasted turkey, a marmalade-glazed ham, his sister's sage and onion stuffing with a side of sea-salted boiled potatoes. Michael's favorite.

"Michael!" his sister hollered out. "So happy yer 'ere!" The family joined round, and everyone shared hugs as the wine poured.

Michael stood at the head of the table, goblet in hand, declaring, "May your troubles be less, and yer blessings be more.

And nothing but happiness come through your door." Hear, hear!

The siblings shared gifts of socks and knitted wool sweaters. Michael unwrapped a gift from his oldest sister... a Silver Celtic 'Tree of life' pendant, placing it around his neck. It symbolized immortality and rebirth as trees lose their leaves, appearing dead in the winter, until the new buds appear, and the fresh cycle of life erupts again.

As he strolled along the River Blackwater of Cork, the wind whipping a crisp December snap, Michael stared out at the shades of green and brown crisscrossing the fields and farms, and the sandstone ridge. He reflected on the nearly seven hundred years that Britain had ruled over Ireland, and how his people had tried and failed several times to rebel with revolution.

Late at night, as his siblings all slept, he sat with notebooks devising ideas. He was more certain than ever he wanted to end British rule in Ireland.

With the prisoners released they needed a new rallying space to continue the fight. Michael emerged as the natural leader after having helped to reorganize the IRB in Frongoch.

It was a biting cold January afternoon when Michael arrived at the home of Mrs. Thomas Clarke, founder of the Volunteer Dependents' Fund, for his interview.

Turning on his charismatic, energized charms, he won her over to the tune of what would be his salary... at two pounds and ten shillings a week. Since Mrs. Clarke had been the wife of the leader in the march, she handed over the IRB list of men to him, which she'd kept safely stored in an empty silver-plated jewelry box should anything happen to her husband.

"Mick, it's yer place now," she said, handing him the list, which he scanned rapidly. "You take over for my husband, yeah? God rest his soul."

"As God is my witness, Mrs. Clarke, I will do good service in the eyes of the Lord," said Michael, taking the list, scanning its names, and then tucking it in his top shirt pocket. "You won't regret this."

She touched his shirt, patting his pocket. "You have the drive and the enthusiasm that will serve our people well."

Michael, having lost both of his parents, loved Mrs. Clarke's parental approval, and bent down to hug her and give her a kiss on both the left cheek and the right. Michael's eyes drowned in hers as they held the moment for her dead husband, her bottom lip trembling. He spoke first. "I want peace and quiet for our country, yeah? I'd die for it."

"You mean you'd kill for it," she whispered. Her fingers shook as she reached up to take his face in her hands. "You go on and do great things, Mick Collins; great things, I tell ya."

And so, the national movement gathered forced. Collins, now in the passenger's seat as Secretary, shared the car with men like Eamon deValera and W. T. Cosgrave elected in Clare and Kilkenny, until soon, he moved up to the driver's seat elected as a Volunteer Executive.

But despite a county of Cork, a country of Ireland, and the blessing of Mrs. Clarke, his most valuable asset was that of Sam Maguire, an old chum who still worked in the post office in London. It was only a matter of time before he'd need him as one of his lead spies.

Chapter Twenty-one

Hazel

It would be months and months, and then years and years, before I could wake in the morning without my first thoughts being 'Dorothy is dead. Mother is dead. Father is dead.'

Evenings I drowned in my dreams a little more every night, with an ocean full of grief, so deep, I feared I'd never swim ashore.

Afternoons the guilt pummeled through me, wishing they were alive to share in the security of my life, wishing they were alive to see Alice grow, and for my mother witnessing that John, for all our ups and down, was a kind and supportive husband.

But I also felt the guilt of not knowing more about the history of my Irish Martyn clan... of my grandparents and our heritage. There was so much I would never be able to ask my father, so much I didn't know I'd need to remember about him since the last time I really remembered him. He'd tucked me into bed that winter's eve, bent to kiss me goodnight, the smell of his aftershave, vanilla and a musky amber, as he took my face in his hands to declare, "My Hazel, you are the best Christmas gift of all. Now night, night and off with the light." And at that, he went downstairs, entertaining guests for the coming new year's celebration.

And here I was now in England, so close to Ireland. So close to my Irish roots. How I longed to understand more of my ancestry and see the beauty of the green isle and its thirty-two thousand square miles coddled by the Atlantic Ocean. Shame, this home of England, just situated to its right had caused so much damage to Ireland's architectural heritage. Dating back to the 17th century, it had towns, castles, and monasteries, or so I read about it in my Cromwell study one rainy afternoon, fingering through the pages of Father's history books that showcased Iron-aged forts and towers. I'd taken it upon myself to inherit my favorite few of his books, and to carve a portion of every morning teatime to read through the rise, fall, and lingering hope of the Irish.

As I placed the history volume on the second bookshelf, my fingers flitted through the binders on the third shelf which housed Father's other books. The literary side of Ireland... James Joyce, one of Mother's favorites... how I wish she'd lived to read his latest short-story collection Dubliners.

Recently there had been that up-and-coming poet... oh what was his name... William Butler Yeats. Oh God, why was I so bad with names? Just last year Yeats told me how much I would adore Ireland when we shared supper in Mayfair. "Long live the Irish!" we toasted our champagne flutes... adding that I'd be a welcome and cheery addition to a dismal England... much more than I could say for the recent Irish turmoil and the Movement formulating in Ireland.

As I moved from the bookshelf grinning to myself, John entered the study. "I've been looking all over for you," he said with fists on hips.

"Oh?"

"Our Alice let the dog out of the pen, and there's a doo-doo on the oriental runner."

"Did you find Aida?" I asked, not wanting to escape my Irish fantasy. He shook his head 'no' and I burst into thought, "Johnnie? What was the town William Yeats said he was born in? The town he said I'd adore..."

"Sandymount. Why?" asked John.

"Is it near to Dublin?"

"Yes," said John, annoyed by my sudden fascination with all

things Irish. “It’s a rather affluent coastal town just outside Dublin. Right up your alley, dearest.”

Moving toward him I gently whispered with a sudden and gentle Irish brogue, “Oh, how I so loved that toast ye made. The one with Yeats. You know... ‘For each petal on the shamrock this brings a wish your way. Good health, good luck, and happiness for today and every day.’”

“Marvelous!” said John, brushing dog fur from the sofa to sit, “But may I remind you that you’re married to an Irish man so what more of Ireland do you need?” He patted the cushion next to him for me to sit.

“Yes! The more the merrier that I married an Irish man! And we’ve your friend... what’s his name? George?”

“Bernard Shaw. What of him?” asked John, stretching out his legs and circling his wrists from arthritis.

“Nothing, except he’s Irish, too.” I handed John a piece of paper tucked in my bosom. “I wrote this for you...”

“Oh?” he said, with curiosity, and putting on his glasses examined the page. “Why it’s a poem... how delightful.”

“Go on, read it,” I coaxed.

He cleared his throat bringing the page under his nose. “Popes, Kings, and Queens, he paints; wives, daughters, dealers, saints. Heedless of their complaints of lamentations...” John put the page down. “Quite clever, but it doesn’t rhyme.”

“Keep on...” I said, waving playful fingers at him.

“Fine,” said John, going back to where he left off on the page. “His wretched wife starving at home, gets scarce a single bone...” John slammed the letter on his knee. “Good God woman, you’re barely starving!”

“Please finish,” I said, my voice deliberately softening to his.

John raised the paper up to eye level. “Yet glories in his name, and wallows in his fame. And tries in vain to claim public attention.”

Silence and then John shook his head. “What is the meaning of this?" he asked, perturbed, placing it on the tea table, and rubbing his wrists more methodically.

"I was thinking..." I said, changing the subject... sort of. "Wouldn't it be grand if you created an Irish collection of paintings documenting the political events of those men who are dedicating their very lives to Irish independence?"

"Why on earth would I want to do that?"

"Why wouldn't you? You just reminded me that you're Irish!" I said, taking his hands and massaging his wrists. "Oh dear, are your hands still bothering you? It is arthritis, isn't it? All that painting... your joints in the same position... for all those commissions."

"Yes, commissions that afford your lifestyle."

I ignored his comment. "Might you not choose to do something you really want to do?"

"Who says I really want to paint the Irish?"

"For history Johnnie, for history's sake. It was you who taught me all one needs for a good portrait is to capture the mood. You could capture the mood. Capture the mood of heroes in war..."

John moved a throw pillow to settle his back comfortably, hands now crossed behind his neck, ruminating the idea...

Chapter Twenty-two
Hazel & John (in War)

That year, 1914, John agreed, and we arrived in Dublin at the Shelbourne hotel. We were barely out of the car when young boys wearing tweed page caps ran through the streets waving newspapers and shouting. "It's war! It's war!" When we read the headline, John and I shared a look. We knew we'd have to go home. Immediately.

World War was upon us...

And so, by boat, we quietly returned to London that night, to find St James Park in an uproar, already being set up as an armed camp. It was then John insisted he must paint his first war picture, and who could blame him? It would be hypocritical having carried on and on about painting the Irish renegades when here at home we had our own men... our own soldiers, fighting to save England. With John's God-given talent, he could do more for our country with a paintbrush then he could with a rifle. And so, he did...

My patriotic John painted "The First Wounded in London Hospital" a stunning portrayal capturing a nurse in the forefront, bandaging a young soldier's arm, while in the background wounded men lay dying in hospital bed, resigned from life.

John's forte became the war at sea and its Navy as he witnessed it all firsthand. Since John was a well-established painter, the art world afforded him a great deal of latitude while his society world turned its back, not interested in the grim reality of death from battle.

John was one of eight artists picked to represent every branch of the British navy. Dispatched to the north, he found his creative and harshest reality in "Hell's Gate" in the Orkneys with its tall sandstone cliffs and seal colonies. Previously the area was best known for the 12th-century Vikings until war again put it on the map.

From there, it was onto painting the troops at the Front at Southampton and Dover.

His painting *The Entrance, Dover Harbor* depicted an area elaborately protected by ranges of anti-submarine netting. Something about the tranquility felt like an homage to the artist Turner. As John covered war, I chose charity work with other expat ladies. We planned an American Peace Ball which I dubbed "Illinois" at the Albert Hall, named for my home of Chicago. It was the only way to raise funds, to help the needy, as the horrors around us unfolded. The Belle Epoque of France, called the Gilded Age in America, was now over. It had all been the calm before the storm of war.

Doing my best to be a positive influence, I became an active member in the Italian Red Cross Matinee at the Savoy in December where I posed as a Madonna for a stage play, an event that inspired John to later paint me as "A Modern Madonna."

The war felt forever, and all socializing ended except for the occasional joining of friends in our parlor. It would be three years later when twenty-one German Gotha biplanes attempted the second aerial bombing raid on London all clearly visible from John's studio at our home at Cromwell Place.

As I hovered in the window, kneeling before a statuette of the Madonna, the battle raged in the skies, vivid orange, purple, and red, above and outside our floor-length windows.

"Don't' move," said John, circling me as my hands clung to the sofa's edge. "Let me sketch you. Right there! Just like that. The way you fret."

"Have you gone mad?! Paint me? Now? I'm frightened," I said, lowering myself, and ducking in and out. I was worried our destiny might be death as the battle raged beyond the safety of John's studio.

"Stay watching the sky and the explosive lights," said John, as he sketched wildly. "I'll make this a painting for all of England. A painting for everyone who shares your fears."

"At any moment a bomb can explode into our home!" I said, now turning toward him with tears. "At any moment life as we know it, could be over... again."

That painting, raw with emotion at the fear of possible demise, would go on to become one of John's most arresting pieces, titled "The Studio Window."

While I'd lived to see much trauma and loss in my life, I understood that random occurrences could end my life, too... or so I would learn when later that summer we were victims of a taxi crash on Park Lane. John suffered mild amnesia, while I was taken unconscious to the hospital.

Upon waking up later that night, I slipped into some sort of panic attack. The history of my life caught up with me, morphing into nightmares of John dying on the front lines while trying to capture a canvas image. It was something I just couldn't bear. Enough was enough...

Later, my wounds were dressed, and I was coherent, so we returned home in an ambulance, where I laid in bed fighting post-traumatic depression for much of the next few months. Alice was constantly within ear shot. My sudden separation anxiety kept John close to me, too, so he painted now, only in the studio. The three of us, the dog, and our beloved Aida.

One day John and Alice, now a teenager and full of attitude and opinions, stood bed side. "Mom-ee!" declared Alice. "Time to get up and grow up. Time to rise and to shine!"

"Yes," I agree, said John, sitting on the bed edge where Alice had just plopped down to the other side. "I couldn't say it better. Wakey-wakey! Rise and shine!"

"You've a world that needs you," said Alice. "What's past is past."

Squeezing my daughter's hand, I studied the beautiful young woman she'd become. I'd certainly done something right in this life. Tossing back the sheets, I agreed, "Fine, the world needs me... you win! I'm up."

"Fine, indeed," said John, "And the housemaid's left a black and gold gown for you in the dressing room. Put it on. I have a plan."

"It's a brilliant plan, Momsie."

"Is this your way of saying it's time to paint me again?" I asked, leaning in for a kiss.

"Yes. Is there any better sitter in the entire world?" said John, puckering up.

"I'm a pretty good one myself, Daddy-O," said Alice.

We were family. And we held hands.

"Oh, I love you so..." I said, taking her into my arms and bestowing a more sentimental and maternal love than my mother had ever bestowed upon me.

Turns out, not only was I John's best "sitter in the entire world" but the painting would become one of John's signature creations titled *Hazel in Black and Gold.* Of course, I had been apprehensive about being painted but we were approaching the end of John's wartime commissions, so I agreed, supportive, as ever, of my husband's interpretation.

Standing posed, my figure at a left angle, I glanced over my shoulder at the painter. In hindsight, the portrait underscored the personality that surrounded both the artist (John) and his sitter (me). I stood proud, shimmering from head to toe, for the sake of our country, for the sake of whatever John needed me to be at that time so he might capture the glory and the agony of battle. Yes, I was rested and fully committed to his needs.

The resulting composition was a graceful harmony of black and gold. The black of my gown represented darkness and war, the gold tones of my shawl representing hope. And the red shoes, my choice, just to add a touch of what life once was, despite black being the overall dominant shade. Crowning my head, I wore a wreath of golden leaves which London fashion-savvy women were eager to copy. Whoever thought a little girl from Chicago, with big dreams and a hunger for her father, would wind up being part of a married pair that would make us leaders – the very avant-garde – in contemporary taste.

"Darling?" called John as I spray-misted the palms, ferns, and potted citrus tree in the solarium.

"In here, Johnnie!" I called out.

"Ah yes," he said, "Seems we've received an invitation from the Duke of Westminster inviting us to his shooting lodge in the Landes, in the Nouvelle-Aquitaine."

"In southwest France?"

"Yes, exactly. Will be lovely; agreed?"

"I'll only agree to visit on my terms."

"And what are the terms, Hazel?" John's voice dipped.

"Well," I said, going to John and placing my hands on his shoulders. "The terms are that I refuse to cross the front threshold without all of us together. You, me, and Alice as a family!"

"Agreed!"

We arrived safely in Paris and what a Paris it had become! The streets were filthy, shutters buttoned up, the people hostile and miserable from war. The cafes on the grand boulevards filled with strangers, everyone looking so sad. John commented how different it appeared from that of London, where a grim, 'don't-care' look prevailed with business as usual.

Even John's favorite Latin Quarters lay quiet, as if a deadly plague had swept through the streets. What on good God's earth were we thinking? Fortunately, John's old friend Jacques Emile

Blance ushered us into his studio, but it too had a look and feel of desolation.

Pulling Alice to my side, Monsieur Blance said, "Bonjour, mes amis!" and we smiled as he and John exchanged handshakes. Then upon seeing Alice and I in summer dress, Monsieur Blance declared in a disapproving voice of broken English, "French ladies dress in black at this time."

John attempted a subject change. "I expect you have sent a great masterpiece to the Salon."

But Monsieur Blance seethed at us. His French accent accentuated. "Ahhh, you English, you do not know what we French must endure. It is hell! There is no Salon. No one paints!" He tossed his hands around, knocking over some of his works that crashed to the ground as if they didn't matter.

"I'm so sorry Monsieur," I said, "C'est dommage." It is too bad...

With that we were off from the dead of our beloved Paris to a small chateau in the middle of a lake, near to Bordeaux, where, for a healing time, we were able to forget the War. John flourished with his inimitable brush, while I focused on my daughter's needs which meant her reading, her studies, her pianoforte, and our shared needlepoint. We, too, took endless strolls talking mother and daughter confidences and future aspirations.

We traveled to St Jean de Luz, where John painted five different views of the harbor with small steamers. The vibrant blue Cote de l'Atlantique and its serenity was hugely different from life back in London, where word traveled fast that women were entering the work force.

Apparently, Aida, our maid, ran away to work in an ammunition factory and fell in love with her boss. But Alice was of teenage years now, not requiring a nanny, and quite frankly enjoyed spending her time, when not in school, completely with me. It was my mother and me again, only better, since I had no desire to control whatever my daughter desired.

Early 1918, we returned to London to the most incredible news...

With universal approval, my Johnnie was to be Knighted "Sir John" for his paintings as a war artist. Winston Churchill made it clear in his telegram to John that he was chosen for his power of concentration and his ability to cope at any means in capturing war motifs. John Lavery had mesmerized the nation, and I was as proud as a wife could be.

As John flattened out the official document, he turned to me with a very earnest face. "It is you that should be rewarded, Hazel, not me."

"How so?" I asked, moving to his side, and taking the letter in my hand.

"An artist is but nothing without his muse. You have cared for me, understood me, and taken care of our daughter and our home."

"Well, thank you, Sir John," I mused at his title. He placed his lips on my forehead. "But it is you who has captured the pain of war and captured the hearts of England."

"Hazel, you're far too kind. You've forfeited your own talents to nurture mine."

Later that night, quietly from my room, I reflected on what he said. It was true. I'd put my own artistry aside to be caretaker, wife, and mother. Was that so unusual of any woman in childbearing and childrearing years? If I was indeed his muse, the muse is not the prize but the method in which the prize is won. And the prize would be the Knighted Sir John Lavery...

Telegrams of congratulations poured in from friends like Lord Wimborne and Lord Donoughmore, now making John and I, more than ever, the focus of public attention. It meant I would have to find a way to carve my own path as not only John's companion and partner, but as a woman who might have influence on the British population.

This also meant, from that day forward, I was now formally referred to as 'Lady Lavery.'

My best friend, Clementine Churchill, Winston's wife, had fun with my new title. Or in other words, say my name too fast, after too much sherry, or without proper annunciation and it could be mistaken for 'Ladies Lavatory.'

Chapter Twenty-three
Michael

"Have you read about this Irishman, Michael Collins?" I asked my daughter, as we sat sharing newspapers over porridge and tea. She shook her head.

"He's certainly quite a public figure..." I delved into the second page. "Well-read in modern literature and drama, and keen to talk about it..."

Hazel continued to absorb the article. Michael was on the right side in the many battles in which Sinn Fein fought. He was a strong influencer in the Gaelic League, in the Gaelic Athletic Association, and finally in the Irish Volunteers...

"Listen to this sentence, Alice... Irish writer and historian named P. S. O'Hegarty writes of Michael in a London opinion page that there was 'very little of the young Mick Collins of those days to give promise of the man he was to come.'" I placed the paper temporarily onto my thigh. "Hmmm, I'm intrigued," I said, but Alice didn't respond. So, I raised the paper, straightened it to firm it upright, and learned some more...

Apparently, Michael was on the run, mostly by bicycle, fighting for freedom, organized as he was energized, with a grand and complex personality. On one hand he was learning to build bombs, on the other donating second-hand clothes to those volunteers in need. A different man to so many different people, he was always kind and persuasive to anyone who crossed his path.

Michael cared deeply for the elderly, while with children he was a prankster with funny faces and jokes, making them laugh and bringing them gifts. But always, most always, he was just a compassionate boy from Cork.

Holding onto that boyish charm and courage he won over all the Irish, who fed, sheltered, and ran messages for him. There was his friend the electrician who networked by moving from house to house 'on call' for lighting services. There were railway employees, hotel staff, sailors at docks, postal workers, ladies delivering wicker baskets full of dried herbs and apples, with rifles lining the bottom, and even the dairy farmers, where Michael could stop for a glass of buttermilk while delivering a code.

Initially he kept his contacts compartmentalized. And he always dressed the part of leader wearing a dark grey suit with a fedora felt hat and an overcoat...

I folded the newspaper and picked up my teacup sipping. "He's like a chameleon... a military leader, a business tycoon...all in one."

"Who cares, Momsie," said Alice. "Though clearly you're smitten."

"Well, he's certainly someone to be admired," I said, my tone as defensive as my truth.

Michael set up his offices at 32 Bachelor's Walk, and there he would work his magic over the next four years until the end of the Anglo-Irish war. On the wall he hung a poem from A. M. Sullivan's *God Save Ireland*:

'God save Ireland,' said the heroes,
'God save Ireland' said they all,
'Whether on the scaffold high
Or the battlefield we die,
O, what matter, when for Erin dear we fall!'

The spring of 1918 with the First World War still in progress, the tide turned towards British favor. But the English still felt they needed fresh troops to finish the job, so Parliament passed a law calling upon all Irishmen to join the British army. A crowd surrounded Michael at 'the green' in Dublin where he spoke from the steps persuading his people not to join.

As he spoke, he quoted his father. "The Irish people will be free when they own everything from the plough to the stars!" The crowd cheered as he spoke. "Britain wanted us for her own economic ends, as well as to satisfy her love of conquest. But Ireland is not an easy country to conquer, nor to use for the purposes for which conquests are made! We have a social system of our own!" The crowd roared and waved Irish flags with pleasure. "We had an economic organization. We have a code of laws that fit us!" Flexing his verbal muscles he ended his speech by saying, "So join me, all of ye! Give us the future! We've 'ad enough of the past! Give us back our country to live in – to grow in!" The crowds roared, applauded, and stomped their feet calling out, "Mick Collins! Mick Collins!"

And then right before them, Michael was placed in handcuffs and arrested for fear his speech would provoke the end of the Crown. Dragged off to Sligo Jail, he hollered back to his fans, "They're a bunch of eejits! We've only begun the fight!"

The crowds screamed out "we love you Mick Collins! We love you!" while some screamed in Gaelic, "*Go n-eiri an adh leat*" which literally means "That luck may rise with you!"

Over eighty members of Sinn Fein were arrested on charges of being complicit to Collin's in arranging to be involved with the Germans for another rising.

Arms were compiled in the countryside from Neill Kerr, an IRB friend, who resided in Liverpool England. Since he was employed on a steamship, he was able to ship ammunitions to Dublin on cross-channel boats.

When Michael was released from jail – not on a technicality and not by trial but by the key belonging to a friendly warden who set him free – Michael set out to draft a new constitution.

On one occasion, just past midnight, Michael secretly showed up at the police headquarters on Brunswick Street, Dublin. He had an 'in' with the door guard, who allowed him entry down a dark narrow hallway and up the back rickety staircase. Once inside, he would examine confidential documents.

Leading the way, by flashlight, the guard led Michael and his friend, Harry Boland, to the small room where Collins sat in the corner on the floor, copying notes by hand, and reading through file after file, report after report, until one caught his fancy.

"Get a load of this, Harry...about me," Michael chuckled. "Says 'he comes from a brainy Cork family.'"

"Says right!" Harry guffawed.

As the General election for an alternative Republican party became a massive victory for Sinn Fein, Michael was appointed Minister of Home Affairs. But he was unable to attend the newly established Assembly in Ireland called 'The Dail Eireann' because he was detained rescuing Eamon de Valera, his friend, from Lincoln jail.

While many of the prisoners were kept in 'muffs' which was a type of straight jacket used for the insane, fortunately, de Valera wasn't one of them. Instead, he sat in his cell without restraints which allowed him to bond with the guards and get messages to Michael.

The only way to get 'Dev' out was with some crafty maneuvering that involved the stealing of keys from the chaplain's keyring who served daily Mass to the prisoners. Collins would have to get a duplicate key into the keyhole of de Valera's cell. How did he do this? It was achieved by convincing a guard to create a wax impression of the Chaplain's key while he napped.

They melted the warmed wax from the candles in the sacristy. Returning the key to the ring, the Chaplain never knew about the wax, or the outline made of the key on paper and pencil. Between the two impressions, Collin's team was able to make a duplicate key baked inside an Irish crème cake, delivered to the inmates.

De Valera got the first slice, knowing it was under the higher side of the cake's frosting. Sucking the frosting off the metal – very tasty – de Valera slid the key up inside his sleeve. Later that night, as the inmates slept and guards slowly worked the halls, de Valera moved the key into the lock, jiggling and jiggling it.

But it didn't work...

Once again, on the next day, and as the Chaplain slept, the guard stole his key and ran the same drill for a second time. Only this time, a guard was paid to slip de Valera the duplicate key and allowed Michael and Harry into the inmate facility to assist.

"Dev!" whispered Michael. "Dev, it's me."

"Michael! Harry!" said de Valera, a bit too loudly. "Over here! Hurry!"

Michael inserted the key into the padlock, his brow gathered in a frown of concentration, his ear listening for the 'click.' Nothing. His hand trembled, tense, as he twisted with just a bit too much pressure. "Bollocks! It's broken! In half! In the lock! Bloody hell, Dev. I'm sorry." Michael blessed himself rapidly twice and gazed up to the heavens.

De Valera tried desperately to thrust his own key from the original copy into the lock from the other side, hoping to loosen the broken one, but to no avail.

"Try again," hissed Michael. "I think the good Lord is with us, yeah?"

"I can't. It's too late. Go before they catch you?" said de Valera, falling against the concrete wall in surrender.

"No Dev! Don't give up! Give it a lash. C'mon!"

De Valera stood forward, exhaled, and with one solid jab moved his own key through to the broken key which clanked to the floor. Voila! The gate opened.

"Quickly!" said Michael, tugging de Valera by the arm. Harry covered him in the disguise of a fur coat and feather hat. He pulled de Valera into his side, as though they were a 'couple' visiting someone in the jail. This was typical as nearby soldiers and girlfriends from a military hospital often visited the prisoners.

"Well, this is original," joked de Valera, examining the furs.

"Shhh!" said Harry, "Just go along. You make a good-looking Colleen."

Michael chimed in glancing back as they hastened their steps to the gate, "Follow your heart, acushla!"

"What does that mean?" asked Harry, bringing de Valera closer to his side.

"Darling," joked Michael, adding a sexy wink.

With ease the three made it through the gate and across the farmland, stumbling through the fields and often using their hands to feel the way, when out of nowhere they came upon a wayward soldier shuffling drunkenly through the streets. He creased his brow and casually offered, "Cheerio, Mates. Wanna share a pint?"

"Cheerio, yourself, Mate," said Michael. "Go home. Get some sleep, it's late." The soldier chuckled, not recognizing Michael, who kept his face tucked downward. The soldier stood unsure which way to go, while he watched Michael, Henry and Dev make their way to a waiting taxi on the other side of the road.

After a never-ending ride through the hills of pin-hair turns, they were taken to the station, where they boarded a train to London. A soft drizzle fought over the sun at dawn.

On board, and as the train roared down the tracks, Michael blessed himself three times before grabbing de Valera's hand in one and Harry's hand in the other, squeezing their fists together.

As his adrenaline subsided, Michael glanced over at Harry, his best friend. Unbeknownst to Harry, his girl, Kitty Kiernan, had fallen in love with Michael, who knew it was wrong to be with his best friend's fiancée. He knew it could harm their friendship, but he also knew all was fair in love and war. And right now, he had to focus on the war.

He thought about the squad they'd formed with a group of their men including Mick O'Reilly and Vincent Byrne, and how the group of them were referred to as "The Twelve Apostles." They were young – nineteen, twenty, twenty-one.

Alas, Michael took no pleasure in killing. Yet, if it hadn't been for Michael, the group of them were all certain they'd forever be under British rule.

All you had to do was meet Michael and you knew he was a breath of fresh air. Full of ideas. Certain they'd succeed. And his mind... always lucid, always roaming, always analyzing to figure out the next thing, the next move... until finally, the methodic rhythm of the train comforted Michael to relax. He was knackered. His eyelids, heavy. His head fell back against the window longing for sleep, bobbing in and out of slumber… until he dozed a good length.

Finally, the train pulled into the London station and Michael sat up straight, getting his wits about him, before placing an arm around Harry and drawing him in with a whisper,

"There is no crime in detecting and destroying in wartime the spy and the informer, yeah?"

"Aye."

"The British have destroyed without trial," said Michael. "I will pay them back in their own coin..."

Chapter Twenty-four

Lady Hazel Lavery

The drawing room was a flutter with politics and conversation. Finally, I piped in.

"Quite the contrary, I'm just a simple Irish girl at heart," I repeated, like some sort of ongoing mantra. "Simple" sounded silly as I sat there in an ornate sage-colored tea party dress with intricate embroidery and delicate tailoring in tiers of gossamer finery. Of course, we knew I was anything but a simple Irish girl, though I had a dreamy romantic view of what it might be like. None of them dared to shatter my fantasy.

Our neighbors, Winston Churchill and his wife Clementine, along with the group of politicians were dumbstruck by my Irish beliefs as we gathered in my home for afternoon tea at 5 Cromwell Place.

Nevertheless, when none of them challenged me, I carried on, speaking of the kindness of Ireland, how my Father had raised me to believe in my heritage and how we planned to someday explore Galway to meet the rest of the Martyn clan. Without him I'd have to do that on my own... "Although my beloved John did take me for my first visit to Killarney House, to see Lord and Lady Kenmare," I said, "They seemed smitten with my love to learn about all things Ireland." Leaning over, I patted John's hand. "When was that, my dear?"

"1913," said John, proud of his timeline skills.

"And we went again just a couple years back to Lord

Wimborne, the Lord Lieutenant, who was serving, of course, during the time of the Easter Rising. His home was stunning. Reminiscent of our American President's White House. I've profound sympathy for the Irish and their welfare." As my lips moved verbal stories of my ancestry, I knew my auburn hair glowed that feisty flare of being Irish. My eyes blinked a delicate green that day, more than hazel brown. Yes, Ireland beckoned my soul, and my Irish eyes were finally smiling. "So," I exhaled, "If indeed you want the Anglo-Irish war over, dearest Winston, then tell Lloyd George to give the Irish their independence."

"Are you out of your bloody mind?!" snapped Winston.

Leaning forward, I refreshed his Earl Grey tea from the silver pot that sat between us for pause. "No," I said, "I'm bloody serious." Then setting down the pot, I sat back cool as a cucumber as the men broke into an awkward chuckle. "Laugh if you like, but Winston, if you want something to turn out different then you have to do something different." They infuriated me but I had to hold my ground, glancing over at Clementine for female support. All she could do was shrug. My eyes egged her on.

"Maybe Hazel has a point?" Clementine added.

"You too?" said Winston. "My own Mrs.?"

"Winston, really?" I said, "Do you want to control something or someone that doesn't want to be controlled? Have you considered just sitting down and perhaps, well, speaking to them?"

"I'm not sure that's such a good idea," John piped in.

"Precisely," said Winston, placing down his Earl Grey cup to grab a ginger biscuit from the tray. "Those Irish boys have committed treason, the entire lot of them! Then they disappear into the night. Like cowards!"

"But..." I interjected.

"But nothing, Hazel," he scolded. "This is more complicated than feasting over a turkey dinner to sign some documents with the enemy. If they indeed are cut from us, it could mean the end of the British Empire!"

"Oh, dear," said Clementine.

Winston continued. "Not to mention the large Protestant population in the north – in Belfast – well, they refuse to join the Catholics of the south for their ridiculously sought independence. What am I to do? Just abandon Northern Ireland who have been true to the Crown?" Winston dabbed the napkin to his mouth and rearranged himself in the chair. "Hazel, I cannot, I will not, go down in history as that Secretary of State, who took on the Irish plight."

"You're right dear," said Clementine, dabbing the linen napkin to her lips. "That Michael Collins is behind all of this political division."

"Oh, pish posh," I snapped. "It's how the press has portrayed him, is all."

"I have to agree with my wife," said John. "Go on and tell them, Hazel. Tell them how you met the Michael Collins years back..."

Winston stopped nibbling his biscuit. All other teacups came to a standstill. "You've met him?" he asked.

"Yes, at the post office, nearby in Kensington. It was quite a while back. He was young but quite charismatic. Very polite." I swallowed hard. "And if I do dare say, an extremely handsome fellow."

"So, I've heard," said Clementine, giving me a quick wink. "They say he's like a movie star. Constantly surrounded by women. They'll go to great lengths to do anything for him."

"Well, that's rather suggestive," said Winston, surprised by his wife's sexual innuendo...

The next afternoon John was painting a Lady Somebody-or-another who wanted her portrait to hang beside a Gainsborough in her husband's ancestral hall. On the final day of the finished portrait, the Lady arrived with her husband who examined the portrait closely. His eyes roamed the canvas beginning at the head, then with his hand he traveled downward across the painting.

The husband finally spoke, "I pass the forehead and the eyes."

"Very good," said John, nodding.

"I pass the nose, the mouth, and the chin."

"Excellent!" said John.

But then the man roamed his hands lower over the painting around his wife's throat until he came upon her chest. "What is this flat-chested modernity that I see?"

"Pardon?" asked John.

"Where is the snowy amplitude of Her Ladyship?"

The man's wife interjected. "I will not have an eighth of an inch added! I refuse!"

On cue I walked into the studio to interrupt, moving toward the painting but not before making eye contact with the husband. "So sorry, I think it's quite lovely. Just as is," I said to the man. "It captures her stunning beauty, her adoration of the man she's gifted the painting to... you." I let loose a big toothy smile and he smiled back.

"Well, if Lady Lavery thinks it's fine..."

"I do... think it's fine," I said. "More than fine." And I moved toward the wife. "Look at how beautiful she is and look how beautifully John has captured her… ah, sexuality ever so discreetly."

"Yes," said the man, inspecting the painting again. "By George, I think she's right!"

And at that, everyone shook hands, and the deal was done. Off went the painting and the couple.

Left alone with John, I cornered him. "Sit, love, here." And I pointed to the two chairs.

"Yes, my love," said John, his tone suggesting he knew something was coming.

"It was lovely of you to paint Sir James Barrie last week. And it was so darling of him to gift me an autographed copy of his most treasured Peter Pan..."

"Yes, Hazel," said John, wondering where this was all going.

"And I love when Sir Barrie dines with us. He's always such a fan of my duck sauce."

"Undoubtedly your biggest fan. Most certainly in the top ten of male admirers."

"Right," I said. "And I adore him." I paused for effect, moving forward, and taking John's hand in mine, the sun streaming through on various canvases and catching my expression just so. "And he so loved when you did that portrait of him as a favor to me... the one where you made him pose as if working on that wooden bench, with the bench in semi darkness to camouflage his height. Would you say he's about five feet?"

"Five foot, yes, dear," assured John.

"And when I suggested we might donate the painting to the National Gallery of Scotland, well, he was thrilled and..."

"Hazel. What is the point?"

"The point is Mr. Barrie would love to meet Mr. Collins." "Mr. Collins?!" questioned John with sarcasm in his tone. "Is that what we're calling that Renegade these days, Mr. Collins?"

"Well, it is his name," I said, with sarcasm. John said nothing, only huffing under his breath. "Oh, Johnnie," I begged, "please paint Michael Collins and the others from Ireland." John eyed me up and down, the look on my pleading face not budging. "Just for historical reasons."

"It would be fine, my love, except I have so many commissions lined up. And now I'm training Winston to paint, good God. Now they're calling him my pupil."

"Which, of course, is highly flattering," I interrupted. "But you know it was me who taught him to paint. It's how he got the bug to be an artist."

"Yes, you certainly did," said John. "And how you ever convinced him to paint a still life of an empty bottle of spirits and a crystal bowl of fruit..."

"Well, he was a lovely student," I said.

"Oh, Poppet," sighed John, using his pet name for me, then pulling back his hand from mine he rested it in his lap with a deep sigh. "Darling, I just don't know that I have the time..."

"Yes, but time does not count where a masterpiece is at stake," I said, scanning his many portraits. "So, you will, won't you Johnnie? Won't you..."

Chapter Twenty-five
Michael

When Michael and his men returned to Dublin, de Valera took part in the ongoing 'Dail', establishing his own parliament, government departments, and a court system. De Valera, now elected President, nominated the following men as his ministers:

Arthur Griffith for home affairs, Cathal Brugha for Defense, Count Plunkett for foreign affairs, W. T. Cosgrave for local government, and last but certainly not least, Michael Collins in charge of finance. "You'll be responsible for seeking out a national loan, Mick."

"From whom?" asked Michael, mystified.

"Grass root supporters," said de Valera. "Congratulations! Your country loves you." As he shook his hand, Michael noted a strange sarcasm in de Valera's tone.

It wasn't known then, but much later, and when the loan closed, Michael reported that the donations in Ireland surpassed the anticipated one-hundred and twenty-nine thousand pounds to three-hundred and seventy-nine thousand pounds. It also wasn't known then either, but de Valera was feeling threatened by Michael's popularity.

By now the Irish Republican Army's guerilla tactics were at full escalation. To help the British police, the English sent in additional backup with a recruitment group that the Irish had nicknamed the "Black and Tans" because their uniforms were the colors of the uniforms they initially wore, a mixture of worn black and khaki. The wretched *Black and Tans* gained a notorious reputation for vicious attacks on civilian Irish by delivering bullets and grenades in their faces. Properties were raided, their homes burned, and their farm animals stolen or slaughtered. At a minimum, there was much looting as their rifles aimed to shoot the fear-stricken crowds.

The *Black and Tans* were mainly unemployed British soldiers who had fought in the first World War, now sent to Ireland to suppress the IRA which by now had established law courts, Trade and Commerce, Agriculture, a Department of Defense and so on. A real threat.

By now, all of England was reading about Michael daily, soon learning that Michael was now not only the founder of a spy network who had infiltrated the British administration, but had been named Director of Intelligence, and had founded two underground newspapers. And then too, he was President of the Irish Republican Brotherhood and Minister of Finance. Yes, Michael was many things to the Irish...

But the one title that fascinated folks the most was that of 'escape artist' as he continued to avoid capture by the enemy. Sinn Fein housed their headquarters at 6 Harcourt Street, temporarily of course, as they had to keep moving about due to the police raids. In one instance a large group of police with fixed bayonets surrounded the building and stormed the offices, in search of Michael Collins, who was seated at his desk doing paperwork. The out of breath officer scurried round the corner meeting Michael straight on: "Do you know where we'd find Michael Collins?"

"That traitor to the Crown?" asked Michael, staring back.

"Yeah, that one!"

Michael stood up and pointed out a window. "Saw a man go through there. Earlier."

Just then another Officer rounded the corner. "Sorry to intrude, Captain," he said, apologizing with a nod to Michael Collins. "But they think Collins has already escaped."

"Move it!" shouted the captain, before turning back to Michael. "Sorry to disrupt. Thank you, Lad."

"Not a problem at all," said Michael. "Hope you find that Collins."

Once the Captain departed, Michael slipped carefully through the top floor window, out onto the slanted roof navigating chimney stacks, and leaped from one roof top to the next, straddling sideways. He was about to consider the slide of a drainpipe when he came upon the Standard Hotel and its skylight. But as he was ready to jump, his equilibrium was off when he saw a khaki helmet appear below, so he waited for him to move on, then said a prayer and flung his bag before him. Realizing a leap through a stairwell would lead to death, he hung from the skylight rods, swinging his body over the banister, and clearing the opening by only a mere two inches.

A car rounded the corner and waited for him across the street of the back hotel kitchen alley.

The irony was that Michael was always in a suit and tie, so he wasn't suspicious. Sometimes he added a woolen overcoat with a pocket watch, which made him an upscale looking 'thug.' Not a person or policeman would suspect of being the real Michael Collins.

Eamon de Velera paced his kitchen. Michael leaned over a wooden chair and listened as he spoke. "By birth right I'm an American citizen," claimed de Valera, "so I'm proposing a trip to America to enlist additional support. And I'll publicize the Dail Loan, among the Irish communities."

"Agreed," said Michael, who was on the same team though they often shared differences. "I've got people in Boston," said Michael. "I can get ye across the pond. They'll be there to greet ye..."

"I'm naming you acting President in my absence," said de Valera.

"It would be an honor, Sir..."

Turns out, Michael not only helped secure de Valera's safe journey, but faithfully visited Mrs. de Valera and her children every Sunday after Mass while her husband was gone. "Please be sure to get this to Dev, will ye, Mick," she asked, handing Michael love letters to deliver to her husband during his absence.

As weeks turned into months, it was Michael who personally financed Mrs. de Valera's trip to visit her husband.

That morning in the London newspapers as John and I prepared our trip to Ireland, I read to John what Simone Tery, the French war journalist – and one of the few to have met Michael – said of him. "At first sight the Minister of Finance looks like a 'bon vivant.' Thirty years old, thick dark hair, open forehead, full face. When he is serious one notices his keen eyes are piercing; he has a square jaw, tight lips, and energetic chin. And, when he laughs... the sight of such good humor should be enough to invigorate the whole of Ireland!"

"On the other hand, listen to what Oliver St. John Gogarty, the Irish poet, politician, and well-known conversationalist says." I cleared my throat to read to John. He says, "'I lit up at the mere mention of Michael Collins. The unlined face of Collins... the beautiful almost womanly hands, and the ivory skin; he's a genius as much as he is an enigma.'" I rearranged the paper. "And listen to this, 'As a matter of fact, it is often the women of County Cork and Dublin who support Michael's efforts as intelligence agents. They have their own network who act as couriers, secretaries, offered nursing services, or just cook a good hearty meal and provide clean clothes.'"

"Yes, Hazel," said John, his tone tolerant at my fascination, "clearly at only thirty-years-old, Michael Collins is now the most notorious and the most beloved man in all of Ireland!"

"Oh, Sir John, don't get tail-ruffled..."

"I'm not ruffled, at all, Hazel!" his voice rose. "We're off to Dublin, aren't we? If it keeps you stifled, I will indeed paint his portrait."

"Brilliant!"

"And stop patronizing me. Referring to me as Sir!"

"Yes, Sir," I said, flirtatiously and winking with delight.

One day, the office at 6 Harcourt Street buzzed with business, when one of Michael's assistants popped her head into the door. "Hey Mick, sorry to bother yer, but ye got a massive pile of fan mail." The assistant dropped the box of envelopes and packages on his desk with a deliberate and humorous thump.

"Aren't you a cheeky bugger," said Michael, fingering through the envelopes and separating them. Donations too, dropped out of the letters onto his desk. A pence here, a pence there. There was a lot to sort – brown envelopes, parchment envelopes, large and small, and one rather very large one with green official markings. Michael flipped it over, back to front. More of a diploma than a piece of correspondence, he ran his finger along the seam to open it. Then unfolded the letter.

Inside, an official request from the British government.

Michael knit his brow. "Am I reading this right?" He handed it to the assistant who read it for him.

"Says a Sir John Lavery is coming to Ireland and has asked permission to paint yer."

"Wants to paint me? Me?" Looking to his assistant for a response, she struggled to contain a giggle. "Fucksake!" said Michael, bursting into laughter. And now the laughter was contagious. Michael slapped his desk in humor. "Jaysus, Mary and

Joseph, what the heavens for?"

"Wants to hang your portrait on his wall," teased the assistant. "Thinks you've got a handsome mug."

"Ahhh, don't go taking the piss out of me."

"Swear on the good Lord. Says it right here, look..." She handed him the second page. "Handsome mug."

He scanned it, laughing. "Does not say that. Besides, I'm only handsome by a blind woman's standards." He dropped the letter on his desk and looked up to the assistant.

"Why do you suppose then?" she asked.

"This is some bloody plot, I tell ya. A plot to get me to sit in a room and then kill me!"

"Naw, don't think so, Mick," she said. "They say he's a very famous portrait artist. Never 'eard of him me self but doesn't mean he ain't famous."

"Surely I read about this Sir John Lavery," said Michael, his eyes focused on the corner of the room, deep in thought, "And his wife, what's her name?"

"Lady Lavery." said the Assistant, picking up the page and reading from the request. "She believes in us. Says she's sympathetic to the cause."

"She's a Yank, yeah?"

"Think so."

"Then she can't be trusted. And I certainly don't trust 'em. He's from Belfast," said Michael pondering and biting his lip before adding, "Tell her and her fancy-pants husband to bugger off. There'll be no portraits of Michael Collins, not today and not ever."

Chapter Twenty-six

Hazel in Dublin

The housekeeper and the butler bustled about assisting me with a wide assortment of luggage; hat boxes for me, attaché cases for John, and his painting supplies, packing them tightly into the car boot. Alice and the dog followed outside to the car.

"You look lovely, Momsie."

"It's very Irish," I said, of my green cloak and matching green felt hat. Then, kissing her on the lips and petting the dog, I promised we'd be home in no time.

The butler opened the car door for me. "Me Lady..."

"Thank you, Mr. Wallace."

Mr. Wallace nodded and secured the handle before he sprinted to the other side doing the same for John. "All set, Clifford," said John to the driver, "Ready when you are!"

"Yes, my Lord," said Clifford turning the ignition over, and off we went.

"What took you so long, Hazel?" asked John, turning to me. "We were to leave hours ago?"

"I had religion classes. Father Leonard in Twickenham was in the study this morning. Didn't you see him?"

"So then, you're really converting?"

"Yes, while you were painting, I've already become a Catholic."

“Beg pardon and congratulations! I hadn’t realized you went through with it.” John looked stunned. “I suppose it’s quite efficient that Father makes house calls,” he added, gazing out the front window at the city.

I knew what he was thinking...what he’d told me a million times before… that Cromwell Place was the place where many people congregated not to see John, but to see me. Fluffing at my dress hem, I played into it... that and the fact that Ireland lay ahead on our new life’s journey.

“Didn’t I tell you what Alice said?” I asked. He shook his head. “Alice said, ‘why do you want to be a Catholic? You’re already a very bad Protestant.”

John chuckled. “Now, that’s funny, dear.”

“Right,” I said, changing the subject again as we circled the park. “Isn’t it marvelous that I’ve pulled some strings, so you’ll be able to paint not only the political but some religious figures for the Irish collection, too?”

“Yes, Hazel, I’m deeply thrilled,” he said with sarcasm.

“Come now, Johnnie. It’s the Archbishop! This will be brilliant for your knighthood.”

“Yes, yes, yes” said John, getting comfortable in the back seat, stretching his legs. “And what’s next, Hazel? A four-course meal with the rebels? Champagne with a side of sorbet?” I said nothing, only giving him a look that suggested I might do exactly that. As if he could hear me thinking, he glanced up at me, “Don’t you even dare...”

Clifford’s eyes scanned us in his rearview mirror as I sat back quietly in my seat. Perhaps Clementine was correct when she said, “Marriage isn’t love. It’s compromise.” John was thirty years older than me and had become an old curmudgeon. And me, what was I? A woman in constant search of identity. In Chicago it had been society, in England it was politics, in Ireland... Well, what was Ireland? I guess it was the search for religion and home...

“What are you thinking, Hazel? I see the mind churning trouble,” John asked, breaking me from my thoughts with the tap of his hand.

"Oh, John, why always so droll? Why not take a chance..."

"Darling, I can't imagine Michael Collins allowing me to paint him. He's in hiding. If I paint him, then they'll all know what he looks like. For capture!"

"Well," I said dismayed, "I hadn't thought of that. But just think of all the good we can do while we're there. Get to the bottom of this terrible war and report back on it..."

"And just whom are we reporting to?" John rolled his eyes. "What are we now, secret agents? Have you lost your marbles?"

"Well, the Prime Minister will want to hear my observations."

"I see..." said John, placing his head back on the backseat headrest and closing his eyes. Clearly, he thought I was deranged.... clearly, he underestimated the power within me.

"Come along, Johnnie," I said, as we arrived at the train station. "Let's get our bags organized. The porters will be taking them to the taxi."

We arrived in Dublin where I was dismayed that it didn't look as I remembered. Since metal armor covered the side windows of the car for fear of a stray bullet, the front windshield gave only a clear view for the driver and for us. Sadness and an odd white film covered town shops and the trees like the first snow of winter. 'Tans' and armored trucks were everywhere, and the only bit of noise were people running for safety during the town curfew. "Oh God, this is worse than I imagined, Johnnie," I said, clinging to his arm for support as we walked up the steps to the hotel lobby. Police and guards surrounded the building, nodding to us.

John tipped his hat and leaned into me, "The newly formed Auxiliary are well-armed."

"It's frightening," I said as we went through the double doors.

"Their mobile units are everywhere," whispered John. "Set to wipe out IRA groups from the city to the sea to the countryside."

"What do we do?" I asked as we reached the lobby desk, and the porter put the bags at our feet. John tipped them generously, and after signing the room paperwork, turned to me.

"What do we do, dear?" he repeated the question. "Why, we draw a warm bath, open a fine bottle of bubbly, have an early supper and tomorrow I paint; that's what we do..."

The next day we lunched with the Unionist Lord Mayor of Belfast who found my fascination with the Irish charming and intriguing, though I bit my tongue in mentioning Michael Collins. Later we traveled into Armagh, which had two church headquarters both occupying the hills and facing each other as if to hug the community. Armagh was overwhelmingly Catholic and Nationalist in many villages, so many bitterly resented the decision to keep South Armagh in Protestant-dominated Northern Ireland. As John explained to me, this led to massive support of the IRA. It was there in the city in Northern Ireland where John would complete a portrait of Cardinal Logue. It was there that John received a threatening letter which he never read, but I did, before discarding its threat that John was a "parasite" and "should be exterminated."

"What is it?" asked John, turning toward me and away from his subject.

"It's nothing dearest," I said, smiling at the Cardinal. "Carry on..."

And he did, trying to capture the little old man with round sloping shoulders, and a face that shot out of his torso as if he hadn't a neck. He had the most ridiculous long upper lip and beetle brows that screamed for a good barber's trim. But worst of all he was a Cardinal and it made John nervous to paint someone so close to the Lord. Later that night, John teased that he still couldn't really see the color of the Cardinal's eyes. I suggested he tell him that.

When the Cardinal returned, John said, "Your Eminence, I have not yet seen the color of your eyes." As the Cardinal focused on me, widening his pupils as if in shock, I could see them. "Alas!

They're Irish gray, your Eminence."

"No, they are black, or perhaps grey with the years," he said. Then rearranging himself in the chair he told us a very self-deprecating tale. "When I was a young priest, a young lady came to me in confession and after the act of contrition continued, 'Father, I have a mortal sin to confess, but I cannot tell it because it is about a Priest.' Immediately I worried what the Priest might have done to the young woman, so I told her that when she confessed, she was also confessing to God. She looked at me and explained, 'Yes, Father, but when I go to Mass on Sunday and look up at the altar and see you there, I can't help thinking, surely that is the ugliest man God has ever made!'"

At that John burst out laughing,

I realized the Cardinal told the story to humanize himself to his painter... thus allowing John to feel more at ease with such a high clergyman.

John completed the portrait days later. "Now then," said John, turning the portrait around for the Cardinal to bear witness.

He stared at it for a long time before declaring, "The last artist who painted me made me look like a monkey in a bush."

John looked at his painting, then at the Cardinal and back to the painting. In a strange way, or so we joked about it later in private, John had done the same.

Nevertheless, the Cardinal paid a hefty tip in addition to the agreed commissioned rate, an amount that John never once discussed with me as he felt it was his duty to financially care for our family.

Thanking the Cardinal, I bowed to kiss his ring, a band of gold with a Sapphire gemstone and a coat of arms of the Pope. I wanted him to feel like we were nobody when in his presence, so I suggested, "Your Eminence, clearly you will forget all about us when we are gone," and he declared, "Well, I'll remember the color of your eyes. Hazel. As your name."

Next on the list was a trip to Mount Stewart and the painting of the archbishop dressed in head to toe black, and rather boring. But he possessed a short grey beard with a clipped and dramatic point. Later that evening, I ever so gently reminded me of our duty to Winston, desirous to know the state of affairs. With some minor input from John, I wrote, though John took credit for the letter...

My Dear Minister of War,

You asked me the other day what I thought of my country's state, and I had not the courage to tell you. But if one artist may speak to another, I will give my beliefs. The Prime Minister has said that he is prepared for a million casualties and a five years' war. I believe that ten- or fifty-years' war would not bring about the result he desires.

I believe that Ireland will never be governed by Westminster, the Vatican or Ulster without bloodshed. I also believe that the removal of the "Castle' and all its works, leaving Irishman to settle their own affairs, is the only solution left.

I am convinced with the knowledge I possess of my countrymen that such a situation would make her one of your staunchest allies instead of an avowed enemy for all time.

In the words of my beloved wife, Hazel, "Love is stronger than hate."

Yours

It was back in Dublin that I received an invitation to meet David Lloyd George at dinner at Sir Phillip Sasson's home. Lloyd George was appointed Secretary of State for War but was frustrated by his limited power clashes over strategy with the military establishment. Somehow Lloyd George felt I might soften his daily frustrations, allowing him distraction as our 'circles' had it he'd become intrigued by my love of Ireland.

"Go on, Hazel," insisted John, "This is your chance to finally do something for the Irish."

I thought on it, having converted to Catholicism despite my family's strong Episcopalian background. My daughter, Alice, had already received Catechism classes years prior at Assumption convent in Kensington Square. Clearly it was time, if I were to truly be Irish, I too, must behave as an Irish Catholic woman, and so I did.

The next day as we drove to Connemara, a remote town where I believed I'd find my ancestors, John persisted, "Hazel, you must meet Lloyd George. What are you waiting for? Reply already, woman!"

"Perhaps. Yes. But for today...well, today is about my family," I said, sadly, and reminiscent of Father, Mother, and Dorothy. As we pulled up onto the gravel driveway to the abandoned farm once part of the Martyn family, I lit up, declaring, "Johnnie. Let's buy it! We'll make it the Martyn and Lavery estate!"

"That's a wonderful idea, Hazel. But let's sleep on it first."

Returning to Dublin I did dine with Lloyd George on a sumptuous dinner of duck, fennel, and orange, but to no avail could I persuade him. As the wine was poured, Lloyd George said with mischievous delight, "This Michael Collins is an incredible escapologist."

"Among other things," I said. "Clearly a man with the skills, wit and intelligence of many men." Lloyd George toasted my goblet, his eyes fluttering and his mind ticking. He was charming and flirty as any man I'd ever met, and so crafty, that we never brought up the situation. Though I did add, "I'm certain, so certain, that you feel sympathetic treatment of the Irish."

But the next morning, I read in The Times that "Lloyd George had the trouble well in hand and that some thousand Black and Tans had landed and were terrifying the rebels into submission and getting their own back." Then a sentence, "We have murder by the throat."

"I am furious! I am livid!" I declared to John. "Lloyd George lied! He intended to do nothing to help the Irish." Crinkling the paper into a ball and tossing it to the table, I looked to John, "It's time. Enough Sirs, and Knights, and Queens, and Kings. You are to paint Michael Collins. It will be our excuse to get to him and get him to come to England for a truce."

"And do you know what Winston said when I told him you're forever persisting?"

"Oh, who bloody cares," I said, glancing away and then raising my chin upward, egging him on. "Well, all right, tell me, what did he say?"

"He said, 'Be careful, my dear John, our men are not all good shots.'"

"And what does that mean?" I asked with a snippy tone.

"It means, if he's in the same room with me and a soldier should walk in, he may not have a good shot. And shoot me!"

"Oh," I said. "Is that all?"

Chapter Twenty-seven
Michael

The most gut-wrenching emotion for Michael was the awareness of the number of hostages and prisoners being executed. He knew it had been on his watch, and he had been the man behind bringing about this war.

Years from now a rebel ballad would be sung called "Kevin Barry" in remembrance of a young medical student who was out collecting bread at a bakery just before he was to take his medical exam at University Dublin. But a raid was taking place that day, and in the confusion, young Kevin was captured and sentenced to hang. Because he was only eighteen years of age, the circumstances drew a lot of attention. Michael saw to it that the spotlight shone on Lloyd George who refused to exonerate young Barry. A crowd of 5,000 gathered around young Kevin Barry's jail cell, singing hymns, and saying the rosary, as Barry was murdered.

The Irish had reached their endurance. Or as Eoin MacNeill composed in an epigram...

> In prison we are jailers,
> Or trial their judges,
> Persecuted their punishers
> Dead their conqueror.

On another occasion, several of Michael's men were being held prisoner in Dublin Castle and about to be transferred to Beggar's Bush. The men were shot while trying to escape, but not before they were tortured, their bodies loaded on a lorry, and their faces ignited with a torch. Michael was devastated at the news.

As doctors opened the coffins to examine the bodies a crowd gathered outside the morgue. "Excuse me, pardon," said Michael making his way through the crowd disguised in a tall hat and long coat, whisking past the detectives and spies. At the back of the mortuary, he knocked on the door. A clergyman was hesitant to unlock it, instead calling out to the priest, "Father! Father, someone is trying to break in!"

Father came running, his feet moving swiftly under his robes to bar the door.

But then he recognized the face. It was Michael, mouthing the words, "Father, let me in." His hands formed a prayer pose; genuflected a nod.

"Right away, Mick," whispered the priest, opening the lock from the inside. Then looking left and right over Michael's shoulder. "Hurry!"

"Thank you, Father," said Michael, grasping the priest by his elbows, and looking at him face on. "Where are the men? I want to see their bodies."

"Their faces are burned off, Lad. It's Satan's doing, I tell ya."

"We must see them dressed in Volunteer uniforms for a proper burial."

"As you wish, Michael. This way." The two scurried down the hallway and into the morgue where the bodies now lay cold and quiet.

"Help me, Father," said Michael, pulling clothes out of the duffle bag to dress the corpses. When they lifted the coffin covers, Michael flinched at the sight.

"We can't have an open casket, Lad," said the Priest. "It wouldn't be right."

"Then it will be our secret that they were at least dressed properly to meet the good Lord, yeah?"

Father agreed, and together the two men ran a knife down the back of the uniforms to loosen them, thus allowing the flexibility to dress the stiff corpses.

On the day of the funeral Mass, Michael refused to fear the bombardment of the Auxiliary, instead, and against all odds, attended his friends' funerals. He had a hat that dipped low over his face and a scarf wrapped round his neck so that he blended in with the other gentlemen in attendance. Later, he carried the coffins to the hearse for their final resting place...

But there was no rest for the weary. That year ended with the city of Cork ambushed, buildings set aflame, shops looted and much of St Patrick Street completely gutted. Townsfolk were numb to the combat that lined their roads even in broad daylight. But worst of all, priests as well as civilians were repeatedly shot in the head without cause.

As the *Black and Tans* grew more frustrated, they knew if they couldn't get to Collins they'd get to his family estate, and so they did, heading out to Woodfield, where John, Michael's oldest brother, resided with his eight children. His wife had died from consumption.

Without a second thought, the Essex Regiment burned the house and all its contents.

The children, with little more than the clothes on their back and one brooch belonging to their mother, wailed, sobbed, and huddled in a corner of a nearby shed until their Uncle Mick arrived, though not in time to see John arrested and taken to Spike Island prison.

For Michael, this was his most testing hour. Despite turmoil, warfare, near death and so much responsibility, he always relied on home as a place of safety. Now the one place that reminded him of his beloved mother and father, was burnt to the ground, demolished in flames.

Michael would forever be responsible for his several nieces and nephews left homeless.

On the other side of war, the final blow to the British was the burning of Custom House which collected all their records for local government, Inland Revenue, and pertinent legal information. Once the IRA checked the corridors, as well as the stairwells, one hundred and twenty Irishmen joined forces to destroy the building, sprinkling petroleum on the structure's exterior.

The people of Dublin took refuge in their homes, sheltering inside doorway vestibules and huddled along hallways as the enemy's spotlight shone upon them from military tanks that carved through the streets. The occasional sound of a lone harmonica filtered through the air. Ironically, as doom continued to fall upon the Irish, David Lloyd George, now the Prime Minister, felt he was making progress. There would be peace talks after all.

That's when The Archbishop of Perth, born in Clare County Ireland, arrived in Dublin as mediator to meet with Sinn Fein.

Michael sent his pal, O'Reilly, on bicycle, through the hilly terrain of Killiney with a letter to Clune that he would meet the archbishop at a newly disclosed place. Afterall, there was more danger in exposing Michael publicly and risk capture, than any promise the Brits might make in negotiations.

Michael kissed the archbishop's ring and genuflected, before looking up to his face. "Forgive me Father, but I can't be a part of peace talks."

"You can, my son. And you will. God has a higher purpose for you."

"I'm a soldier, not a talker."

"It is your destiny," said Father, taking Michael's hand and directing him to sit in the easy chair.

"Father, please understand. I can't have my military situation turn into a political one."

"What makes you think that God isn't interested in politics, eh?"

"Father, they've murdered my people! My friends!"

"Befriending enemies makes you stronger, kinder and wiser," said the archbishop, patting Michael's shoulder. "So be smart, Lad. Do it for the good Lord, eh?"

As Archbishop and Lloyd George persisted, the secret meeting was held at Dr. Farnan's home despite the danger that negotiations might also cause the archbishop as well.

An agreement was made that the Irish would temporarily halt all violence in a truce so long as the Dail Eireann would be free to meet without interference from the authorities. The archbishop traveled to London with the news which Lloyd George told him that only if the Irish surrendered their arms would the British negotiate.

Michael reminded the archbishop that they wouldn't budge. "Tell Lloyd George it's a mistake if he thinks he can kill us and still be friends..."

This went back and forth and back and forth via the archbishop until, on December 23rd, 1920, the Government of Ireland Act was passed. It declared that Ireland would now have two governments – one in Dublin and one in Belfast, for the people still believing in the Crown.

To celebrate what seemed like some hopeful news of a truce, and because it was the week of Christmas, Michael gathered friends at the Gresham Hotel. The Gresham was one of the fanciest hotels in all of Dublin, just on O'Connell Street, despite being damaged during the raids, and was going through refurbishment. Nevertheless, Waterford chandeliers still hung proudly in the central dining room.

But as the group arrived, carrying Christmas gifts and bottles of cheer, Michael found the private dining rooms already booked, which would seat him in the center of the public dining room. The men shared awkward glances, awaiting Michael's decision to sit. Which they did. There was silence for a bit, the group of his men nervous at the eyes of the dining room guests fixated on them.

The waiter brought appetizers of cured salmon, soda bread, and at Michael's insistence, a bottle of "yer finest red." Together the men toasted, "To Christmas! To a New Year. God Bless! Erin go Bragh!!" Michael nodded his head, clanking the goblets of each of his men – Rory, Gearoid, Tobin, and Cullen and...

Suddenly the Auxiliaries raided the hotel lobby and burst through the dining room past the piano player, securing the windows and the kitchen entry. The conversation and the clanking of forks and knives suspended, succumbing to the sound of soldier's boots.

"Stay calm," whispered Michael to his men who looked to him for direction.

The Captain of the Auxiliaries roamed from table to table, searching the faces of each patron, hands on his belt in case he needed his gun.

One of the soldiers approached Michael, patted down his jacket's front pockets and found a flask of whiskey in his lower hip pocket. "It's a Christmas gift," said Michael, gazing up at the soldier. "For me landlady."

The soldiers shared a look as the captain came forward, taking Michael by the arm and pulling him to his feet, "What's your name?"

"John Grace CPA," said Michael.

"Accountant?"

"Yes, that's right," said Michael. "Just over on Dame Street."

"So, you're not Michael Collins?" asked the officer.

"Michael Collins? The IRA fugitive?" With a pathetic shake of the head, he continued, "Officers. You're not a bunch of eejits. Do you honestly think I'd be in the middle of a public dining room sharing turkey and Christmas pudding if I was indeed Michael Collins?"

"Pat him down," said the captain, sternly.

Patting him down with more force, the officer found a note in his pocket that read "Rifles."

"Rifles?!" asked the captain.

"It's refills, not rifles," said Michael, "For my notebooks. See..." and Michael pulled out his notepad which fortunately hadn't any recent war strategies. Instead, it contained a scribble of a Christmas tree and the list of gifts he'd be dropping off to those who fed and cared for him during the past year.

"You're being quite contrary," said the officer, grabbing Michael by the hair at the back of his head, then pulling his face up to the light to compare to an old grainy photograph the officers were using to find Collins. Michael was certain he was doomed, as his eyes shifted to his friend, Tobin, who sat there with a look of 'grab his revolver.' But just as the men were ready to leap into action, the officer let him go.

"Wrong guy," said the captain. "Too old to be Collins."

Michael rearranged his jacket sleeve, then fingered his bangs back into place.

"Care to join us, Officers?" asked Tobin.

"A little Christmas cheer," said Michael, who was fortunately a bit inebriated, having had a glass of wine and some earlier whiskey which allowed him to remain relaxed.

"No, we've work to do," said the chief. "Sorry for our confusion."

"Not a bother," said Michael, toasting the officers.

With the sideways nod of his head, the Chief signaled to the men to leave. "Merry Christmas to all," they said, tipping hats to the guests.

"And to all a good night," toasted Michael's friends at the table. As they gulped down the wine, Michael peered over his goblet until the last of the Auxiliary were gone... then he let out a huge exhale.

For Christmas Eve, with no place to go, no family home to go to, and with his brother John's children with relatives in various Cork homes, of which he visited everyone, he found himself knocking on the door of Eamon de Valera's house in County Wicklow.

It had been a long time since the two men had laid eyes on each other... de Valera overseas in America on a financial mission, and Michael, having changed and grown, not to mention the fact he'd now eclipsed de Valera in fame and power.

"Mick!" said de Valera, looking lean, weak, and worn out, but surprised at his guest.

"Merry Christmas, Dev. Tell me, how was it? America?" said Michael, coming in for a hug and handing him a gift-wrapped box of cigarettes.

"What does it matter," he said with an uneasiness, his voice tired and hoarse, too.

"You're the big fella! From here to the New York Times, I tell ye. It's all anyone talks about. The great Mick Collins! You ought to run for President."

Michael could again sense a certain resentment in de Valera's sarcasm. He turned the conversation back on him. "And Harry? My best friend?"

"No plans for him to come home," said de Valera, pouring Michael a whiskey. "He's become a true IRA presence in the States, despite his home sickness and some girl he's in love with." He handed Michael the glass and slapped his back. "No time for women in war."

"No time indeed," said Michael toasting de Valera. His mind shot to Kitty, the girl both he and Harry were smitten over. The girl that had since fallen in love with Michael.

"Come sit," said de Valera, leading Michael to a chair by the fire and across from the Christmas tree. He called out to his wife, "Sinead, set another plate!"

Michael exhaled hard, while running his hand through his bangs. "We'll need a lot of money to build up after all the destruction. So many of our people are dead. So many have died for the cause, too..."

"I couldn't believe my eyes when I saw the destruction left just here in Cork."

"You should see Dublin. All of it. A bloody mess, yeah? Literally a bloody mess!"

"It's why you need to be in America, Mick. With Harry. Raise more funds to rebuild all of Ireland. Make us stronger..."

It was at that moment Michael realized de Valera, his friend, the man whom he'd saved from jail, the man he confided in, would do everything in his power to be rid of Michael Collins. And what better way than to send him to America. Except Michael would have none of it. And neither would the people of Ireland. They needed him here for the country and the negotiations.

As Sinead entered the room, asking, "Who's carving the turkey?" Michael gazed at de Valera and the irony of the question. He knew the old adage to keep your friends close but to keep your enemies closer...

A truce was indeed set between the IRA and the British Army where all fighting would cease until July 11, 1921. At that time, Michael was selected to come to London for peace talks. This gave the Irish a moment to breathe so that men might creep home to their families. Children were able to play in the gardens and parks again, and women could stroll for an afternoon walk.

Remaining in Ireland as a "Symbol of the Republic" de Valera decided it would be best to send Arthur Griffith, Erskine Childers, and Michael Collins to the delegations. But Michael wouldn't hear of that either. "Dev, why are you putting me in this position? It's yer job, not mine. I'm merely a soldier."

"If we're to be taken seriously," said de Valera, "then you must go to negotiate in England on our behalf. You're the strongest card, Mick."

"You're bollocks, Dev! I can't just go public! I've been in hiding all these years."

"Won't matter. The truce will end the war and you'll be free to roam the streets once more with no need to stay hidden."

"From your lips to God's ears..."

Michael and his two men arrived at 22 Hans Place just south of Knightsbridge, London, England, where the bold, graphic, whitewashed words 'Collins the Murderer" were painted outside their guest quarters. As a result, Michael chose to live separately at an undisclosed place. I would later learn it was 12 Cadogan Gardens.

Of course, the weight on Michael's shoulders was heavy, though the gossip by now was that British society secretly admired him.

Lloyd George had confided to John and me over champagne, "It's infuriating! Ten thousand pounds upon Collins's head and he rides around on a bicycle!" Even Lloyd George's Cabinet Secretary, Tom Jones, was quoted in The Times, "The tenacity of the IRA is extraordinary. Where was Michael Collins during the Great War? He would have been worth a dozen brass-hats!"

Yes, he was extraordinary and soon I'd have him here at the studio so John would paint his portrait.

What John and Lloyd George didn't know was that I had already contacted Michael's sister via the post and sent funds for his orphaned nieces and nephews. And she had informed Michael that someone named "Lady Lavery" had sent the funds.

As God as my witness, I was certain Michael Collins would visit 5 Cromwell Place in the very near future...

Chapter Twenty-eight
Hazel & John
(& Michael)

John stood behind his easel deep in thought at the canvas...deep into his 'clair-obscur' style, which is to say a certain use of contrast between light and dark. I was his focus. I was his light. John, most of the time, my dark. He relied on me to be his best sitter.

The portrait of me had a complicated past despite its harmonious colors. While John started the painting in 1892, as a portrait of Mrs. William Burnell, at around 1912, he transformed it into a portrait of Sarah Bernhardt, the French stage actress whose performance of Alexander Dumas's play prevented her from returning to complete the sitting. War too, prevented her from traveling from Paris to England.

So here it sat, unfinished for probably another ten more years, when John decided to morph it into me, now dressed in red, purple, and gold. My body language told John I was anxious to get on with my afternoon, having some correspondence to tend to.

"Still, Hazel!" John hissed. His eyes set on me as if on a zoo animal. He raised the sable brush vertically. I stifled to stillness, appearing naturally relaxed in my pose. I couldn't help but circle my right shoulder from where my arm was positioned high above the chair, all blood now drained from my limb and fingers clutched awkwardly onto a red rose. Its thorns pricked my thumb.

Waiting was never my strong point… waiting for a portrait sitting… waiting for John to find that blue pool of inspiration… waiting for Michael to walk through the door. My bosom rose and fell beneath my lace corset at the thought of him. An occasion for passion.

John smiled and nodded. I smiled and nodded in return, lowering my eyelids. Little did he know what I was thinking...

It's not that I didn't love my husband –I did! John Lavery was wealthy, kind, talented... albeit utterly dull.

Yawning, I drew a tiny watch tucked inside my cleavage and peeked at the time.

"Don't move," John demanded, plunging back into the canvas with a groan. Biting my lower lip, I fidgeted, slouching into the red velvet cushion of the mahogany chair, which in and of itself was a problem as I am a bed woman, a bathtub woman, or any woman who is best and happiest horizontal, not erect. A fantasy of a random lover lowering me to the duvet flickered in my mind. It had been so many years since a man ran his hands over my body, since a man loved me, kissed me, caressed my every curve.

"Turn, just a bit," said John, with well-honed impulses. "Yes. Bit more. There! Yes! Brilliant!" With my last bit of patience, I exhaled; the fingers of my left-hand dangled at the chair's spindles, but my mind wandered beyond my gaze. If the painting was to be called *The Red Rose* why did I wear purple? And velvet? So gauche. Why not shades of green– like England's Sherwood green, hunter green, or silken pine, or…

My head went to Ireland. To Michael. Shamrock green, Kelly green, moss green… Michael will adore when I wear my Gloucester sage cloak, which is to say more of a gray, like a thicket, covered in the sweet spring of April showers which are never-ending in my beloved Emerald Isle...

As John dabbed brush bristles to the palette's yellow ochre, the double doors swung open. It was the butler, clearing his throat. "So, so sorry," he said, aware that he wasn't to disturb. "You have a 'private' guest is what he told me, Sir."

"Did he say give a name?" asked John, perturbed.

"The big fella."

"Send him in..." said John.

He's here! Gazing over at the door, I felt a leap of excitement but remained positioned. My letters to the British delegates including de Valera had worked! They saw the importance of this portrait!

And then...

Arriving like a thunderous clap of lightning, Michael lowered his head under the door jam. A spy, IRA soldier, revolutionary, charmer, now stood in the center of the room and towered over my husband, John. I noted he was much more handsome than I had imagined.

"Mr Collins!" said John, moving to shake his hand. "Brilliant!"

"Dia Dhuit," said Michael, Irish for 'Hello.' He unleashed a smile and wasted no time. "Shall we give it a lash?"

"We shall indeed!" John scanned Michael. A tall, robust, Hercules with a bright face, twinkling eyes, and a playful smile. "Here. Allow me," said John, helping Michael in removing his heavy, wet, woolen overcoat.

"There's a gun in my pocket," confessed Michael.

"Understood," said John. "Not a problem at all." John extended his hand, directing Michael to a stool in the corner.

Rising from my chair, I met Michael's eyes. Despite the entire width of the room between us, my jubilance was practically transparent.

"Welcome to England," I said from a few feet away, my tone deliberately casual but sincere. "So delightful you've responded to my inquiry."

"Mrs. Lavery, such a pleasure," said Michael, coming forward and leaning over to kiss my hand. "So very kind of ye to put this portrait into motion, yeah?" He gazed into my eyes, holding the stare in a very charming way. He then took both of my hands in his, and with such warmth and sincerity, he added, "And thank ye so much for your generous donation for my nieces and nephews. God bless you."

"Yes, but of course. Thank you, Mr. Collins," I said, with a nod under lowered lids. A noble movement.

"Please, call me Michael, or Mick..."

"Michael..." I said my voice lingering as I circled the room to gain my composure.

Michael's underlying complexities permeated the studio walls. We could feel his energy, his greatness, his integrity, and a good dose of his fear. He sat on the stool but faced the door. Always on alert.

John placed a hand under Michael's chin, tipping his head up just so. "Michael," said John, pausing to surmise his subject, "Brilliant jaw structure." Then clearing his throat and moving back to his easel, as the sun set outside, John added, "There is no greater charm than the mixture of the violet twilight and the orange lamplight to illuminate the way."

"A beautiful sentiment, Mr. Lavery," said Michael, gazing around the room at various canvases. Most of them were of me and I could tell by the look on his face, his eyes scanning up and down them, that he was pleased. He caught me watching him and bit his lip before speaking. "Have you students, Mr. Lavery?" asked Michael. "Of art?"

"I think every art student starts with the belief that when he has gained a knowledge of the language, he will be able to say something on canvas that has not been said before. I am always fascinated by the few students I've had but most especially Winston Churchill."

"Churchill?" repeated Michael with concern.

"Yes," said John. "And he's a big pushover behind a canvas. Ask Hazel. She was his first teacher." But I flitted my hand toward John to continue. "If the student artist is a wise man, he turns his training to account by becoming a teacher, provided he has the power to impart what he has acquired; a critic, if he can express himself in words; a curator of a gallery or a dealer..." "Or Secretary of State for War," chimed Michael, glancing over at me with a smile.

"Yes," said John, "or Secretary of State for War..." He allowed the words to drift...

And so, John began – plunging into the portrait. My eyes darted between them – my husband and Michael – the artist and the subject open to the artist's interpretation. Of course, no painter could say more with fewer brush strokes than John Lavery, and no set of eyes could convey more affection than mine for Michael Collins.

"Such a shame," I said, "that we are but one nation, one people, only divided by a strip of water and a lot of hatred."

Michael glanced at me with a smile. "Indeed, it's not as the good Lord intended."

"Halfway measures accomplish nothing," I declared. "It should be all war or all peace."

"Aye," said Michael, nodding and again biting his lip to suppress a smile.

"Perhaps we should pray for all of us. Both sides," I said. "Go to church together."

"I'd like that, yeah?" said Michael, a smile now forming broadly on his lips.

"I suggested to John we invite all the representatives here to London," I said, "under our roof. For a truce." I was standing in front of Michael now. "You know we've guaranteed your men safe conduct if they came here for the conference. And I'll serve the finest dinner! Convince the Brits as to why we must support Irish independence."

"My Hazel," said John. "She has a completely compelling way of persuading the Irish point of view to the English. Thinks a roasted pork dinner and a jelly cake will solve political matters."

For a moment I felt embarrassed of John dismissing my importance by thinking I equate everything with a meal. But then I glanced at Michael. His expression said he believed in me.

Michael chimed in. "I think a roasted pork dinner is a good start."

As John mixed his oil paints in the tray, Michael stared at me in a prolonged and intense consultation. Something was happening in the room. My temples throbbed blood. The unspoken is that I'd already fantasized about him.... longed for his danger, his responsibilities, to be part of his passion for his country. Our country. Ireland.

The silence in the air moved between us as if the brush strokes could speak…

I'd take the ambushes. I'd take an assassination if necessary...

Words from years ago ran through my mind: 'Art... so sacred the love of it covers a multitude of sins, and so, they excuse themselves...'

Chapter Twenty-nine

Hazel & Michael

Lingering outside the Brompton Oratory, I arrived early along the grass-hemmed edge overflowing with scarlet geraniums and coleus planted between cast-iron vases on corners of the courtyard. A garland of petunias looped itself above the neatly raked gravel. How did I know this in such detail? Because I stood there for a good twenty minutes pretending to busy myself with the study of nature. Until, coming from behind, I heard footsteps crushing through the stone. But then they stopped.

I turned...

There was Michael staring at me, staring at him. "Top of the morning, to ye, Lady Hazel," he said, tipping his felt hat.

"Top of the morning to you, Mister, er, Michael," I said, extending my hand which he took.

He patted hand and looped it into his elbow, as we walked, both of our eyes bursting with pleasure. What was supposed to define us – delegates, and hostess to the delegates – was shifting. I was shifting. I was nervous. I spoke. "You know we met long before..."

"Where? Ireland? You a secret spy or something?"

"No, nothing quite so elaborate," I said, stepping forward. "You were a young man working at the Kensington Post Office."

"Guilty as charged," said Michael.

"You don't remember?" I asked. He shook his head. "I thought we shared a moment," I said.

"I'm certain that we did," he paused. "Over the stamps or was it the envelopes?"

"Stamps," I giggled.

"Then, envelopes were with another beautiful woman," he joked.

"Very amusing, Michael," I said, not used to cavorting and teasing. If I dared say so, it was fun. He was fun. When had fun left my life or for that matter, ever existed? Then his eyes darted about the church grounds for anything out of the ordinary. "Nobody will find you here," I assured him, as we strolled out of the garden toward the open door of the church, arm in arm.

"No, I suspect yer right."

"This is a big ordeal. Negotiating for our countries. We owe it to ourselves to be seen in public," I said.

"To put our tryst in the open?" he joked. "In the press?"

"Precisely," I said, without missing a beat. "Better to make it obvious."

He cleared his throat as if divulging further revelations. "If they catch you with me to be sure they'll remove you from every society board in London..."

"Oh, pish-posh to all those society boards," I said, dismissing him with playful fingers. "One can run into boredom before they run out of evening gowns."

He chuckled before shifting thoughts. "Your husband is from Northern Ireland with the Protestants, so I find it odd that his alliance isn't with them. With the Crown..."

"His alliance is with me... as well as what's right and what's wrong with this world."

We were now at the door of the Church.

"After you, Lady Hazel," he said, at the threshold.

"Hazel," I whispered into his ear. "Just call me Hazel."

"Hazel," he whispered back, his breath warm at my nose and near my mouth.

"Yer not anything as I expected," he said.

"And what did you expect?"

"A snobby aristocrat."

"But I am a snobby aristocrat," I said, winking. "Only a nice one."

Michael dipped his fingers into the holy water, never removing his eyes from mine, and then blessed himself three times fast. "Heaven help me, Lord." And he didn't mean help him with the war. He meant with me...

We took an empty pew four rows back from the altar. It was an empty church on a weekday 8 a.m. Mass, except for the handful of elderly widows and widowers.

"Meant to tell ye," said Michael. "Having a tough time sitting still for your husband's portrait of me, yeah? Absolute torture! Me sitting still..."

"I completely agree! I can't sit still either! And I must sit for him all the time!"

"Then yer a brave one."

"Didn't the words 'ye' and 'yer' die out hundreds of years ago? They're archaic..."

"Not in Western Cork. Common word. Like me... common."

"I suspect there's nothing common about 'ye,'" I said, deliberately imitating him. "But I think the word 'ye' is for referencing several people, not just one; correct?"

"Suppose it is. But my poor family wasn't the most educated." And then pointing to the altar. "Here comes Father," said Michael, opening his hymnal as the priest took the podium. He extended his hand out to his parish with a sign of the cross. "In the name of the Father, and of the Son, and of the Holy Spirit..."

"Amen," I whispered, and Michael handed me a Bible and the program. As our hands touched, my heart smashed violently against my chest wall. The strangest creeping of moisture tingled in my undergarments. With a thick swallow in my throat, I knew I must continue to gaze at the priest and remain inconspicuous as possible.

Staring straight ahead, I counted the lilies that lined the altar. The smell of camphor oil rose from the front pews and mingled with our fourth row, so strong that I feared combustion.

Just then Michael's hand reached out to take mine resting on my lap as if he could read my mind and longed to calm me. We stayed that way, hand in hand, until it was time to stand up and recite the gospel responses.

The caterer and staff bustled about all day, with every silver candelabra polished, every tablecloth pressed, portrait dusted, feather pillow fluffed, and every vase of flowers arranged and strategically placed on various side tables and in the foyer hall.

The dinner at 5 Cromwell Place was in full swing, waiters carrying silver trays of hors d' oeuvres full of 'Devils on horseback' and bacon-wrapped oysters. Sipping champagne between bites of beluga caviar, John and I sashayed about eventually landing at the crackling fire by the mantel in conversation with Lloyd George and his secretary, Eddie Marsh.

"Welcome to my home, Gentlemen," I toasted, glasses clinking.

"And what a lovely home it is," said Eddie. "Thank you for arranging this lovely soiree." As I smiled, and nodded, John knew I was a nervous wreck as this could launch friendships before war and peace. A carefully curated guest list had been established as they filtered in one after another. Every so often, I glanced up as the butler spoke... anticipating Michael's arrival.

The butler cleared his throat, "A Mister and Mrs. George Bernard Shaw." Entering the room, the two scanned for John and me, and upon seeing us, waved and headed toward the mantel.

The butler spoke again, "May I present Lord and Lady Birkenhead," who entered next.

Moments later, another ring of the bell. "May I present Mr. and Mrs. Damien Jones of Oxford, previously of Gloucestershire" and just behind them, "May I present Sir and Lady Worthington Evans."

As the party grew more crowded, suddenly Michael and his two men appeared at the open doorway to the grand room, taking in the chandeliers and the posh guests. The butler, unsure how to announce them, leaned into Michael who whispered some advice. The butler nodded and upon clearing his throat: "May I present three men from Cork."

I suppressed a giggle. The entire room went so silent that one could practically hear Lloyd George choking on his skewered nibble.

As the moment passed and the Ted Lewis orchestra played in the background, I whisked my way toward Michael across the room to the radio song, When My Baby Smiles at Me. "Welcome to England, Gentlemen!" I said, taking Michael by the arm and bringing him through the group that parted ways like Moses and the Red Sea. "Michael, this is Mr. James Barrie of Surrey."

"J. M. Barrie? The author?" asked Michael, extending a hand. "Of Peter Pan? In the flesh?"

"In the flesh, my boy," said Barrie, shaking Michael's hand vigorously. "The pleasure is all mine."

As the housemaid lured me away with a question on champagne shortages, I left John in charge of our guests. Winston made his way toward Michael just as John unrolled a large paper. "I have this poster from South Africa, Michael," who examined it and read aloud, "Ten pounds Reward for Winston Churchill, Dead or Alive."

Michael turned to Winston on cue. "Certainly, yer worth more?" said Michael.

"Apparently not as much as you, Mr. Collins," said Winston. "We put a bigger price on you, Sir. I believe it was Ten-thousand pounds."

"Ah, well, inflation, Mr. Churchill," said Michael, and the men chuckled.

I moved to the mantel, leaning upon my elbow, suddenly

feeling relaxed and pleased to watch them mingling. Sipping my Jack Rose of fresh lemon, applejack and grenadine, my friend, Clementine leaned in. "Slow down there, Hazel," teased Clementine, handing me another one which I took and sipped rapidly. "Handsome devil," she menaced, peering over her spectacles, and nodding towards Michael. "I think you're neglecting your hostess duties."

"Oh stop, Clemmie," I said, glancing over at him, and seeing him suddenly standing like a wallflower sipping whiskey as the English men spoke. There was something admirable about him. Unlike me he was an underdog believing in the cause that defined him, but like me, we shared a gnawing at our souls for a bigger and greater purpose. Idealism.

And then Michael shyly glanced my way.

"He's quite fetching," said Clementine, "Keeps glancing over here towards you. Go on, wave." But I didn't. "Fine, then I will," said Clementine, lifting her hand and moving her fingers in a flirty wave to Michael. "Hello there, handsome," she murmured under her breath. The corner of his lip gave a curl, and he waved back. She turned to me grinning ear to ear before adding, "Nothing is more lovely than knowing an old married woman is still desirable."

"Shall I go over to him?" I asked Clementine, pretending to be shy.

"Well, you know, Hazel," she said, "it's not customary for a lady to stroll over from one gentleman and seek out the company of another... but yes, bloody hell, do it!"

And with that I sauntered off to where he had just sat in a velvet armchair. "Hello," I said.

"Hello yerself," he said, eyeing the rest of the crowd, then eyeing me for eyeing him. "Your behavior is recklessly unorthodox."

"Is it?" I asked, leaning in with a little more bosom and bare shoulder than all of England was used to witnessing. "May I see to it that you have a refill?" Picking up his crystal tumbler I rattled it, empty.

"Don't you have staff for that?" he asked, jokingly.

"Yes, but sometimes I like to give it the personal touch," I said.

"I really shouldn't," he said, leaning in and taking in my scent, one he would later describe as delicately floral and European, with a certain connotation of civility, culture. "I can't have my cup of bliss overflow now, can I?" he said. Double entendre. Witty. I was at a loss for words. So, he helped me, "When can I see you again?"

"You're seeing me now," I said, standing up and noticing more eyes upon me. "I... um, how about tomorrow..."

"Yes, please," he said, devilishly.

"Collins, my boy," John called out from nearby with a reproachful eye. "Do join me. We were discussing your discussions of tomorrow's truce..."

"I have but one word for truce," said Michael, rising from his chair.

"And that is?" asked John.

"Freedom," said Michael.

At that the men were taken aback by his gutsiness. A Machiavellian look shadowed Lord Birkenhead's eyes.

"To freedom!" I toasted the Irish trio, coming in for the save, but no one budged. "Agreed?" I asked, knowing it was a hazardous query. I clinked at their glasses but still none of them joined. "To freedom all around!" I continued, "And the avoidance of corruption." As our crystal glasses touched, our eyes met. It was clear Michael was intrigued. I carried on, "It's wrong to have a battle of wits with someone who is unarmed, now isn't it, boys?" They nodded and the mood was lightened.

Michael spoke to John and Winston, "It is only in the remote corners of Ireland in the south and west and north-west that any trace of the old Irish civilization is met with now. In those places, the social side of Anglicization never easily penetrated. Today it's only in those places that any native beauty in Irish life survives."

"Agreed," said John. "And those are the poorest parts of our country. I was born and raised in Belfast. And it's certainly changed."

My eyes moved about the room, darting across the faces. Seemed Lloyd George had already departed as a means of self-preservation for the negotiations. The last thing he whispered to me was that he would be awaiting Winston, Clementine, John, and me to join him for a four-course dinner at Claridge's in about an hour.

It was clear Lloyd was not as taken by Michael as the rest. He felt he was an ambitious and destructive lad, or so he told me. The last thing I said to Lloyd about Michael was that "He is beloved by the Irish, may I remind you, Lloyd, and he's the Minister of Finance, to say the least. Please try to stay positive for both our country's sake."

But he changed the subject, instead referring to our forthcoming dinner and whiskey. "Tell John not to keep the grouse and water waiting." And with that he was out the door.

One by one the guests gathered their coats, did the double-cheek kissing, and were off. John was busy telling George one of his repeated jokes when Michael latched onto my arm.

"Church then?" he asked.

"Church seems to work," I said, unleashing a massive grin to match his. 'But I can't linger just now. Lloyd George thinks..."

"Please don't start any sentence with those three words 'Lloyd George thinks,'" he said, with sarcasm. "He doesn't think at all. That's the problem..."

I giggled. "You're quite amusing, but I do need to win him over."

"Shouldn't be an issue," said Michael, leaning in to peck my cheek. "Good night then, and God bless."

He stood tall and turned back to shake hands with the others who clamored around as he exited the door.

Later that night, I sat at my vanity in a satin dressing gown, applying my ritual cold cream to my face. John approached from behind in his monogrammed robe, placing a tender kiss on my head.

"Well, you certainly did quite a good job letting the fox into the coop," said John.

"Whatever do you mean?" I asked, playing dumb and looking at him through the mirror.

"Collins. You've brought him here to our home. Let alone a portrait, he's becoming a friend to the enemy."

"Well... as I said earlier, 'hatred has no home here.'"

"Yes, well, had it not been for you, Hazel, there wouldn't be a Treaty negotiation."

"I don't need to take credit where credit isn't due. Not yet. They haven't signed."

"No, these negotiations will take time, but you've opened our home, Hazel. Such an opportunity to bring together both sides on neutral ground."

"Yes, I admit to as much. I try to be a steady influence."

John moved to his side of the bed, gathering his books and water glass, and tossed a couple of pills to the back of his throat. "Can you believe how Collins has bonded with the Unionist Lord Birkenhead? Right here in our home. If anyone reaches an agreement, it will be because of the two of them."

"True," I said, rising from the vanity to my side of the bed.

"And I had a good chuckle when the dog pawed at Birkenhead."

"It was horrid! I had to apologize," I said, turning down the sheets.

"Yes, and then when Birkenhead mischievously said to you, 'Oh, I am sorry. I thought you were making advances,' I near died when Collins stood up to defend you." John cleared his throat, imitating Michael's brogue. "'Do ye mean to insult 'er?'" John chuckled. "Good God, Hazel, I was waiting for a bar room brawl!

Right there in the billiard room!"

"Oh, it was nothing, dearest," I explained, climbing under the covers. "I told Michael that Birkenhead was only joking."

"Yes, But the way that Collins defended you," said John. "Has a thing for you, he does, Hazel. I can see it in his eyes." I said nothing. Gathering the duvet under my nose. "Must be your new look," he continued, "The red-purple toned hair and the ruby lipstick. Must see you as someone his age?"

"Oh, stop making a fuss... I always wear festive lipstick."

"Yes, dear, you do. But not on his collar?"

"Good night, Johnnie," I said, changing the subject as he leaned down to peck my lips. Then turning to my side, I fluffed at my pillow. "I've got church tomorrow..."

"You've seemed to embrace the church like never before, my dear, Hazel..."

"Well, I'm a devout Catholic now," I said in the dark and stillness that surrounded us before the sound of his footsteps headed down the hallway.

Then a silence lingered, until my long night turned into a gentle and anxious dawn.

Chapter Thirty
Hazel & Michael

On October the 11th, the Irish Political representatives met the British delegation at a massive round table that included Lloyd George, Lord Birkenhead, Winston Churchill, Austen Chamberlain, Sir Worthington, Sir Gordon Hewart, and Sir Hamar Greenwood.

Because they'd met in past days over the many dinners, teas, and talks of the weather that I'd taken such care to host, it seemed a silent camaraderie existed between the men. Michael later told me that when Lloyd George waved the gents to their seats, they instead stood to shake hands and greet each other, saying what a lovely time they had at my house.

Michael's days became a vicious round of Mass with me, negotiations at Downing Street and then tea or late supper at my home.

Following morning service, we exited the church shaking hands with the priest who wished us a blessed day. As we moved from the Oratory, I chose small talk as the autumn leaves rustled around our ankles in colors of gold and brown. "It's due to a lack of sunshine and much precipitation," I explained, "London just doesn't deliver the tones of orange and red the way they might in Chicago."

"Not to sound cliché," said Michael, running his hand through his bangs, "but we have to stop meeting like this."

"Why?" I asked, with a sudden flirtatious tone, as we hastened to a row of parked bicycles.

"They'll think you're a double spy and shoot ye!"

"Oh Michael, you've been watching too many movies at the picture palace."

"And all this time I thought I had you fooled that I was the head of the IRA, but instead I've been enjoying matinees at the picture house," he said with sarcasm as he headed toward a row of bicycles. He removed his bike from the rack.

"Shall we cycle together?" I asked.

"Are ye riding on my handlebars?"

"No, I've my own bicycle. Just over there," I said, pointing with a giggle, and then securing a pin in my furry-plumed velvet hat.

"Where?" he asked, confused.

I pointed to the side of the church where a Roadster lady's safety bicycle stood, having bought it a few days prior to impress him. "It's your mode of transport, so now it is mine."

"Bloody brilliant!" he said, sounding sarcastically English, hopping on his bike, and circling effortlessly around me. "Let's make a go of it!"

Moving to my bicycle, I lifted the hem of my dress and attempted to mount the step-through frame while grabbing onto its very upright handlebars. As I began to pedal, my feet ready to engage the coaster brakes, I jerked the bike frame left and right, more crooked by the moment, until all balance was utterly lost.

"I can see they taught you cycling in that American boarding school," he chuckled. "Right up there with French and Latin lessons."

"No, they didn't," I snapped. "I taught myself, thank you very much." Forcing the bicycle left and right, my jerky movements were hideous. I attempted to keep my dress hem from the chain.

"You're pathetic, yeah?" he joked.

"Pathetic, no. I beg your pardon."

"Pardoned, indeed," he chuckled. "And note that I'm working on my 'ye' and 'yer's' but it's hard to break a habit."

"Good on you!" I stood up straight, juggling the weight of the bicycle straddled between my legs. Michael guffawed. "Michael, you asked me if I possessed a bicycle. Which I do. You didn't ask me if I could ride it."

"Ha! Yer taking the piss out of me!"

"What on earth?!"

"Oh, sorry. Irish, slang. For being comical, yeah?" "Yeah, nothing. If you want to give me a riding lesson..."

"I'd love to give you a riding lesson," he said, suggesting more than a bike ride.

The moment hung in the air, and my senses scrambled, turning my complexion into a deep rose blush from neck to my forehead. "I'll manage just fine," I said, again trying to coordinate the pedals with the handlebars and practically crashing onto the curb.

Michael cringed. "Look, Lass, don't be stubborn. If I don't help ye, you'll have an accident with that nearby lamppost."

"Fine." At that I stopped and straddled the bicycle beside him.

"I'm glad to see you here every morning, Lady Hazel," he said. "You make me happy and frankly I don't recall the last time I laughed so hard or laughed at all."

"Well, I'm glad to provide comedy at my foolish expense," I said, patting down the ruffles on my dress into place.

He winked at me. "Shall I walk you and your bicycle home, and then I'll come back to fetch mine?"

"Yes, that would be quite chivalrous," I said, flustered and gathering my composure.

He took my arm with one hand, escorting me from my bicycle, then taking the handlebars with the other. As we walked toward Thurloe Square, a traditional garden square in South Kensington and only moments from my house, he stopped to take in the foliage, smelling the air.

"It's quite lovely, isn't it?" I asked, as he looked me up and down.

"Yes, quite lovely," he said, as if suggesting me. We stared for a moment unsure what to do; our sensibilities disappearing with every breath.

"It's a private communal garden, you know." I swallowed. "It's for the residents to gather their thoughts. I love how the Victoria and Albert Museum pokes through over the trees."

"Take me there sometime..."

"I'd love to."

A magpie began singing loudly which sounded more like a dog bark than a bird call. He spoke first, "Said to be one of the most intelligent mammal species." I gazed at Michael, taken with how he studied the bird, its black beak, its striking white breast. "To be free as a bird..." he added with a sigh.

"Are you free, Michael, or have you a girlfriend?" I asked, surprising myself as the words slipped from my lips.

He leaned my bicycle onto a tree trunk, then took my elbows in his hands, facing me full on.

"A girlfriend?" he asked. "Yes, my girlfriend has been Ireland."

"And before that?" I asked.

"My mother and my sisters."

I grinned. Good answer. No mention of the politically naive and emotionally insecure Kitty Kiernan I'd heard rumors of... the girl back in Ireland.

And then, very unexpectedly, he said, "May I kiss ye?" And before I could respond, his face came at mine. At first, I didn't move my lips, stunned by his forwardness, but then slowly my mouth moved on his, until after several discovery pecks, I relaxed so his lips and tongue could travel in and out of mine.... first gently and then hungrily, as though all the world's intention could be filled through our affections.

As we stayed kissing, my mind roamed. All my life I'd been searching for Father and found him in John. All my life I'd married or almost married the younger men that Mother had given or assigned permission. But this... no, this was different.

As my mind convinced my lips to forge forward, I caught my breath, before devouring him more and more. A gentle moan slipped from Michael as I slipped my fingers from my white gloves, tossing them to the ground, then moving my hand up around his neck, drawing him closer to my face, taking in his scent, – Heaven! – an intoxicating and mysterious smell, he was vigorous with Levantine spice and Irish moss, tangled riverbanks, and crisp moonlight.

When we finally broke, I stared into his hooded hazel eyes, contagious and full of vitality. I studied the corners of his mouth and the way it twisted up almost to the corners of his oversized ears. I dabbed at his playful bangs, dipping into his bushy brows. His chin quivered. I stood on tiptoe to kiss it, my mind racing through my lifelong narrative. We may have only just met, but I felt this was a long time coming... some sort of delayed gratification. Something I'd earned after a lifetime of proper discipline.

As I finally pulled back, I placed my finger to my lip as if to seal his taste. "Forgive me for being so bold. I don't want to force your hand," he whispered.

"And I don't want to twist your arm," I countered.

He giggled. "Please twist anything you want, Hazel Lavery." He gathered my bicycle and took my hand. "This must be romance, eh?"

"Romance is an art, but not every man is an artist."

"Your husband is?" he said very deliberately. Catching me off guard.

"Yes, he is an artist. Of the canvas, he is indeed."

"Indeed," he said, surrendering, and then pulling me in again and we both giggled.

"Michael," I said. "We have to stop meeting like this."

"Then you have to wear a different dress."

I gazed down at my wardrobe. It was nothing out of the ordinary, but I suspected that for a boy from Cork my blue velvet ensemble with the tightened corset was quite fetching.

My heart thumped so strongly I thought I would faint on the spot and so I decided to change the scene, first grabbing my gloves from the ground, then carefully placing each finger through the fabric, and finally began walking at a quickened pace. He followed behind.

We arrived through the other side of the park and just across from my front door. I exhaled as we crossed the street and changed the subject. He spoke first. “All the women I’ve ever known... well, they pale in comparison to you...” He slung his head down with guilt. “But I’ve not been honest with you, Hazel.”

“Oh?”

“There is a woman. Well, was. Her name is Kitty and she’s a lovely girl from back home... but not...”

“It’s fine, you owe me no explanation,” I said, raising my hand up calmly and eyeing my front door in case John might be glancing out the window.

“You are all I’ve dreamed of in a wife and so much more,” he said.

“That’s lovely. But we’ve a problematic wrinkle.”

“What’s that?”

“I’m married,” I said, definitively waiting for a response but he said nothing. “Besides, what do you know of marriage, Michael? You’re married to a cause.”

“But when the cause is over, I’d like to be married to a real woman.” He took my white gloved fingers and studied every one of them, massaging them in his big, rough, bare hands. “For now, we’ll be soulmates if not bedmates...”

“I can barely breathe,” I said, as he let my fingers go.

The butler was in the window, moving the curtain to peek and heading undoubtedly to greet me at the front door...

“Ah, Mr. Wallace is there,” said Michael, pointing.

“Yes, he seems to be everywhere. Sometimes I think there are ten of him,” I chuckled. “I’ll see you this evening, Michael...” my tone changing back to that of Lady Lavery.

Michael hung his head. "Goodbye then, Lady Lavery." And then he called out, while trotting backwards away from me, "Anyone ever tell ye, you're like a fancy meat scrap?" I shook my head 'no.' He continued, "Like the kind you feed your dog for a treat. The kind of portion that leaves the dog longing for more..."

I bit my lip to contain a giggle. "Good day, Michael," I said, and moved up the threshold. Then turning, "Until tonight..."

"Yes, to be sure. Until tonight. I'll be thinking of nothing else but the delegates and the negotiation." As if to say his body parts were throbbing and thinking so much more.

And with that the door swung open. "Welcome home, Your Ladyship," said Mr. Wallace.

"Mr. Wallace," I said, nodding, monotone and nonchalant.

"Will Mr. Collins be joining us for tea?"

"No, Mr. Collins has work to do," I said, dismissing the recognition.

"Alice and Eileen have arrived," said Mr. Wallace. "They wanted to surprise you," he said, taking my hat, gloves, and shawl.

"Alice and Eileen? The Girls?" I asked. "Home? Together? Oh joy! Please let them know that I'll be right there."

"They're in the kitchen eating eggs and soldiers."

My mind still a flutter; somehow, in the moment, that comment had a different meaning than the British term for eggs and strips of white toast. "Thank you, I'll join them shortly. That will be all, Mr. Wallace." As Mr. Wallace departed the foyer, I stood perfectly still, my hand clutching the other side of the door handle. My head and heart were still racing.

Oh Michael, Michael, Michael... God, he was thrilling! And he tasted delicious! I longed to taste him some more, but what was I to do? Take to bed with him? Could I? Should I? Was I a natural rebel? Did I have it in me? I've yearned for breathtaking experiences, but at the cost of a bullet? My countries – both – needed me. Perhaps, even depended on me! This was crazy. And deliciously dangerous!!

And at that, the girls were there, cackling their shoes across the buffed black and white checkered limestone floor, dashing to my arms.

"Darlings!" I blurted out, taking them both to my side...

Chapter Thirty-one

Michael & Hazel & John

The restaurant was abuzz when Michael and I entered. All the scenarios came at us, the ones where you see someone you know – Oh, hello; and the one where you see someone you'd like to know, or they might like to know me. But most of all, the people that shouldn't be seen together. I suspect those people were Michael and me, given the whispers and head turns as I waved at my friend, Horace Plunkett, moving towards his table.

We were dining in Kingston-upon-Thames to meet Horace, a Christian socialist, who stood to greet us as we approached.

I spoke first, "Sir Horace, allow me to introduce my new friend, Michael Collins."

"Michael, lovely to make your acquaintance," said Horace, behaving as jolly as one would hope. "And this is my wife, Piaras Beaslai."

"Piaras, lovely to see you," I said, kissing her left cheek and then the right. "Michael," I said, "Horace is an Anglo-Irish agricultural reformer, and Unionist MP, a supporter of Home Rule, and lately, well, an author."

"I especially love the last bit," said Michael, taking Horace's hand with a firm shake. "A big fan of your work The Rural Life."

"Well, the chap's well read," joked Horace, lighting up and nodding satisfaction at me.

It was a festive and animated gathering since among many things, Horace had just founded the Irish Dominion League, and in the very near future, he'd become a member of the first formation of Seanad Eireann, the upper chamber in the Parliament of the new Irish Free State. But for now, he was here as a dear friend, my friend, who admired my determination to bring the English and the Irish together. Horace promised me he'd make Michael feel welcome. And he did.

Later, upon arriving back at 5 Cromwell Place, it was evident that Michael and I got a wee too tipsy.

"Come, Michael, and stay the night," said John, escorting us to the drawing room, where I flung my velvet coat onto the silk ottoman. Michael sank into the club chair, stretching his feet to the logs in the fire. John moved to the liquor cart allowing himself a generous pour of a twenty-year-old Scotch.

"I love it here by the fire, you know," said Michael. "It's been so long since I've had a place called home."

"Well, 'notre maison est votre maison,'" I said.

"French! For our home is your home," John said.

"And I've said it before and I'll say it again," raising my nightcap to a toast. "A place where there's no room for hatred."

After more shared spirits, John insisted Michael spend the night in the guest quarters rather than risk being out in public, since his guard was down, or in other words, he was inebriated. But Michael refused and continued to thank John for all his hospitality, and the marvelously completed portrait that was quite an accurate resemblance of himself.

"Glad it meets your satisfaction," said John.

"Fer sure. It's better looking than the real thing, yeah?" joked Michael.

"Hardly," I chimed in.

Michael moved to the series of portraits completed so far. Leaning against the wall for pickup. There were the other Irish men.... Robert Barton, Gavin Duffy, and Arthur Griffith among them.

"If I do say so," said John, "You have a charisma unlike the others."

"You're far too kind," said Michael, returning to his chair by the fire.

"And on that note, I shall excuse myself to retire to bed." John moved to peck me on the cheek. "The maid has turned down your bed, Hazel."

"And yours?" I asked, since John always slept in his own quarters.

"Yes," he confirmed, "Good night to both of you."

"Good night," said Michael and me in unison.

Left alone in the room, I sighed a grand exhale, and moved to the mantel to rest my elbow, my profile reflected in the glass behind me.

"Fucksake! I'm so sorry," said Michael, standing erect now and moving toward me.

"Please, no need to apologize. I knew exactly the risk of dining out with you publicly, with God knows what snipers might be lurking," I said, warming my hands in the rising flames. "I just wish we could get out of here...."

"Out of here, where? I have a responsibility to Ireland..."

My mind raced for a plan. "Paris would be lovely, or America, or Tangier, if we must..."

"Is that what you want?" he asked, standing now beside me.

"I can't have what I want."

"Yes, ye can," he said, turning me into him. "But my life at this moment is bound by Dublin, Cork and apparently London and Liverpool. Surely that's boring..."

"There's nothing boring about you, Michael, that's the problem," I said, moving closer into his chest, the smell of his masculinity rising. "When I discover someone or something wonderful, it stays in my heart." I closed my eyes and exhaled, "Forever."

"I long to kiss you, again, but not here... it's not right. Sir Lavery is just..."

"Agreed," I said, "then where?"

"Tomorrow, after church, yeah?"

"Yes," I said in starving desperation.

"You sleep in separate bedrooms?"

"For years, sadly. Truth is I've not felt the arms of a man..."

His arms drew me closer. "You're beautiful."

"You're beautiful, too," I said as he pulled me closer, and we swayed for a long moment. "Oh, how I long to take ye to Garryvoe..."

"Garry who?" I chuckled, pulling back.

"Garryvoe is a where, not a who," he said, looking down at my face. "It's ideal, Lass. Open land, and sea and intimacy. The golden sandy five-mile beach, the view of Ballycotton, and its lighthouse..."

"There's a lighthouse," I asked, smiling.

"Eternal and dependable. Built in 1840 she was."

"Well, aren't you the historian."

"No, I'm a feckin eejit, is what I am..."

"You're not an eejit," I said, attempting to imitate his brogue. "I long to be your – what do you call it? – your Colleen," I added, slang for an Irish woman.

"Very amusing, Hazel. If I wanted an Irish girl, I suppose I'd have one. It's the American woman I want. It's you..."

"I wouldn't mind so much just being an Irish girl," I said. "Once my mother and I stopped at a pub on the way to someplace or another and we came upon a small town. The people inside the pub were happy and gay with the simple existence of life. No drama. I liked that. I wanted to stay and talk to them and share a pint, but Mother wouldn't even allow me to speak to them. It was a horrible thing to do. They were people. No different than me, or you, for that matter."

"Is this yer way of saying ye want me to take you to a pub?'

"No. Yes. Take me anywhere." I let go of his arms and listened in the hall to be certain no one was eavesdropping. "What about this other place you mention?" I asked. "Clonakilty? Tell me about it."

He moved back towards me, stroked my hair and let out a sigh as though the word hit a nerve and took him back to his past. "It's the heart of my home. Family, farming. Has a pub. Several, to be certain. Famous for black pudding."

"Black pudding? Sounds lovely," I said. "We'll have some."

"Silly woman, it's not dessert. It's made from pig's blood," he chuckled.

I stuck out my tongue in disdain. "That's Clonakilty's claim to fame, yeah? Pig's blood?" I said, imitating him again.

"Yes," he whispered, "Behave. It's late." He gathered his hat and coat and headed for the door.

"But I don't want to behave. I'm tired of behaving." He said nothing. "Michael," I called after him. He turned and met my eyes, puzzled by the tone in which I summoned him back.

He answered in an almost obedient fashion. "What is it, Lady Lavery, my love..."

"I'm sick to death of seeing you leave..."

He sighed, "It's only until tomorrow. Promise."

"Promise?"

"Cross my heart, hope to die."

"Don't say that!" I snapped. "It's a bad omen."

He went to give me a gentle peck under the chandelier of the foyer. The house was still except for us.

"Until tomorrow?" I asked like a small desperate girl, reminiscent of when I last said goodbye to my father and there was no tomorrow.

"To be sure," he said, squeezing my hand in his. "Good night and..."

"God bless," I added, beating him to it and he threw his head back laughing.

As I held the door behind him, he tipped his hat, his eyes glancing left and right until a car pulled up to gather him. And then he was gone.

I stayed in that door jamb until the last of his brake lights were out of sight.

Love, I thought. It's as mysterious as the lover. When you walk on a path of the discovery of love you get a feeling that will transport you in a way that is not rational...

So, what do you do?

You stay on the path. And you run as wild as your feet will take you to the very end.

Chapter Thirty-two

Hazel & Michael

We squeezed hands, secured in the church pew, as the priest's sermon quoted St Matthew: "Blessed are the Peacemakers" having undoubtedly figured out who Michael was.

Father went on about Patriotism and love of country and it was soon clear that he was focused on Michael's best interests. He had our back. Kept our secret. He ended his sermon by uttering, "God's house is all man's safe house..." And cast his eyes at Michael.

We said our ritual goodbyes to the priest, Michael tipped his hat to the other patrons, until we were out of sight at the side of the building. Michael placed my cloak around me, rubbing my shoulders from the chill of the air, gallant-like. His eyes were always on alert, his hand near his pocket for his gun.

"Where's your driver?" asked Michael. "Ye know, Clifford? Baldwin? Er?"

"Clifford. He's not here. C'mon," I said, "My car is out back."

"You're driving?" he asked, off guard.

"Yes."

"I hope you can drive better than you steer a bicycle," he teased, glancing around. Nobody. Nothing. Only the whip of a late autumn breeze freshened our faces.

We were in the car now. Me on the driver's side. I looked up at his handsome features and began to spill my plan. "I've arranged a room at Claridge's which seems, of course, overly obvious as I dine there frequently, you understand, but by hiding you in plain sight the staff will never suspect a thing."

"Claridge's? Fancy," he said.

"Yes, I'm quite friendly with the staff for charity events," I said, stopping to catch my breath and compose myself. "The plan is to park the car on Mount Street, stroll leisurely to Davies Street and enter the hotel through the back, then go to the front desk to obtain the key. After a short while, you follow only a shorter route, Mount Row to Brook's Mews. We'll meet at the top of the staircase, end of the hall, second floor."

"Clearly you've thought this out," he chuckled, amused.

"Yes, all of last night."

He tipped his head in a flirtatious manner. "So, you're seducing me? To bed?"

"Yes, every bit." I said, surprising him with my assertiveness, which felt darn good.

"And here, wear this," I said, handing him an old frumpy Homburg hat of John's. And a long scarf to cover his face.

"And she's gone as far as providing a disguise," he said, biting his lip, and examining the items, before leaning forward to kiss me. I pulled away, staying in business mode.

"Just one question," I asked. "Have you ever been with an older woman?"

"Ummmmm..." he said, taking a long time to respond as if to say he'd been with so many women.

"I'm being serious," I asked again.

"Why? You're older than me?" he asked, with a massive grin, closing my car door, then looking around the vicinity once more, before going around to enter the passenger's side to join me.

I'd already started my engine...

Lingering at the hotel stairs in its art deco splendor, I was nervous. This was a place favored by royalty – Queen Victoria and Prince Albert – and the most distinguished of our generation, and heads of state, which I suppose were the people I already associated with.

My heart pounded nervously as an elderly couple strolled by followed by bright young things with bobs and flapper dresses. I turned to face the wall, my face draped by a thin veil. From the lobby, tunes of Gershwin played jazz, a bit too festive for this dramatic luncheon moment.

And then I turned. And Michael was there. At the bottom of the staircase, a near-perfect study of disposition, albeit dressed in that oversized hat and scarf. He gazed up, grinning, hand on the banister, never taking his eyes from me as he leapt the steps two at a time... beckoning to come please me.

If I'd had one afternoon to sum up all that ever mattered until the day I died, it would have been that afternoon...

He took me gently down to the canopy bed, kissing me for the longest time, nervous to move forward until finally, I sat up at the edge, and began to undress rather shyly, one layer at a time as he assisted with the tiny buttons on the back of my satin dress while I loosened the sleeves.

Standing and turning to face him, I allowed the dress to pool to my ankles revealing a corset, and lace panties with garters and hosiery.

A sly grin formed in the corner of his mouth as he stood back, watching me undress. As I was about to remove my brassiere, he undressed himself frantically like a teenager, anxiously removing his suit pants, belt, shirt, undershirt, and knickers, then standing there all at once, glorious, and foolish... completely naked except for his socks. His eyes never left mine. We both giggled awkwardly as he came toward me, running his hands down my back and cupping just above my thighs. He kissed me full on the mouth before effortlessly picking me up in his arms and placing me ever so gently on the muslin sheets of the mahogany bed.

And then, he was on top of me, devouring me, every bit, starting at my mouth and making his way down to my breast with such tenderness and passion as if every kiss, every move of the tongue, was an art. He moved down to my stomach and hips, turning me over, kissing the curve of my spine before turning me over again, moving his tongue inside my thighs and to private places no one had ever ventured, places I didn't even know existed. I could feel his hardness pressing into me, throbbing large and ready for me to receive him.

And receive him I did as though a dam burst, the rushing waters filling every bit of me and then some. We moved slowly at first and then with more thrust, creating a dance, the most perfect union of man and woman. He was the best lover I'd ever known and after he climaxed, we fell back on the sheets, breathless and panting, separate but still together, as he reached out for my hand and took it into his.

It had been more than I could have ever dreamed for a mere socialite from Chicago who thought she'd had it all and seen it all. Clearly, I'd been missing the most important bits of life. To feel alive. And with Michael Collins. I knew, no, I was certain, he was more than I could ever need or desire until the end of time. Because to want something and then to get it is the most rewarding, the most incredible experience, surpassing all others.

"Where did you go?" he whispered, propping himself up on his elbow and staring at me.

"Nowhere, everywhere," I said, running my fingers down his profile. "I'm here, don't worry. Completely and utterly here."

"Good," he said, "me, too."

He fell back on the pillow. "I can't imagine a woman of yer class and elegance would want a simpleton farmer boy like me..."

"You're so wrong. You're that and so much more," I said, curling into his arms and kissing him more and more. "I chose you. I choose to be with you!"

His mouth intensified on mine, thrusting his chest, his hips, and his hardness into me yet again, until I could hardly believe it, but he wanted another go. Spreading my legs wide,

I wasn't nervous now. Instead, I let myself fall off the cliff of passion and when I did, something glorious happened. I felt faint, and chilly, warm, and tingling as suddenly we built to a synchronized crescendo of excitement... crying out and clutching onto each other. My body released a rush as I quivered from head to toe, climaxing for the first time in my entire life. Who knew a woman could feel such pleasure!

Then, all was quiet again.

And I lay still, at peace, next to my secret, satisfied. Let me die, just here. Just now.

This was truly mad, passion, abandon... and I wanted more and more and more of it...

After what seemed the entire afternoon, he left the hotel first, and I freshened up before taking the short jaunt to my car parked as I left it on Mount Street. Turning the ignition, I decided to take the long route home, circling around Green Park and Buckingham Palace, along Westminster, over through Belgravia, then along the bottom of Hyde Park to Knightsbridge. God, how I loved London. But God how I loved him. Lifting my fingers to my nose, the smell of him still lingered everywhere. Good Lord, I never wanted to bathe again!

But I had told Michael I couldn't leave John, an old man who would die soon and then we could be together. It was the right thing to do, though my heart and soul longed for all the wrong things.

In bed I had poured my life out to Michael. My upbringing, my father, my mother, her death, Ned, his death, my sister, her death, and all my various illnesses, I felt I'd had to grow up fast. He told me too, about his parents' death, his brother's murder, and the many tragedies he'd endured in losing loved ones and friends to the cause.

We agreed that death hardened us as much as it softened us...

As I lay in his arms and he asked me about John, I explained the long journey we'd taken to finally be man and wife. It was then Michael wondered why I'd want to toss that all away over a stupid infatuation with an Irish renegade. Surely, my life would be better and calmer with John.

But that was the problem. Life had become dull... I didn't want calm. I wanted to feel, to kiss, to swoon, to live! But maybe Michael was right. Not the just-an-Irish-renegade-bit, but his concern which stimulated my own concern. I was an older American socialite parading around London and all the world as Lady Lavery. Why would a hot Irish man want me? Was this my last attempt to hang onto my youth?

Clementine kept teasing that I was forty now. Old! Certainly, this robust Irish man could have any young woman in Dublin, Cork, Kenmare, or all of Ireland.

My mind raced to all the men of my past. Ned, bless him, was an honest husband, and had meant well but fumbled through lovemaking, his hands best used as a surgeon. And, that crazy Len in Italy was a wild playboy with little skill other than to admire his own shortcomings, as it were. And John, bless him, too, had been tender and gentle, and not much of a lover and not often... his passions poured into his canvas instead of me as if I were a porcelain doll that he was afraid to break.

On the other hand, Michael told me he'd only been with two women, which piqued my curiosity. "Do tell..." I teased and he blushed.

One, named Dilly Dicker, whose name as well as actions seemed out of a novel. While the two had courted, she'd dressed as a man and sneaked onto mail boats in wicker baskets and steel drums to steal mailings and correspondence between London and Dublin Castle.

The other, he said, was the most recent – Kitty Kiernan. Rumors circulated in Ireland that she was his partner and next thing, his fiancée, but it just wasn't as he'd hoped since they barely saw each other these days. Besides, she challenged him with every political move he made, asking question after question, often to the point of exhaustion...

As I pulled the car up to 5 Cromwell Place, I stalled out front, the afternoon again flickering movie reels in my mind. How I lay my head on his heart, running my fingers through his moist chest hair, his breath rising and falling gently, content. My eyes teared up as I had explained to him that I'd spent a good deal of my life pleasing others and entertaining the most boring people at dinner parties, social and charity events, not because I'd chosen them but because they'd chosen me.

Michael assured me that our future would be solid with none of that. I thanked him and kissed him as we made love all over again. It was then between those sheets tangled in our love that I realized he'd given my life purpose. A purpose greater than anything I'd ever known. By loving him, by befriending him, I could convince him to be calm, to negotiate, and to make our countries one as our hearts.

But he had reached over to the bedside table, the gaiety fading from his eyes. He pulled out a British memorandum typed on an Underwood typewriter dated October 27, 1921. "De Valera has put me in a very tough position," he said, handing it to me.

"And Shane Leslie is utterly jealous of our closeness," I said, my mind ticking.

"Who?"

"Shane Leslie, first cousin to Winston. Sends me hideous love poems. Spells out my name and uses the first letter like this..." clearing my throat, I faked a man's voice. 'H: how can I tell you. A: All the deep nadirs of despair I know. Z: Zeniths of joy... and so on, until he spells Hazel."

"Jesus, Mary and Joseph," he said, "But can ye blame him? Yer like a drug to us idealistic men."

Sitting up, I gathered the sheets around my waist, shook the paper out straight and read its contents from the English to the Irish. "The Crown is the symbol of all that keeps the nations of the

Empire together. It is the keystone of the arch in law as well as in sentiment...

"The British Government must know whether the Irish Delegates are prepared that Ireland should maintain its ancient allegiance to the Throne, not as a state subordinate to Great Britain, but as one of the Nations of the Commonwealth, in close association with the Realm of England, Scotland, and Wales.

Scanning the pages – and there were many, more a book than a memorandum - it went on and on about Common Citizenship, Defense, Trade and Commerce, and Finance.

Placing it alongside of me, I lowered my body and took his head onto my chest. "Don't give in," I said, and then gently, running my fingers through his bangs as he lay on my breast. "You have a lot to contend with but don't give in."

"I just want it to all be over," he whispered. It's when I realized our hearts and souls had both been deeply tried in their own way. The room at Claridge's didn't stir just then. The silence lay on us with the weight of things final and irrevocable. After a long while, I moved downward to put my face next to his. "We'd have been happy."

"Because we're not?" he asked, looking straight into my eyes, and crawling back on top of me.

This was love. The words were yet to be spoken, but implied. Until now...

"I love you Hazel Martyn Lavery." He quivered as he spoke.

A long smile crossed my face as I stared deep past his eyes into his soul. "I love you too, Michael Collins." Forgive me, Father, for I have sinned. I've committed adultery....

As we clung to each other and he thrust inside of me, the rhythm of his moves matched the rhythm of my thoughts...

Each time you happen to me all over again…

Each time you happen to me all over again...

Each time...

Chapter Thirty-three

Michael

It was late November, and the Anglo-Irish negotiations were making progress. They had begun to divide into smaller conferences so that they might have more direct negotiations. On certain days Michael was hopeful – as was I – that he'd be bringing a new Republic back to Ireland. On other days, things would go terribly wrong, the English insisting they'd only come to future agreements and eventual peace if he accepted the Crown.

Because of Michael's association with John and me, I decided that enough was enough. If Michael and I were to ever have a real life together, these negotiations needed to wrap up. By Christmas. Oh, how I wished he'd spend Christmas here...

But I knew in my heart the Irish delegates would head home for the holidays. And once home, with no guarantee that the negotiations would be completed, why would they bother to return to England at all?

There had to be a way! I paced my boudoir as the sun came up over the park just outside my window, the park where Michael first kissed me. If I had to see the darn treaty signed and framed at 5 Cromwell Place, by George, I would! But what could I do?

Clementine confided in me that Winston had told her that Michael had lost his patience and had begun to show his temper. As my home played a central diplomatic role during the treaties, I arranged a few meetings. On one occasion, Lloyd George stormed out of my house, and I ran after him, in the light falling snow, which made for a lovely effect, as I begged him to give me an hour. I would convince Michael and deliver him the next day myself to Downing Street for final negotiations.

In the meantime, I tried to convince Michael, left brooding, pacing in the drawing room, to take what negotiations he could get now and get the rest later... not too dissimilar to our romance in which rumors had been circulating.

People wondered if I was just a kind and decent woman making allies, bringing peace to the world, while others were jealous and thought I was seeking attention. At one point, Winston told Clementine that he thought John and I were angling for knighthood except John already had that, so what was it we wanted? Clementine knew of my truth but kept mum. And John, his head barely out of the paint-pot, suggested I not spend so much exclusive time with Michael for fear he was confiding matters with me that were compromising to the negotiations.

On top of it all, we'd begun receiving piles of hate mail calling me a "traitor" and I should be "murdered." Hiding the letters from John, and when he was in his study, I simply tossed them into the fire. Certainly, the police would have little sympathy for me sleeping with the enemy! Let's face it, I'd finally made the biggest name for myself by being practically 'wanted' but not only by my lover... instead by Irish terrorists and British Intelligence!

Michael felt we provided sufficient gossip to fuel speculations from both sides. I agreed.

To lessen the gossip, I turned the situation back on the English, continuing to remind Lloyd George, Birkenhead, and the others, that John had a Patriotic duty. He must finish the paintings that would represent the Treaty for the Irish collection. It would be historical, monumental, or whatever dignified words I could conjure up at this point, all to avoid the obvious. I needed to keep them all nearby so I could keep Michael nearby. This was love.

And a dog...

John was in his study beginning a painting of Earl Mosley Addressing the House of Lords, on a massive canvas of 50 x 40 in all its grandeur when I entered with a barking pup.

"And who have we here?" asked John, reaching down to pet the dog who ran in circles, tail wagging frantically.

"It's a Kerry Blue. A gift from Michael."

"Oh?" John looked at the dog and then at me. "Have you named him?"

"Mick!" I said proudly, patting the dog along the backside. "Stay! Down boy!"

"Quite amusing! Why aren't I surprised?"

"Apparently they're bred to control vermin and badgers and foxes," I said, proudly. "Good working dog for sheep herding."

"I'll keep that in mind should I ever own a flock." John chuckled at his own joke. 'Mick' growled at John who set down his paintbrush and put out a hand to pet him. "I suspect that the dog is intended to frighten away everyone except Collins."

"The painting is coming out splendid, Johnnie," I said, ignoring his previous comment. "Look at the details of the assembly. Rich and mellow in color... the effects are quite beautiful and dignified." The dog ran around, batting his tail and knocking over John's paint cups. "Let me deliver Mick to Mr. Wallace. He'll need a good bath, a walk and some training."

"Not necessarily in that order," said John, going back to his canvas as I exited with the barking dog...

Perhaps the dog was Michael's way of letting me go. For now. Because for days he suddenly went missing.

At the Brompton Oratory – our usual 8 a.m. church date – he was no place to be found, three mornings in a row. When the phone rang, I leapt with hope in front of Mr. Wallace, but it was never him. At a certain point, I began to think he'd been secretly murdered.

Later that night, I woke up sitting upright and screamed in my bed.

"What is it?" asked John, dashing into my room, and pulling on the light switch.

I tried to get my bearings in the dark, and then went silent with a panting perspiration beading around my forehead.

"What is it, my dear?" asked John again, taking me by the shoulders.

"Oh, John I had a terrible nightmare," I said, "a premonition of sorts. It wasn't good." I fell into his arms, and we sat there, him petting me down.

"You must tell me, Hazel..."

I pulled away and pulled the sheets around my neck, lying down slowly and staring at the ceiling. "It was a bad dream. They were carrying Michael away covered with blood."

"There, there. It's only a dream, Hazel. It's not true." He pulled me in and stroked my back like one might do to a child...

The next day there was a knock at the door, and as Mr. Wallace opened it, I was already standing behind him. There was Michael at the door. Thank God!

"Sorry to be MIA from the IRA," said Michael.

"Not amusing. You had me petrified," I said, as Mick the dog jumped round Michael's legs in excitement. I asked Mr. Wallace to take the pup as I took Michael by the hand into my drawing room and closed the double doors, exhaling loudly.

"I've been worried for days!" I said, going in for a massive hug.

"It's gone crazy," said Michael, his voice vibrating off the walls as he backed up and rambled. "More and more responsibility rests with me. I've been held up with Lloyd George upstairs and then I'm back downstairs with Birkenhead and Churchill, and then all of us together. Me, outnumbered by the three of 'em!" Michael began pacing, practically crying and at times raising his voice, his face turning red with upset. "Lloyd George has bullied me!"

"What?" I said, myself pacing with intensity.

"The bias of his speech is either accept the terms or we go to war, yeah?"

"Oh, dear," I said, lost for words.

"I've until 9 pm tonight. Tonight!"

"Tonight? Just like that?" I asked, going to him, but he moved to the other side of the room, one hand on his hip and the other under his chin. "I've written to Dev. Told him this is a real nest of singing birds! They chirrup mightily one to the other, and there's the falseness of it all, because not one trusts the other." He began pacing again. "Lloyd George's attitude, well, I find it to be particularly obnoxious. He is all comrade-ly – all craft and wiliness – all arm around shoulder, all old friends' act. But that's it. It's an act! Not so long ago he would have joyfully had me at the end of a rope! He thinks that the past is all washed out now, but that's to my face. What he thinks, no doubt, is behind my back. Well, makes me sick at the thought of it..."

Just then John was at the door, having been listening in after hearing raised voices from his study. "Michael, calm down, my friend. Let me mix you a drink. Maybe ole George is only bluffing."

"Bluffing? I wish, John," said Michael. "Just have a look out yer window!"

And at that, John moved to the window to see the military guarding their home. "Heavens! Is that Scotland Yard?"

"Aye!" said Michael. "They're outside my residence at Cadogan Place, too. Right now! All week, yeah."

I led Michael to the sofa and took his hand in mine. John went around the back side of the sofa, placing a hand on Michael's shoulder. As John and I shared a look, one that said Michael was in grave danger, I declared, "Perhaps it's best you stay here. For now. Go no place."

"Yes," said John, on cue. "The thing is good boy, no one knew what you looked like before. Now, with all the press and all the parties, you'll be a moving target."

"Do you think it would help if I spoke to Lloyd George?" I

asked, looking to John for guidance. “Throw a gathering?”

“Good God woman, no!” said John standing and pacing now himself. “This is hardly the time for one of your gin and jazz-fueled soirees!”

“Isn’t it? Because they seem to work,” I spat. And then, I bit my tongue. Cautious not to say more. John never took me seriously while Michael did nothing but take me seriously.

Then John looked down at Michael, who had turned white as a ghost. “I think you’ll have to sign, Lad. Ireland can’t survive another war even if I can get a group of us to finance you...”

“And then what?” said Michael, looking up, “Go home? To my country? Tell ‘em I signed, and they are still swearing allegiance to the Crown?”

“Oh, poor dear,” I said, taking Michael into my arms on the sofa, but awkwardly as he wouldn’t budge, and besides, John was right there watching. Michael dropped his face into his hands and sobbed. Like a child. Not childish but childlike. I looked at John, who shrugged his shoulders. He was at a loss. This wasn’t good. Far too much for one young thirty-year-old man to handle. All this negotiating, all this friendship, all this time and no resolve.

John moved to the liquor cart, pouring equal parts tomato juice and vodka into a glass. Stirring it he began to sip.

“Johnnie, what on earth?” I asked.

“Called a Bloody Mary. It’s the latest fashionable drink from Paris,” said John. “Seems appropriate for the moment.” John handed a full glass to Michael who shook his head ‘no’ so John drank his anyway. “Yes,” said John between sips and speaking very matter-of-factly. “You sign the treaty. And I’ll be sure to give Winston and Lloyd George a piece of my mind.”

“John’s right,” I said, “You sign now, to avoid war, and you tell your people that. You don’t want them slaughtered. And then, in time, you negotiate on the backend. As a stall tactic.”

“Hazel’s correct, Michael,” said John. “For now, you compromise. You’ll be a hero if you sign to spare your people any more bloodshed.”

"I'll be a dead man not a hero is what I'll be..." said Michael, and at that, John chugged the rest of his drink and moved on to drink what would have been Michael's.

"Right," I said, standing up, opening the double doors, and calling out, "Mr. Wallace?

Mr. Wallace!" But he was already there. "Oh, yes, Mr. Wallace. I need you to get Lloyd George on the phone for me. Tell him I'll need a car. He's to call off his guards. I'll be personally delivering Michael Collins to Downing Street, tout suite!"

"Hazel, you can't!" said Michael, now standing.

"I can and I will."

And then John chimed in, "Once she's made her mind up, there's no stopping her..."

As Michael got up to head to the door, John came over and whispered in my ear. "Be careful there." His words meant many things.

"Yes, of course," I said, looking deeply into John's eyes and never intending to hurt him.

"Alice and I need you," he whispered. "Eileen, too."

"Yes, I know, Sir John," I said, "And Mick needs me, as well." On cue, the dog was back, jumping about.

Chapter Thirty-four
Hazel, Michael & a Treaty

The night of December 6th was exceptionally long. I paced from room to room in my dressing gown and robe, the only sound coming from the ticktock of the grandfather clock in the marble hall... until, finally, the bell at the door chimed. "Got it Mr. Wallace! Not to worry..." I hollered behind me. "Go back to sleep."

"Very well, My Lady," he called out, shuffling back to his quarters.

As I pulled open the door there stood Michael, no bodyguards, and a full face hung low. "Michael!" I exclaimed, grabbing his arm to take him inside and then glancing over his shoulder and down the street to where the sun would soon be rising.

"No need to worry about them now," he said, "I've done it. I signed the bloody thing..."

"Brilliant!" I said, taking him in for a hug. He allowed me to just hold him as he stood stiffly and defeated. "Oh darling, it's over now. You've done it!"

He pulled back. "No, I didn't do it. God made it happen. Peace for Ireland." He smiled, gazing down at me, his face sleepy, "And I wanted to say goodbye. Gotta go home."

"Understood," I said. "But you must eat. Breakfast now, a bath and a rest? You must be exhausted. Shall I get the room made up?"

"No, Hazel. I must return to Ireland. With the treaty."

"Now?"

He nodded 'yes' and then commented. "At 2:30 a.m. – could the day have been any longer? But they had indeed typed a final redraft of the treaty. Griffin said to Lloyd George, 'Mr. Prime Minister, the delegation is willing to sign the agreements,' and so we did."

"And then what?" I asked.

"It happened." He exhaled hard. "And as Birkenhead handed me the pen for signature, he remarked that he was signing his political death warrant."

"What did you say?"

"That I might be signing my own death warrant."

His tone scared me. "Oh Michael, no," I said. The look on my face turned to fear.

"Don't worry," he said, pulling me into his chest. "I'm not going to die."

"How do you know?" I said, whimpering.

"Because a good Irish man never does what's expected of him. And I'm expected to die." He kissed my head and then took my face in his hands.

Then he pulled back and reached into his pocket. Pulling out a pen. "Here. It's all yours," he said. "The pen we shared to sign the bloody agreement."

From a distance we heard John approaching. Michael leaned in to kiss me tenderly on the lips before studying my face as if it were the last time that he might ever see it. "I can't greet John just now. Please, thank him for everything and his support," and then Michael was out the door, dodging the public, the world, and the still of the night.

I was left standing in an empty doorway, suspecting that in the long run, loving him might be a losing battle...

When John entered the room, I was at the window. He watched me watching Michael go down the street. "Bravest man I've ever met," said John, shaking his head. "Sadly, his people will turn against him. As a traitor."

"Don't say that, Johnnie! Why will they turn? He hasn't betrayed anyone. He's saved his country!!"

"Yes, but there are some Irish who still believe Ireland isn't ready for peace. They prefer gun powder."

I couldn't let Michael go alone, so I followed him.

To Dublin. We met at the Shelbourne hotel.

The press began to target Michael's behavior, describing him as "Passionate, forcible, and at times almost theatrical" which I saw as translation to: 'purely fed up with the entire set of circumstances.' He was exhausted. They went on to make a celebrity mockery out of him. "His flashing eyes, firm jaw and thick black hair, through which he ran his fingers from time to time, were all revealed under the dazzling lights of the electroliers." And in the evenings, he shared and read to me the speech he intended to give the following day.

"How about I give this a go..." said Michael clearing his throat to begin: "In my opinion, the treaty gives us freedom, not the ultimate freedom that all nations desire and develop to, but the freedom to achieve it... we have stated we would not coerce the North-East. We have stated it officially. I stated it publicly in Armagh and nobody has found fault with me. What was the use of not agreeing to the partition of our country? Surely, we recognize that the North-East corner does exist, and surely our intention was that we should take steps that would lead to mutual understanding."

"It's good," I said, hesitating. "But reinforce the point of what the goal intended to be. Even after the signing."

"Yeah?" he asked, then crossing out a sentence and adding in this: "The Treaty has made an effort – to deal with on lines that will lead very rapidly to goodwill and the entry of the North-East under the Irish Parliament."

"Perfect!" I said, going in for a hug as I tussled playfully at his hair.

As the treaty was debated by his peers, I enjoyed holiday season shopping for Eileen and Alice, and a new leather flask for John. I enjoyed breakfasts with George Bernard Shaw, lunched with our family friend, J. M. Barrie, and supped with Lady and Lord-Lieutenant of Ireland. But I reserved my most special nights for Michael, even though near misses filled his days.

On one afternoon, a young man held Michael at gunpoint, but thankfully he managed to disarm him. But the near miss bullets followed too, day after day. And the constant screams at his back, "Traitor!"

The angry Irish had little understanding of the pressures Michael was put under and why he finally had to sign. Instead, they were certain Michael and his colleague and friend, Griffith, were drunk or drugged or both, when signing the treaty. For Michael he had the added "sex-crazed" man, which couldn't have been further from the truth, but we couldn't go public as I was a married woman in an affair. But his behavior in the early days of the IRA had been sleeping in the guest beds and sofas of those who helped him hide and escape, which was anything but romantic. Both Michael and his men knew what it was to spend a night, literally within seconds of their deaths. Oh, why would his own people turn on him now?

More crazy rumors began to escalate to the point that he'd broken up a royal romance with Princess Mary. And Michael himself was to wed her, making him First Governor. Foolishness! He'd never even met the woman!

We tried to make light of it, but I could see the pain in Michael's face that his own people – the ones cut from the same plain cloth as he'd come from – had trivialized all that he'd done, all that he'd accomplished.

The sad bit was that for all the rumors of the IRA boys being "womanizers" they returned home to Ireland, relieved, and short of Michael, all wed into strict Catholic marriages.

And then there was Kitty Kiernan, the woman Michael really had been involved with sending him letters of love and anger. Letters he shared with me as the only person he could trust and who understood him.

But Michael defended his people despite their uproar. He heard his people's pain. Like them, he didn't like the treaty he signed with England despite his allies believing it was the first step to not only uniting Ireland but giving them full independence...

It was clear just before Christmas, that the press and public reaction was mostly with him. For the time being, all was safe and sound...

Chapter Thirty-five

Hazel

The Dail recessed on December 22nd, when I returned to England to celebrate Christmas with John, the girls and 'Mick,' our jumping, drooling, misbehaving dog.

Home-made Christmas cards had become popular, so the girls and I worked at the kitchen table constructing unusual shapes with foils and ribbons. When we walked to the post office in Kensington to mail the ones not too fragile to go through the slot, I was reminded of the first time I met Michael in this very place. But now, a new young eager clerk smiled and assisted Alice and me. In addition, I made a daily jaunt to the pillar box to drop a letter to Michael in Ireland. My only way to stay connected to him...

It seemed that wherever I was, whatever I did, Michael was with me or so I told him in our latest holiday correspondence... and of course, despite the turmoil he was dealing with, I tried to find the positive in all of it....

> My dearest darling, my secret, my love,
>
> I was so excited to read the details of your military welcome in Dublin. You are on the cover of every newspaper I can get my hands on. But it's made more special to receive the personal notes from you detailing your emotions.
>
> Christmas is always a sentimental time of year for me. I

reflect on my father and how Christmas was the last time that I saw him. December 25th has become a time when I long to be close to those I love. That includes you.

And I will think of nothing but you as the priest delivers midnight mass and communion. I'm sure he'll be wondering where you've gone off to, but I'm certain he also reads the papers. I keep you in my heart and thoughts and will light the biggest possible candle at Mass to burn in your victory...

As I celebrate Christmas with orange-zest hot toddies and spiked holiday punches – John's latest concoctions – how I wish you were here with us and Alice, and of course, Eileen, who you've yet to meet – and our dog, Mick, who wags his tail at the mere mention of your name. I adore him, and who at this very moment is at my ankle gnawing on the biggest bone that Mr. Wallace has snuck him from the kitchen scraps.

Oh dear, wonderful Michael, please don't despair that you're alone at the Gresham hotel much of the holiday. Christmas is only one day of the year. And what you're doing is the final round of the final round, and by next year at this time, we might all be together, celebrating. And Ireland will be free. They'll be celebrating YOU!

Besides, you'll see your best friend, Harry soon, finally back from America. He'll be by your side for those negotiations in Ireland, and I shall be there the early part of January when we will celebrate our own private little Christmas. I long to be by the fire, snuggled in each other's arms. Heaven!

Until then, let me know you are safe and warm and loved by friends and family. In haste just now, as I'm dashing to the kitchen. Alice has taken to baking our favorite shortbread biscuits and the timer has just alerted us that they're ready to come out of the oven.

Merry Christmas, darling. With love as ever, xH

This was a festive holiday, a relief of sorts, having spent the last year and a half with a home full of dignitaries. It was lovely to experience my home without responsibility... lovely to attend other friends' social events, the envelopes of invitations piling at the foyer table... to let my hair down and stay in my dressing gown all day as the girls opened their gifts under the seven-foot fir tree with German glass ornaments. We purchased a new RCA radiola with loudspeaker for fun, in addition to the things they'd need for their own homes – more Bone china settings and silver to add to their collections.

There were the latest flapper styles. John got such a kick out of the girls in matching dresses completely covered in fringe that shook on their bodies when they danced, revealing a slip of leg. John and I had everything we could want in the material sense, so Old Saint Nick seemed to know we could use a new Victrola. John, of course, being Old Saint Nick.

"Johnnie, you shouldn't have!" As he kissed my forehead, I could sense an understanding in the exchange between us.

"Thank you," he said, his eyes moist with emotion.

"Always, my love," I said, and squeezed his hand, reading between the lines.

"Enough Momsie. It's time to open our final gift," she said, kneeling at the tree to gather it. "Eileen and I bought it together."

Alice stood over me as I unwrapped the box from Selfridges, a high-end clothing store founded by our friend Harry Selfridge who was always spoiling me with specials and alerting me to seasonal sales. The tissue paper crinkled from my anxious fingers. I removed a lovely embroidered shawled dress which was all the rage in high society.... "Oh, Girls, it's stunning!" Of course, my mind went right to Michael. "Emerald color! My favorite!" I said, standing and pinning the dress against myself as I twirled. "Irish green," I smiled. "I love it, my girls. And I love you!"

But as the season ended and the new year was upon us, all I could think of was Michael's situation in Ireland, still far from over...

On January 7,1922, as I paced my room in the Shelbourne hotel of Dublin, sixty-four voted in favor and fifty-seven against ratification. Two days later, Michael's 'friend' de Valera - resigned, opposing the treaty. A slap in Michael's face as he was the one to send him to the negotiations in the first place when Michael knew that it should have been de Valera to represent the Irish. In my way of seeing things, de Valera had always chosen to sit in the trenches sipping champagne while Michael had long fought the war in a field and from behind a Downing Street conference table.

The good news, if there could be any, was that all over Ireland, the red, white, and blue British flags came down the flagpoles, and the green, white, and orange flags were hoisted up.

A provincial government was set up consisting of Michael, W.T. Cosgrave, Arthur Griffith, Eamon Duggan, and Joseph McGrath, now President of the Dail. These were worthy men who had stood by Michael fighting for their country.

John had painted every one of their portraits during the negotiations in England. There was also one of Kevin O'Higgins and Harry Boland added to the group, Michael's best friend.

Elected as Chairman, Michael had a new and daunting weight on him to implement and uphold the treaty, which in fact, was not only unacknowledged by the British, but had picketers of anti-Treaty-ites forming everywhere all over Ireland. The north of Belfast and surrounding areas were still pro-British and remained Protestant to their core.

At times Michael was unsure if what he'd stepped into was a choice between the Treaty and a Civil War, or between an independent republic and British rule. The lines often blurred.

In August that year, Michael's best friend, Harry Boland was mortally shot; Arthur Griffith, who had been by his side from the start, died of a heart attack.

And within weeks...the worst of all...

One afternoon a handwritten letter marked "private" arrived at the Shelbourne from Winston. Running my finger along the seam of the seal I opened it to reveal these words:

> My dear Hazel,
>
> I had a very pleasant talk with M.C. this morning and hope to see him again on Monday. I am very glad he and his colleagues are dining with you tonight. I am sure your influence will be exerted in the cause of peace... I ought to let you know 'confidentially' that my colleagues take a most grave view of the Constitution...

It was then that I realized Michael's frustration of yet another political battle in keeping the Constitution separate from the Treaty...

While I had many trips back and forth to Ireland in the early part of the New Year, it was on one night, months later, in August, when Michael and I had been dining with Horace Plunkett. Horace had become increasingly important in my life. While I didn't tell him romantic details as I had with Clementine, it was clear every time that Michael and I dined with him. Though, of course, we only made it all seem official business.

Over baked pork chops, Michael explained in detail his great ambivalence over Dublin and the Nationalists. Michael informed me he was off to Cork where he would finally reunite with his people, to inspect a tour of the south and bring the fighting to an end.

"But you're feverish and not feeling well," I insisted. "And your men – your friends – are all being murdered!"

"I've got to go..." he insisted back. "There must be peace. Just last week I attended a funeral. The Mass was heartbreaking... the poor women weeping and almost shrieking for their dead sons. Someone's sister and one wife were there, too, and a few small children." Michael shook his head. "It's enough, Hazel. I must seek peace among my own, yeah?'

I slid over and took the seat between Michael and the window, only to later discover I'd been blocking the view of a gunman all along. How did I know this?

Because later as we entered my car, the three of us huddled in the backseat before dropping off Horace, the same sniper shot half a dozen bullets at our vehicle. Michael grabbed my torso and lowered it quickly to below the windshield level as glass shattered.

We escaped narrowly around the corner from Horace's house which no one suspected as a destination since no one knew we were dining with Horace. The driver pulled onto the curb and silenced the engine, lowering the headlights. As we exhaled, we held hands, the three of us, relieved to be alive.

"The bullets must have gone over our heads!" said Horace, stunned that none of us were hurt as the driver got out to examine only a few deep 'dings' in the side of my car with a torchlight.

"I should have had a bodyguard," said Michael turning to Horace. "Forgive me."

"It's all well and done. I'll be fine," said Horace. "But you Michael, well, all our thoughts and prayers are with you."

"Surely they'll find the sniper," said Michael.

"Who?" asked Horace.

"An ex-Connaught Ranger, Dixon, I suspect," said Michael.

Horace shook Michael's hand, looked both ways, exited the car, and then lowered the brim of his hat to head down the street.

"God bless you," said Michael as he lowered the window to call back to Horace.

Horace formed a prayer pose and kissed the tip of his fingers, slanting them toward Michael.

I then asked the driver to give us a moment, so he remained outside of the car and lit a cigarette. Michael turned to me in the backseat, positioning himself to take me square by the shoulders, "My love," he said, "I am sorry to put your life and that of your friend's in jeopardy."

"It's quite alright, darling. So long as I'm with you. I think you're probably invincible. Either that or I'm a feckin eejit!" I added, imitating him.

We both giggled in relief and he bent forward and kissed me gently before pulling back to speak. "Let me make it clear that I look forward to when this is all over. God knows, after last year, I never want to spend another Christmas held up alone in a hotel room where the only gift I get is a handwritten note slipped under the door wishing me "Happy Christmas" from the hotel manager.

"You won't, I promise," I chuckled, trying to make light of it, my gloved-pointy-finger outlining his profile, as he never took his eyes off me. "Next Christmas and every New Year and even Easter, somehow, some way we'll be together," I assured. As my finger outlined his mouth, he nibbled it playfully between his teeth before whispering into my ear, "I love you.'

"Fer sure!" I said, imitating him again, and pecking the side of his neck, inhaling the scent that belonged to only me, to my heart, to my soul. My Eve to his Adam.

He closed his eyes in happiness, a look that would stay with me forever and a day...

...because everything I believed in, everything I hoped for, was about to change in an instant. With a bullet...

Chapter Thirty-six

Michael

For weeks I would repeatedly read the police transcript, comparing it to my love letters for their date and time, as if it would make a difference. As if it would change something. It didn't. But I did the best I could to piece-meal the answers of what the final moments were... which went something like this:

Michael's convoy left Portobello Barracks, Dublin at 5:15 a.m. that Sunday of August 20th, making his first stop at a place where he spoke of transferring some of the prisoners out to Gormanston camp to relieve the overcrowded conditions.

As the convoy headed to Roscrea Barracks, he and his men had breakfast before the inspection. Over eggs and coffee, General Eoin O'Duffy discussed ending the Civil War now. With the shake of a hand, Michael headed to Cork City which would have taken some four hours, so he stayed the night in the military headquarters in the Imperial Hotel.

Every day along his journey he wrote me a short note, posting it from each destination, so I felt I was with him on his adventure home. He told me that he'd had a reunion with his sister, Mary Collins-Powell, and her son, and that the rest of the evening, over a very fine whiskey – and since John and Winston had spoiled him for such – he spent in consultations with General Emmet Dalton. Together the two felt that normalcy would not be too far off. That made Michael's "heart swell with pride for his people" or so his letter told me.

The next day, Monday, August 21, he spent the morning with General Dalton. Together they visited the Cork Examiner to discuss the general Free State position with the editor, Tom Crosbie, who he said was a very likable lad. For lunch, instead of eating, he visited some of the local banks to trace republican/IRA/anti-Treaty funds from during their occupation of the city. It was worth a try since over 120,000 pounds had been collected in customs revenue and kept stashed in the accounts of sympathizers. Michael told me that he told the bank managers to lock the doors. He was only allowed to reopen if they cooperated. He then had the bank identify the suspicious accounts via a forensic investigation and said that upon his return, they'd decide how best to handle the missing funds. He shook the bank manager's hand, who wished him well. Michael had incredible integrity where money was concerned.

Again, he visited with his sister for tea and biscuits. They shared stories of their parents and their childhood on the farm. And before he departed, asked her to be sure to get the next letter to me in the Post. Yes, apparently, he told her all about us and the hope for our future. In that letter he told me she gave him her blessing, which meant the world to him, despite her concerns that he was a devout Catholic who had been committing adultery with a married woman. We recognized the hypocrisy, but our intention was to someday make it right and wed.

Michael's day ended over dinner thirty miles away at Macroom, where he met Florence O'Donoghue, a leader of the IRA in County Cork. He felt Florence could offer some advice on how to stop the Civil War and assist in future consultations. She assured him he'd done good by his people.

He wrote the next letter on August 22, 1922, as the sun came up over the hills. He could imagine a new life and a day, every day, with me. He drove in a yellow Leland Thomas Straight Engine. Emmet Dalton was in the front seat, so it allowed Michael to write a letter to me, as his driver, Private Michael Smith Corry, whisked him through the countryside. M. Quinn was the reserve driver, sitting in the back seat with Michael.

Behind them, a Rolls Royce Whippet armored car nicknamed the A.R.R.2, was carrying Captain Joe Dolan. A man named Jim Wolfe was the driver, Jimmy “Wiggy” Fortune the co-driver, and the machine-gunner on the armored car was “Jock” McPeak.

As I read that letter, something pitter-pattered in my heart. Some instinct. Some stirring worry that the military backup was not enough to protect the Free State Commander-in-Chief. They were, after all, traveling through many active anti-Treaty areas of South Cork.

When they stopped the convoy in Macroom heading towards Beal na Blath to get directions in the early morning, Michael picked a dried wildflower from the side of the road and pressed it in the clasp of the ruby brooch possessing my photo. He told me he couldn’t stop removing it from his chest pocket to steal a glance.

They stopped for lunch at Callinan’s Pub in Clonakilty. The men greeted him as they did with one fist slapped into a palm, and pats on the back. It was there he had a half hour to write me a proper letter. Or so he’d begun writing it, and then was called back to the truck, by the others, knowing he’d finish it later when he arrived at the hotel.

He attempted to finish the letter to me. “...we will go further with the British government once there is peace here in Ireland. I believe now that the British have given up their claim on us – though I hope that doesn’t include you, dear Hazel – then we might work together to help those in the northeast.” Michael meant Belfast by saying “the northeast,” and it caught my attention as that’s where John had been born a lifetime ago into poverty.

“I’m feeling sentimental now and must end this letter, until later. We’re about to drive by the remains of my childhood home, Woodfield, burned practically to the ground.”

I later learned from Dalton that Michael was quiet as they departed his family farm. He didn’t say much on the road toward Bandon either, except he kept closing his eyes to rest, reaching in his chest pocket, and pulling out a rosary in one hand and my brooch in the other.

As the convoy left the Eldon Hotel and headed back to Cork there were many roadblocks due to many of the roads being destroyed. As bombings during the war destroyed the bridges, they had no choice but to circle back around to Clonakilty. As they carried through, Michael thought of those who wanted him dead. Leaning forward to the front seat, he patted Dalton on the shoulder and said, "Yerra, they will never shoot me in my own country."

"Don't be so sure," said Dalton on the road out of Bandon heading north. "As you said before... after signing the treaty, 'will anyone be satisfied with this bargain?'"

"If we run into an ambush along the way, we'll stand and fight 'em," said Michael.

Dalton later told me he didn't know how to respond, so he said nothing.

And an ambush party there was.

The ambush met in Long's Pub and spotted Michael's party as it passed through Beal na Blath. The men were officers trained in guerrilla warfare though unaware that Michael, who they wanted to kill all along, was in their vicinity, until early that morning. They stopped an innocent Clonakilty local named Jeremiah O'Brien, who was only delivering cartloads of empty mineral bottles to Bandon. Together they surrounded his cart, removed one of the wheels, which would force the cart to block the road. They also put a mine in its place, which would force Michael's convoy to unexpectedly stop.

The ambush party was approximately thirty men, who took turns waiting in place in the hills. But as the ambush party surrounded the area with weapons and waited in place most of the day, nothing happened. It was because Michael's men had returned the way they came in, due again, to the multiple roadblocks.

When Michael's convoy came into view, just before sunset, at approximately 7 p.m., the first shots were fired. Dalton looked to their driver and called out, "Drive like hell!"

But Michael, being Michael, countered the command with "Stop! We'll fight 'em!"

And fight they did or so the newspapers reported. Michael and Dalton first fired from behind their armored car. "There! They're running up the road!" Michael shouted, taking aim.

But the machine gun in the armored car jammed up several times, allowing the IRA fighters to take advantage. They shimmied on their belly, closer to their target...

For whatever reason, Michael ran about fifteen yards up the road, dropped into a firing position and continued shooting at the men, which must have saddened him as they were once his own comrades.

"Emmet, I'm hit!" was the faint cry Dalton heard coming from Michael. Commander O'Connell ran over to where Michael was now lying face-down on the road. Dalton examined him and found a massive wound at the base of his skull behind the right ear. Michael knew his comrades were there but was unable to speak.

They rolled him over gently.

O'Connell knelt beside the dying, but conscious Michael. As though he could read Michael's wide opened eyes, he began to recite the words of Act of Contrition. "O my God, I am heartily sorry for having offended Thee: and I detest my sins most sincerely because they displease Thee, my God, who art so deserving of all my love for Thy infinite goodness and most amiable perfections: and I firmly purpose by Thy holy grace never more to offend Thee."

A small smile crossed Michael's lips and with a slight squeeze of O'Connell's hand, he murmured a word.

"What me Lad?" asked O'Connell, leaning his ear into Michael's lips.

"Haaa-zel," Michael struggled to form the word. His final thought.

Very gently, O'Connell placed Michael's head on Dalton's knee and attempted to bandage him, but the size of the wound and the amount of blood made it near impossible.

A cold grey death spread over Michael's face.

The thirty-one-year-old idol of the Irish was lying in the mud, his head cradled in Dalton's hands, all but twelve miles from Clonakilty, where it all began, murdered not by the English, but by his own countrymen.

Michael Collins died that day, but as a soldier, not a politician, which is what he would have wanted.

His body was placed in the car for the sad journey back to Cork City where they pulled up outside of The Sacred Heart Mission at Victoria Cross. Father O'Brien administered last rites. As Michael's body was loaded upon the steamship SS Classic which left Penrose Quay sailing down channel, General Dalton sent a telegram to the Dublin Headquarters:

Chief of Staff Dublin. Stop. Commander-in-Chief shot dead in Ambush at Bealnablath near Bandon approximately 6.30 Tuesday evening with me. Stop. Also, one man wounded. Remains leaving by classic for Dublin today, Wednesday, noon. Arrange to meet. Stop. Reply. Dalton.

Shortly after, the press was notified... and so was the world...

First in *The Day*, a three-cent paper in Ireland with the headline:

"DRAPED IN IRELAND'S TRICOLOR FLAG, BODY OF MICHAEL COLLINS LIES IN COFFIN IN DUBLIN HOSPITAL."

More papers followed:

THE BIG FELLA IS GONE!!!

Chapter Thirty-seven

Hazel

The maid came in earlier than usual with my English Breakfast tea tray, pulling the satin cords to the blinds of my room to distribute the light. John usually came to greet me, but I was certain he was in his studio allocating the final touches on his recent portrait of Lord Carson of Duncairn.

"Good morning, my Lady," she said, before adding quite casually, "They have shot, Mr. Collins."

"What?" I snapped, immediately alert, and gathered my robe and slippers. "Who did? Is he alive?"

"All in the newspaper, it is," she nodded to the newspaper before quietly excusing herself. Dashing to the tray table my hand shook as I lifted The Times bringing the headline closer:

MICHAEL COLLINS KILLED! A national tragedy. Killed in native country.

I let out the loudest scream as my body gave way to the carpet, reaching for the nearby table for support. Crawling to my fainting couch, I clutched a throw pillow, burying my face into it. The first thing I thought was this was all my fault. Every man I'd ever loved was bound to die.

A second unrecognizable sound radiated from my body; a moan so deep from the pit of my stomach to the depths of my soul. As my world came down around me, I curled onto the carpet, my knees under my chest, rocking myself, bent in a mantra of pain.

After a while, I sat up, lifting myself from the floor and through blurred eyes I scanned the article rapidly to gather information faster than my tears hit the ink. "Killed in an ambush in Cork despite Emmet Dalton pleading with him not to set off that day as though he could see it coming..."

Lowering the paper to the carpet, I stared into nothingness. Panic gripped me. It was as if the past tragedy of family deaths was merely a warmup for the most heartbreaking and personal of all. Michael.

My mind flickered to the bullet points of the man that was Michael Collins. I could write one-hundred things I loved about him in an instant, and then turn the list into one-thousand things even faster. The way you ran your fingers down my spine tickling my buttocks, the way you buttered your toast in the early mornings, the way you squinted your eyes with pleasure, the way you tipped your hat...

The clock on the mahogany sideboard ticked the time, the seconds, the minutes – 7 a.m. – with many seconds, minutes, hours, days, months, and years, I would now live without him.

We had planned a future together. To do everything together. Except to die.

Gazing bleary-eyed up to the ceiling in my room, and then to the wall where a crystal lamp shone on a Dublin landscape that I'd hung next to a small picture of Father from my youth. Ireland and Father. Michael and Ireland. Michael and Father. And now in heaven, he's with you, Father. Please welcome my Michael with open arms. Mother and sister, too...

My door swung open without a knock and for a quick second my mind played tricks on me, telling me it was Michael coming to say his death was all a lie. He was still here. But it was John. I screamed out, "Johnnnnieee! Say it isn't true!!"

"I wish I could, my dearest," he said, dashing to my side. "I'm so sorry, Hazel. I tried to get to you before anyone else did. I just learned myself. Winston rang. Saying it was urgent." John gathered me into his arms, pulling me up from the floor like a ragdoll and back onto the couch. He tossed a copy of another paper from

London onto the table. It was *The Star*, whose headline was caught in a glimpse, right to the point.

MICHAEL COLLINS SHOT DEAD.

As John rocked my body, I glanced at that headline again, which would never vanish from my mind. I could almost hear Michael saying this about himself with a tease, "The worst four bloody words I'd ever hear, yeah?"

"There, there, Hazel," said John, holding tightly though I barely felt his arms. "This is a terrible sin. Shot dead in an ambush. Slain by his own people in Cork." John exhaled and drew me closer as I sobbed all over again. "When Winston rang to tell me the news, I told him that when the Irish chose to slew the Irish they killed all of Ireland as a force for good and greatness in the world... when every horror is committed in the name of nationalism."

I had no idea what he was babbling, and I said nothing as John held me. It suddenly occurred to me I had dreamed of his death only the night before; his face covered in blood.

My mind, my heart, and soul began to drift elsewhere...

Was it brief? Did you suffer? Oh, how I wish I could have held you as you lay dying... I will never know what you would have been and what we might have had. I will never see our dreams come true and our life realized. I could make another list of one thousand more things of what life would now be. Without you.

And then I sat up very solemnly, "Johnnie, I need to be alone just now. I'll be downstairs shortly."

"Of course, Hazel. I'll get arrangements sorted immediately. To get us to Dublin."

As he gently closed the door, I curled up further into the couch. The room was still for a very long time. And so was I.

When I finally stirred, I thought about what little time Michael had with me, but we had known complete love. Of that I was certain. Everyone should know a complete love at least once in this life. Michael Collins, beautiful Michael Collins, soldier, renegade, politician and mostly just a man... was my complete love.

The tragic news reached America appearing in *The Boston Post* and soon after, all the world's cover stories of Michael Collin's death. *The New York Times* said, "Irish appalled at death of Collins; fell fighting with victory at hand... Dail meets soon to seek a new leader..."

The rumors instantly circulated into conspiracy. Whodunit? Was it a friend? An enemy? Was it an Irishman or a Brit that shot him?

Eamon de Valera had hoped to see Michael the day of his death and was within a few miles from the site of the ambush though since resigning, he had little influence over the IRA and zero military influence at all. Yet, de Valera did go to Long's Pub to meet Michael, but he was already gone. Rumors speculated de Valera attempted a ceasefire but to no avail. Further rumors circulated that he tried to prevent the ambush but was ignored.

Whether that was true or not, we'll never know. But we do know on learning the news of Michael's passing, de Valera was quoted in the press: "A pity. What a pity I didn't meet him that day. It is very bad that this happened to Collins, as his place will surely be taken by a weaker man."

Richard Mulcahy, as Free State Army Chief of Staff, issued the following message to his Army:

"Stand calmly by your posts. Bend bravely and undaunted to your task. Let no cruel act of reprisal blemish your bright honor. Every dark hour that Collins met since 1916 seemed but to steal that bright strength of his and temper his brave gaiety.

"You are left as inheritors of that strength and bravery. To each of you falls his unfinished work. No darkness in the hour: loss of comrades will daunt you in it. Ireland! The Army serves — strengthened by its sorrow."

Chapter Thirty-eight

Hazel & Michael (once more)

Michael's body was brought back to Dublin. Only family and close friends were admitted to the mortuary chapel, which was eerily hushed when John and I entered.

Slowly, together, arms and hands entwined, John and I made our way to the casket, almost expecting it to be someone else. Almost expecting it to be a mistake.

But when I looked down, staring in disbelief, there was no mistake. It was Michael. Pale and lifeless. All his dazzling flamboyance, gone. A Free State Flag covered his body with a crucifix on his chest.

John spoke first. "He's like a Napoleon in marble as he lies here in uniform." Then shaking his head, "Such an unnecessary tragedy." Taking a deep inhalation and then exhaling a 'huff' through his nostrils, John added, "If I leave you here to gather my painting equipment, will you be alright?" I nodded.

If you can believe it, John was commissioned to paint Michael's portrait in death titled Michael Collins: Love of Ireland. Morbid but somehow miraculous...it was typical of dignitaries to be painted when lying in state. It would allow a physical point of reference to his last moments before the casket lid was shut.

As John moved to the door, I called out. "John," just whispering in a tone audible enough for him to turn. I was about to say, "Forgive me on this judgment day for having loved him," but the look in his eyes met mine, and it was understood.

Left alone now at Michael's side, the mercury of the room seemed to fall to frigid cold, as I was the only living warm-blooded creature there with my lover's corpse.

For the last time, I studied his eloquent features so at peace. In politics he was a man of few words yet somehow managed to convey the most. He had fought and worked harder than any of his colleagues. There had never been any happy-go-lucky Irish man about him.

He was now my dark angel.

Leaning over to kiss his lips, cold and hardened, the warmth of love gone, he had been the man who slept secretly and often, though not often enough by my side, but always waking with a smile. How I could still see the morning light bathing his face in sheer and utter joy. How I longed to feel his fingers run through my hair, my eyes closing in restful satisfaction. Why did this happen? What God would do this?

As I stood beside the casket trying to memorize his face that I would never see again, my mind wandered: Did I make the most of loving you? I gazed up to his sealed eyes hoping for an answer but there wasn't one. Staring at his lips they remained so animated that at times they played tricks on me. Moving. Oh Michael. My Michael...

And then John was back. I hadn't even heard him enter until he touched my arm. "We've not much time, Hazel," he whispered, "and I must get this portrait right. It's the last and only thing I can do for the Lad."

After some setting up and arranging his easel to the proper light, John dabbed his pallet knife into the flesh-colored tones of buff titanium beige and some white, mixing and mixing, looking at me and then to the casket, and back to me again. Nothing needed to be said. It was understood. I would go home now...to John and to my life in London.

Sitting quietly on a nearby chair, John glanced up with an exhale, "God knows I'm attempting to do Michael justice."

"I know you are," I whispered, my tone somber.

John came to my side at Michael's casket where he examined his profile, before moving back to his canvas, examining the comparison – dead man to portrait of dead man. "Any grossness in his features," said John, "even the peculiar little dent near the point of his nose, I'll make disappear, I promise."

No need, I thought. He's perfect.

Four soldiers entered now, standing around the bier. The stillness broke at long intervals by someone entering the Chapel on tiptoe, paying their respects, kissing his brow, then slipping out the door.

Michael's sister, Hannie Collins, with whom he lived when he first went to London and worked at the post office, arrived. She took one look at me as I stood to greet her.

"Are you..." she asked, hopeful.

"Hazel, yes, and you are Hannie? He loved you so."

Hannie came in for a warm long hug and then pulled back, keeping her palms at the base of my elbows. "We had planned a long holiday for early September," she said, her lips trembling. "But that morning of August 23rd, when I arrived at the post office in West Kensington, I was taken into the superintendent's room. I asked what I did wrong, but they told me I'd done nothing. There was a rumor my brother had been shot."

"Oh, poor dear," I said, playing the part of widow and gathering into my arms the woman who might have been my real-life-sister-in-law.

"I'm not surprised," she sobbed. "I had a premonition he'd been killed. He was so unhappy for so long. Except about you, Hazel." I smiled at that thought coming from his sister. "At the moment of his death the load went from his mind, and so it must go from mine."

"There, there," I said, rocking her gently.

"Thank you for paying for my train ticket from London," said Hannie, pulling away and opening my hand to put something in my palm. It was a small and wilted shamrock. She closed my hand tight, holding onto my fist. "From where Michael fell."

As Michael laid in state before the funeral procession, the closed casket was now draped with the flag. The mourners lined the church steps, kneeling and praying all around the block. I cut through the crowds who stood to make way for me to pass, the last to enter the funeral at the church. The patrons gasped and whispered as I strolled up the aisle, wearing lace and black satin from head to toe. A veil covered my tearstained face. I slid in the pew next to Hannie and John.

Glancing around discreetly, tipping my eyes up from under my veil, I saw a woman who stared at me from a pew to the left and in the front. I was certain she was Kitty Kiernan, also dressed in black from head to toe and wearing a thin veil. For a split second I caught her staring at me, and our eyes clung in a strange acknowledgement that we were two women in love with the same man, who in return had loved the same women. Or it was just my perception as perception alters everything. Perhaps Kitty shot icy daggers, I don't know. But what I know for sure is that Michael Collins was mine in life, and now in death, he belonged to no one. Only God.

Emmett Dalton came to my side to greet me and offer condolences as I did him. Taking me gently by the elbow he moved me to the casket for the final time. It was there I placed his rosary beads around a floral wreath. But Emmett retrieved them, returning them into my hand, and clasping my palm shut. "Don't you know someone will steal them?"

I gazed up at him grief-stricken and declared, "If someone wants to steal them that badly, then let them take them. It won't bring my beloved back."

Oliver St John Gogarty was already whispering gossip into Lady Leslie's ear. Later I would discover that he spoke in a spirit of mockery, "We have Lady Lavery in widow's weeds, full of confidence in Collins. And his ex-partner, sitting nearby and seething!"

I later learned from Dalton that on Michael's body were found three items aside from his gun and rosary beads.... and they were delivered to me by his sister Joanna. "He loved you..." she said, trembling. She took my hands as if touching me would be like feeling her brother's hands again.

The first item was a peculiar one. It was a piece of paper soaked in blood with a description of a portrait of me that Shane Leslie had written entitled, 'To a Portrait of Hazel as Leda or Rose O'Grady.' Shane's words went on to describe my "beauty" in detail though the paper was torn and fragmented keeping only the best parts.

Second, more fragments of paper from letters that had passed between us. One was dated the day he was killed. It contained these words: Hazel, My Dear, Dear, Hazel, I read your letter again this morning before going to sleep. When I woke, the pages were by my side. God Bless you, '*mo mhuirnin*' (Irish term for endearment 'my darling') I too wish it was tomorrow'– with all my love, yours. M.

Third, and turns out, fourth, items were the small red ruby brooch belonging to me with a clipped piece of my hair, which he wore in his scapular case, also soaked in blood.

Father Joseph Scannell, Army Chaplain and Father Joe Ahern recited the funeral prayers. Hannie spoke at the podium, unfolding a letter from George Bernard Shaw, who sat near to me in the pew. His words – which Hannie now read – summed it up quite stunningly:

Don't let them make you miserable about it; how could a born soldier die better than at the victorious end of a good fight, falling to the shot of another Irishman – a damned fool, but all the same an Irishman who thought he was fighting for Ireland; 'A Roman to a Roman?' I met Michael for the first and last time on Saturday last and am very glad I did. I rejoice in his memory and will not be so disloyal to it as to snivel over his valiant death. So, tear up your mourning and hang up your brightest colors in his honor; and let all praise God that he had not to die in a snuffy bed of a trumpery cough, weakened by age and saddened by the disappointments that would have attended his work had he lived.

And then Hannie broke into sobs, folded up the paper and returned to her seat.

Dalton moved to the podium quoting their friend Griffith who had died of a heart attack the year before. "I said it before and I say it again, Collins was the man who made the situation; he was the man, and nobody knows better than I do, how, during a year and a half, he worked from six in the morning until two the next morning. He was the man whose matchless energy, whose indomitable will, carried Ireland through the terrible crisis; and though I have not now, and never had, an ambition about either political affairs or history, if my name is to go down in history, I want it associated with the name of Michael Collins."

"Hear, hear!" chimed some of Michael's men from the pews, though some of his most important allies were not present. In the end, trying to do the right thing, he'd split hairs with de Valera and Rory O'Connor and quite a few more. Or as Michael said in one of his final letters to me, "They are all knifing me now..."

It was then, I excused myself from the funeral and walked back down the aisle, out the door and down the steps. If I were to go down in history, and as God was my witness, I would find my own reason to do so, but I too, would like my name to go down in history with Michael Collins. But would history even care to remember him?

Focusing on the future, I would somehow adjust back to a life without him. And, I would see to it, somehow, that the world – our worlds of England and Ireland – would give peace and unity a chance. Just as he intended.

Until then, he deserved a proper burial, and I would also see to it that his brothers and sisters had the financial means to have the monument they desired erected in his honor at Glasnevin cemetery in Dublin. It would be an anonymous gift "on behalf of an American Lady." It would be a limestone cross, and it would need to be approved by the State as his was considered a military grave.

What I didn't know is that it would end up taking many years – until 1939 – to get the grave erected properly because of much political red tape. It turned out at the base of the problem and the stalling had been one man with an exceptionally large ego: Eamon de Valera. Even in death he still fought over Michael 'Mick' Collins and his immense popularity.

Eventually, the Dublin Cemeteries Committee approved the grave which would be a plot four feet wide, and eight feet deep. And eventually, the 'Celtic Cross' would be eleven feet and six inches high in memory of Michael. Around the base would be plenty of space for visitors to drop off flower bouquets into the tall metal urns which gave the illusion of a flower field in his beloved Cork. The epitaph, chiseled in stone in his beloved Gaelic, translated to this:

'In loving memory of Michael Collins who was born on 12 October 1890, and who died on 22nd August 1922.'

Below it:

May God give him eternal happiness.

And at the bottom:

Erected by his brothers and sisters.

On the back:

Michael Collins

And then:

God have mercy on us.

Chapter Thirty-nine

Hazel

John and I returned to Cromwell Place that August, but only for enough time to pack and gather our daughter, Alice, and my dog, Mick, so we could visit the Fords in North Berwick. We rented a houseboat on the Thames. The buoyancy of the waves cradled me in an unexpected peace, as the water separated me from the earth and from reality. It was there on the river that I wrote in my diary about the secret I had been keeping for the past two months...

I saw my Michael impromptu that very last hour when he started out for Cork. It was early morning Sunday when I was to tell him that I suspected I was pregnant with our child. But with our car having been ravaged by bullets, the timing seemed too stressful. And Horace was with us, too. So, my next plan was to tell him in Dublin...after his tour of Cork... after the tour that would never bring him back to my arms...

But tell God you have a plan...

God had a different plan...

Upon returning to London and learning of Michael's death, my body went into trauma, and I collapsed in my bedroom while packing for Ireland. My maid came dashing in after my pleas for help. I was losing our baby in the most horrific way, blood all around, not much different than the way Michael lost his life.

But it was a hushed circumstance, one I kept cautiously from

John since he was never clear why the doctor came to examine me. I explained it was stress-related and my years of illness come to the forefront; enough of an excuse to appease my elderly husband.

But while I believe it was wonderful to carry our child, to have a living and breathing part of Michael inside of my body, it was God's will that I didn't carry it to full term. What kind of life might my child have had to be the baby of Michael Collins? Would he or she live a life at risk? I couldn't live to lose them both to tragedy. Instead, our unborn child's soul now lives with Michael, in heaven.

Grief all around. Grief is the price we pay for love.

I have been sick in soul and body since, but this sane, healthy, normal place on the Thames and the great content of Alice and John with this sporting life here, makes me less miserable. The soft, strong air is a great healer. I dread going back to London. Instead, I have been idle, only walking and reading and alas, thinking more than is good for me of that tragic Ireland, and what it has cost us all...

When we returned home, I had a lengthy list of suitors waiting to take Michael's place as if that were even a consideration...

Shane Leslie, first cousin of Winston Churchill had always been in love with me, or so Clementine continued to remind me. But he was annoying, and more interested in society, gossip, and every angle rather than caring about me. Nevertheless, to get a rise out of me he authored a beautiful poem upon seeing John's portrait of the dead Michael Collins.

> What is that curling flower of wonder
>
> As white as snow, as red as blood?
>
> When Death goes in flame and thunder
>
> And rips the beauty from the bud.

They left his blossom white and slender
Beneath Glasnevin's shaking sod;
His spirit passed like sunset splendor
Unto the dead Fiannas' God.

Good luck be with you, Michael Collins,
Or stay or go you far away;
Or stay you with the folk of fairy,
Or come with ghosts another day...

Shane pursued me but to no avail, though I was touched by some of the kind words spoken of me by him in a newspaper article. "...of Hazel's achievements in bringing about the Irish Treaty of 1921, I know no historical comparison, save the Princess Dorothea de Lieven's diplomatic cleverness amongst the statesmen of the drawing room in bringing about the Treaty of London in 1827 by which the Powers recognized the Independence of Greece.

It was from her salon, which was also her husband's studio, that Hazel set out to inveigle English and Irish statesmen from the summits to descent and know each other personally, as well as politically. Many such as Winston Churchill and Lord Birkenhead or Michael Collins and Arthur Griffith had reason to remember number 5 Cromwell Place (an ironic name for omen) during the twenties."

Another potential suitor was Charley Londonderry, Minister for Education in the Northern Ireland Government. For quite some time he refused to meet Michael during Treaty negotiations because he disagreed profoundly with Michael's theory on Government, and because it was a "very unhealthy curiosity to meet this celebrity." But it wasn't Michael's celebrity that had bothered him, or so he admitted to me after Michael's death, it was that he was jealous that Michael had stolen my heart. Were we that obvious? Charles said "oh, yes," Michael and I were that obvious. But he also confessed that in hindsight, he was happy to have finally decided to meet Michael – engaging, chivalrous and certainly charming – just before his death to understand why I wanted Michael and not him.

Charles strolled with me one day to the Grosvenor Gallery where my portrait of *Rose and Grey* hung alongside Michael's portrait.

"How are you holding up, lovely Hazel," asked Charles.

"As well as can be expected," I said, "And sheltering John from the truth...though I'm certain he knows. Men sense those types of things," he said. I opened my clutch purse and pulled out a letter. "What is it?" asked Charles.

"A letter that Michael had in his final belongings. One that Shane wrote to me."

Charles stopped and we sat on the bench. He looked at the words: "A 1000 ships launched Helen, poets relate, yet Hazel is content with ships of state." Charles folded up the paper, handed it back to me, shook his head and exhaled. Then he stood up, took my elbow and we walked into the next gallery. Silence ensued as he glanced at the portraits John had painted hanging side by side, and then at me, before declaring, "I didn't stand a chance of winning you over during Michael's life, and I suspect I have less of a chance after his death."

I could only nod. He was right.

Another possible lover had come forward following Michael's death, and rumors had swirled that he replaced Michael Collins. His name was Kevin O'Higgins. He made his longing for me clear in poetry albeit not such good poetry. Certainly, O'Higgins' poems were lovely, and I didn't want to hurt him, so I befriended him as best I could. We often shared tea and I edited through his political speeches, as we talked of what might have been if Michael lived.

But I held Michael and all that we shared close to my heart. By comparison, all men paled to Michael Collins.

Nevertheless, O'Higgins wrote me many letters, and I to him, too, as the situation in Ireland grew more dire...

Dear Lady Lavery,

Your letter of Wednesday reached me here yesterday. I have been recalled from the Army and have been asked to take on 'Home Affairs.' There are times when the only safety-valve is work, things so terrible that one dare not to stop to think on them. There is work enough in our hands, God knows, and there is the clear duty to carry on and endeavor to save Michael's achievements for the country from destruction.

...Childers is no fool. He knows that when he destroys property, bridges, railways, etc., he infuriates the people, but he is prepared to go on infuriating them, hoping for a social and economic collapse, hoping for a point when the people will kick out blindly at an intolerable condition regardless of the question of who caused it. He and De Valera know that their following is criminal in motive and in act; they are prepared to go on using that criminal instrument in the hope of crumbling foundations. This is ghoulish – but I think it is true.

I wish I could write you in a cheerier vein, but the position is too grim. We will get on with the work – and you, whom Michael loved so well, will pray for success, and will help when you can in the way that only you can. I wish you could realize how much all of us here appreciate your help and sympathy.

Greetings,
Kevin O' Higgins

One day, O'Higgins came from Ireland to John and me, saying that he favored John for the Lord-Lieutenant of Viceregal Lodge, which was the official residence of the President of Ireland in the Phoenix Park in Dublin.

I was so proud of my John, as the position was only given to a nobleman holding wide statutory powers. "My Johnnie, my Sir John," I said, patting his back, "a mere boy born into poverty, has certainly come a long way." But with the Irish Act of Unions, the duties attached to the Lord Lieutenant had become nothing more than ceremonial in nature. Nevertheless, we were heading out to dine with Winston and Clementine to celebrate.

Winston raised a flute of champagne, "Well, John, are you getting ready?"

"Ready for what?" asked John, pretending that he did not know what Winston was referring to.

"The Vice-Regal!"

"That's a dream of O'Higgins," said John. "To see Hazel in the Vice-Regal."

"Either way," said Winston, "we are in favor of it."

Hear, hear! Clemmie and I toasted at the idea, though I knew I needed some space and time to mourn to truly understand my heritage before John assumed the post...

While on a solo trip to Ireland to visit Michael's grave, I stood in the pounding Irish rain and told Michael of our unborn child. I asked him to forgive me for not telling him in life. I told him to watch over his soul in heaven. Waiting for a reply or a sign, none came, which was odd. They say that those who die in turmoil do not settle their souls in peace.

Leaving his grave, I explored every bit of our country and my Martyn ancestors of Galway. One distant relative brought me into his home for dinner, claiming that I couldn't be a Martyn as they'd never had a beautiful woman in the family.

For days I kept diaries, exploring every corner of the country. And while the violence ensued, and despite my connection to the Treaty, I hoped there wasn't a revengeful man that might turn his gun on a woman. On me. Thankfully, and with God's guidance, I was right.

But I couldn't help but be curious, if Father were alive to see

I'd discovered politics, would he see red? Or would he be proud of a woman who got a Treaty signed for our fatherland?

Upon visibly witnessing the Lodge in Phoenix Park in all its glory, I knew I belonged there. Seeing it as something tangible made me realize what a great honor this was for John, and for me, as his wife. The edifice was reminiscent of the American White House, all Eighteenth-Century feeling, solid, white, and regal; the drive from Dublin Gate to Castleknock Gate more than two miles long. Such grandeur! The grounds were well maintained, with topiaries, mazes and pathways all bordered by beautiful plantings.

That August of 1923, John and I attended the unveiling of a monument in honor of Arthur Griffith and Michael Collins on the Dublin lawn of Leinster. The Viceregal party were our escorts. I was dressed in black, short of a tiny white rose bud banner on my hat. Hannie Collins insisted I sit next to her.

Upon returning home to England, I learned that the position of Lord Lieutenant was abolished as the Irish Free State took hold. The Chief Secretary's Office would eventually be abolished in October 1924, too.

The short-lived dream of becoming Vicereine of Ireland.... of a future, living there, full time in Ireland, was once again shattered. Instead, steady and dependable as ever, our home with its lacquered black door and gold knocker at 5 Cromwell Place in Kensington continued to service Irish political crises. As a matter of fact, it had earned a nickname "That Irish place" by taxi drivers who dropped off dignitaries.

Chapter Forty
Hazel
(Undeniable & Unstoppable)

At a certain age, and certainly once one hits forty, the years pass quickly. It was almost Christmas 1927. By now I'd become a major supporter of several organizations that focused on education, hunger and mostly those of peace missions. One of them included a charity on financing the Irish Sisters of Charity hospital in Cork for incurable diseases.

Just that year I became part of the Folklore of Ireland Society... a voluntary cultural organization set up with a mission of collecting, preserving, and publishing the language and culture of Ireland. Folklore collections began to pour into the Society from patrons in Cork, Kerry, Donegal, Counties Antrim, Derry, Galway, Mayo, Monaghan, Tipperary, and Waterford.

As I check-listed horizons Michael would have been proud of, I took it upon myself to learn to speak Gaelic. It was challenging to memorize another language, as the mind doesn't absorb to the degree it used to by the time one is forty-seven.

But the words '*Beidh grá agam duit go brách*' for 'I love you forever' were always on my mind... and repeated in a whisper since I knew Michael was always with me, and especially at morning service Mass at Brompton which I rarely missed.

As the melancholy of the holiday season kicked in, I was

reminded of how once-upon-a-time, Michael and I agreed it would be the last holiday we'd spend alone.

It was the night before Christmas eve...

Alice was out on Regent Street for drinks at the Café Royal, a thriving Victorian restaurant known to cater to the upper crust and apparently British spies. And then she was off to the Savoy for dinner with her international crowd. Like mother like daughter, I suppose. Christmas eve she'd be traveling to Ireland, spending more and more time in Kilkenny. She even had dreams of living there. I suspect my Irish bug bit her, too. And she even expressed it to me in a letter:

> Dearest Mommy,
>
> The Irish are such delightfully kind and amusing people. It is nothing like English hunting, either field or country, everyone helps everyone else, and no one swears at anyone and you're always welcome in the country if you're a stranger.... I think Ireland is the freshest, simplest, nicest country and people I have ever met, and I love every inch of it, so you can say 'I told you so' and crow over me to your heart's content now. You were right! And I love you!

My stepdaughter, Eileen, wrapped gifts in the parlor. Nearby were her daughters, Ann Moira and June Mary, which now made John and I official grandparents.

Winston and John were in the library deep into cigars, gin and political talk with our son-in-law, William, while Clementine and I sat sipping sherry in the drawing room, the doors closed.

My newest friend, Jessie Louisa "Louie" Rickard, an Irish writer, whose romantic novels we all devoured, joined us, listening on as Clementine cackled about some latest fashion. My eyes watered up for the tenth time that day. I didn't intend for her to notice but she instantly figured it out as I turned the other way to avoid eye contact. "Hazel," said Clementine, leaning in, her voice full of pity, "Hazel, look at me." I turned as she gained my full attention. "You must gather yourself, darling girl."

"Oh Clemmie, I don't know how to..."

"Of course, you don't. You're American," she said, patting my hand. "But try you must."

"He was the love of..."

"...your life, yes, I know. But he's gone. It's been years," said Clementine. "Those chapters of life are best left unpublished." Then she eyed my wardrobe, black from head to toe, compared to her layers of lapis and pitch blue – a bias-cut dress with belted waist and large yoke collar. "And Hazel, dearest, you're not in mourning, you're married..."

"Well, I suppose marriage is a form of mourning." The three of us women shared a look. "Fer sure," said Louie with her Irish brogue. She was sporty. Wearing high waisted sailor pants and striped blouse.

As I admired their zest for life in the present, I longed to tell them right then and there that I mourned not only for Michael, but for our unborn child, and the recent loss of yet another one of Michael's friends. "It's been so difficult, ladies. You're the only ones I can confide in except for Michael's sister, Hannie. We've stayed close. My love for him is always with me. He once said we were like swans who mate for life."

"Pain comes from always wanting..." said Louie, trailing off and turning the other way, like a true romantic writer, gazing out the window. Whenever she spoke, rain practically fell on cue.

Clementine began pinching the puffed sleeves on her dress and then gazed up at me, clearing her throat to speak. "I have five tips for any woman where the living men are concerned, not the dead ones."

"Oh?" I sat up, eager.

"Firstly," said Clementine, "it is important that a man hires you a skilled staff and has an admirable career. Second, that he makes you laugh. Third, it is important to find a man you can count on who doesn't lie to you. And that this man loves you and spoils you.

And, finally," she added, "it is most important that these four men don't know each other!" A pause, and then Clementine burst out laughing.

"Oh Clemmie, you're wretched! Is this your way of saying I should have an affair?"

"It's time dear. It's time."

"I concur!" said Louie.

"But I'm a Catholic now," I declared, "I don't believe in divorce."

"Nobody is saying to divorce, just have a good ole roll in the hay with a man more your age," said Louie, tipping her head to suggest John was very old.

I regretted the way that I segued into the next words that fell from my mouth since rumors had already begun circulating about me. "And Kevin O'Higgins is dead, too. Michael's friend."

"Another one?" asked Clementine. "Dead?"

"Yes, back in July, didn't I tell you then... though it feels like yesterday. The assassins poured lead into his body just like they did to Michael except they murdered him on his way to Mass."

"Disgraceful!" said Clementine.

"Sometimes, I just feel frozen in misery," I added.

"""So, you were close, yeah?" asked Louie.

Trying to avoid the question instead reframing with a different answer. "I was watching polo at Ranelagh when I was told the news. The first thing I thought was the same thing I always think when I hear of the death of a man close to me. It's always the men close to my life who die." Leaning forward I poured more sherry, and topped Clementine's off, too. "O'Higgins so much wanted to see Michael's achievements and endeavors for the country. They're saying he was perhaps the greatest diplomat of them all. You know, he wrote me the most charming note. Ended it by saying he wished I could be there as his Parliament meets again. And then he went on about how much the Irish appreciate my help and sympathy."

Clementine studied her sherry glass, took a sip, and then spoke,

"Hazel, I suspect that your views of Ireland are unsuited to the harsh reality of sectarian strife."

"But I love Ireland so. It was purely by accident of birth that America claimed me. Although," I said, easing back into the chair and pouting, "Perhaps John was right. He once said that 'Hazel's Ireland is as unreal as a mirage in the desert.'"

"Well, he could be right," added Louie. "Come to think of it, after O'Higgins assassination, an Act was introduced that allows the killer to be arrested and get the death sentence if he's caught with illegal firearms."

"Yes," I said, "but they passed an Electoral Amendment that each candidate for election must swear to take the Oath of Allegiance within a given time or vacate his seat." Louie knit her brows, so I explained, "It was when the Fianna Fail finally entered the Dail. Ludicrous! It was the Fianna Fail party responsible for O'Higgins murder!" I said, my voice trembling.

"Oh Hazel," said Louie, "I cannot bear to think of you suffering as you are and can see how this grief has caught you with such cruelty. Oh, my dear, for the sake of all of us who love you... try to swim hard. Stay afloat. I know your courage... that wonderful gay courage of yours, which is part of your beloved self, and it will return completely. I promise."

Clementine sighed. "Right, then. All you can do now is focus on doing the best you can for your beloved England, and well, maybe a bit for Ireland, too. Besides, you don't even realize it but you're someone to be admired,"said Clementine. I creased my brow. She continued, "You aren't just one of the ladies who lunch, but a lady who lunches with a purpose. An entire Treaty was signed thanks to you."

"And as a result, Michael probably died thanks to me," I said.

Clementine stretched her neck to see that our husbands weren't listening. "You need to focus on the living. You. John's not getting any younger and neither are we. Have an affair before you turn into a spider granny. We only have a couple good years left if we're lucky."

"Being forty-two is ancient!" I scowled. "Don't remind me."

"And I'm right behind you," said Clementine. "End of my thirties!"

"You should talk. I'm older than both of you," said Louie. "I'm well into my forties."

We sighed. "Well, at least we're wise and old," I said. "I just wanted my last few years to be with him."

"Yes, well it's time to put him in the past," said Clementine, again. "It's not like one hundred years from now anyone will remember Michael Collins."

"You don't think so?" I asked, sitting forward, and considering her advice.

"No, history will forget." Clementine raised her glass for a refill, jiggling it. "I should talk, delivering all this advice," she said. "Truth is I'm going mad deep inside."

"Oh?" I asked.

"I need to find something to do with myself," said Clementine. "Winston is driving me crazy. Has the political bug for good."

"What do you mean?" asked Louie.

"He's still carrying on," said Clementine, leaning in and whispering. "Saying that he's known since he was a boy that someday he'll be Prime Minister."

"Oh stop!" said Louie, chuckling, "Winston Churchill, the Prime Minister?"

"Though honestly it's not too far-fetched an idea," I said, hunching my shoulders.

There was a slight knock at the door and Mr. Wallace was there. "So sorry to disturb, your Ladyship, but Sir Lavery requested that the ladies join him in the library."

"Will do, Wallace," I said, standing up and taking Clementine by the arm and squeezing it. "Thank you, my friend..." and then taking Louie's arm, too. "And thank you, my new friend."

We moved down the hallways of my beautiful home, the three of us locked arm in arm, past the gorgeous sculptures and paintings and furnishings, though in my heart I knew none of it mattered. Love was not material. Love is all that we take with us in the end.

My son-in-law bypassed us to check on my granddaughters, their echoes heard giggling from another room.

"Ahhhh," said Winston, "Alas, here they are." Clementine moved to Winston's side, and I moved to John's with Louie, "What were you ladies gossiping about?"

"The usual," I said.

"Yes, needlepoint and bridge club," Clementine lied.

"To friends," I said, raising my glass.

"And secrets," said Louie, winking.

"Hazel," said John, "I could give up the paintbrush for the simple joy of seeing your great gifts gloriously framed for the benefit of Ireland. The Ireland of your own creation..."

"I'm sorry, but I'm lost, Johnnie, what are you saying..."

"I've a splendid thought thanks to your pal, Bodkin... who used his influence to give you lasting recognition."

Winston chimed in. "Yes, and I'm all for it."

John looked at me proudly to explain. "Mr. Cosgrave and the currency commission have come up with the idea of recognizing your services. They've commissioned me to paint your portrait to be reproduced on the bank notes. Ordinarily it's Royalty that appears on bank notes but let's face it, you are royalty in your own way, Hazel, and..."

"What?" I asked, confused.

John continued, "President Cosgrave said in his very charming way, 'every Irishman not to mention the foreigner who visits Ireland, will carry Hazel next to his heart.'"

"Or fondle you from his pants' pocket!" added Clementine.

The men chuckled at the sexual innuendo.

"Well, I'm flattered and stunned," I said, trying to contain my enthusiasm by speaking politically. "Certainly, I admire the First President of the Executive Council. And let's face it... no other statesman could achieve what he intends to bring to Ireland... but really... this?"

"Yes," said John.

"You're being far too humble, Hazel," said Louie.

"We all admire you, Hazel," said Winston. "Godsake, it was you who taught me to paint!"

"And it was a pure joy!"

"But beyond that," said Winston, "you've taken great risk in getting Protestant England to see some virtue in Catholic Ireland."

"Well, thank you, Winston," I said. "I tried."

"And the death of Collins has clearly not stopped you in the role of correspondence for Irish politicians," Winston added.

"How true," said John, "She's the house Diplomat in more ways than one." A sarcasm in his remark.

"And John, bless him, has had to put up with me," I said.

"So, you'll be the face of the banknote?" asked Winston. "Allow John to paint you?"

"Yes," I said, "I suppose I'd endure a ten mile walk across a muddy, wet field, if that's what the Irish want."

"You won't have to do that, my love. We'll pose you in the studio."

"Then it's a 'yes?'" asked Winston.

"Yes, I'll do it," I said, and then with self-deprecating humor. "Only because John won't have to pay a sitter."

As we tossed our heads back in laughter, we toasted our flutes, and sang out, "Merry Christmas!"

Chapter Forty-one

Hazel
(Social Influencer)

The contract for the commissioned painting of the bank note said I was to look like an average Coleen otherwise every Irish woman would raise concern as to why I was chosen over any one of them. "I see you as more a glamorous Gibson Girl," said John, lifting his brush. "More the standard of beauty, fashion, and manners through World War." My lips curled at the sentiment. "More to the left," he demanded. "Yes, there, that's it... the woman who satisfies that need by captivating the imagination of the country... providing a perfect image of femininity."

"I'd prefer to suggest neither superiority nor inferiority but of equality with all."

"And you have," said John, pausing to take in my thoughts. "I'm quite impressed with all that you've become, my dear. The female personification." He dabbed a final spot on the canvas. "That face of Ireland."

John captured me at an angle, with an easy poise, my long nose tipped downward, and the dark circles under my eyes of all that I had endured erupting on canvas. But in my eyes, having posed for over four hundred of John's portraits, I knew exactly how to deliver the pain that came through from the soul. Not because I was 'posing' this time, but because it was real.

Pain comes from always wanting him. And the longing and the

luminosity somehow mixed into my sad Irish-eyed expression.

John fussed with the shawl on my head, pulling it back, suspending his brush midair. "I imagine an interpretation of Kathleen ni Houlihan," he said. "

"Katherine ni who?"

"The legendary heroine mythologized by our friend Yeats."

"Oh," I said, not sure to whom he referred. My shawl was pulled a bit more back, providing a peekaboo of my hair's fringe at the crown of my head. My fingers rested under my chin, and my arm rested on a harp, the symbol of Ireland. Behind me, John chose a landscape – Killarney – though I wanted it to be referred to as Galway since I had an affection for the 'West' being a Martyn. Either way, the background on the note was many shades of green the way Michael had always described Clonakilty. All hills and sea, a muted Irish landscape that matched my hazel eyes. Smiling inwardly, I thought of the poem Michael had once written to me now taped in my scrapbook. He was never Yeats, but knew I adored his awkward poetry attempts. It was the thought that counted...

> Oh! Hazel, Hazel Lavery;
> What is your charm Oh! say?
> Like subtle Scottish Mary
> You take my heart away
> Not by your wit and beauty
> Not your delicate sad grace
> Nor the golden eyes of wonder
> In the flower that is your face.

At times over the past several years and since his death, I felt like the little girl I once was, navigating those Chicago blizzards; snow falling in sticky measure, my boots moving as fast as I could, but then defeated I would give in to its force, the wind whipping in my face as I trudged off, surrendering to the white-out blindness of nowhere.

But time and history moved on... the Irish forgetting the hatred, the Civil War and the Treaty that followed. Instead, they focused on the future and the rebuilding of all that could once again be glorious Ireland...

Who am I now? I asked myself that question as Vogue photographers roamed my home time and time again to capture my life, only this time for a series where I leaned against the toile wallpaper... the one wall where Michael and I often kissed in the foyer.

Who am I now? Ah, the answer. I am a mother, a stepmother, a grandmother, and a wife, blessed by my tragedies. Yes, you heard right. Blessed. It is said in an Irish sentiment "that the living go to bed with the dead." It took close to three decades to realize that all those I've lost are all those I've become.

In the name of my sister, Dorothy, whose clock ticked expiration long before mine, I focused on feeding the hungry. In the name of my father, I focused on Ireland and keeping its folklore alive. In the name of Mother, I continued with charity work.

It was Hannie and the Collins siblings who told me I am "mentally well endowed," as I helped them – financially and emotionally – whenever the need occurred.

Yes, survival is a skill that's repeated itself in my life in the most unexpected ways. Death created an urgency to get out there and live. Those years since Michael's passing had been the ultimate awakening. It taught me that what remains must be the most poignant of years...

"Ah, voila!" said John, stepping back from the painting. After several versions, the currency portrait was complete. He placed down his brushes in the jar and came over to take me by the hand to witness the result. But I didn't want to see it. I wanted to wait and be as surprised as the Irish people when it was unveiled...

"Did you hear me, Hazel?" asked John. "I said, from 1927 onward, you will be the acclaimed face immortalized and gracing every Irish Free State banknote!"

My profile and "delicate sad grace" as Michael once called my expression, peered from the ten- and twenty-pound banknote until about 1963, when I was demoted to the one-pound bank note. In 1976, I was replaced by Irish writers and Celtic themes. Of course, I was long gone from this earth to know any of that.

After the bank note, my face adorned an advertisement for *Ponds Cold Cream*. In women's magazines read the words "The Greatest Beauty since Lady Hamilton" a fanciful tribute to a favorite character, a woman who was an English maid, model, dancer, and actress. She became the mistress of a series of wealthy men, culminating in the naval hero, Lord Nelson. Yes, it seems Lady Hamilton and I had much in common...

Chapter Forty-two
Hazel
(Real, True & Infinite)

I lived long enough to return to America one last and unexpected Christmas with John and Alice. We stayed at the Ambassador Hotel while Alice went to Connecticut to visit my childhood friend, Marie Truesdale, from Chicago boarding school. While we were in New York, I insisted that Alice visit the Trudeau's, her biological father Ned's parents, in Saranac Lake. My theory about life was that if we live long enough, it all goes full circle, and we make peace with all those whose lives we touched or those whose lives touched ours.

I lived long enough to visit old American friends and see how 'un-Irish' they made me feel with their pettiness, though we loved when they asked John, "Does it make your blood boil to see how we've robbed you of your art treasures?" Quite the contrary, John explained that Americans beautifully cared for his treasures. And then paid hefty sums for them, too.

John's fans approached him in droves, as he obtained commissions in Philadelphia, Pittsburgh, and other cities including Chicago. His exhibition of "Portraits, Interiors and Landscapes" opened in Palm Beach, Florida, which only pained me in realizing that I would never really be home again until I could again go home to England...and to Ireland.

In October of 1929, I lived to see the new Belfast gallery open its doors with a special 'Lavery Room' in which my favorite full-length portrait called *Hazel in Green and Mauve* was previewed. Of course, this caused problems in Dublin, where we had to assure them that there were two separate collections in both the north and south of Ireland.

Thankfully, I lived to see my daughter, Alice, wed Captain John McEnery, in Cannes, France, on March 5, 1930; her wedding announcement traveled as far as the New York Times. It was a beautiful church on Suquet Hill, a place that back in 1815, Napoleon had attended early Mass, though I do confess, just like my mother, I did not approve of the union. And, like my mother, I tried everything possible to stop it including placing a nail file in the pocket of the groom as it was understood that a Catholic marriage could be annulled should a weapon be present at the ceremony.

Dramatically, Alice threatened to run away to a convent, and it was then I controlled myself, remembering how badly my mother's negative influence affected my entire life. But as I confided in Clementine through gritted teeth, "The groom is nothing but an unsuitable swain – a common farmer from Kilkenny – marrying my only child!" I stopped myself, realizing that Michael Collins had been no more than a common farm boy inside a Revolutionary.

John walked Alice down the aisle, and later she toasted him, saying she always wished he were her biological father. On her honeymoon she wrote me a note:

> Dearest Momsie,
>
> The more I think over all you and Popsie have done for me all my life, the more unable I feel ever to thank you enough and looking at it like that it does seem very ungrateful of me to have married anyone you don't like. I can only hope that one day you will feel differently about Jack and that our horses may be of some success."

And success the horses were indeed! Their horse 'Red Park' was the winner of the Irish Grand National and Galway Plate in 1933. But the best prize was living long enough to see my first biological grandson, Martyn, with his flaming red hair christened Catholic in Ireland.

I lived long enough to befriend Noel Coward. In the early 1930s, at Noel's persistence, I had what others called "Hazel's Boys." They were young men, like sons, whom I championed and groomed to be proper contemporaries for the future. God knows we needed more gentlemen for the next generation. Even in my old age, at fifty-two, I loved sporting them around in my chauffeur-driven brown Renault. Wallace was gone now, and we had "Jasper' as my driver. Did I mention that Winston and Clementine's son, Randolph Churchill was one of the young men I groomed?

The last person I lived to befriend was Evelyn Waugh. Twenty-three years younger than me, I suspect he could have been one of "Hazel's boys" because I encouraged him to write. I shared in his success, even hosting several book parties in his honor.

I wouldn't live to see it, but in 1946 he'd dedicate *When the Going Was Good* to the memory of me, which was kind, as towards the end he found my fondness of him "suffocating" though I always adored his company.

I lived long enough to see my friend Louie Rickard write of me as her heroine in her 1927 novel *A Bird of Strange Plumage*. Louie would tell me on my deathbed that she would miss a life without me sharing secrets. A debilitating stroke in the nineteen-fifties left her paralyzed on one side. She taught herself to write with her left hand, with characteristic courage. In her later years, she lived in the Montenotte home of Denis Gwynn, my daughter Alice's second husband, an Irish journalist and professor of modern Irish History, who served in World War I. Yes, you heard it... second husband. I never lived to say to Alice, "I told you so," though Mothers are always right. I knew the first husband wasn't worthy of my daughter. Nevertheless, my friend, Louie outlived me by thirty years and died in January of 1963, buried in my beloved Cork, in Rathcooney cemetery.

I lived long enough to see my stepdaughter, Eileen, remarry the love of her life, William Francis Forbes-Sempill, from the House of Lords. But I didn't live long enough to see Eileen die of tuberculosis, at the age of forty-four, only eleven years younger than me. And only six months after my own passing.

I lived long enough to see friends die... Lord Birkenhead in 1930 and others. As they departed this earth and I felt that the balance of those I loved were mostly in heaven, I began to slip into a deep depression, suddenly inefficient to cope or engage in this life in general. You can take the girl out of Chicago, I guess, but you can't take Chicago tragedies out of the girl.

As I moved through my fifties, nephritis returned, and my youthful beauty began to lose its dewy and rosy complexion. Makeup didn't help, though I slathered it on. Like my mother before me, so much time went into the prepping of my face – patting my powder, coloring my ruby lips and wistful almond eyes, their lids covered in layers of blue eyeshadow. John would say if someone asked, "She's in the bedroom... painting."

It's a sad and funny thing about aging. If you were always an attractive woman, you somehow incorporated your 'looks' into your seduction routine. But when the looks are gone, you must rely solely on wit and wisdom. I'll take youth and beauty any day... because no woman wants to try so hard to be funny when she reaches fifty.

But *Vogue* didn't see it that way as Cecil Beaton, who became one of my young protégés, was the last to photograph me for the fashion magazine in March 1933. The caption of the painting made my heart soar to the realization that even others saw me as Irish. "Lady Lavery, wife of Sir John Lavery, the celebrated painter, here wears her little white fur jackets which are so chic for early Spring and so becoming to her dark Irish elegance."

I was sad to live long enough to see de Valera replace President Cosgrave following the victory of Fianna Fail, and Labour in the Irish general election of 1932. I was sad to see Anglo-Irish diplomacy crumble.

As the Great Depression set in, and art consumption was

strained, our finances became precarious. Though rich or poor, John would undoubtedly paint until his hand could no longer lift a brush.

And finally, I lived long enough to sink into a deeper illness brought on by the simple removal of a wisdom tooth in 1933 with gas and anesthetics. The procedure caused an inflammation of the walls of my heart which had a troubling heart murmur.

It was quite serious, and the nurse forbade visitors or even simple phone calls.

But when the pleurisy turned into double pneumonia, I felt more isolated than ever. Alice had given birth to her second child, and I longed to return to the responsibilities of mother and grandmother to her new baby girl, Mary, but time was not on my side.

Now I only wanted the comfort of my "Boudoir prison" as John called it, a place to reminisce about life, about Michael, and about death. Number 5 Cromwell Place – which once entertained the heights of political, aristocratic, and occasional bourgeois types – had become the home of an invalid. Me.

John and I reminisced as he painted a final portrait of me in my bed cushioned by feather pillows on all sides. First, we spoke of the magic of Tangiers and our last visit. Two years prior, we passed through the Straits of Gibraltar for the final time. Then we talked of his enjoyment watching me make a life out of being interested in meeting all types of people – men and women, rulers and writers, soldiers, and painters, too. And he reminded me that while I too had once been a painter, my true art was undoubtedly bringing all these people together at 5 Cromwell Place.

"Hazel," John called out from across the room where he painted me lying in my bed. But I could barely respond. He spoke nonetheless, assuming I was listening. "I will never know how many sitters I had through the years thanks to your friendships. I will always lift a brush and assume somehow it had to do with you."

"You painted the Queen before you knew me," I murmured.

"True," said John, "But how Lord Lonsdale loved to have you talk to my sitters. I believe it was Lord Lonsdale who once said, 'My dear Lady, you have revolutionized the sitting!' and he was correct, my love." I smiled, contented. Happy that John was happy.

The next day my portrait was completed. John turned the painting around for me to see, and I witnessed echoes of Whistler's work again in everything he did. Here I was on the canvas for the last time, in a very large picture, bedridden, framed by pink awning curtains. "It's sad, Johnnie," I whispered. "What's it called?"

I closed my eyes as he spoke. "It's called *The Unfinished Harmony,*" he said.

"Well, I look like the imaginary child of Mahatma Gandhi and Lady Oxford!"

"Ha! I'm glad your comical nature is still surfacing," he chuckled. "And on that note, Alice is here to see you."

As I visited with my darling daughter and grandchildren, John did his best to carry on in finding the best doctors and specialists… but to no avail...

Chapter Forty-three

The Unfinished Harmony

It was the day before the New Year, 1935, but I no longer wished to ring in beginnings...

My heart could only take so much.

For as long as you were alive, I was alive inside. But without you here, Michael, I have done my work to please your cause, so my life is done.

I lived long enough to conquer my own self... having had more vision than end-of-life hindsight. I believe I lived long enough to change the world, to leave my mark. Yes, I tried to make a difference. Historians will continue to debate my existence where my affair with you was concerned. Some saying he was some "romantic attachment" that I conjured in my mind. A "figment of [my] imagination," said others. Pish posh! Others said I was what the French call an "enfant terrible...," a social influencer whose naïve fervor aroused comment.

Many years ago, I was at the Savoy and saw Lloyd George dining nearby, so I quickly moved to his table as he smoked a cigar. "I want to settle this Irish dispute tonight," I demanded, as onlookers Noel Coward and movie star Douglas Fairbank were seated just one table over, and the press at another, always quick to capture me and my antics. From my bed I raise a strained chuckle in memory of that moment with Lloyd George.

But now, John will have had the final word, putting the finishing touches of the portrait of me in death, lying in my bed, surrounded by rich colors, my complexion so pale. His interpretation will be that of forever slumber... making me more abstract than any of his past works.

"Johnnie, it's so very macabre. I do not like leaving such a sad souvenir of myself."

John came to my side of the bed to kiss my forehead. Our marriage had long ago become duty over desire.

Running his fingers tenderly over my cheek, he whispered something about "when illness took my hand from the pulse of the lives of others, that I would die." He kissed me again, a tear falling onto my forehead as I slipped into a dream-like state, though I heard him declare that the final painting of me would describe what he always knew and loved of me...

I suspect he meant this: That I was at times unobtainable, but always undeniable, and unstoppable... the traits to be admired, to be captured on a canvas, but never truly understood... as if I still held onto a secret even in passing.

Bless you my Johnnie, for all you've been. I thought I'd be burying you first, but God wanted you to protect me until death, just as you always have... in my life.

I believe we have many loves in our lives at different times of our lives. John was my first, Michael was my last.

As my body gave way, my last thoughts were of Michael and what we shared. Like him I will now live in a place between our dreams and our memories.

Once he wrote me a poem on route to Ireland that Christmas, sitting in that lonely hotel room before the final negotiations of the New Year. Memorizing it, I recited it day after day, though I never learned what a '*Cucugan*' meant...

Cucugan I call thee,
Cucugan the dove,
Because of thine eyes and the voice that I love.
Cucugan I call thee.

Hast thou no fear, little bird, little love,
I am an eagle and thou art a dove
Hast thou no fear of me?
Wild is my nest in the mountain above,
Wilt thou fly there with me lovely white dove,
Shall my wings carry thee...

And carry me he did. As I died, my face pale but tranquil, I saw him in a mirage, arms outstretched standing outside our Brompton Oratory once more, with his tender smile and that playful curl at his lip. It was then, I felt my soul and my spirit roll through the clouds, plowing straight to heaven's light, and into his arms.

For all of eternity.

Epilogue

A poet from Northern Ireland named Medbh McGuckian studied under Seamus Heaney. His studies included Sir John Lavery's, *Hazel, The Green Coat*, 1926. McGuckian summed it up best, by crediting John Lavery for giving me life beyond physical death:

> He has been able to bring your inner sun
> to full view, a real heartbeat, and a lucid mind
> inhabiting a body degrading into matter.
> One can't argue with that...

John didn't put the final touches on that final portrait of me for a month. Instead, it sat turned to a wall. He couldn't face it. In fact, he knew it would be useless to try any sooner as it would bring back too many memories that, as he might say, "would crowd round him. It would spoil the reality of the picture."

My funeral mass took place at the very Brompton Oratory where I became a Catholic and where I fell in love with Michael at our daily Masses. In Dublin, a Memorial service was held at St Andrew's Church in Westland Row, because Cosgrave's government insisted.

One of those who attended my funeral was Cecil Beaton who wrote:

> "Not only has one of my first and favored stars ceased to shine, but I have lost a true and sympathetic friend. When I started my career, Hazel was one of the first to overwhelm me with encouragement and kindness. She sent notes, drawings, criticism, and suggestions. She sympathized with my despair. And now, poor Hazel has been laid in her coffin... a living spirit has become a thing of the past. Those who loved her will perhaps make a legend of her, decorating her memory with the tuberoses, orchids, and crimson roses that she surrounded herself with in life. But soon, and inevitably even those dearest friends will be busy going out to lunch with someone else."

Two days after my funeral service, John paid his solo tribute by charcoal sketching my coffin as it lay draped with flowers in my small bedroom surrounded by flowers, a dim light, a crucifix, and tall tapers. A death chamber for certain, the painting was titled "It is Finished."

My stepdaughter, Eileen, also died the same year as me, with John by her side during the previously mentioned tuberculous. She took my sick bed at 5 Cromwell Place and for that I am grateful and would have found comfort.

My Johnnie continued to paint for six more years before he joined me in heaven. He gifted many portraits of me to friends like J. M. Barrie and Clementine Churchill. And he visited America, this time back to visit Mr. Frick in New York and to see his new gallery.

In 1936 John went out to Hollywood and I can just imagine him saying that the lighting effects were changing all the time, what at one minute was black darkness was the next brilliantly lit. Yes, Johnnie, it's called a movie set.

On those movie sets he painted and flirted with Loretta Young and Maureen O'Sullivan with her 'Irish eyes.' There were cocktails and dinners with Marlene Dietrich too, and a young actress named Shirley Temple, America's number one box office draw. But when Johnnie stayed at the Palm Springs retreat of our friend Gordon

Coutts, he realized he didn't have the spirit to start a new life and a new adventure... and certainly not in America, though he tolerated the country more than I did. He felt an affection for the people as America had once brought him, me. In Dublin he received 'The Freedom of the City' award where at a celebratory luncheon he paid affectionate tribute to me for dominating and influencing most of his life.

John visited one of the galleries in Dublin two years after my death. W B Yeats wrote about me in a poem titled "The Municipal Gallery Re-visited."

> Hazel Lavery living and dying, that tale
> As though some ballad-singer had sung it all...

The works of Sir John Lavery now appear in museums worldwide in Aberdeen, Belfast, Buenos Aires, Dublin, Dundee, Edinburgh, Glasgow, Luxembourg, the National Museum of Wales, National Portrait Gallery (London), National War Museum (London), the Art Institute Chicago, and the Uffizi Gallery (Florence.)

After my passing there were times when John wanted to throw up his arms at everything and return to the happiest days of his existence as an irresponsible Bohemian, which is probably why his final painting was *Gipsy Encampment* in 1940, of peasant-like people sprawled out on lawns with wagons in front of them.

But he knew that Alice and the grandchildren needed him. With her help and insistence, he began writing his memoirs. He no longer longed for 5 Cromwell Place... not anymore. Not without me. He asked Alice if he could come to live with her in Kilkenny Ireland.

John passed away in Alice's home of bronchial troubles in January of 1941.

My body is buried in Putney Vale Cemetery, England, next to John for all eternity...

But my heart, oh my heart, resides in Dublin with Michael...

It took until 1939, four years after my death, to erect the limestone cross at Michael's grave where the only people present were Johnny Collins, Michael's brother, a priest, an altar boy and a gravedigger who questioned why the press wasn't present. It was because Eamon de Valera wanted to keep the celebration of Michael's life to a minimum.

After close to two decades of dilly dallying and much political red tape, de Valera signed the document to get the order executed to erect the cross just as World War II broke out. Rumors had circulated for years about his jealousy of Michael Collins. Not only did he run blockades on giving Michael the marble shrine that should have been erected back in 1922, but Representatives of the Army were forbidden to attend any annual commemoration service for their first Commander-in-Chief until 1971.

The name Michael Collins was also left out of a 1965 guide-book entitled, Facts About Ireland, produced by the Department of Foreign Affairs, which had to eventually be reprinted to include information about Michael Collins. Finally, after much uproar by the Irish, Michael's grave was added to the list.

A year later, on the 50th anniversary of the Rising, Masses were said in over seventy churches in county Cork alone, where hundreds of thousands of people per year began to visit Michael Collin's gravesite at the Glasnevin Cemetery. His grave is the most visited in all of Ireland. He is considered a national treasure right up there along with the Cliffs of Moher, the Guinness Storehouse and St Patrick's Cathedral.

One hundred and eighty-three soldiers of the Irish Free State are buried around Michael, as well as the most prominent national figures which included his friends and colleagues, Daniel O'Connell, Founding Member of the Provisional Irish Republican Army; Charles Stewart, Dominant Member of the Irish political movement; Arthur Griffith, friend of Michael's and President of the Dail Eireann; Erskine Childers, Irish Nationalist and writer, executed by the Irish Free State government; Kevin Barry, the young medical student executed "Kevin Barry!" for his role in the Irish War of Independence; Kevin O'Higgins, friend of Michael

Collins and assassinated Vice President of the Executive Council; Brendan Behan, author and playwright; Kitty Kiernan, girlfriend of Harry Boland and Michael Collins; Harry Boland, friend of Michael Collins and anti-Treaty politician; and of course, most ironically, Éamon de Valera who lived a long life and died in August of 1975, fifty years after the assassination of Michael Collins.

As for Winston Churchill, he did indeed become Prime Minister in 1940 and I was sad to have missed that celebration. John and I would have thrown the grandest of parties for him. One can only imagine the look on Clementine's face when the circumstances came to fruition.

Winston died in 1965 and is buried in the Parish Church of Saint Martin Bladon in Bladon, just at the foot of Blenheim Palace near the charming village of Woodstock, England. And, Clementine, my Clemmie, bless her, lived to the ripe old age of seventy-seven dying just before Christmas in 1977.

She was so certain that no one would remember Michael Collins, but each year twenty-thousand people visit the Michael Collins Center in Clonakilty. His fan base is the general population of Ireland. And of Irish descendants worldwide.

But I am certain that I remain his biggest fan of all...

THE END

ACKNOWLEDGMENTS

Someone once said something like, "I wait until a book gnaws at me, insistent on my involvement, before I sit and decide to write it..."

The idea for this novel first came to me from my very enthusiastic friend, Rebecca Dunn.

"Lois, you *must* write this novel!! Hazel had an *incredible* life with fascinating and famous friends...and lovers!" Then she went into hush-hush tone as if divulging some juicy secret, "Hazel is *you*, Lois, only from another century." I chuckled at the comparison but politely declined, "I love you, Rebecca. Thanks, but no thanks."

Like every other genre in publishing, the historical fiction climate kept changing. Back then it didn't seem like the right time. But I also didn't see myself writing a book of historical fiction having just come off the high of my first novel, *PLAN C: Just in Case,* a screwball Sex-and-the-City-ish comedy published by Bloomsbury. It hit #1 as a UK best-seller. No, I was certain I'd write *that* sequel until suddenly *that* climate changed too. My publisher just wasn't interested. But she did publish my novella on love, loss, and mothers, entitled *Court of the Myrtles.*

About a year later, I glanced at a file in a desk drawer entitled 'possible projects.' I began wondering about this Hazel Lavery and googled her. That's when the gnawing began.

The publishing market suddenly had a desire for untapped women who changed the course of history. I had always been an American history buff, so I'd enjoy the research of this hidden figure; and if I could give high-society-Hazel a romantic, playful element, all the better.

When I learned that Hazel Martyn had married Sir John Lavery and was rumored to have had an affair with the charismatic IRA hero, Michael Collins, I was certain that there was something there. *How could this woman not be known? How come there hadn't been a novel, movie, or streaming series about Hazel Lavery?* Besides, much like my own personal past, Hazel had played inspiration to two famous men in *their* careers. I was tired of beautiful women being reduced to backdrop; intelligent women reduced to muses. Yes, Hazel was my girl!

But I worried I wasn't capable of writing Hazel's story until I found myself at lunch with my friend, Erica Jong, who clicked a champagne glass to mine and said, "You *can,* and you *should* write this book." Erica watched me light up when I spoke of Hazel's young life at boarding school where she too, like me, always knew she was different. Not special, but different. And we both shared a void from MIA fathers. Our adult life was practically a mirror image of love, loss, pain, lovers and husbands all surrounded by a variety of celebrity artists.

Next, I rang my friend, Renee Rosen, who writes about iconic figures. I had once helped to edit her novel entitled, *Park Avenue Summer.* The premise was about Helen Gurley Brown who had been like a second mother to me. *I knew Helen's voice, but Hazel's?* Renee confirmed what I needed to hear: "Take the aspect of Hazel's character to show who *you* are because those are the things you are going to identify with...what you're going to explore." Thank you, Renee.

About fifty pages in, it was time to ring my friend Rebecca and tell her I was tackling the novel about Hazel. She was overjoyed as I thanked her. "You were right, Rebecca!" But I think that she thought the book would be written in a matter of months, and that it would be in bookstores within a year. She was already sorting out plans for a book party or two. Every month she'd ring, and I'd explain that it took at least two years to research and write, followed by the process of selecting an agent - several literary agents wanted to take it on. But upon submission to publishing houses my agent, Alexis Hurley, learned that editors "loved the writing, loved the research, loved, loved, loved," but, but, but... it seemed a story of a "white Irish girl" was undesirable in a time when the publishing tides had *again* turned. It was post-George Floyd. They wanted diversity and underrepresented voices, not an expat socialite!

I give my heartfelt thanks and admiration to Alexis – an American/Irish agent, btw – for believing in me and my novel. I love you! Always.

Thank you to my incredibly wise editor with her Southern Belle charm, Dee Marley. Your patience astounds me. And of course, thank you to the many designers, and team at Historium who moved this manuscript into an actual page-flipping book.

As I went deeper down the Hazel rabbit hole, I devoured so many insightful non-fiction books. These authors helped to educate me on the Irish, Sinn-Fein, the IRA, Churchill, etc. I highly recommend these publications for further reading if you choose to know more:

The autobiography *The Life of a Painter* by Sir John Lavery allowed me to capture John's comical voice. It was such an enjoyable read as a standalone, never mind as material for my novel. I could feel John Lavery coming to life, feel his wit and his intelligence. No wonder he captured Hazel's heart. And mine.

Thank you to W S Sparrow, *John Lavery & His Work*, which was also helpful.

Thank you to all the museums who protect and share John Lavery's works with the world. But especially to The National Gallery of Ireland in Dublin and the Rothe House & Garden, Kilkenny, where a lovely employee let me sneak up the stairs to view the three Lavery paintings before she closed for lunch. And in England, the always incredible, National Portrait Gallery.

It was an overwhelming journey delving into the world of Michael Collins. A massive shout-out to Tim Pat Coogan (wherever you are, I owe you a martini. If it's Ireland, I owe you a pint!) I adore you for writing such an in-depth biography, *Michael Collins*. Initially I dreaded having to read 510 pages but soon found it to be so interesting simply for pleasure. Coogan's book read like an animated history class with all the anecdotes and insider's information that any novelist could only *dream* of for reference. Ditto for your book The *Twelve Apostles*.

Peter Hart, thank you for *Mick, The Real Michael Collins*, another 485 pages of information. I burnt many Jo Malone candles while reading. Between the two Collins biographies and taking them to bed with me for late night highlighting, I felt like I *slept* with Michael Collins for over six months! And btw, Michael Collins was a rock star. Super crafty yet diplomatic, poetic, courageous, flirtatious, and so handsome, that I found myself beginning to fall in love with "The Big Fellow" until I had to remind myself that A: he was practically half my age, and B: he's dead.

There are countless articles on Michael Collins. The book *The Path to Freedom: Articles and Speeches,* gave me true insight into how he sounded when he spoke.

The book *A Will to Power: Eamon DeValera,* by Ronan Fanning and Paul Bew's *Churchill & Ireland* were very insightful.

Burning the Big House came out post-completion, but I referred to it in the aftermath for accuracies and to further understand what Irish country homeowners experienced in the time of Revolution (and why these houses became such a target for political purposes.) And to Clive Aslet for your gorgeous and descriptive book *The Story of a Country House* for the history of the upstairs/downstairs staff/Lords of country homes.

Saving the best book reference for last...thank you, gracias, merci beaucoup, and every language of gratitude, to my hero, Sinead McCoole, for your beautifully written, and heavily researched biography entitled: *Hazel: A Life of Lady Lavery*. Your academic and historical masterpiece broke down the timeline of Hazel's life. But more importantly, I was able to utilize and quote the actual tone and voice of both Hazel and John from their initial love letter correspondences.

As for films there were Neil Jordan's, *Michael Collins,* starring Liam Neeson, as well as H C Potter's movie *Beloved Enemy,* which was based loosely on Collins and Lavery. The latter was a silly interpretation that felt more like the Christmas classic, *It's A Wonderful Life.* Also, *The Wind That Shakes the Barley* with a plot about Ireland 1920, helpful about safe houses and weapon stashing.

Thank you to my dear and wise friend, Tony Byrne, of the Oxford Book Festival, for suggesting so many publications and for always educating me about the Irish. You are a walking, talking encyclopedia! How I adore you, Tony! xo

And how can I not thank the people of Ireland with their "Big Irish Energy!!" Thank you to Jamie Murphy from Michael Collins House for answering my often-silly questions in emails and for being so enthused when I visited Clonakilty. You rock, Jamie! Michael Collins would have adored you and your list of resources. https://www.michaelcollinshouse.ie/media/articles-research/

Thank you to Tim Crowley, a relative of Michael Collins, and for your narrative tour of Clonakilty. And to Dolores Crowley, your generous wife, who gifted me a copy of your book *In Search of Michael Collins.*

To the many delightful and often amusing people I met along the way in the towns of Dublin, Cork, Kilkenny, Kinsale and Clonakilty. The Irish are so warm and real. I always thought I loved the English most, but I've had a true awakening. The English are complicated moaners, whereas the Irish are easy-going, inviting, with big smiles and lyrical tales of fairies and folklore. Buy them a Guinness and they'll give you an earful, I promise. Thank you to the Emerald Isle with your wind-whipped ocean and your 50 shades-of-green rolling hills pounded by rain: Lime, Emerald, Jade, Moss, Olive, Chartreuse, and Celadon, I love you.

And that's because Ireland is in my heart, and apparently in my blood. While I barely knew my father (he left when I was two years of age) my grandmother on my father's side was a Wyatt of Scottish and Irish descent. Her father was Ira Wyatt, and her Irish mother was Joanna Donophan. I'm not certain of the spelling as I only have a very tattered letter explaining my family's ancestry written by an elderly aunt who had flamboyant penmanship.

However, my grandfather was William Cahall of English descent, and his grandparents were all born in England. His father was Oliver, and his mother was Edna Clongle (or was it Clough? I can't be sure. Again, an old aunt's penmanship.) Nevertheless, I've always felt torn between the English and the Irish, just as my soul sister, Hazel fluctuated between the two countries.

Lady Hazel Lavery (exhale) I feel like you are my new BFF. Your spirit is forever with me. Thank you for allowing me to take creative license to 'zhuzh' up your love life in fiction. There are so many books on Ireland's history but there aren't many love stories *in* its history.

To my reader: Thank you for taking this fictional journey with me. I've done my best to maintain historical facts and not tamper with war, politics, treaty signings, and the Collin's assassination. And, as always, to keep Hazel's intent and integrity intact.

To librarians and Booksellers: I founded and direct both the Cape Cod Book Festival and Palm Beach Book Festival. My heartfelt thanks go to all of you who truly *care* about reading, who have the sense to see our novels, memoirs, and all genres, find their way into the hands of the curious to the bookworms. Independent bookshops are kind of like the middleman of chocolate truffle makers. There are the people who *make* truffles (author) to people who *sell* truffles (bookstore) to people who love truffles (readers.)

I suspect Hazel loved chocolate truffles. According to legend they were invented by French pâtissier, Louis Doufour, who first displayed them to his customers for Christmas day, 1895 in Chambray, France. Hazel would have been fifteen by then, and with her mother dragging her around Paris and into the countryside she'd have sampled one for sure.

Here's my excuse for the truffle segue: To my beautiful daughter, Maxine, with her French-inspired chocolate business. She read my first pages and listened to me clacking away on the computer keys thereafter. Yes, giving my daughter a shameless plug here. www.maxineschocolaterie.com

And finally, thank you to Matthew. You provide me with contentment and consistency. Bless you for your patience, your steadfast kindness, and your enthusiasm for *my* enthusiasm for Hazel. But mostly for your driving skills... for your ability to navigate a rental car on the wrong-side-of-the-road in Ireland, while I'm pointing and shouting out, "Wait! Stop! Look at that over there!" Brake slam. You are my "luck of the Irish" which is amusing because you are English. Albeit *never* a moaner. I love you.

HISTORIUM PRESS

www.historiumpress.com

www.thehistoricalfictioncompany.com/historium-press

NEW YORK, NY / MACON, GA

www.ingramcontent.com/pod-product-compliance
Ingram Content Group UK Ltd.
Pitfield, Milton Keynes, MK11 3LW, UK
UKHW041740190125
4173UKWH00044B/1756